WITH BLOOD AND IRON

Douglas Reeman joined the Navy in 1941. He did convoy duty in the Atlantic, the Arctic and the North Sea, and later served in motor torpedo boats. As he says, 'I am always asked to account for the perennial appeal of the sea story, and its enduring appeal for people of so many nationalities and cultures. It would seem that the eternal and sometimes elusive triangle of man, ship and ocean, particularly under the stress of war, produces the best qualities of courage and compassion, irrespective of the rights and wrongs of the conflict . . . The sea has no understanding of righteous or unjust causes. It is the common enemy, respected by all who serve on it, ignored at their peril.'

Reeman has written over thirty novels under his own name and more than twenty best-selling historical novels, featuring Richard Bolitho and his nephew Adam Bolitho, under the pseudonym Alexander Kent.

WORLD WAR II NOVELS BY DOUGLAS REEMAN

A Prayer for the Ship
High Water
Send a Gunboat
Dive in the Sun
The Hostile Shore
The Last Raider
With Blood and Iron
HMS *Saracen*
Path of the Storm
Deep Silence
The Pride and the Anguish
To Risks Unknown
The Greatest Enemy
Rendezvous—South Atlantic
His Majesty's U-boat *or* Go in and Sink!
The Destroyers
Winged Escort
Surface with Daring
Strike from the Sea
A Ship Must Die
Torpedo Run
The Volunteers
The Iron Pirate
In Danger's Hour
The White Guns
Killing Ground
Sunset
A Dawn Like Thunder
Battlecruiser
For Valour
Twelve Seconds to Live
The Glory Boys

THE ROYAL MARINE SAGA

Badge of Glory
The First to Land
The Horizon
Dust on the Sea
Knife Edge

WITH BLOOD AND IRON

DOUGLAS REEMAN

Essex, Connecticut

An imprint of Globe Pequot, the trade division of
The Rowman & Littlefield Publishing Group, Inc.
4501 Forbes Blvd., Ste. 200
Lanham, MD 20706
www.rowman.com

Distributed by NATIONAL BOOK NETWORK

British Library Cataloguing in Publication Information available

Library of Congress Cataloging-in-Publication Data

Names: Reeman, Douglas, author.
Title: With blood and iron / Douglas Reeman.
Description: McBooks Press paperback edition. | Essex, Connecticut : McBooks Press, 2023. | Series: The modern naval fiction library | Summary: "In 1944, ace commander Rudolf Steiger takes a U-boat flotilla out into the bitter winter seas, where he faces a new and deadly enemy-his own nagging doubts about the outcome of the war"— Provided by publisher.
Identifiers: LCCN 2022054153 (print) | LCCN 2022054154 (ebook) | ISBN 9781493071609 (paperback : alk. paper) | ISBN 9781493071647 (ebook)
Classification: LCC PR6068.E35 W58 2023 (print) | LCC PR6068.E35 (ebook) | DDC 823/.914—dc23
LC record available at https://lccn.loc.gov/2022054153
LC ebook record available at https://lccn.loc.gov/2022054154

∞™ The paper used in this publication meets the minimum requirements of American National Standard for Information Sciences—Permanence of Paper for Printed Library Materials, ANSI/NISO Z39.48-1992.

Contents

Author's Note

Nearly thirty years have passed since the Battle of the Atlantic reached its peak and began to swing in favour of Britain and her Allies. It was a battle which started within minutes of the outbreak of war and continued to the final shot. It gathered momentum so that both sides were lost in such a wave of desperate ferocity that the hard-won rules of combat were thrown aside.

At the turning point of that battle, when the new weapons of radar and improved escort vessels were beginning to take effect, the cost was already too high. Thousands of Allied seamen, hundreds of ships and their desperately needed cargoes, littered the bottom of the greedy Atlantic.

We who took part in that battle hardly thought of the enemy as something human, as flesh and blood. We feared him because he was invisible yet ever-present, and out of that fear grew hatred and the power to hit back with ruthless determination.

Now that time and understanding have soothed, if not completely healed, some of those memories, I have tried to see that same war as it was experienced by the men we fought for so long: the crews of the U-boat Service.

From first to last they never faltered. When Germany's hopes were shattered, and the Allies drove the road to victory, these men lived and died by their code. Their motto, 'We serve with blood and iron', took on a grimmer meaning.

This is not the story of that early part of the war, but later, at the turn of the tide, when the Germans knew the desperation of encirclement and defeat, as we had once known it.

In his foreword to the German book *U-boat 977* Nicholas Monsarrat once wrote of this aspect of naval warfare: '. . . it is cruel, treacherous and revolting under any flag. There is a current Anglo-American illusion, skilfully fostered during the war, that whereas the Germans used *U-boats,* which were beastly, we only used *submarines* which were different and rather wonderful.' A shrewd observation indeed. Can anyone fight with such weapons and not become tainted?

1: New Year

Major Fritz Reimann, Garrison Commander of St. Pierre, stepped out of his commandeered Citroën and scowled at his driver.

'Wait here!' He pulled his thick greatcoat carefully across his corpulent body and stared with something like hatred at the tall fence of gleaming barbed wire which spanned the entrance to the small harbour. The very sight of it, with its armed naval sentries and alien newness, made his bald head break out in a sweat beneath his cap in spite of the icy January wind which swept up from the Bay of Biscay and swirled about his polished boots.

Almost overnight, or so it seemed, the quiet orderliness of this small French town had been transformed into a whirlwind of action and organisation. Major Reimann pulled his heavy chins tightly into his collar and marched past the saluting sentries. He should have guessed what was happening when they built the two U-boat pens inside the harbour. His superiors had said that they were for temporary use or something of the sort, but as usual nobody told the truth any more. The navy had moved into his domain, and already three submarines lay alongside one of the two long stone breakwaters, and another was inside its new pen undergoing repairs. They had commandeered the only large hotel as their headquarters, and even the school and some of the harbour buildings had been taken from his command.

Major Reimann was fifty-three but looked ten years older. As an artillery officer he had originally been drafted to this sector of the French coastline to arrange and build the local coast defences. The four concrete gun emplacements which faced the restless Bay had been his greatest pride until now, and his additional powers as garrison commander had been the culmination of his military ambitions. Unlike many of his contemporaries, who were dotted in their thousands throughout occupied

Europe, Reimann was content with his command. With the growing slaughter on the Russian front he had at first been left with boys and old men for troops. Now the boys had gone and he was left with elderly or unfit soldiers who, like himself, were quite content to avoid the mainstream of war.

He paused at the end of the coast road and glared down at the small harbour. The bay itself was protected on either side by twin hills which ran right down to the narrow shelving beach and seemed to crumble into the layers of black rocks which littered the windswept foreshore. Cut into the side of one of the hills the U-boat pens made an angry concrete scar which, although concealed from the air by camouflage nets, were glaring enough to make his temper rise yet again.

He had telephoned his Divisional Headquarters several times about this intrusion, but had stopped even that when he had been told with unconcealed delight that the naval commander of the Base was the general's cousin.

Reimann peered up at the whitewashed hotel and swore beneath his breath. Well, we shall see. Cousin or no, I intend to show him a thing or two!

Ten infuriating minutes later he was ushered into a long handsome room, the broad windows of which seemed to span the whole bay and the angry sea beyond. There was a smell of fresh paint and polish everywhere, and Reimann's anger changed to jealous bitterness when he saw the coloured charts which covered two of the walls and the map-tables with their flags and counters of different hues, all of which seemed to emphasise his own inferiority.

Behind a wide desk the one-armed naval officer regarded him with a slight smile. Reimann noted the four gold stripes on his remaining sleeve, the decorations, the air of alert arrogance which the man seemed to generate.

Captain Hans Bredt pushed the silver cigarette box towards the fat, bald-headed soldier and then drummed on the blotter with his small, neat hand. He recognised all the irritating symptoms of non-co-operation immediately but smiled in spite of this fact. Bredt, like Reimann, had his present appointment because he was no longer fit for an active command, but unlike the corpulent officer he was well aware of his own importance, and that of his job.

Bredt was just forty years old, but his short blond hair and round youthful face made him appear too immature for his rank of senior captain. Had Riemann been more observant he would have recognised the intolerant ruthlessness in Bredt's restless eyes, but he was not, so he imagined for a few more minutes that he was still in command of St. Pierre.

In his thick, guttural voice he rambled on a while longer about the town and its merits. Of the difficulties he had surmounted, without recognition, and of the high state of efficiency of his small garrison. The coming of the submarines and their crews might well alter all that. St. Pierre would tempt the R.A.F. beyond Brest and Lorient, and might even arouse resentment in the French themselves to a point when some hot-head might form a local Resistance movement.

Bredt listened to the flat, aggrieved voice and marvelled at Reimann's stupidity. He himself had commanded a U-boat in the first days of the war. In six months he had sunk thirty thousand tons of enemy shipping, won four decorations and lost an arm. How he remembered those distant days of triumph with pride and excitement, each passing month adding to his belief that they were the finest times of his life. Time had blotted out the memories of pain and suffering, of frustration and fear, and only the symbols remained.

'I can assure you, my dear Major, that I will do all in my power to see that things remain as they are. I have no wish to attract attention from the enemy air forces, any more than I want interruptions to the workings of my base here. But this war has been going on for four years, it may well continue for another ten! In that time it seems probable that we will see some changes.' He allowed a little sarcasm to filter into his tone. 'I am sure that even the army will appreciate our usefulness here.' He waved his hand towards the wall-charts. 'Our submarines span the Atlantic. Even at this moment our men are sinking enemy ships. Ships carrying guns and tanks to the Russian front where they would be used to kill your own colleagues. But the price is high. Our submarines get no rest, and when they are in port they must have instant attention.' He permitted a small smile. 'The crews, too, must have some diversions to renew their energy!' He frowned and pushed a folder across the table. 'I have here a list of my requirements in the town and facilities I still require.'

Reimann purpled and lurched to his feet. 'You must understand my position! The mayor here, *all* the leading citizens, they look to me for instructions! It is unfair to force your affairs on me like this!'

Reimann spun round as a third voice cut across the room. He

had been so intent on watching Bredt that he had not noticed the other officer who had until this moment been sitting in a deep chair facing the windows.

'If you are not fit to control this flea-pit, Major, perhaps we can get someone else!'

Bredt coughed. 'Major Reimann, allow me to introduce Commander Rudolf Steiger. He is to command the flotilla. At sea he will be my opposite number.' He smiled at Reimann's confusion. 'My other arm, so to speak!'

Reimann was about to lose his last shred of self-control when the other officer moved away from the windows, so that the shadows cleared his face like a cloud. Reimann was an unimaginative man at the best of times, but immediately he could sense the danger which seemed to surround this man who was called Steiger. He was tall, with the wide shoulders and small waist of an athlete. He stood quite still, his neat brown hands hanging at his sides, his head jutting forward in a slight stoop. But Reimann's attention was riveted on Steiger's face. Beneath the short, glossy black hair his features were quite still and impassive, yet his cold grey eyes and straight controlled mouth gave the immediate impression of tremendous concentration and disciplined strength. Like a cat, Reimann thought, like a *wild* cat!

Bredt cut into his thoughts smoothly. 'I expect you have heard of Commander Steiger? One of our greatest U-boat aces. He is to take command of one of the submarines here as well as his other duties.'

Steiger turned his back on the soldier and walked again to the windows. The harsh light reflected from the sea played across his impassive face and upon the angry white scar which ran down his left temple to the corner of his eye. Over his shoulder he said: 'Today is New Year's Day, Major. Four years of war, and yet there are still people like you who know nothing about it!'

Reimann turned to Bredt. 'How can you allow him to speak to me like that? What *right* has he?'

Bredt lit a cigarette. 'Every right, Major. Take a good look at him. *He* is a fighting man! He does not merely wear a uniform. He knows what war is, and goes looking for it.'

'Perhaps if I had been younger——'

Steiger cut Reimann short. 'My God! How many times have I heard that! "If only . . . perhaps . . . given a chance . . . etc., etc."

When people whine to me of war's futility I tell them that only the people are futile!'

Major Reimann gathered the last of his dignity. 'I must leave now. I have to inspect the coastal batteries!'

Steiger laughed shortly. 'Look to the road, Major!' He turned to watch the angry bewilderment on the man's face. 'Your guns point out to sea, Major. But when the enemy comes he will come down that road!'

Major Reimann slammed the door behind him, and Bredt frowned at his cigarette. 'You were a little hard on him, Rudi? I have dealt with many of his kind. They don't worry me any more.'

Steiger spoke as if he had not heard. 'Those damned people! Clinging to their petty little dreams of power!'

Bredt frowned. 'Well, let us get on. I think you have the whole situation at your fingertips now?'

'When do I take command of *U-991*?'

'She docks tonight. She has been on a three-month patrol, as you know, in the Central Atlantic.'

Steiger interrupted. 'And her captain is dead. Very convenient.'

'He was apparently killed when the submarine was surprised by an aircraft some four days ago. I have seen all the signals, but a full report will be necessary when they dock.'

Steiger said slowly: 'I knew her captain when he was at Lorient. Captain Maazel. When my own boat was sunk I somehow knew I would get his command. He has been going downhill fast. A bad captain, I would say. Now he is dead. Another name for our memorial!' There was no bitterness in his voice, and Bredt eyed him warily.

'You never change, Rudi. You never seem to get excited about anything.'

Steiger stared through the wet glass towards the nearest hill. Bending in the stiff sea-wind, a line of trees ran up one side like a group of ragged fugitives fleeing towards the summit.

'What is this flotilla going to be? Misfits? Or something worse?'

Bredt sat back in his chair and stared moodily at the nearest chart. The coloured lines which depicted the enemy's convoy routes and patrols moved towards the British coastline like arteries, which indeed they were.

'No, Rudi. This flotilla is to be something better! For years now we have grouped our submarines in the bigger ports, Brest,

Lorient, St. Nazaire, Kiel and all the rest. They go to sea and scatter. They are homed on to targets by aircraft or their own sighting reports. They attack in wolf-packs. But the casualties are heavy. By decentralising the bases and having smaller groups we will be able to control our movements and patrol sectors better.' He coughed. 'Of course, we are getting some rough material to work with. All the boats in this flotilla are from other groups which have been broken up.'

'Sunk!' Steiger said flatly.

'Even so, they have to be formed into one new team. Eight boats with you in command of the group. Group Meteor.'

Steiger listened to Bredt's smooth voice as he outlined the new role of St. Pierre and its base. He is like Reimann, he thought. Bredt still fights his war from memory, just as the Major fights his from hearsay.

He stared out over the craggy breakwaters and moored submarines and across the limitless wastes of the Bay of Biscay. The Atlantic. The most ruthless and savage battleground in the world. He wondered what he would find in his new command, and why Maazel had died. Returning from a fruitless patrol. All torpedoes fired, but no sinkings reported. He must have been a useless commander. Everyone on board thinking of getting home and dry, and thanking God for being spared. His lip curled slightly. At that moment, and under that set of circumstances, a U-boat was at its most vulnerable. The sudden roar of propellers as the unseen aircraft dives out of the storm, the rattle of gunfire, the frantic order to dive, sometimes given too late. At least for Maazel it had been too late it seemed.

He heard Bredt say, 'Your last boat hit a mine?'

He nodded absently. 'In the North Sea. I was on the bridge with the lookouts. Just the five of us. I saw the mine as it bobbed up by the bows. I had time to see it was one of our own!'

'Bad luck.'

'Mines are like the people who sow them. They lack discrimination!'

He closed his ears to Bredt's voice. Words, words, words. They were not needed by those who really knew what was happening at sea. The moment of realisation, followed immediately by a blinding flash. He could not remember any explosion or sound, except, of course, for the screams which came up the bridge voice-pipe before they were strangled and finally silenced as the U-boat dived beneath him. He and the lookouts were thrown clear, although two of the seamen died almost at once from shock. An E-boat pulled the last survivors aboard and cruised slowly back and forth across the patch of oil. Two dazed seamen, and their captain. He remembered looking down at the widening circle of oil, the few pieces of flaked paint and a solitary life-raft, and thinking, So that is what it looks like when you die!

'You were lucky again, Rudi!'

Steiger turned away from the window. 'I am still alive.'

Bredt pointed at the wall-charts. 'St. Pierre is the first of many new bases. In one year our submarine production will have doubled. The enemy will not know which way to turn!'

Steiger smiled for the first time. 'Doubled? I will be content with what we have now, so long as it gets better support. Like all forms of power, enough is plenty!'

'How much tonnage have you put down now, Rudi?'

Steiger shrugged. 'I forget. Two hundred thousand tons, I believe.' He ignored the mixture of admiration and envy on Bredt's face. 'I never think of them, only the one in my sights.'

A telephone jangled and Bredt lifted it to his ear in one quick movement. His face became formal and stiff as he listened. He put it down and said: 'Your boat has been reported by our air patrol. She will be alongside in four hours.'

'Another boat. Another struggle against personal feelings.'

Bredt stared at him with surprise. 'I imagine that you will soon make a real ship out of her, eh?'

Steiger eyed him calmly. 'A U-boat is not a way of life. To me it is merely a weapon! A soldier lying in the mud should not have to wonder about the rifle he holds in his hands. He should only have to know how to fire it. That is how I am with a U-boat!'

Bredt looked closely at the quiet, watchful figure facing him across the desk. He had met many commanders, some boasters, some deliberately casual, others left no impressions at all. Steiger was none of these. He seemed to smell of submarines, to represent in a slight gesture or sign all the terrifying dedication required by a U-boat captain who had managed to survive throughout the whole war.

Bredt thought of all the great ones who had gone. Gunther Prien, Johann Mohann, Rosenbaum and Kretchmer who was a prisoner of war. He looked at his own empty sleeve with sudden emotion. I might have been as great as any of them, he thought. Now I am as much a memory as they. He realised that Steiger was watching him, his eyes wrinkled in a small smile.

'Do not worry,' Steiger spoke almost softly. 'You have done more than most. If you do a good job here that will be enough for Germany!'

Bredt stood up and paced across the room. 'If only I could get back to sea. If only I could . . .'

Steiger watched him without speaking. Emotional, he thought briefly. He was lucky to escape with the loss of one arm. Aloud he said, 'Since the British perfected their radar detectors life has become much harder in the Atlantic.'

Bredt returned to his chair. 'We will beat them.'

'We will. But it needs more cunning now. We must teach these new men to be aggressive! The wolf-pack system was good enough a year ago, but now the enemy escorts are better and stronger. Radar has made it more difficult to surface to charge batteries. They can smell a U-boat before you can whistle!'

'We have the new Snorchel, surely that makes it easier to charge batteries at periscope depth?'

Steiger shrugged impatiently. '*Very* good on paper. Almost useless in anything of a sea. If you could see it operate actually on patrol you might change your opinion.' He saw the flash of hurt in Bredt's eyes and started to regret his own intolerance. But he hardened his heart almost as quickly. If Bredt was unable to forget his own past and concentrate on his new task then he deserved to be hurt.

Steiger tried to relax his aching limbs, but his self-imposed alertness remained. His scar felt hot and irritating, and almost involuntarily his hand moved up to touch it. They had stalked a British tanker for three days. They had attacked it with the last two torpedoes, and then closed in to finish off the precious cargo with gunfire. Even though the tanker was doomed and ablaze some few fanatical beings had manned the tiny deck gun and returned their fire. One small shell had exploded on the U-boat's casing, and one white-hot splinter had branded Steiger for life. He often wondered about that nameless British seaman who had aimed and fired that gun. Even as the oil had exploded, and the tanker had rolled over on to a sea of flames, that man must have seen the U-boat commander fall. What had he felt? What did anybody feel?

Bredt said suddenly: 'The British newspapers have printed your name again. How do you like being called a war-criminal? They say that you fight with any method at your disposal.'

Steiger shrugged. 'My father once told me that the only crime to commit in wartime is to lose!'

He stood up, and even Bredt was conscious of the sense of latent power and danger which seemed to surround the man. He knew that Steiger was thirty years old, yet he could have been any age. It was said that he had no other life but the submarine service. He had few friends, and only a handful of those knew much about him. He had become a legend, a real symbol of Germany's greatness.

'I am going to my quarters. Perhaps you would let me know when my boat is sighted?'

'Certainly, Rudi. Is there anything I can tell the other commanders who are already here?'

Steiger rubbed his chin. 'Tell them to get their men properly dressed and turned out when they are in harbour. I don't care what they look like at sea, but here in France we represent the German Navy, and I will not tolerate a group which looks like a gang of pirates!'

'Is it that important?'

Steiger paused by the door, his grey eyes suddenly alive. 'To make a man fight well you must first make him proud! Not just of some stupid bundle of patriotic sentimentalities, but of himself!'

Bredt shook his head. 'You never change, Rudi. Do you fear nothing yourself?'

Steiger smiled slowly as if at some old memory. 'Only failure. By concentrating on that, death has become merely incidental!'

The door closed, and Bredt was left staring at the charts and his small paper flags.

Rudolf Steiger turned up the collar of his greatcoat as he stepped from behind the shelter of a long harbour shed, and felt the full force of the stiff west wind. Over and beyond the two stone arms of the harbour the empty sea was lashed into countless lines of whitecaps, which as they approached the foreshore merged into impressive curling breakers and threw themselves with mounting fury against the glistening rocks and along the full lengths of the breakwaters. Apart from the seething whitecaps, the predominant colour was grey. From the tossing desert of water to the invisible horizon the whole coastline seemed to merge into one threatening pattern of grey hues. Low overhead the clouds scudded after the breakers as if to add their weight to the onslaught, so that spray and drizzle mingled as one, and broke the shoreline into unnatural brooding shapes behind a shifting curtain of mist and haze.

Nothing human moved on the foreshore, although Steiger had the impression that many eyes were watching from the small, ugly houses within the harbour limits and from the bare concrete gun emplacements.

Through the mist a green light stabbed with unexpected brightness, and Steiger quickened his pace along the breakwater. From one of the sheds a handful of seamen in oilskins shambled without enthusiasm towards an empty berth, while an officer waited until the last possible minute beneath the shed roof, his face hidden in his upturned collar.

Steiger walked past them, his eyes ignoring their incurious glances, and peered over the stone rampart towards a darkening patch of grey as the familiar shape manœuvred towards the narrow harbour entrance.

The rain and spray ran down from his white cap and across his neck but he watched unflinchingly as the buffeted U-boat thrust her sharp stem midway between the two stone walls and pushed eagerly into the calmer waters beyond. He watched her reduce speed, his practised eye taking in the slime and weed of three months' patrol, the bullet scars across the forecasing and conning tower, the listless seamen who stood with the bow and stern lines, and the small group of officers on her bridge.

A small patch of bright red flapped from her ensign staff, and Steiger noticed that the flag was at half mast. Overhead two Messerschmitt fighters burst across the harbour with their familiar throaty growl, the black crosses on their clipped wings gleaming momentarily before they turned and swept out to sea. Steiger saw an officer on the submarine's bridge start and peer upwards at the two aircraft, his tired features suddenly apprehensive. Across the narrowing gap of churning water the officer seemed to see Steiger, and for several seconds he held his eyes in what appeared to be a questioning stare. Then as the U-boat manœuvred closer to the jetty he turned away, his arm waving to the waiting shore-party.

The propellers churned astern, and heaving lines snaked across to the eager hands ashore. Springs and mooring wires followed, and as the boat nudged against the rubber fenders she seemed to shudder, and fell silent. Only a pounding generator continued to send a haze of diesel fumes above her aft casing to mingle with the spray and float around the bedraggled ensign.

Steiger walked back along the jetty. Already his new crew

were scrambling ashore and falling in on the jetty. The Base staff were taking over, and harassed petty officers were shouting out names and checking details against sodden lists and signal pads. Then the men shuffled to attention and began to march towards the buildings beyond the new pens. This was to be their new home for as long as they stayed in harbour, for as long as they stayed alive. Yet none of them even glanced at the town, and when a petty officer bawled, 'Eyes left!' and saluted Steiger, their eyes were dead and unseeing.

Steiger raised his hand to his cap, his face unmoving. As the crew marched past him he noted every telltale detail. The familiar pallid faces, unkempt hair and straggling beards, the worn leather jackets and salt-caked boots. He saw, too, the young inexperienced faces made suddenly old, broken here and there with the face of a professional submariner. Even these latter few looked downcast and beaten.

Next came three of the officers. The slim one in the forefront whom he had seen on the bridge must be the First Lieutenant, Heinz Dietrich, and the others probably the Navigator and Torpedo Officer. The Engineer was evidently still aboard. Like most of his kind, he was probably unwilling to hand over his machinery to base workers without some last-minute precautions.

Steiger turned his back and hurried towards the hotel. There was no point in confronting Dietrich the moment he stepped ashore. He had seen the immediate caution on the young lieutenant's face, and something more besides. Guilt? Fear? He was not sure, and in any case Steiger rarely trusted first impressions.

Steiger walked past the hotel and peered back at the U-boat. Already the power lines were snaking aboard, and oilskinned figures clambered along her narrow decks. Her number, 991, stood out clearly against the dull plates, and Steiger noticed, too, the buxom mermaid which was painted on the front of the conning tower. Life-size, she wielded a large axe, and glared with bright blue eyes towards the bows where the torpedoes would be waiting to fire.

The submarine was two years old, so the mermaid was probably a legacy from her first commander. Steiger dug his hands into his pockets and trudged along the sandy road parallel with the new barbed-wire fence. When that mermaid had been added to the boat she had been symbolic of the times, he thought. The Atlantic war at its peak, with the enemy losing more shipping than he could replace. The heyday, the climax of a new submarine warfare. That was the sort of war Bredt remembered, he thought. A band to play you out of harbour, flowers and Iron Crosses to greet your return. Now the war at sea had changed to a higher gear once more, and both sides fought with uncompromising desperation, with no quarter given or asked.

Now there were always new weapons followed immediately by new counter-measures, fresh tactics to be studied with too little time to practise. There was always so little time, and Steiger knew that each passing month demanded more and more of every commander who took part in the Atlantic war. Every time you sailed the odds mounted against you. If you were lucky you might escape with a sharp warning. If not, you died. Now that I have lost a boat, but kept my own life, perhaps I have gained more time? Or are the odds all the greater now? Unexpectedly, he smiled, and realised that he had reached the end of the wire fence.

Through the wire he could see some French workers loading an ancient lorry with timber. They seemed cheerful enough, and quite unlike those in Lorient and other big French towns where the streets were always thronged with field-grey uniforms, with German sailors and the busy cars of the S.S.

Here it was evidently quite different, and Steiger knew it was because this small town had been by-passed by the war. He remembered Major Reimann's angry face and his spluttering complaints. It was amazing how many Reimanns there were in this war, who imagined that if everything stayed as it was, the war would end on its own, in its own good time.

He wondered briefly if the other seven submarine commanders would approve of this new base and Bredt's ideas of strategy. He had at least one friend amongst the seven. Alex Lehmann had been with him both at Lorient and at Kiel. An unruffled, dependable man, he would make all the difference in a flotilla of strangers.

He reached the hotel and handed his dripping coat to an orderly.

Some white-jacketed messmen were banking up the fires and putting up the blackout shutters. In one of the rooms Steiger could hear a piano being played rather sadly and the buzz of conversation. Already the hotel was losing its earlier appearance and function, but seemed somehow glad of the change.

Just before the last blackout shutter was hoisted into place Steiger got one more glimpse of the sea. Beneath the black clouds and darkening sky it looked threatening and cruel. As always, it was waiting. It never grew tired of the game which they had all been made to join.

Steiger sighed and climbed the stairs to his room.

▪ ▪ ▪ ▪ ▪

In his oil-stained leather jacket, heels together and cap gripped firmly beneath his arm, Lieutenant Heinz Dietrich stood motionless in the middle of the long map-room. He could feel the fatigue sweeping over him like the effect of a drug, and the details of the room seemed to fade so that he was made to concentrate his attention on the desk and the one-armed captain who sat behind it. He waited in silence as Bredt leafed through the stained logbook and the sheaf of sighting reports. Outside the shuttered windows the wind howled across the Bay and rattled the glass with savage persistence. Dietrich looked down at Bredt's sleek, well-groomed head and stifled the resentment and uneasiness which the man's silence made him feel. Across the room he caught sight of himself in a tall gilt mirror. A slight, youthful figure, with three months of beard that seemed to accentuate his boyish features, which now looked so strained and grim. His hair was long and very fair, and seemed to clash with the cold, troubled eyes that stared back at him from the mirror.

Bredt cleared his throat. Without looking up he said sharply: 'This seems in order, Lieutenant. Captain Maazel was on the bridge with you when he was hit by the aircraft's bullets, and then the submarine dived?'

'Yes, sir.' Dietrich answered briskly and remained staring over the Captain's head.

'The lookouts had already gone below?'

'Yes. I had given the diving alarm. We were already flooding.'

Bredt's small hand began to drum on the desk. 'Why was it that you did not see the aircraft in time?'

For the first time their eyes met, and Bredt felt conscious of the young officer's hostility.

As if he was repeating a lesson, Dietrich said flatly: 'There was a heavy sea running. We had surfaced an hour earlier and we were charging batteries. It was very dark with thick cloud formations. Our radar detector was non-operational because of the bad weather, and the noise of the storm must have drowned the sound of the aircraft's approach.'

'Must have?'

'Nobody reported it,' Dietrich answered with stubborn finality. 'I pressed the diving button and cleared the bridge. The Captain remained and was caught by a burst of machine-gun fire.'

Bredt continued to drum his fingers. 'The aircraft saw *you* all right, then?'

Dietrich stared fixedly at the wall-chart beyond the desk. Oh, you stupid swine! Of course the Tommy saw us! We were lit up by his searchlights, pinpointed on his radar, and were lucky he did not have any depth-charges. Aloud he replied, 'He used lights, sir.'

'I see.' Bredt looked up swiftly. 'Why did Captain Maazel remain so long on the bridge?'

Dietrich steeled himself. This was the moment. 'He was shouting, sir. I think he was suffering from strain.'

Bredt stuck out his chin. 'Strain? Do you mean he did not *realise* what was happening?'

'Yes, sir.'

'But he was your commanding officer!'

Dietrich swallowed hard. As if *that* made any difference!

As Bredt turned his eyes back to the reports again, Dietrich swayed on his feet and tried to blot out the picture of Maazel's distorted face, ghostlike in the blazing searchlights. The room seemed to fade and he heard again the roar of the storm and the growing thunder of the aircraft's engines.

Maazel had been shouting at him. Screaming abuse like a madman. All the pent-up fury and frustration of the patrol had burst from him like a flood, so that he seemed quite unable to move. Maazel, with his fat, unhealthy face and protruding eyes. Dietrich had never believed he could hate a man so much. Now he was dead. He remembered with sudden clarity the savage, sneering voice changing to a cry of agony as the bullets had struck sparks from the rim of the bridge and hurled him to his knees. Already the water was roaring into the saddle tanks and the deck was tilting into a dive, but Dietrich was held mesmerised by the man who quivered at his feet. The man who had tried to break his spirit, who was going to destroy him when they reached base. In an instant he had changed into a shapeless, whimpering creature which pawed frantically at Dietrich's boots.

Even as Dietrich leaped down through the hatch and groped for the locking wheel the water had come cascading over the conning tower. Not before he had seen Maazel's staring eyes and clawlike hands, nor before he had time to realise that he had deliberately left him to die.

'You would say, then, that the Captain was too badly wounded to be saved?' Bredt's voice jerked Dietrich back to reality.

'Yes, sir.' His answer was firm, but he felt his heart pounding against his ribs like a hammer. When they had surfaced the following morning Maazel's body had still been there on the bridge. Held in position by one of the steel safety belts. Dietrich had stared for endless seconds at the sodden, bloated mass which had once been the force that threatened to destroy him. There had been only one bullet hole in the slime-streaked oilskin. He could have been saved. He *would* have lived. With the aid of one of the seamen he had rolled the body over the side. He had kept his secret.

'Your new captain is Commander Steiger.'

'Yes, sir.' Dietrich had recognised Steiger on the harbour wall. Who in the U-boat Service did not know him and his reputation? So now that Maazel was gone, Steiger would be in command. He would be quick to notice any fault or weakness. It *would* be Steiger!

'Very well, Lieutenant. Tomorrow your men can take some local leave. You will receive all your Standing Orders in the morning when you can take Captain Steiger over your boat. This will be a first-rate flotilla, and I will not tolerate slackness or failure! Germany requires maximum effort from every officer, especially from the U-boat Service!'

Dietrich felt the weariness tightening around his skull like a steel band. This damned idiot kept him standing like a recruit just for the pleasure of hearing his own voice. He heard the rising howl of the wind and felt slightly sick. The short respite in harbour would soon pass, and then they would be back again in the Atlantic. It had been bad enough with Maazel. *He* had been a coward. Steiger would drive them all until they dropped.

'Permission to fall out, sir?' Dietrich kept his voice toneless.

'Very well. But go and inspect your crew's quarters before you dismiss yourself. Always put duty first, Lieutenant!'

Dietrich clicked his heels together and strode from the room. Bredt looked with irritation at the two small oilstains left by the young officer's boots on the new carpet, and then walked to his map-table. With great care he removed the last flag from the Alantic and placed it alongside the rest of the new flotilla.

2: U-991

The low-beamed café was situated on a corner of St. Pierre's cobbled square and seemed to lean against the other buildings for support. It consisted of one very large room with a raised portion at one end for the private alcoves and small circular tables. The air was filled with the buzz of conversation and laughter, and an unmoving cloud of blue smoke hung like a sea fog beneath the worn beams of the roof. A fat, grey-haired man sat beside the kitchen door, his eyes closed in concentration as he squeezed a large accordion, the music of which hardly penetrated the noise about him.

The tobacco smoke eddied momentarily as the street door opened and a gust of wind billowed against the thick blackout curtain, then as the three naval officers entered the packed room a silence transmitted itself across the seated customers so that the accordion intruded upon the café like a fanfare.

The three blue-clad figures moved through the silent throng and up the short flight of stairs to the balcony. There was only one table vacant, and an elderly waiter in a long apron guarded it apprehensively as the officers converged on it with silent determination.

'I am sorry, *m'sieu*,' the waiter swallowed hard, conscious of the faces which watched from every side, 'but this one is reserved.'

Karl Hessler, *U-991*'s Torpedo Officer, raised his massive eyebrows and stared bleakly at the frightened waiter. Then with a nod to his companions he sat down heavily at the table, his square, stocky figure upright in the chair like a rock.

'But, *m'sieu*!' The waiter flapped his soiled napkin and peered helplessly at the three seated figures.

Hessler said quietly: 'Stand *still* when you are speaking to a German officer! We require some good champagne and perhaps later some brandy. Do you understand?' He looked up calmly, his deep-set eyes gleaming beneath the great tufts of hair.

The man stammered, and then, realising that the first round had gone to Hessler, scurried away into the smoke. Slowly the conversation and noise returned, and Hessler placed his red hands carefully on the table. 'Insolent swine!'

Franz Luth, the Engineer, leaned against the balcony rail and looked down at the packed heads below him. There was not a single German to be seen, and Luth sighed with deep contentment. His lean bony figure seemed lost within his uniform, and the melancholy face and brown eyes gave him the appearance of a village priest. 'This is more like it!' He finished his careful scrutiny and turned back to his companions. 'You can almost retain the delusion that we are on holiday!'

Hessler grunted impatiently. 'Damned Frogs! If they try to be clever with me they'll be sorry! I've not been sweating blood in the Atlantic all this time to be treated like some sort of unwanted guest!'

Luth smiled. 'Perhaps they don't realise the sacrifices you have been making for their benefit?'

Gunter Reche, the Navigator, groaned and ran his hand across his thin receding hair. He was a paunchy young man, and his sallow skin looked unhealthy and raw from the unaccustomed use of a razor. 'Now then, you two! Can't you stop goading each other for a moment?' He gulped as the waiter put the bottles carefully on the table and licked his lips with anticipation. Half to himself he said: 'Three months I have been waiting for this. By God, it's going to taste good!'

Hessler lifted his glass and tossed the champagne down his throat. He slammed it in front of the waiter and waited for a refill. 'Gnat's water!'

Luth ran his tongue around his dry lips. 'Excellent. Probably made this morning, but still excellent!'

Two bottles were emptied with hardly a word more being said. Slowly the room seemed to get smaller, and the alien voices and movements to fade beyond the small world of their table.

Luth said at length, 'Well, what do you think of Rudolf Steiger?'

'I knew him before.' Hessler stared moodily through the smoke. 'Cuxhaven it was. He was only a lieutenant then, but I knew he'd do well.'

'So he should, with his background.' Reche sounded petulant. 'A naval family for God knows how many generations, he could hardly go wrong!'

Hessler laughed harshly. 'You're like all the damned amateurs! In peacetime you sneer at the regulars, and when you get hauled into the service you're jealous because you're so damned useless!'

'Don't forget, Karl, I was in the Merchant Service!' Reche's feverish eyes burned with indignation. 'All the finest navigators come from there!'

'Naturally. You had nothing to do all day but gape at the sky! You *should* be good at it!'

Luth grinned lazily. 'We have been in port two days, yet in that time I should think that our new captain has been over every inch of the submarine. He bombarded me with questions about everything! Had me worried more than once!'

Reche said slowly: 'We must sail again in three days. It's not fair. We've never had to sail so soon after a patrol before.'

'This will be different.' Hessler spoke with complete confidence. 'Just a short patrol to see how the flotilla works together. Not a bad idea, really. It's always bad policy to give the men time to brood. Keep them on the jump, and keep them busy, that's what I say!'

Luth yawned, the champagne making his bones feel like rubber. 'Never mind. This will be a nice place to come home to!'

Hessler lifted his hands, and Luth thought they looked like two red crabs.

'That's right, Franz!' Hessler was suddenly speaking loudly. 'A couple of weeks and I'll have a nice little chicken to take to bed with me, eh!'

Luth felt his face was split into an uncontrollable grin, but no longer cared. It was always the same after a hard patrol, perhaps more for him than anyone else aboard. In charge of the submarine's engines and electric motors, responsible for immediate diving and surfacing of the boat under every conceivable condition, he had little time for fear or conjecture. Immediately afterwards was the time for that, and drink, preferably champagne, was his remedy. It might be a nice change here, he thought vaguely. A small town like this could offer much more than those damned great targets like Lorient and Brest. It would be possible to go for walks over the two hills, and sleep at night between clean sheets without the nerve-tearing scream of air-raid alarms. Yes, it might be just right. And at sea with Captain Steiger they must surely be safer than with Maazel, who had nearly driven them mad with his tirades and insults. Poor Heinz Dietrich, the First Lieutenant, had borne the full brunt of those attacks, had been a human buffer for the rest of them. Even with the ratings nearby Maazel had not hesitated to curse him. Once, Luth had gone to the Captain's cabin for orders and had heard the Captain scream, 'They'll be surprised in Germany when I tell them about you!' And Dietrich had burst from the cabin, his face white. As white as the night Maazel had died.

Hessler poured out the last of the champagne with an unsteady hand. Then with a belch he lurched to his feet. 'Silence!' His harsh voice echoed and bounced round the long room like a gunshot, and a sea of faces turned up to him as if on hinges. Hessler lifted his glass. 'A toast! Lift your glasses and drink to the U-boat Service!' Nobody moved, but as the old accordionist jerked upright in his seat his instrument emitted one doleful squeak. Somebody laughed nervously, and Hessler's face flushed with sudden anger. With a flick of his powerful wrist he hurled an empty bottle across the room so that it shattered against the far wall with a splintering crash. Hessler beamed, the sweat running down from his close-cropped hair. 'Now drink, you frog-eating swine!' Mugs, glasses and coffee-cups were raised aloft, and Hessler downed his last drink with a grunt of satisfaction. 'Now we can go back to the mess,' he announced calmly.

As they walked down a hastily cleared passage between the still standing Frenchmen, Luth said quietly, 'You certainly know how to further the ways of German culture, Karl!'

Hessler regarded him blankly. 'Yes, I do!'

Luth shivered as the Atlantic wind lashed him in the face. Hessler was a good man to be with in action, but perhaps in future he would come ashore alone.

Long after they had crossed the square the café was still completely silent.

. . . . .

The dawn, which a few minutes earlier had been a mere grey smudge across the harbour entrance, pushed with slow insistence against the dripping stone breakwaters and glittered dully over the heaving water.

Rudulf Steiger tightened the white silk scarf around his throat and shrugged his shoulders deeper inside his stiff leather coat. It was strange how new and alien his clothes felt. Everything fresh and unfamiliar, nothing to touch or see which would bring some old memory alive. He shut his mind to the picture of his old metal sea-chest and those other well-used clothes. They were lying with his last crew on the bottom of the North Sea. It had not been deep where the U-boat had made her last dive. Not like the Atlantic, where the great depths would crush a sinking boat like a fish tin, with its tortured crew dying a terrible death in darkness, in what was said to be the worst agony known to man. No, his old boat would lie undisturbed for the rest of time.

Some of the compartments might even remain intact, mechanical tombs for the men who had stayed at their posts.

He looked up sharply as the steel plates beneath his feet began to shake with a steady and insistent vibration. The grey light was even stronger, and he could see the shadowy figures of the deck-party moving about the forecasing below him, and the glint of ice-rime along the jumping wire. Less than a week in harbour and the U-boat was all ready to leave again for the Atlantic. Her six bow tubes were loaded with new torpedoes, as was the one in her tail. Reloads lay gleaming in their racks, and the long hundred-and-five-millimetre gun on the forecasing was no longer streaked with weed and salt but shone beneath a blue coat of oil and grease.

The mooring wires dipped and tugged across the trapped water alongside, and Steiger could see the men on the jetty, their hands moving impatiently to release the submarine from the land. They wanted to be rid of her, to return to the peaceful life of the Base, to the attractions of the town.

It had been a busy week for Rudolf Steiger as he had played his dual role ashore and aboard his new command. He had met the other commanders, had many conferences with Captain Bredt, and spoken to the Headquarters at Lorient. It had left him no time for personal thoughts, and he was glad of that. He was glad, too, to be rid of the shore. He could not put it into words, he did not try. But as the submarine lurched against her fenders, and the familiar orders were barked along the narrow deck, he felt the old, testing strain replaced by cold excitement. Like the sense of lust mingled with fear experienced by a hunter, which indeed he was.

It was a pity he had not found more time to meet his officers and men. There would be little enough opportunity when they reached their assigned area, but then there was never time for anything any more. He thought of his First Lieutenant's face the previous night. Together they walked along the windswept sea wall until they were above the silent submarine. Dietrich had started to ask about the exercise the flotilla was going to carry out when Steiger had interrupted him.

'You might as well know now. There have been fresh orders. The flotilla is to sail at dawn without further delay.'

He remembered the pounding of the breakers along the beach and the measured tread of a nearby sentry. He had sensed the bewilderment and disbelief in the other officer, and had felt it change to shocked anger.

'But, sir! It's not fair! We're worn out, exhausted! It's madness to send us back so soon!' Dietrich had thrust his head towards Steiger so that he could see the eyes burning like twin fires in his pale face.

'They are my orders, Lieutenant.' Steiger spoke calmly, but there was nothing mild in his tone as he added, 'While I am in command all orders will be carried out without question!'

Dietrich's slim shoulders seemed to sag. 'Then the men will make mistakes. They are nearly all new men. It was bad enough on their first trip, the last captain was at least . . .' he faltered, and Steiger added quietly:

'Afraid? Is that what you were going to say?'

Dietrich turned away as if to hide his face, and Steiger continued evenly: 'He was a submariner before you entered the service. When Germany struggled to prepare for this war, when attack by Britain and her allies was inevitable, it was Maazel and many just like him who gave us the breathing space. Had he been killed or replaced in those early days his name would have been revered. As it is,' he shrugged, 'he died too late.'

Dietrich said in a muffled voice. 'He was a hard man to work with, sir.'

'Too hard, perhaps, so that he could not bend. Instead he broke!'

While they had stood looking down at the submarine, Steiger added: 'Every man aboard will have his own personal battle, but you and I can only afford one. Never forget that, Lieutenant.'

As he stood now on the vibrating bridge Steiger remembered that short conversation and those he had had with his other officers. Captain Maazel's stupidity had done its work well. The officers were no longer a team, they were small confused islands, dispirited, perhaps even afraid.

He could see Captain Bredt now, shining in the harsh dawn like some figure out of history. The empty sleeve which he wore with such pride looked rather pathetic, but Steiger dismissed him from his thoughts. Bredt had wanted to rouse the crews an hour earlier so that he or Steiger could address them. Steiger had merely said: 'They will do as I tell them. That is enough.'

It was odd the way Bredt accepted his uncompromising rebuffs. Bredt was a senior captain, just as he was in overall charge of operations. But Steiger knew his weakness. He needed a prop for his authority. Rank and officialdom were not enough. They never were with men like him. Although Bredt hung fast to his submariner's pride, he knew that he no longer belonged. To the men who served in U-boats he appeared little different from any staff officer. To them there was no one who counted but their own commander and Admiral Dönitz himself. Anyone between merely had to be obeyed or tolerated.

A grey hull slid past, the brief wash making the deck stagger beneath him. Alex Lehmann's boat. Now they had all sailed. The time was nearly ready. He remembered with sudden shock how tired and haggard his old friend had looked. He hardly spoke, not even of his wife in Germany whom he had married and left within days. Steiger frowned. It was wrong for any officer to marry in wartime, and for a commander it was madness. Any distraction could be fatal, and where an operation, the submarine and its crew depended on one man's eyes and judgement at the periscope it should not be allowed.

The voice-pipe squeaked and a petty officer bobbed his head to listen. 'Control room reports ready for sea, Captain!' The man's eyes were white in the gloom as he stared at his commander. 'Engine room standing by!'

'Good. Shut all watertight doors.' It would be well to take normal precautions even in St. Pierre. A stray mine, a badly handled French merchantman, anything like that could soon settle a slow-moving boat leaving harbour.

He adjusted the strap of his binoculars about his neck and stepped up on the small grating in front of the bridge. 'Stand by! Let go stern rope!'

There was a faint splash and then the clatter of feet as the men whipped the wire aboard before its eye could foul the propellers. He felt the fresh breeze against his cheek and watched with narrowed eyes as it pushed the wallowing hull away from the jetty. He frowned. Too slow. He had to remember that this was a bigger, heavier craft than his last one. 'Slow ahead starboard!' He tapped the toe of his boot slowly against the grating as the order was repeated down the voice-pipe. With a shudder the screw on the opposite side to the jetty began to thrash rhythmically at the dull water which surged along the curving ballast tanks. Very slowly the U-boat began to move ahead. The wire spring from the bows rose dripping from the water and tautened like a bowstring. As the raking stem surged against its unwanted bridle the stern reluctantly swung out into the harbour.

Steiger noticed that his mouth was quite dry and spoke harshly to cover his irritation. The boat handled well. It was a simple operation to spring the hull clear of the jetty. And yet . . .

'Stop starboard! Let go forward!' He watched the darting figures of the deck-party driven and controlled by Lieutenant Hessler's squat shape. Soon he would know them all. But first they would become a crew. Then the individuals would emerge. The weak and the strong. The genuine and the shams.

'All gone, sir!' Hessler's harsh voice carried clearly above the growling diesels.

'Slow astern together!'

The water beneath the pointed stern erupted into a thrashing maelstrom as the twin screws dragged the long grey hull back towards the centre of the harbour. Steiger glanced astern. The town was just visible in the growing light, the low roofs wet and miserable.

That was far enough. Ahead of the bows the narrow harbour entrance lay clear. Through it he could see the white-flecked waves and the shadowed sides of the big breakers. 'Slow ahead together. Starboard ten!' The boat rocked gently in the backwash and then thrust forward to meet her element.

A quick glance at the compass repeater. 'Steady, steer two-six-five!' He felt the boat steady about and settle on her first course. A good coxswain, at least, he thought.

He noticed that the deck-parties had fallen in forward and aft, their ranks swaying to the boat's easy motion. Bredt was a tiny figure now, his hand raised in salute. Steiger touched the peak of his white cap, the symbol of every U-boat commander, and dismissed the land and Bredt from his mind.

The harbour entrance seemed to widen as they approached, the two curved arms open like a child releasing a toy boat. There it was. The Bay of Biscay. Part of the Atlantic, the hunting ground.

He did not duck as a fine curtain of spray lifted over the bridge, the salt keen against his mouth. Overhead, two early-morning gulls dipped and screamed around the periscope standards and the damp, flapping ensign.

The flag was no longer at half-mast. A U-boat had lost its captain, a captain had lost his U-boat. Brought together they had given each other life again.

'Half ahead together! Steer two-seven-oh!' The sharp stem bit deeply into the first long roller and sliced through it with eager contempt. The broken wave thundered along on either side of the narrow hull and joined the churning white froth at her stern. She leaned very slightly as she curved on to her new course, the increased speed pushing her through the broken water with ease.

Around the small bridge the four lookouts were already in position, their glasses trained to cover every arc of danger. Behind the conning-tower the four-barrelled Vierling still wore its spray shield, but the magazines were loaded, and its gunners stood ready, their eyes towards the low clouds.

A signals rating hauled down the flag and rolled it carefully into a bright red bundle.

Steiger gripped the rim of the bridge as another roller loomed ahead of the raked bows, as if he were riding the U-boat like a charger. He watched the rating with the flag slide gratefully through the oval hatch and disappear. The deck-party were still working on the bucking forecasing, making sure that everything was secure for sea and the first dive.

He tightened his mouth into a sharp line. The flag had been taken down and stored away until their return. It was not needed any longer at sea. They were ready now. Ready for anything. A shaft of watery sunlight lanced briefly through the low clouds and flashed across the grey horizon line. Steiger settled down to watch it with the patient fascination of a hunter.

* * * * *

As the U-boat steadied on her now westerly course across the Bay of Biscay the seamen on the forecasing moved awkwardly back and forth along the narrow steel deck securing the mooring wires and other unwanted equipment in readiness for the first dive.

As their seaboots skidded on the slippery plates and their gloved hands grappled with newly greased gear they glanced occasionally at Lieutenant Hessler who leaned moodily on the slender guardrail, his eyes fixed on the creaming water as it sluiced alongside and over the rounded saddle tanks.

Max König blinked rapidly as he was caught unprepared by a sheet of icy spray flung over the bows, and wiped his lips with the back of his glove. Like most of the seamen around him he was working slowly, unwilling to leave the movement and life of the sea and sky about him, to exchange it for the muffled silence of the sealed hull below his feet. He squinted through the spray towards a dull grey shape which lay to the north like a cloud which by a freak of nature had fallen into the sea itself,

That must be Belle Île, he thought. His strong teeth showed momentarily in a grin of satisfaction as he added the new-found knowledge to all the other things he had learned since he had joined the U-boat. Astern the land subsided into the murk, and he gave a great sigh of satisfaction. Whatever danger lay ahead of the submarine, he was among friends. His new life had started three months earlier when he had joined the boat for its last patrol, his mistakes and clumsiness had been taken for granted amongst a crew comprised almost entirely of other new recruits, and had been readily forgiven by the harassed officers because of his willingness and apparent unruffled calm under all the harrowing weeks of patrol which they had endured.

Whatever happened elsewhere he was now Max König, seaman gunner, a small part of Germany's élite.

The roar and hiss of the turbulent water lulled his mind like music, and he allowed his thoughts to drift back to the spring of nineteen-forty-three. Almost a year ago, he thought with sudden surprise. He remembered the rawness of his lacerated hands as he had shovelled away rubble and blasted stonework, his empty stomach revolted by the stench of the bombing, the stink of burning flesh which seemed all around him. It had been in Hamburg, but it could have been anywhere. Each day the wretched inmates of the concentration camp had been crammed into trucks and driven to wherever labour was required. He had been strong even then, after six months of living death. Six months of beatings and humiliations, of interrogations and a nightmare of hopelessness.

Then they had been sent to the Naval Recruitment Depot in Hamburg. It had been dawn, with tiny patches of bright blue sky showing through the twisting palls of smoke which hung over the battered town. The Depot had been straddled by a stick of bombs, and the long, cheerless huts had been set ablaze by the incendiaries which followed.

Working like automatons the prisoners had blundered blindly through the smoke and crackling flames while the S.S. guards had kept at a safe distance, for once silent and afraid.

It had been an unreal world of pain and noise, and it was while he had been working alone in the semi-darkness that he had found the trapped figure of a man beneath a great charred roof support. He was nearly dead, his powerful limbs suddenly pathetic and useless as he stared with terrified eyes at the fire which moved relentlessly towards him.

Suddenly the world had faded for the prisoner who stooped

warily over the prostrate figure below him. He had half listened to the man's grumbling and pleading as he tried to free his broken legs from the pressure of the beam, but had been aware of the scheme which was already forming in his tortured mind. As he pulled the man clear the body gave a great shudder and life was gone with the suddenness to which the prisoner had become so hardened and accustomed. With frantic desperation he stripped the tattered uniform from the corpse, his fingers clumsy with excitement as he stuffed the man's documents and identity cards back into the pockets of the naval jacket after one quick examination. Max König changed from a dead, crushed corpse to a tall swaying figure who stripped away his own striped prison clothes and stood naked in the swirling smoke. Around him the air was thick with noise and cries, yet still no one else came near. With his breath rasping in his lungs he pulled on the torn trousers and boots and slipped the jacket around his shoulders. The loose prison overall was easy to drape across the corpse, and the ill-made wooden clogs which all the prisoners wore were made to fit anybody. There was just one more thing to do. With his strong teeth gripping his sleeve to withstand the searing pain, he leaned his full weight against the glowing end of the burning beam. He had learned to accept and understand pain quite well after his months under the Gestapo, and the knowledge that the red-hot embers were burning away his flesh and the tattooed identification number gave him just sufficient strength to keep him from screaming once more.

It was a clumsy, desperate plan, the moment's deed, the action of a man driven to the extremes of a trapped animal. If a guard had come to that part of the bombed building, or a man who knew him, he might have suffered in vain. But, instead, a party of seamen had forced their way into the smoke and found him alive but unconscious. They hardly glanced at the dead body in smouldering prison clothes who lay half consumed by the advancing flames, but hurried away with what they believed was one of their own kind.

He awoke in an unreal world of white sheets and silence, and once again coincidence and fate played on his side. They needed beds, and an injured recruit with a deep but safe burn on his arm was nothing but a hindrance. In three weeks he was on the move again, to a Training Depot in Cuxhaven. Every day was a nightmare of suspense and fear, but around him the complete orderliness of service life seemed to exclude discovery, and as the time went by he began to realise that he was safe. No letters came for him, he seemed to have no life beyond the walls of the barracks, and when the chance came to volunteer for the U-boat Service he had taken it. The last link with the outside world would be broken. All the main submarine bases were in Occupied France. Away from the concentration camps, away from Germany, he would be safe in the one place where he would not be hunted.

Lieutenant Hessler's harsh voice cut through his uneasy thoughts. 'Jump to it! Do you think this is a damned pleasure trip?'

König smiled and hurried towards the conning-tower. Even Hessler seemed gentle after the camp guards, and the closeness of his new tiny world made up for the rest.

He glanced sideways at the tall figure in the forefront of the bridge as he reached the hatch. Captain Steiger. A man whose exploits he had read even before he had been arrested by the Gestapo. He was said to be the ace of U-boat commanders, a real hero, and not just some stupid instrument of propaganda. How could a man like that live and fight for Germany with such ruthless dedication when he must know of his country's tyranny and corrupt cruelty?

As König reached the bottom of the conning-tower ladder he saw his new-found friend Horst Jung, a battered-faced boxer from Lubeck, standing with a mug of steaming soup in his outstretched fist. Max König took the mug and allowed his tense mind to relax. This was real. Everything else was conjecture and memory and was no longer to be trusted.

. . . . .

Rudolf Steiger lowered his binoculars and watched the two fighter aircraft skim low over the U-boat's wake and then turn away towards the shore. In a few seconds their wafer-thin silhouettes were lost in the haze which already hid the French coast, and once more the sea was empty.

He leaned his elbows on the rim of the bridge and watched the bows corkscrewing into each successive roller. Behind him he could hear the lookouts shuffling their feet and the steady pulsating beats of the twin diesels. Through the open hatch came the familiar smell of a submarine, diesel oil and boiled cabbage, damp and sweat. He remembered his very first cruise in a small coastal submarine in the Baltic, and the carefree atmosphere of an exclusive yacht which had prevailed. In peacetime they had often visited British ports and had been entertained by the

Royal Navy. Yet always, in spite of the loud-voiced speeches of comradeship and friendly rivalry, there had been an air of tension, as if both sides knew in their hearts that eventual war was inevitable. The British could never win, he thought, in spite of their allies and powerful forces. They made the mistake of over-confidence and the sense of superiority brought about by tradition and past victories.

He wondered briefly how his father would have felt about this war. Rudolf Steiger had found his father's fame, coupled with the long line of naval ancestors, almost a handicap at the beginning of his naval career. It was as if his father had represented something dangerous and alien to the new Germany, a heritage of class and privilege. Rudolf Steiger had been able to ignore these things because he knew only too well the real story and all the suffering which had gone with it. He had been eleven years old when his father, the great Felix von Steiger, had been released by the British at the end of the First World War. He remembered still the impact the homecoming had made on him, and the shock he had felt when he had seen the frail, sick figure who had once struck fear and admiration throughout the world. His father had commanded a commerce raider, a converted merchant ship, and had taken the war against the enemy supply ships deep into the South Atlantic before he was eventually beaten and captured by a British cruiser. His small son had been staying with a simple but well-meaning uncle at the time, and the shock of his father's capture had left him dazed and frightened. His mother had died a year earlier, and the great house which had been the family home for generations on the banks of the Plöner See had become empty and desolate.

He remembered, too, with ever present bitterness, how the house had been bought by a fat Munich banker, and how the money had hardly covered the debts incurred while von Steiger had been fighting for Germany's survival. Those years which followed closely on the collapse of Germany were clearly imprinted on Rudolf Steiger's mind, they had served him as an unfailing warning and incentive at the very beginning of his own career when the new Germany had risen above the wreckage of corruption and anarchy.

His father had been loyal to the old traditions to the end of his life. Even after the naval mutinies and the terrible days when the red flag had appeared in the streets of Kiel, when a naval officer could hardly get enough bread for his family, and when he himself had sold his prized medals and decorations for the sake of his young son, he still maintained his belief that honour and tradition would prevail, that Germany's ex-enemies would not stand by and see a gallant foe allowed to sink into rebellion and shame.

He had died believing those things, his tired mind still critical of Germany's new leaders and the vital, ambitious plans they envisaged. Rudolf Steiger had searched until he had found his father's old decorations and had given them back to him, and even that had been nothing to the pride he had seen in his father's eyes when he had been accepted for a naval cadetship. Steiger smiled to himself. His father had hated submarine warfare in the First World War. He often said it had started the wildfire of hatred which had eventually brought the world against Germany in one combined force. What would he have thought had he lived to see his son driving home the hard-won lessons of those far-off days?

Steiger had dropped all his connections with his past, and had refrained from using the hallmark of the early aristocracy into which he had been born. He had no family, nothing to shake him from his unswerving and dedicated course in his efforts to serve his country in the best way he knew.

In the great sail-driven training ships as a half-starved cadet he had endured the harsh discipline and senseless bullying without faltering, keeping a large portion of his mind occupied with his own future and laying his plans accordingly. He had served under a succession of officers who had left their mark on him one way or another. The good ones he remembered with admiration and critical approval. But even the bad officers found a place in his ordered mind, if only to serve him as a warning.

He recalled the first month of the war when he had been a junior watchkeeper in a submarine patrolling the North Sea. They had attacked a small freighter and had surfaced while the crew took to the lifeboats. He still remembered the feeling of nakedness as the U-boat had rolled uneasily on the flat, oily water with the broken ship nearby, her sturdy hull still refusing to sink. The U-boat commander had waited calmly for the boats to be lowered and the shocked crew to pull clear before he fired the final torpedo.

A year later that same commander had died carrying out the same sort of deed. An aircraft had dived out of the clouds and bombed the submarine to its death. Steiger often wondered what that commander must have thought at that last moment. Did he remember his own words to Steiger a year earlier? He had said then when he had seen the apprehension on the young officer's face: 'In war you must always play by the rules! There is no other way.' He had died doing just that. He was no hero because of his beliefs. In fact he could be looked upon as a traitor, a man who had used his authority to sacrifice a submarine and its crew for some personal satisfaction. War was *not* a game, and Steiger had fought his own battles accordingly. The men who had bought his father's house, who had lived with the ancient oil paintings of the von Steiger family, no doubt believed that *they* had served their own part in Germany's struggle and were moist-eyed and fiercely proud of the heritage they had done nothing to help. Adolf Hitler had done much to stamp out that sort of deception, and after the war they would finish what he had started.

A voice interrupted his brooding thoughts, and he turned to find Dietrich at his side. The First Lieutenant's face was calmer than he had seen it before, almost resigned, he thought.

'Boat trimmed for diving, Captain.' He glanced swiftly along the horizon, his pale eyes empty of expression. 'I have checked all the new stores. Everything is properly stowed.'

Steiger nodded. The first dive after a stay in harbour was always a worry. With full fuel tanks, additional stores and ammunition the density of the hull would have changed quite considerably. 'Very well, Heinz, we will dive in five minutes.'

Dietrich seemed startled at Steiger's casual use of his first name, and Steiger wondered just what sort of a U-boat Captain Maazel had been running before he was killed.

'How long have you been First Lieutenant?' He watched Dietrich's face stiffen into a guarded mask.

'Just over a year, Captain.'

'And in the Atlantic about two and a half, eh?'

Dietrich nodded, and Steiger saw his hands clench inside his leather mittens.

'You should have a command of your own by now. I expect you're more than ready for that?'

'I think so, sir.' His answer was cautious and evasive, and Steiger's doubts hardened. Captain Maazel's confidential log-book was missing. It was a form of rough diary in which U-boat commanders were expected to note down defects of their boats, remarks about their officers' capabilities, etc. As it was made in the heat of the moment, it was considered invaluable by the Naval Staff when they had to assess the standards of their sea-going officers for promotion and training. Maazel's own logbook was assumed to have been on his person when he had been killed. Steiger frowned. Every first lieutenant should be eager for promotion and resentful of any delay in what he would consider his right to a command. Unless he was a coward, or totally unsuited in every way. Dietrich seemed neither, but his reserved and careful answers were surprisingly unusual.

Steiger glanced at his watch. 'Clear the bridge!' He snapped down the voice-pipe cover and turned to watch the lookouts struggling through the narrow hatch. Dietrich took a last glance along the empty deck and followed them below.

Steiger breathed deeply, enjoying the moment of complete peace and seclusion. After this there would be no more leisurely dives, no more calm preparations. In future every action would be sparked off by instinct and danger.

He watched the gulls which still circled hopefully over the glistening whaleback of the hull and wondered if the rest of the flotilla had fanned out to their prescribed routes as he had planned. He wondered also which commander would send the first sighting report to bring the others in for the kill, and who would break first if the odds were too great. With a grimace he tightened his binoculars about his neck and slid down the ladder inside the conning-tower. The electric motors had replaced the diesels, and he could sense the expectancy below him in the control room.

I am anxious about their capabilities, he thought, and yet they are just as much worried about me. Perhaps they think I may have cracked after losing my last boat? He slammed the hatch over his head and gave the brass locking wheel a vicious turn. Perhaps I have? How can any man know until it is too late?

He dropped the last few feet into the control room. 'Flood!' His voice cut across the tense atmosphere where the hydroplane operators crouched over their wheels, their eyes patiently watching the stationary depth needles and where Reche, the Navigator, leaned his elbows on his chart table, his face squinting with concentration as he worked swiftly with parallel rulers and a pencil.

'Flood!' Luth repeated the order into his handset, his calm engineer's face watching the flooding-table where the coloured lights were all showing 'Ready to dive' on each dial.

Steiger braced his legs and stood upright in the centre of the crowded space, his head brushing an overhead pipe, his arm around one of the sheathed periscopes. 'Ninety metres!' He saw Luth nod and glance quickly at his gauges.

'Five, four, three, two—both!' Luth twisted his thin neck to follow the movements of his men as they leapt like monkeys to open the valve levers.

Steiger released his breath very slowly. It was surprising how tense he had become. The lights on the board flickered to show that the valves were open and water was thundering into the ballast tanks on either side of the hull.

'One!' Luth ordered the final valve to be opened right aft. The U-boat vibrated like a finely tuned instrument as the depth needles began to creep round the great dials. Five fathoms, eight fathoms, twelve, twenty . . . the deck canted obediently, and Steiger saw the tiny beads of sweat glinting on Dietrich's pale face as he stood behind the Coxswain, a little weasel of a man from Essen, who gripped the wheel and glared at the gyro compass as if he hated it, and he wondered if, like himself, Dietrich was remembering the boisterous, empty sea above which with every second that ticked away drew further and further from the diving submarine.

A man in the passageway beyond the control room gave a little cry as the metal in the hull emitted a sharp crack, and then looked shamefaced as Hessler barked dourly: 'What are you worried about, eh? It's not everyone who gets buried in a coffin worth twenty-five million marks!'

Still the boat planed deeper. Thirty fathoms, thirty-five, forty . . . down . . . down, the planesmen tensed their bodies and spun the wheels, their combined breath misting the great implacable dials. The boat steadied, and as Luth passed his calm orders Steiger could hear the vents slamming shut and the water already being pumped from forward to aft in the trimming tanks to control the downward plunge.

'Steady at ninety metres, Captain!'

Steiger nodded and half listened to the telephones and voice-pipes buzzing their information from one end of the hull to the other. Like the men around him and out of sight in the other compartments who had to be completely sure of their own tasks, every piece of equipment and mechanism had to be as efficient as the day it was installed. From right forward where the torpedoes lay waiting in their tubes, through the narrow central gangway bordered by the magazines, switchboards, refrigeration compartments, stores, radio room, crew spaces, control room, galley, battery compartments, to the aft section of the hull with its massive engine room and electric motor space, and finally the hindmost torpedo tube, the 'sting in the tail', every inch of space was crammed with wiring, dials, pipes and switches. Every wire was like part of a complex blood and nerve system, which in its turn was indirectly connected to the eye and brain of the U-boat commander.

Dietrich returned from his inspection of the hull. 'All secure, Captain!'

Luth put down his handset. 'Boat correctly trimmed, Captain.'

'Very well. Return to twenty metres.' Steiger turned to Reche. 'Lay off a new course at oh-nine-hundred, and tell the radio room to report every signal intercepted once we surface!'

'Twenty metres, Captain?'

Steiger flung his leg astride the small metal stool which was riveted in the centre of the control room, and rested his hands on the periscope. 'Fourteen metres!'

He waited in silence as Luth controlled the boat's final rise to periscope depth, then signalled with his thumb for the shining metal tube to be raised.

He crouched, his forehead pressed against the rubber pad, and watched as the swirling green shadows in the lens changed to silver and grey, and as the tip of the periscope broke the surface he saw again the low, hostile sky and the great breakers which seemed to rear over and blind the seeking eye with silent fury. A quick look round, and another brief scrutiny directly overhead. No ships, no aircraft. He snapped up the periscope handles and stood up as it hissed back into its tube.

'Surface! Anti-aircraft gun's crew close up! Double lookouts!' He turned to look at Dietrich as the U-boat's silence gave way to bustling excitement. 'Drum into your lookouts the importance of their work in the Bay. The British may not care to attack from the air, but they can pin us on the surface until warships can be sent for. See to it that we see them first!'

He waited a while longer until the hatch was open and the diesels were thundering away once more, sucking down great gulps of salt air to stem the tide of staleness and mould which was never far off, and then he walked forward to his tiny cabin. As the crew were dismissed from Diving Stations they parted to let him through, their faces watching him with awe or apprehension.

He pulled the curtain across his cabin doorway and threw himself on the bunk, his eyes open and unblinking. He had masked his feelings from the others, as he knew he could, but he could not deceive himself. His heart had been beating faster and his mouth had been dry when the U-boat had dived for the first time. With an impatient sigh he rolled on to his side and closed his eyes.

Overhead on the swaying bridge the lookouts and the Officer of the Watch peered steadily at the horizon. Men on a tiny steel island surrounded by the vast, wind-torn wastes of the Atlantic which, as ever, remained indifferent to the ships and men who sailed it. Below the conning-tower throughout the grey hull the other forty-odd men worked or waited for the inevitable. But in his small cabin their captain was asleep.

3 : The Convoy

Heinz Dietrich clung to the wardroom curtain as the deck gave another sickening roll beneath his feet. They had been at sea for over a week now and the weather had deteriorated with each weary hour on watch. Up on the swaying conning-tower Dietrich had at least been able to concentrate on the approaching rollers and prepare his numb body accordingly. It had helped to take his mind off other things and make the agonising hours pass more quickly. Overhead the sky was so dark that the grey sea appeared almost gay by comparison, and as the U-boat swooped and slashed at each white-toothed wave Dietrich found time to wonder at the sea's complete desolation and emptiness.

He blinked in the dull yellow glare from the misted light bulbs, and slid his body along the top of a locker and wedged his elbows on the canting table. His face was stiff with salt and rime, and his eyes felt as if their sockets were lined with dry sand.

Stohr, a torpedoman who served also as officers' messman, poked his head around the curtain and stared at the First Lieutenant with round questioning eyes. 'Eggs and sliced bacon, Lieutenant?' He waited, watching the emotions chasing each other across Dietrich's face. 'We still have some fairly fresh bread,' he added as an additional temptation.

Dietrich shook his head. 'Just tea, Stohr. Bring me some tea with some lemon juice.'

A curtain jerked beside one of the bunks, and Luth stuck his dishevelled face through the opening. 'Bring *me* his bacon, Stohr! Make a nice sandwich!' He blinked at Dietrich and rubbed his eyes. 'What's happening? Where are we?'

Dietrich yawned, the effort making his jaws crack. 'Still steering south-west. Afternoon Watch have just closed up at their stations.' He took the great mug of tea and steadied it against his arm.

Luth received his sandwich and lay back with a sigh of satisfaction. Between gulps he mumbled: 'Well, Heinz, we still get the best food in Germany! I'll bet your brother could do with some of this on the Eastern Front, eh?'

Dietrich shuddered and gripped his mug with such force that the enamel flaked from its chipped surface. 'He's dead!'

Luth sat up with a jerk, the bacon fat running down his stubbled face. 'Dead? My God, Heinz, I'm sorry. I didn't know . . .' His voice trailed away as he stared at Dietrich's stricken face.

'I don't want to talk about it.' Dietrich stared unblinkingly at the greasy surface of his tea and watched it sway towards the lip of the mug, falter, and then fall back to the other side. Around him and beyond the curtain the boat creaked and groaned with each dizzy swoop, and the diesels' combined beat varied with every savage thrust through the broken water. He remembered with sudden loathing the gleam in Captain Maazel's piggy eyes as he had shouted: 'I know of your brother! A damned, gutless coward!' He had waved his little logbook in front of Dietrich's face. 'Shot for cowardice, eh? Shot like a stinking swine of a traitor!'

He had screamed and yelled for several minutes, but Dietrich had shut his mind to the meaningless tangle of abuse. Albert was dead. He could see him now, the thin, frail scholar who had always been slightly amused by his younger brother's obsession with the navy. Albert Dietrich had ignored the changing Germany about him and had concentrated upon his own realistic yet isolated world within the university. He studied Greek while Heinz struggled with the mysteries of navigation and the handling of small arms. He discussed lunar logic of an age which had been in dust for two thousand years while his brother was prepared for a war which would make all others seem childlike in their simplicity of aims.

Dietrich knew his brother was no soldier, how he ever attained the rank of lieutenant was also beyond him, but of one thing he was also just as sure. He was no coward. He had spoken to soldiers in the French hospitals outside Lorient, and had tried to understand from their disjointed descriptions the vastness and the horror of the war in Russia. These maimed and limbless men, pinch-faced and old before their time, had spoken almost casually of places which to Dietrich were unknown. They spoke of them with the ease brought by familiarity. A battalion had been wiped out there, or they had fallen back because they had run out of ammunition and had not eaten for four days. Little sentences, tiny fragments which built up in Dietrich's desperate mind the picture of his brother's last place on earth. Captain Maazel had been informed of his execution by firing squad. Not in order that Dietrich might be spared the horror of the news or have it halved by Maazel's understanding. Dietrich ground his teeth with helpless fury as he recalled the slating words and the threats which Maazel had flung in his face. Dietrich was due for a command, or *had* been until this. It appeared that when the High Command were fully aware of the shame of Dietrich's family a command of anything was not only unlikely, it was an insult even to suggest.

Dietrich ground his teeth even harder as he thought of Steiger's casual questions before they had dived. Perhaps no one else knew yet? Perhaps the logbook which he had flung over the rail with Maazel's carcass was the only record as yet?

I have to get out of this boat. Away from all those who ask questions and make every conversation a nightmare.

Luth said quietly: 'He did not die alone. I hope their sacrifice is not too late!'

Dietrich lowered his head on to his arms. A few months ago and I would have yelled at Luth for his lack of confidence. I used to get so angry with Albert and his cheerful mockery. He was always poking fun at Germany's leaders, the parades, the show of might which I in turn worshipped.

Now he is out there in the snow and mud alongside a million others. What will they care who died valiantly or who died in vain? For them it is too late.

Maazel had threatened, 'Wait until we get back to Germany!' He intended to drag Dietrich's name in the dirt, if only to cover up his own weakness and fear.

I am glad I killed him. He was afraid like Albert, yet he condemned my brother as if to gather strength from his blood.

Franz Luth peered down at the sprawled figure on the table and wondered. He was fond of Heinz Dietrich, yet he did not know why. The exhausted First Lieutenant was a quiet, unapproachable man at the best of times, and although he had always been friendly enough in the past, he had appeared as a listener rather than one of the wardroom's tight brotherhood. Now he seemed so tense, so unbearably overloaded with inner torment, that Luth did not think he could last much longer.

He sighed and rolled on to his back. That was the trouble, really. They had all been at it too long. They knew every irritating mannerism and habit of those crammed alongside them. A second's anger could fan up into a fire which could destroy the boat as surely as any depth-charge.

The scream of alarm bells tore across his troubled thoughts like a razor, and he was out of the bunk, fighting against the curtain and the running figures beyond before he realised what was happening.

. . . . .

Rudolf Steiger wedged his body more firmly into one corner of his small cabin and pressed his knees against the folding desk which was bolted to one bulkhead. He stared at the piled charts and well-thumbed reference books and stifled a yawn, his bristled chin rasping against his high-necked sweater. Everything was damp and grimy, and the cold air seemed even sharper with diesel fumes than usual as the boat rolled and plunged into the teeth of a big sea as it broke across the casing and sluiced against the swaying conning-tower, but the noises were distant and muffled, like the sounds of breakers and surf in a sheltered cove. Only the sickening motion was there to remind him that his boat was still running on the surface and danger was ever present.

As he had expected, a week at sea had broken down the barrier of anonymity in the crew, and already the faces had gained character and personality so that he could watch a man, listen to him for a few moments, and gauge some of his quality. Most of his discoveries had not been encouraging. The ratings, new for the most part to submarine life, seemed loose and aimless in their duties, and their previous cruise had done more harm than good and nothing to bind them into the essential team.

He peered at the spidery pencilled course drawn on the nearest chart to their present approximate position, one hundred miles west of Cape Finisterre. A small convoy had been reported heading for their patrol line, a handful of supply ships outward bound from Gibraltar and making passage to Britain. U-boat Headquarters had signalled that these ships had already been attacked by U-boats operating off Lisbon, without success. Steiger's lip curled with irritation. He could well imagine the battering the grey attackers had received from the British down there. Gibraltar and its approaches had been a burial place for many a German, yet U-boats were still optimistically homed into that area. A couple of years ago, even less, and such attacks would have been easy. He himself had prowled almost within the Rock's shadow to torpedo and sink the precious supply ships. It was so maddening that in U-boat Headquarters and Berlin there were senior officers who still could not appreciate the change of strategy. Admiral Dönitz understood well enough, but even he had to listen to his advisers and pay service to the muddlers in high places.

Dönitz had been right to spread the weight of the U-boat arm. Against the packed ranks of the Allied navies it was suicide to group submarines in a mere handful of tempting target areas. Stretch the enemy's resources to the limit and he was beaten. Finally and completely.

He tensed his muscles as an order was shouted in the control room and repeated by some anonymous seaman. I must try to relax. Every strange sound seems to convey a threat or a new meaning.

He frowned. It was impossible to change now. Other men, in that impossible unreal world of peace, might have one great event in a whole lifetime to consider. With him, every hour of each day might bring just one more threat, one more terrifying obstacle to be overcome, so that he could never rest on his past achievements. He skated on thin ice and must live with it.

A nerve jumped in his cheek as the alarm bells began to jangle their unearthly tune.

He jumped to his feet, his hands automatically reaching for his binoculars and pistol. He always disliked keeping a Lüger with him at all times, its weight seemed to be a constant reminder of what could happen if his own power of command was broken.

In the control room the atmosphere was already tense and apprehensive as the lights flickered impatiently on the flooding-table. The electric motors whined into life, and the deck began to tilt as the hull responded to the urgent demands of the hydroplanes.

Gunter Reche, the Navigator, followed the lookouts down the bridge ladder, his wind-seared face uneasy and strained. For a moment he stood in his dripping rubber suit, his protruding eyes blinking from the depth dials to the helmsman, and then he saw Steiger and licked his lips with quick nervous movements of his tongue.

'Destroyer, sir! Bearing red five-oh!' He faltered. 'I think she's Spanish. Not like any Britisher I've ever seen.'

He paused as Luth called, 'Forty metres, Captain!'

Steiger bit his lip with impatience. Reche was a nervous fool, but it was too late to start explaining things to him now. No destroyer would see a U-boat in this sort of weather. With its low hull trimmed right down and the slender conning-tower blending with the waves which had been their constant companions since they had left harbour, even radar would be baffled.

Reche added miserably, 'The range is about four thousand metres.'

Steiger bit back his annoyance. Reche had already created an unfavourable impression. He was a bully, and his nerves seemed so brittle that he always appeared as if he had difficulty in keeping his actions under control. Because Reche had ordered a dive a fresh decision was required, and at once. If they remained submerged too long they might miss contact with the expected convoy. If they surfaced they might attract the attention of a nosy Spaniard, who in turn could give away their position.

In a flat voice Steiger said, 'Remember that in future you will not give the order to dive unless the range is so small you can be detected.' He looked for some light of understanding in the other man's face. 'We *must* remain on the surface for every possible minute we can!'

Reche dropped his eyes and bit his lip like a petulant child. In his thin receding hair Steiger could see the sweat gleaming like dew, although the air in the control room was still cold-tinged with the icy sea above.

Steiger gestured briefly at Luth. 'Periscope depth!' He waited, feeling isolated and uneasy. It was so difficult to give his whole being to the task in hand when he could not rely on those around him. If only there was more time.

'Fourteen metres, Captain!'

He crouched on the stool and waited for the periscope to slide smoothly from its well. The waves, lopsided and huge, defied every effort to find the other vessel, and Steiger found that he was gripping the handles with his full strength as if to hold back the threatening fury of his frustration.

'Raise her, Luth!' He pressed his forehead against the rubber pad and swung the periscope in a slow arc as the U-boat lifted itself a little more in the plunging water. Her casing was no longer concealed, and she was riding dangerously clear of the water He gritted his teeth. It would be just like some stupid Spaniard to come snooping round here. Probably out of Vigo on some useless mission or other. He stiffened as the low shape floated across the streaming lens and then steadied across the cross-wires of the sight.

'Down periscope! Twenty metres!'

He sat crouched on the stool, his strong fingers twisting at a button on his bridge coat. Between his teeth he said: 'Reche, you are a stupid fool! That is no Spaniard, it's a British escort vessel!'

Reche's pasty face seemed to go grey. 'I—I don't understand, sir! Four funnels, too—too old I thought . . .'

His voice faded as Steiger said harshly: 'One of the old ex-American destroyers given to the British in 1940. Any fool should know their silhouettes by heart!' He raised his voice so that it echoed around the silent control room. 'There is *no* excuse for negligence, and I will not tolerate it!'

He found that his hands were trembling, and he gripped the leather button of his coat with savage force. 'Alter course and steer one-eight-five!' He tried to blot out Reche's outraged face and the shocked surprise of the others, and concentrated on the picture which was so reluctant to form in his mind. The escort ship was steering almost due north. Probably on the right wing of the invisible convoy. It was unlikely that such an old ship would be alone. On the other hand . . . He stopped his racing thoughts with the suddenness of shutting a flood-gate. It was no use. They must surface and risk the possibility of discovery. Every U-boat made a disturbance when blowing to the surface, but the risk had to be taken. If they alone had sighted the convoy then they had the responsibility of informing the rest of Group Meteor.

'Surface!' He dropped the command into the stillness, and found a small comfort from the excitement which moved like a chill wind through the crowded space.

He walked unhurriedly to the ladder and stepped on to the bottom rung. Over his shoulder he said, 'Lieutenant Hessler, bring all tubes to the ready!' He saw Dietrich watching him over the helmsman's stooped shoulders. 'Heinz, tell the radio room to stand by to transmit!'

He watched the depth needles creeping back round the dials, and heaved himself up the ladder. Twenty metres, fourteen, ten, he swung the locking wheel and pressed his shoulder against the hatch. Icy water cascaded over his shoulders and across the upturned faces of the lookouts below him. Then he was through the hatch, his boots skidding on the streaming plates as the trapped water surged through the drain holes and the rest of the hull reared like a desperate shark through the black-sided wave troughs.

Heedless of the spray and the sudden intensity of the wind, he levelled his glasses over the rim of the bridge. There it was, away over the port bow, converging now on an almost parallel course. The old destroyer was rolling through steep, sickening arcs, her four slender funnels moving from one frantic angle to the other. Steiger smiled bleakly. He had heard that these old ships had been designed for the quiet Pacific waters and were no match for the Atlantic in winter. Out of their element, overloaded and top-heavy with extra equipment, they had their work cut out to stay afloat. He swung his glasses carefully ahead, conscious of the lookouts behind his back as they followed his example. He stiffened like a gun-dog. On the heaving, white-capped horizon, in direct line with the U-boat's raked bows, he could just make out the faintest smudge of something moving and alive. Not one ship but several. His experienced eyes remained fixed on the wave-shrouded shapes even though his cheeks ran with tears as the needled spray dashed over the conning-tower and seemed to pierce his very skin. It was the convoy. It looked like a line of merchantmen in the middle of a zig-zag, their ragged shapes blended momentarily into one as they completed their turn. If their mean course remained constant they would run straight across his own approach.

He shouted above the roar and hiss of water: 'Convoy dead ahead! Range five thousand metres!' He waited impatiently as a petty officer repeated the information down the voice-pipe. 'We will attack on the surface. Tell the radio room to signal the group. Position, course and speed of convoy!'

He heard the periscope squeak in its standard behind him, and imagined Dietrich relaying the bearings and distances to the waiting men in the control room.

He turned his attention to the destroyer. It was getting nearer, but its low hull was awash and glistening as it rolled into each new trough. 'Alter course two points to starboard!' No point in inviting danger.

He felt almost exultant as the U-boat's bows slewed round away from the watchdog. The attack by the other U-boats near Gibraltar had done him some good, after all. It seemed as if the British had kept most of their escorts astern of the convoy in case of a fresh attempt to break through. They did not anticipate another group ahead of them.

The voice-pipe crackled. 'Three of our group have acknowledged, sir! They are getting into position for attack. The nearest boat will close the convoy in half an hour.'

Steiger nodded. By that time we will have attacked. We will have been successful, or . . .

'Full speed ahead!' This was no time for stupid pessimism. The boat was committed. *He* had clinched their fate one way or the other.

. . . . .

Dietrich stood watchfully in the centre of the control room. To all outward appearances he was calm enough, yet as the stream of range and fire control orders were passed down from the range-finder and fed into the action plot he could feel his heart pumping in time with the diesels' furious beat. He could imagine the Captain overhead on the narrow bridge, his eyes now glued to the attack-sight—an enormous telescope which was always rigged for a surface engagement—his brain wrestling with every alteration of course and speed from the distant enemy.

Lieutenant Hessler crouched over his torpedo-switch panel, a headset held loosely in one hand with one earpiece jammed beneath the rim of his cap, his deep-set eyes expressionless as he waited for his men at the tubes to report.

'Tubes one to six—ready!' Hessler grunted and flicked down his switches. The bow doors were open, the steel fish were waiting and prepared. From right aft another call. 'Tube seven—ready!' All switches made.

Dietrich wondered briefly if Reche had really thought the destroyer was Spanish, or whether he had been afraid to wait and find out. He had never liked the Navigator, but until now had been prepared to accept his disgruntled and pessimistic attitudes. Steiger had seen through his loud-mouthed defences, and Dietrich knew that in the Captain's eyes every officer and man was now suspect.

The blowers and compressors were screeching like mad things, and Luth winked quickly at his assistant, a bluff petty officer called Richter. 'Soon now! We will be amongst the Tommies any minute!'

Richter forced a grin. 'Let's hope we get it over quickly.'

Luth glanced across at Dietrich. 'The Chinese have a saying. Of all the thirty-six alternatives, running away is the best!'

Richter laughed, but Dietrich's voice was harsh as he barked: 'Hold your noise there! And keep those remarks to yourself!'

Luth flushed and turned his face back to his dials. It was not like Dietrich to explode in front of the others.

Dietrich rubbed his aching eyes with his knuckles. It had only been a casual remark from Luth. Or had it? Did they all know about his brother? Perhaps they had expected *him* to crack, too! As he allowed the thought to play across his raw nerves like a knife he imagined Steiger dying like Maazel and he himself being left in command. Not after a patrol, running for home, but *now*, with the enemy steaming right across the cross-wires.

He could feel the bile rising in his throat, choking him, and he looked desperately at the men crouched over their dials and levers, their faces blank, their eyes empty.

Hessler pressed his earphone closer and nodded. 'Very good. Target red four-five. Range four thousand. Torpedo speed thirty knots, running depth seven metres!' He repeated his instructions calmly in his flat grating voice, and Dietrich watched him as if mesmerised. You never knew anybody until you saw him in action. The trips ashore, the quick furtive moments of forced gaiety, meant nothing. Only this was real now. The neat uniforms, gold lace and proud badges were as much of a farce here as they were on the Russian Front. Men became animals, beasts searching out hiding places and opportunities to kill.

Hessler looked unruffled, concentrating on his torpedoes. Steiger was going to fire from the bridge controls, yet Hessler did not seem to notice. Any other torpedo officer might have thought that the Captain did not trust him to complete the firing, or perhaps, after all, Hessler was no longer keen on responsibility.

'Stand by one to four!'

'Ready!' Hessler caught Dietrich's fixed stare and shrugged.

'Fire!' The boat staggered as up forward the first fish leapt from its tube. At intervals of just over a second the next three followed, while Luth's men pumped water forward to compensate for the sudden loss of weight. It had often been known for a submarine's bows to rear right up at the moment of firing, and at this speed of eighteen knots a boat could be rendered helpless for the next vital moments.

'Hard a-starboard!' The voice-pipes crackled and squeaked, yet above all other noises Dietrich could hear Steiger's sharp voice, his tone unchanged by events, his orders clear and impersonal.

'Shift target! Stand by five and six!' The range-finder crew shouted out the fresh information as it was fed down from the great unwinking lens, their voices hoarse and excited. 'Target green oh-five . . . range static . . . same running depth!' The torpedoes were set to pass beneath the enemy ships so that they would be fired by their magnetic pistols.

Dietrich found that his face was ice-cold with sweat, and he had to bite his lip to retain his concentration. His eyes passed quickly over the helmsman and hydroplane operators. The latter were waiting tensed in their seats for the moment to dive. It could not be long now. That destroyer must have spotted the U-boat by now! How could Steiger sound so sure of himself and hold his targets in the slender sights when all the time the moment of discovery drew closer?

There was a hollow boom, followed immediately by a second explosion, and Hessler threw back his thick neck and laughed 'A hit! Two hits, by Christ!'

Dietrich tried to smile, but his face felt frozen.

'Fire!' The next two torpedoes flashed from the tubes, and again every man's heart leapt in time with the vicious little thuds as the glittering monsters tore through the water and curved away on to their prescribed courses.

The hull shuddered again and the steel plates seemed to hold the echo like a memory. The sounds of the distant explosions were impersonal, thunder across a line of hills, or a roll of drums beating a dirge. But Dietrich knew well enough what they meant. The great white curtain of water as it rose alongside each stricken ship, the savage blast which tore open a hull with the ease of a wolf ripping the skin from a rabbit. Then the flames, the tiny ant-like figures fleeing from the explosions and the fire; the empty, bobbing lifeboats; and, above all, the once proud ship rearing and rolling, ugly in its death agony.

The radio operator called out: 'Someone's sending! "German

submarine . . . under attack . . ."' He waited and then added. 'No more signals!'

Hessler glanced at Reche, who crouched over his chart-table. 'Pity he didn't have time to give his exact position, too. It would have saved *you* a bit of work!'

The Navigator did not seem to hear, but stared fixedly at the pencil which he held like a talisman.

The bell jangled, and Luth's men jumped at their controls. 'Flood! Emergency dive to ninety metres!' Already the lookouts were falling down the ladder, their shining rubber clothing making them appear like seals caught in a net. The hatch clanged shut as the motors whined to full power and drove the hull into the great tumbling water so that the hydroplane fins bit into it and thrust the bows down into a steep dive.

Steiger clung to the bottom of the ladder, his arms spread out as if he were crucified. 'Shut off for depth-charging!' A nerve jumped in his cheek as the watertight doors slammed throughout the tilting hull, and the men in each compartment looked quickly at each other and then looked away.

Down . . . down. Forty metres, eighty, ninety. The boat seemed heavy and unmanageable as it pulled on to an even keel. At this great depth every plate and rivet creaked and moaned, and the lights flickered across the taut faces of the electricians who waited to repair any circuit which might fail. The motors were reduced to a smooth purr, and above the sounds of straining metal and uneven breathing they all heard another noise. Again it was a noise with no warlike connection. A distant steam train, or a motor mower. The hydrophone operator moved his headset gingerly away from his ears. 'Destroyers at close quarters! Six different propellers turning!'

The thunder of the racing propellers drummed nearer and nearer. Steiger said quietly, 'Starboard twenty,' and watched as the polished spokes were put over. The roar was deafening now, right overhead. 'Midships. Steady.' The helmsman hunched closer to his wheel, his eyes glittering in the compass light.

Dietrich held his breath counting seconds. The destroyers had passed overhead. The depth-charges must already be falling through the grey water towards them.

. . . . .

The magazine for the U-boat's main armament was situated just forward of the control room beyond the thick pressure bulkhead, and as the oval door slammed shut, and the clips dropped into place, Max König glanced quickly at his companions. Mostly gunners like himself, they were wedged into a small shapeless group, their faces strained, listening and apprehensive. He looked again at the bulkhead door and wondered what would happen if the hull was burst open.

Horst Jung sat down on the steel gratings and spread his thick legs out in front of him. His creased boxer's face seemed relaxed and calm, and the mass of scars and lines on the wind-chafed skin gave him a kind of sad dignity. He prodded König and gestured towards the side of the hull. 'Keep clear of that, lad. When the charges go off you could get your back broken!'

He spoke to König, but the other men shuffled away from the dripping steel, silently obeying the older man's warning. In silence they listened to the propellers overhead, and König wondered how he would react. On the other cruise they had escaped any serious damage, and Captain Maazel had never got very near to his proposed targets. This was very different.

'They've passed over!' They were all looking upwards now, as if to pierce their steel shell and see beyond towards the surface.

The first pattern of depth-charges exploded with a deafening roar which seemed right alongside. The hull staggered and rocked almost on its side, sending the dazed seamen into an untidy heap. Before they could recover another charge exploded with a single crack, so great that the sides of the hull appeared to shrink inwards with the force.

König clapped his hands over his ears as he felt the pain darting into his skull like two hot needles. He saw that some of his companions were rolling on the deck in agony, and blood gleamed brightly in the harsh lights from noses, ears and from cuts sustained as they were flung against the sharp unyielding equipment around them.

Another pattern of charges and yet another. The world had become a tiny terrifying place which tossed and swooped beneath them as they stared at each other with mounting horror.

Petty Officer Hartz, the gun captain, clung to a fire extinguisher and glared at them with forced fierceness. 'Silence there! Keep still!'

All the lights were suddenly extinguished as if by a hidden hand, and for several moments they sat mesmerised until the emergency lighting flickered on. They were covered with flaked paintwork and dirt brought down by the force of the detonations, and some of the men were so dazed with shock that their bodies rolled limply on the tilting deck as if already dead.

There were two muffled clicks outside the hull, and König felt the vomit on his tongue. Jung had told him earlier that if a depth-charge was really close you could sometimes hear the pistol firing inside it as it reached its correct depth. He had heard just that, and as his shattered mind groped with this realisation the two charges burst as one. The submarine gave one great leap, tossed out of control like a blinded marlin, and slewed on to its beam ends. The lights vanished again, and König found himself in a struggling, gasping heap of clawing figures, his breath stifled by the weight of the others, his ears deafened by screams, shouts and the clatter of falling gear.

A fist gripped his arm in the darkness and Jung's hoarse voice seemed to be right inside his head.

'Here, hold on, Max! She's diving!'

A heavy body fell across König's spine before he could answer, and another voice screamed: 'Christ! She's going to the bottom! We'll be crushed alive!'

König let his body go limp as the others fought to get to their feet, only to be knocked half senseless by another explosion. The U-boat was already running deep. If she was blown deeper or went out of control she would soon pass below the safety level. Beneath thousands and thousands of tons of water her hull would be flattened like a fish tin. Slowly and relentlessly, before the water was mercifully allowed to enter and finish their agonies.

A telephone buzzed, and he heard the petty officer cursing as he struggled across the pitch-black compartment, His torch flickered across the distorted faces and white-balled eyes and then settled on the telephone. He wrenched it from its clasp as the deck swung through another crazy angle and the whole steel frame boomed like a giant oil-drum.

'Magazine, sir? Yes, sir? Very good, sir!' Down went the telephone and simultaneously the lights flickered on once more.

Hartz pulled himself across the deck, his grizzled face angry. 'Look to it, you swine! Check the hull! Replace any broken lamps at once!' He wiped his lips. 'We're not done for yet. Not by a long chalk!'

A small gunner named Krieger burst from the huddle on the deck and flung himself at the massive door. He beat on the grey metal with his fists until the blood poured off his broken knuckles and spattered across the men behind him. 'Let me out! Christ Jesus let me free!'

Horst Jung wobbled on to his knees and hit the wretched Krieger hard in the kidneys. One blow, upwards, and very sharp. With a small cry the man rolled on to his back and hugged himself in agony.

The petty officer nodded briefly. 'Good. Well done!'

Jung glanced at König, who was still lying on the deck plates and eyeing him curiously. 'I had to do it,' explained the ex-boxer. 'Anything like that and you've got real trouble on your hands!'

König sat up, realising as he did so that the deck was steady again. There were still plenty of explosions, but after the last close ones they seemed distant and unimportant.

Through the hull they could hear the sound of tearing metal, and Jung said shortly, 'Ship breaking up somewhere.'

König felt weak and sick. 'God, I thought it was us!'

Petty Officer Hartz looked down at him with disgust. 'There's still time yet!'

The loudspeaker on the bulkhead crackled and then burst into life with a loud hum. They watched it, fascinated, waiting to hear their fate.

But a harsh, unrecognisable voice roared: 'Tubes one to six reload! All sections report damage!'

König levered himself to his feet and swayed dazedly against the cold steel. In the midst of all this the Captain was preparing for the next round!

Jung was talking to the petty officer, the only other seasoned man in the compartment. 'That's the trouble with U-boats. Too much work and not enough damned fun! When I was in destroyers we always had a laugh or two, even when things were bad. Down here, apart from a game of Skat and a good sleep, what have you got?'

Hartz laughed and relaxed for the first time. He kept his eyes on the shaken seamen as he said: 'Ach, you're right! And these stupid bastards don't help matters!'

Jung winked at his friend König. 'They'll learn!'

Hartz hurried to the buzzing telephone. 'Not at the expense of *my* life they won't!'

Beyond the steel door Rudolf Steiger clung to the periscope and dashed the sweat from his eyes. His hand brushed against the white scar on his forehead and he touched it with something like surprise. In the middle of all this hell the scar was like meeting an old friend.

Dietrich said in a strangled voice, 'No damage reported, Captain!'

'Very well.' Steiger crossed the control room and peered down at the chart. His boots crunched on the carpet of broken glass which had burst from every dial and light when the last charges had fallen. Very close. The closest yet. He shut his mind again. That could wait.

'Periscope depth! Stand by one to six!' He looked through Dietrich's white face and ignored the fear and defiance which hung in the air like a gas. 'We are here to attack a convoy, gentlemen. Not sit on our backsides like . . .' his eye fell on Reche, 'like a lot of Spaniards, for instance!' Surprisingly there was a ragged laugh from the men nearby. Not much, but Steiger treated it like a small spark in a damp fire. Slowly he said: 'Not a bad attack. But we will have to do much better!'

'Fourteen metres, Captain!' Luth sounded the most normal, but Steiger could not see his face.

'Up periscope!' He bent his tall frame and waited. Not a bad attack, he had told them. It had been terrible! But were they really to blame? He had always maintained that a U-boat was as good or as bad as its captain. He sucked in his breath as the furtive lens broke the wind-torn surface and he saw the pattern of black smoke, orange flames and frantic stammer of signal lamps.

A destroyer was end-on to him. Its back was turned for a moment. A captain *had* to be right. Had to be right every time. The sweat ran down into his eyes as he stared at the destroyer. With a great effort he moved the periscope very slightly.

The cross-wires hovered across a careering freighter like a giant web. In a toneless voice he said, 'Stand by one, two and three!' He had to go on with it, but suppose *he* was at fault now?

'Fire!'

4: Men Overboard

The Morning Watch had almost dragged itself to its miserable conclusion yet still the dawn had not appeared in any recognisable form. Franz Luth, *U-991*'s engineer, sucked in his frozen cheeks and clung to the rim of the bridge, gloved fingers slipping on the fine coating of ice-rime, his sleep-starved body swaying to the hull's fiendish motion as he ducked to avoid another curtain of flung spray. The long gusts of wind had touched gale force and seemed to blow right through the triple layers of clothing and pierce his thin body as if it was an old curtain. In spite of the unaccustomed discomfort of watch-keeping on an open bridge, Luth found the change welcome, if only to keep out of the reeling, stinking hull below his straddled legs. Captain Steiger kept the boat on the surface for long periods, regardless of weather or daylight, and old, stuffy but peaceful watches far below the boisterous wave crests had become a thing of the past, a collection of memories.

They had been at sea for three weeks, and every day had added to the tension and strain which seemed to hold the crew in its grip like pack ice.

Two weeks had passed since Steiger had begun the attack on the convoy, and Luth still had to think very hard before he could sort his recollections into some kind of sane order. After the combined attacks he had felt weak and sweating, his hands and limbs refusing to answer the demands from a shocked mind. Attack after attack, always with an aftermath of depth-charging, frantic alterations of speed and depth, and fresh demands from the well-tried hull which shuddered and cracked with every assault.

In the past Luth had confined his thoughts and ideas to his duties with the engines, it had helped to keep his mind from straying to the ever present possibility of death, but the Captain's unrelenting pressure, his spine-chilling dedication under the most impossible conditions, had made all those delusions harder to entertain. They had cut right through that convoy and had torpedoed three freighters and one of the escorts as it chased after another U-boat. Other hits had been obtained, but in the confusion of burning ships, exploding ammunition and charging destroyers no one seemed to know the exact results.

A day later the U-boats had drawn together to re-form, and as the remnants of the convoy steamed on they counted their own losses and looked to the future.

Only five of the eight submarines had actively engaged the convoy. Of those, one was missing and two were limping back to St. Pierre. Now there were five. Strung out in a ragged line, forty miles between each boat, while the January gales screamed across the great grey furrows and crumbled the long Atlantic rollers with each savage gust.

In *U-991*, at least, there was little time for speculation and open despair. The Captain had driven them all, officers and men, without let-up or pity, until they had grown to curse the sound of his voice. He changed the ratings round at their jobs so that torpedomen stood lookout, and artificers and stokers struggled with ammunition and the mysteries of seamanship. Luth had to keep a watch on the bridge in turn with the other officers, while Lieutenant Hessler prowled around the engine room, his deep-set eyes for once apprehensive as he bombarded the Chief Engineroom Artificer with questions.

Luth tucked his stubbled chin into the sodden towel about his neck and wondered. Did it really matter that they could do each other's work in an emergency, or was Steiger merely forcing them to keep going in the best way he knew? He did not seem to care for their bitterness, even hatred, but perhaps he thought that was the only way left to pull them all together.

In the past fourteen days they had sighted and attacked a small convoy and a single merchantman. The latter had been Swedish, but Steiger had remarked almost indifferently: 'They know this is a restricted area. That is all there is to it!'

He had at least allowed the Swedes time to abandon ship, and had then ordered the gun to fire on the vessel's waterline. Twenty shells were needed, and the crazily rocking casing had made the gunners' aim haphazard and clumsy. The neutral merchant ship had been pockmarked with glowing holes before a lucky shot had given her the mortal wound. The U-boat altered course and increased speed into the white-capped waves, while far astern the tiny lifeboats tossed and swayed at the mercy of the storm.

Luth wondered if Steiger had really dismissed them so easily, or whether he found time to wonder at the fate of helpless men adrift in open boats. It was impossible to tell from Steiger's impassive features, and for that reason alone the crew had come to fear him. This was no Maazel, no blusterer or tyrant.

Steiger seemed to depend on no one but himself, and by his own tireless example drove everyone else to a point of collapse.

A lookout reported thickly, 'Looks like the dawn on the port quarter, sir!'

Luth rubbed his sore eyes and peered at the sliver of silver below the black clouds. The dawn. Just a brief indication of another day, and another search.

It would soon be time to go below and struggle with breakfast across a table gone mad. Then a few hours in the bunk. His mind was already slipping away so that he could endure the pounding of the spray and the piercing intensity of the wind. He thought of the little Baltic steamer in which he had been a gawky third engineer. In that other world he had become old before his time, and had allowed personal enjoyment to replace ambition. Sweden, Norway and Denmark, the little timber ship had plied with slow regularity between all three, and Luth had waited with cheerful indifference for the old Chief Engineer to die or retire so that he could get promotion. His own father was dead, but his mother and three sisters lived in Emden, well away from the Russians and seemingly free from too much bombing. It seemed to Luth that his family life consisted merely of letters from home. First the Baltic steamer, now a U-boat. But recently at least he had been able to make their lives a bit easier. With a few luxuries which he had obtained in France and Holland and with gifts sent via trusted friends, Luth hoped his family of women would not worry about him so much. Not that they ever heard much at home to worry about. The news was always bright and optimistic even although the streets were full of crippled and wounded soldiers and the night skies throbbed with enemy bombers.

Luth was a thinker and had always respected the truth, and it angered and troubled him to think that the war was doing away with it completely. He had once mentioned it to Dietrich, only to receive the reply, 'In war, morale is more important than truth!' Luth smiled. Poor Heinz. He was so young and had gained his small experience of life from the navy. He had learned to obey orders and do his duty, to respect his betters and hate enemies of the Fatherland. All very neat and tidy, but to Luth it was also impracticable and distasteful.

Perhaps that is why I like Heinz Dietrich, he thought vaguely. I am thirty-one, one of the oldest men aboard, and Dietrich seems to look to me for something. Security or friendship? What does it matter?

He jumped, guilty and startled, as Dietrich appeared out of the semi-darkness. Dietrich said briskly: 'All quiet? Good. Go below and get some hot sausage inside you.' As the lookouts stumbled below to make way for their replacements, Dietrich said in a quieter tone, 'I am sorry that I have behaved so badly lately, Franz.' He looked away towards the reluctant dawn. 'I have had a lot on my mind.'

Luth pulled his waterproof hood tighter and moved clear of the fresh lookouts. 'I am in no hurry for my breakfast. Why don't you tell me about it?'

The sea noises intruded into the small bridge, and Dietrich felt the misery and bitterness welling up inside him like a flood. For a split second his old defences dropped into place, but at the sound of Luth's quiet voice those same defences crumbled.

He kept his eyes averted from the other man's face and moved closer so that the lookouts should not hear. 'My brother was executed for cowardice,' he began.

. . . . .

Rudolf Steiger entered his cabin and hung up the heavy torch with which he had been inspecting all the hidden and inaccessible places abaft the engine room. The deck was swinging repeatedly through an eighty-degree angle, and one extra savage lurch caught him unawares so that he pitched across the tiny cabin space and fell headlong on to the bunk. Slowly and painfully he pulled his legs after him and lay face down on the rough blankets. His sleep-starved body cried out for rest, yet even in a state of semi-exhaustion his ears probed beyond the swaying curtain, his brain remained keyed-up and ready to trigger into a fresh emergency. Against his cheek he could feel the damp of the blanket with its attendant smells of mildew and oil. In this bitter weather it was quite impossible to relax either mind or body, just as it was beyond the powers of his weary men to introduce a little comfort into the restless dripping hull. Steiger had ordered that the electric radiators should be switched off at all times to save any additional drain on the batteries, so that the men off watch could no longer attempt to dry their clothes, and instead sat or lay in listless bundles, their bodies lost beneath layers of damp and dirty garments.

Steiger rolled restlessly on to his back and thought about the neutral ship he had sunk. It was strange how his men had looked at him when he had ordered the gun to be turned on the Swedish freighter. It seemed that to them a flag, an emblem, still meant something. They could see no further than that. A convulsion of exhausted anger ran through him and he glared up at the streaming deckhead. Do they imagine I do these things for effect? For some stupid personal satisfaction? Who can *dare* to call himself a neutral in this war? The Swedes sat smug and safe in their sterile country trading and growing fat with both sides. Their ships crossed the war-torn seas with calm indifference while Englishman and German struggled with every last ounce of strength just to survive. That lone Swedish freighter was in a recognised Restricted Zone. She was probably running an illicit cargo to the British unbeknown to anyone but her owners. Well, she would not do it again. He ran his fingers across his scar and wondered why he was even attempting to justify the sinking in his own mind. For a moment longer he tortured himself with ruthless self-criticism, testing the weakness of his own defences, sneering at his mind's vague explanations. For once the game gave him neither comfort nor satisfaction, and he turned his attention to his recent inspection of the boat.

Everything was a battle, there was never any let-up. In three weeks at sea he had welded the dispirited, untrained crew into a small team, if only by making them hate him. He gave them no peace, and had not spared them a second to find the time for fear. In three weeks he had stamped out the clumsy incompetence which had been bred during the previous three months and had made a rough surface on which to work his plans. But now the boat itself had started to weaken. After the last convoy attack a depth-charge had fallen very close once more. By some strange coincidence it must have exploded within feet of that other terrible salvo which had almost sunk the boat during his first attack on the other convoy, and when he had crawled through the aftermost confines of the narrow hull he had heard quite distinctly the uneven beat of the starboard propeller. Instead of the usual confident rumble it was more like a hollow thud. He had told Luth, but the Engineer had merely shrugged as if he could no longer trust his own opinions. A propeller blade was probably bent or broken completely, or part of the shaft itself might be damaged externally. Either way it could not be ignored. So far, it was not affecting the steering or fuel consumption, but the noise alone was enough. Any enemy listening device woul not fail to pin-point the grating thud no matter how slow the engine was running, and once bracketed by depth-charges who could say what further damage might do to the hull? If only the weather would moderate. They could surface to full buoyancy and put relays of divers overboard to examine the affected area. There would be few volunteers to swim in ice-cold water, but if necessary he would go over the side himself. Once again he found himself looking inwards even as he thought of the idea.

Suppose I am getting like the others? Is all this forced example really for the men, or is it for me? Perhaps I am more use at the Base, like Captain Bredt. Another self-conscious hero from the past for whom the present has no reality or form. He dismissed the idea with a bitter smile and tried to imagine Bredt at sea in *U-991*. The dirt and discomfort would be enough let alone the constant sense of frustration and baffled bewilderment which this sort of fighting had introduced. Like the machinery of war the men themselves needed constant stores of energy, precious fuel indeed. But whereas the powers of destruction were constantly being improved and enlarged, the strength of their users was daily being diminished and sapped by the mounting strain.

Large supply submarines had been introduced to fuel and store U-boats at sea so that the patrols could be doubled and the maddening loss of time it took to get a boat to its allotted area could be overruled. But how many men could stand that double amount of strain without seeing a tree or a rain-washed village, or hearing people laugh once more? And how many commanders could be expected to remain alert and vigilant like the wolves they were supposed to be?

Most of the bigger boats were now fitted with Snorchels so that they could cruise submerged yet use their diesels. It meant that they were safe from the searching and invisible eye of radar, but, again, how were men expected to stay whole if they never tasted fresh air and never saw a star above the horizon? After a few days of patrol at Snorchel depth Steiger had seen men change into living corpses, their skins dead white and almost transparent.

That was why the war had to be won soon. Germany possessed the means and the courage. But Germans were only human, and if the war dragged on for another four years or so the overwhelming weight of the Allied material power would begin to weigh in the balance.

He heard a man laugh in the passageway and smiled in spite of his troubled thoughts. They curse me because I cut down their heating and change their duties. Yet if we stayed on patrol for another six months they would accept it like dumb beasts. They have become part of the boat, sections of a weapon which I alone must use.

He started as he realised a figure was standing in the cabin entrance. It was the Chief Engineroom Artificer, Richter, whose grimy face was creased with worry.

'Lieutenant Luth's respects, Captain, he wishes to stop the starboard engine.' He stepped back a pace as the deck wallowed heavily and a bundle of books were hurled from their rack by an invisible hand.

Steiger threw his legs over the side of his bunk and swallowed hard. His stomach felt sour and empty, and he wanted more time to rest and think. Instead he asked sharply, 'Is it the propeller again?'

Richter nodded. 'The shaft is shaking so much now that we think the gland will be irreparably damaged if we stay on the surface.'

Steiger sighed. On the surface in these mountainous seas they could not keep control of the rudder with only one engine. Submerged, the shaft might be safer but the noise would guide the enemy like a radio beacon. He stood up, his shadow covering the other man like a cloak. 'Very well. Pass the word to the Officer of the Watch for Diving Stations. We will go down to ninety metres and then cut out the starboard engine.' He gave the other man a hard glance. 'But tonight we surface come what may, Richter, and I want some men overboard to check the extent of the damage!'

Richter nodded. 'Yes, Captain.' He licked his lips and paused half inside the doorway. 'Lieutenant Luth thought you might wish to return to Base, sir.'

Steiger was buttoning his jacket. 'But then Lieutenant Luth is not in command, is he?'

Richter looked at the uncompromising smile on Steiger's mouth and hurried away with his report. As he pushed his way through the bunched figures and enquiring faces Richter wondered how some of the new men would fancy the idea of taking a cold bath in the Atlantic. He thought of Steiger's cold face and grinned in spite of his apprehension. With Steiger you at least knew where you stood. Not in the grave, but damned near it!

'Diving Stations!' he yelled.

* * * * *

The seamen in the main forward mess crowded around the narrow slung table and used each other's bodies as props to ease the discomfort of the metal lockers upon which they sat. The mess was situated just forward of the control-room bulkhead between the magazine and the main switchboard. To make room for the evening meal the narrow pipe-cots had been folded against the deckhead and the spare hammocks which were used to store tinned food were slung above the central gangway so as not to bang against the heads of the men around the table.

Max König used his strong fingers to wipe the remainder of his fried bread around his plate to soak up the last of the stewed veal. The bread was extremely stale, but fried and well dipped in fat it made a good buffer against cold and hunger. He concentrated upon the small piece of table directly in front of him and only half listened to the voices of his companions. By weighing his words before he spoke and enjoying the freedom of his own thoughts, König was able to avoid the everyday pitfalls into which his false background might otherwise throw him. He was Max König, an ex-printer's assistant, just as it stated in his records. That other man, the beaten and tortured inmate of a concentration camp, had died in an air-raid. He no longer existed, or so he repeatedly told himself.

He found his new role easier to accept than he had expected because his earlier life had become so unreal and terrible in his imagination, and all the former things in which he had lived and believed were as dead as the prisoner. As dead as Gisela, the girl he was to have married. He clenched his hands in his lap as the nightmare picture moved into his thoughts with stark clarity. As a student he had first joined the Communist Party almost as a joke and at the same time to pacify Gisela.

On that last day the Gestapo had brought the girl into the room where he was being questioned. He would have admitted anything, confessed to every crime he knew if only he had been able, but he knew nothing. He had pleaded and struggled, too desperate and horrified to understand that the Gestapo men were determined to finish what they had started whatever he said.

They stripped the girl and tied her on the table opposite him. Her long blonde hair shone in the harsh lamplight, and against the black uniforms her skin looked like marble.

The officer had struck him again and again in the face. 'Confess!' he had screamed. 'The names of the swine who belong to your unit!' But he could not answer. He had attended a few meetings, distributed leaflets, and in secret had condemned the Nazi Party. But of the more active Communist organisations he knew nothing.

The Gestapo men by the table had bent over the girl with what looked like piano wire, the ends of which were fashioned in arrow-headed hooks.

He did not remember how long it had gone on. Twice he had fainted and the picture of the twisting naked figure had mercifully faded away. They revived him with cold water and kicks, and the nightmare went on. Her screams seemed to scrape the innermost membranes of his ears so that he did not hear his own cries or the laughter of the tormentors. When she eventually died they tipped her from the table so that her mutilated body lay on the bloodied floor at his feet. The girl who had walked through the fields at his side, who had laughed at his bourgeois upbringing, and whom he had loved more than anything in the world, had gone. He could feel nothing, and even the jeers and blows which drove him back to his cell did not seem to reach him. In the concentration camp he had waited for madness or death to destroy him. Instead he had found an inner strength which even now he did not understand.

Horst Jung, the boxer, downed the last of his tea and banged the mug on the table with a satisfied belch. 'Good food and fresh air! What more can a man want?' He glanced across at his friend. 'Well, Max, and what are you so deep in thought about?'

König forced a grin, caught off guard. His face had gone very pale and he knew the others were watching him. 'A bit seasick, I think!'

Some of them laughed and the small spark of tension was extinguished. It was strange how small things became so vital and challenging in a submarine. Any careless word or action could dog a man for days, follow him on watch or into his bunk until it became a major issue.

Rickover, the youngest man aboard, who had just passed his eighteenth birthday, nodded gravely and glanced up at the curved deckhead. 'When we surface they are going to send some of us overboard to look at the starboard screw. *I* might volunteer.' He looked round challengingly, his round face pathetically youthful against the bearded seamen nearby. Despite all his hopes he was still unable to get anything to grow on his pink face, and the others pulled his leg unmercifully. He was known as Moses throughout the boat, a name always given to the youngest member of a U-boat's crew, and this small notoriety allowed him to get away with high spirits which in anyone else would have been regarded as insolence.

'Yes, *you* volunteer, Moses!' Michener, the dour ex-policeman, nodded grimly. 'We might get a bit of quiet in the mess then!'

Schultz, a stick-thin man who had once been a successful photographer in Frankfurt, gave a low groan. 'My God, I shall be glad to get ashore. France, anywhere, just to get on dry ground and feel safe again!'

Michener sneered. 'Safe? Nowhere's safe today!'

Jung pulled a strip of cheese rind between his uneven teeth. 'You wait until you've been in the service as long as I have! Ach, you make me sick! A few little depth-charges and you all whine for your mothers!'

Nobody challenged the battered boxer and he continued dreamily: 'I remember when I was in a little coastal submarine at the outbreak of war, we had a commander who made Captain Steiger seem like a saint! We were based at Cuxhaven.' He paused, aware that König was immersed in his troublesome thoughts again. 'Do you know Cuxhaven, Max?'

König pulled himself together and nodded. 'Yes. I used to go to the regatta there with my family before the war.'

Michener leaned forward, his policeman's face frowning. 'I thought you used to be a printer's assistant? That regatta was only for the well-offs!'

König felt a wave of panic swoop over him and heard Jung interrupt irritably, 'Anyway, at the start of the war——'

Moses Rickover leaned forward, his smooth face innocent. 'Er, which war would that be?' he asked politely.

The line of weary faces broke into laughter and König forced himself to join in. That was a near thing. I can never relax my guard again.

He looked up. Michener was still looking at him, his dour face thoughtful.

The loudspeaker rattled into life. 'Attention! Stand by to surface in ten minutes' time! Gun crews to muster!'

The men's faces immediately became masked in apprehension as they began to stow away the table and plates. The small items of escape and relaxation were packed out of sight. They were to prepare themselves once more for whatever lay waiting on the surface.

König buttoned his oilskin coat and waited by the magazine door. Jung ran his eye over the small mess and grunted. 'That'll do. Now let's get to our stations.' Aside to König he added: 'You want to watch that Michener. He looks like an informer!'

König stared at him, stunned. '*I've* got nothing to hide!'

Jung shrugged, his eyes lost in the battered creases of his face. 'Maybe, and maybe not. But these days it doesn't seem to matter much, does it?' For a long second he stared at the other man and then shuffled away after the others.

• • • • •

Heinz Dietrich pulled himself upwards through the oval hatch and slipped the dark goggles from his eyes. In spite of the usual precautions, however, it was several seconds before he could accustom his vision to the complete blackness which enshrouded the surfaced submarine like a cloak. The wind which had made watch-keeping a nightmare seemed to have fallen away completely and had been replaced by a flat unmoving coldness like that which in northern waters heralds the approach of icebergs, and the great tapering white-capped waves had been smoothed and rounded into one unbroken black swell.

Both engines had been stopped, and the U-boat rolled sickeningly over each successive hump of shining water, its yawing motion only part soothed by the crude canvas sea-anchor which Hessler and his deck-party were paying out from the bows.

Occasionally the pointed stern rose cleanly out of the water, its fins momentarily shining in a bright pattern of green phosphorescence which seemed to accentuate the helplessness of the surfaced hull. Doubled lookouts peered into the darkness, and shadowy figures slipped and stumbled across the wet casing as orders were called in unnatural whispers. Through the open hatch Dietrich could hear the stammer and buzz of morse from the radio room where the operators listened for any sign of an enemy patrol vessel or an inquisitive neutral.

He gripped the rim of the bridge with all his strength as the first of the torches were switched on and a handful of the best swimmers slipped over the side. He ground his teeth with helpless fury while these men paddled clear of the plunging hull, their bodies only visible because of their bulky lifejackets and the thin lines which kept them moored to their parent craft. When they had made a protective semicircle around the starboard quarter Dietrich saw two more men follow them over the stern itself. The waterproof lights gleamed with fierce brightness, so that Dietrich nearly cried out as the glare lit up the full length of the shining hull and the white faces of the men around him. Then the lights faded as the two swimmers pulled themselves under the hull. Seconds passed, and then the two men were heaved aboard and two more took their place. The first ones staggered to the bridge ladder and blundered up on to the bridge. Above the moan of the sea Dietrich could hear their teeth chattering and the gasp of air in their frozen lungs. As they vanished below Steiger climbed up from the casing and stood beside his subordinate.

'No luck that time, Heinz.' His voice was calm and showed neither disappointment nor strain.

Dietrich winced as a beam of light broke the surface and shone directly towards the sky. 'Christ, look at that!' In spite of his guard the anguish burst from him like a torrent. 'Any half-blind pilot could see that! What a chance we're taking!'

Steiger shrugged. 'By day it would have been worse. We would have been at the mercy of every ship which moved. In darkness we can at least have room to manœuvre.'

'If we returned to Base we could soon get the thing repaired,' Dietrich persisted stubbornly. 'The risk is too great here!'

'We must make the effort, Heinz. Every hour in harbour is one wasted. Every day away from the patrol area is helping our enemies!'

Two more half-naked engineers staggered past the officers on their way below, and Steiger called: 'There is brandy waiting for you! Well done!' In a normal tone he added: 'We are not alone, Heinz. Alex Lehmann is out there somewhere.' He signalled vaguely towards the invisible bows. 'We had a signal from *U-985* to say they would stand by in case of accidents.'

Dietrich swallowed hard with frustration. What good would Lehmann or any other submarine commander be if a destroyer swept out of the darkness?

'Well, sir, I think we have done our share on this patrol. No one else seems to have sunk so many targets!' Conviction gave an edge to his voice. 'The men are worn out. Three weeks at sea following immediately on top of three months under Captain Maazel is surely enough?'

'Are you asking or blaming me, Heinz?' Steiger had half turned his head, but Dietrich could not see his face. 'Do you think I am enjoying all this delay and discomfort?' He gave a short laugh. 'I have not been back to Germany for two years, but I know that rest from duty is not the answer to anything!'

There was a shout from the deck and Luth ran quickly along the swaying casing to the foot of the conning-tower. 'They have located it, Captain!' His face looked like a white egg in the darkness, and Dietrich felt Steiger tense at his side as he leaned over the edge to hear Luth's hoarse voice.

'One blade sheared off and another ready to go, I think!' Luth paused as if trying to read Steiger's thoughts.

Dietrich felt his hands trembling with excitement. They would have to return now. Even Steiger would not risk the Atlantic with one propeller.

After a brief pause Steiger said: 'Very well, Chief. Get those men aboard and secure the upper deck. Report when ready to start the port engine.

'Make a signal to Base, Heinz, and tell them we are returning from our area. Inform Alex Lehmann that he is to take over command of the Group.'

'What's left of it,' added Dietrich. He winced as Steiger swung him round against the periscope standards.

'I heard that!' Steiger twisted the front of Dietrich's oilskin until the material bit into his chest like a steel band. 'I *heard* that! Well, just you remember, Heinz, that we will go on fighting if there is only one boat left in the Group, in the whole U-boat fleet! By God, you cannot measure a man's requirements in time of war!' For several more seconds they swayed together, the lookouts rooted to their posts by the intensity and hatred in Steiger's voice. More calmly he added, 'When you have a command of your own you will remember——'

He broke off as a seamen yelled: 'Aircraft, sir! Port beam! Listen!'

Steiger swung his head like a wounded stag, his fingers still gripping Dietrich's oilskin, as faintly, then more confidently, the aircraft's engines throbbed across the unbroken water.

Steiger barked: 'Diving Stations! Clear the bridge!' And as the men tumbled below he called to the few figures who still clung to the swaying casing: 'Get below! At the double!'

The electric motors hummed into life, and Dietrich realised that Luth was already in the control room. Still the boat remained unmoving in the swell, and Steiger called again: 'Lieutenant Hessler! What in hell's name are you doing? Get those men *below!*'

Hessler's voice was harsh even above the drone of the circling aircraft. 'There's a man caught, Captain! His lifeline's holding him against the rudder!'

Dietrich breathed in deeply. They were helpless now. A poor wretch was trapped against the hull, his half-frozen body preventing them from starting even one of the propellers.

A gasp went up from the deck-party as a parachute flare burst high above the water. As their seared eyeballs peered round at the nakedness of their boat they all saw the flurry of foam as another U-boat dived in the far distance, also the momentary glitter of light reflected across the underside of a giant bomber as it broke through the low clouds.

Dietrich's voice broke. 'We can't wait! We'll all be killed!'

Steiger stared at him and then called sharply to Hessler, 'Cut that lifeline, and get below!' Then to Dietrich he added: 'No, we can't wait any longer. Once more, we haven't the time!'

The propellers thrashed madly at the water and the air hissed through the vents as the U-boat buried its snout to escape the blinding light and the roar of aero engines. Four bombs roared deafeningly into the empty sea, and with a bellow of frustration the bomber swung away towards its far-off base.

The flare extinguished itself in the great empty desert of water, and the lone swimmer who screamed and pleaded at the night sky was soon swallowed up and lost in its vastness.

5: Recriminations

Rudolf Steiger moved closer to the tall window which spanned the side of Captain Bredt's handsome office and stared absently at the harbour below him. Nothing seemed to have changed in the month he had been away, yet he could sense that everything was different. The clouds were high and unbroken, but a pale watery sunlight gave the illusion of warmth so that he imagined he could feel its feeble strength against his cheek.

He had docked the damaged submarine the previous morning, and already it was snugly secured inside one of the deep pens receiving the attention of the Base staff. The grey hulls of other U-boats lay alongside the harbour walls, and he could see the ant-like figures of seamen and mechanics moving in deceptive confusion across their narrow decks. The tide was low, and the rugged stonework of the jetties showed a glittering waterline of brown and green weed which contrasted sharply with the harsh grey and silver of the sea beyond.

He turned his head slightly to watch the soldiers on one of the tall flak-towers as they swung their gun-barrels after a friendly aircraft as it swooped towards the hidden town. More troops were drilling stiffly by the harbour sheds, their strutting N.C.O. made ridiculous by distance.

Behind his back Steiger could feel the uneasy silence of the six other U-boat commanders of the Group. They sat in a listless semicircle facing Bredt's empty desk, each man immersed in his own thoughts. Against the bright paintwork, coloured charts and the pretentious carpet they looked faded and unreal, and Steiger tightened his lips into a frown of annoyance. When he had signalled his intention to return to harbour Captain Bredt had immediately recalled the rest of the Group, or 'what was left of it', as Dietrich had so rightly if incautiously observed. They had arrived within hours of each other, the five submarines returning to rejoin the two which had already limped home to repair their damage. One missing. Steiger mentally shrugged off the loss. Nowadays it was inevitable, and with a new Group working together for the first time it could have been much worse. He tried to remember the missing commander, Karl Schubert, but already the impression was blurred and indistinct. Just another shadowy figure like the six behind him. Like me, he thought grimly.

The door clicked open and Captain Bredt strode briskly into the room, accompanied by an elderly commander who assisted with the running of the Base.

Steiger turned and stiffened to attention as the other officers dragged themselves to their feet. Again Steiger was struck by the contrast between the people who lived and worked ashore and those who fought even for the privilege of living. Bredt, in his immaculate uniform and freshly laundered shirt, gave off his usual air of alertness and petulant disapproval, his round face shining as if from a cold shower. Steiger compared him with the crumpled figures around him, their blue uniforms hurriedly dragged from damp tin boxes, their shirts probably still unironed. Their faces, too, were so different. Hollow, sleep-starved and sharpened by strain and fatigue, they regarded Bredt with something like hatred.

Bredt sat down and gestured for the others to follow suit. He allowed a brief spasm of annoyance to cross his smooth face when Steiger remained standing by the window, but apparently decided to ignore it. He cleared his throat and began to drum on his clean blotter. The neat hand beat its little tattoo for several seconds, watched by seven pairs of red-rimmed eyes.

Steiger found that he wanted to laugh, but checked himself as Bredt began to speak.

'Well, gentlemen, so ends our first patrol. I think we did quite well up to a point, but I will go into that in a moment.'

Steiger saw Alex Lehmann watching him from across the room, his eyebrows raised in questioning amusement. Bredt's *our* and *we* had caused a ripple of life to move through the little group, and several of the commanders were looking at Bredt with undisguised amusement.

Bredt frowned and the smiles vanished. 'However, one boat has not returned. That is most serious and brings disgrace upon all of you!'

Lehmann half rose to his feet, but Steiger waved him down. With his eyes hidden in the shadow of the window he said flatly: 'Losses are to be expected surely? Schubert is merely the first in this Group!'

Bredt regarded him stonily, and Steiger thought he saw a flash of triumph in the officer's pale eyes.

'You have obviously not been informed about Schubert?'

Steiger forced himself to remain still and patient. Bredt had changed out of all recognition in the month while they had been at sea. He was more sure of himself, less ready to compromise. He had even declined to see Steiger alone when he returned, but sent a message to announce this meeting with all the others present. Steiger cared little about this treatment. He was used to the strange ways of superiors, and was even glad that a clear margin had been drawn between Bredt and himself.

Bredt banged the blotter with sudden vehemence. 'Schubert surrendered!' He glared at them singly, holding each man's eyes for a long second until his gaze finally fell on Steiger. Coldly he continued, 'The shame and humiliation he has brought will be hard to wipe off the slate!'

The commanders moved uneasily in their chairs, and some glanced at each other with suspicion, as if each saw a potential coward and traitor.

'I shall take steps, *any* steps, to see that such sickening behaviour does not happen again! I have informed U-boat Headquarters of this betrayal, and they have ordered that Schubert's records and decorations be annulled and destroyed. His family and all those with whom he had dealings shall be made to understand what he has done!'

Steiger wondered briefly what had made Schubert take such action. He had been on the right flank of that first attack, so it seemed unlikely that he had been severely handled by the convoy escorts. It was almost as if it had been a deliberate act of surrender. It was unheard of, but such things could spread like disease. Steiger recalled Dietrich's relief when they had turned for home, Reche's fear and the shocked disbelief of his crew at each aggressive attack on the enemy. Steiger began to pluck at a button on his jacket. It was as if the thrust and power of the U-boat arm was becoming blunted and tired. He half listened to Bredt's monotonous ranting and knew that his tactics could only add to the damage.

Then with a start he realised that the anger he felt against Bredt was only an excuse. Schubert's action in surrendering his boat had affected him more deeply than he yet understood, and because it had given Bredt a new power, that, too, added to his sense of personal betrayal.

Bredt was warming to his theme of self-righteous indignation: '. . . and I cannot impress upon you too much the importance of your task! More effort, more definite action, with less thought of the consequences, that is the sort of imaginative strategy which will serve Germany!'

Steiger glanced slowly at his companions to see how they were reacting. His friend Alex Lehmann sat bolt upright, his narrow, sensitive features pale with anger. Busch and Wellemeyer, the two commanders who had brought their damaged boats back to Base after the first engagement with the convoy, stared glumly at the carpet as if they felt in some way responsible for the whole affair. Otto Kunhardt, a bright-eyed fanatic with over a hundred thousand tons of enemy shipping to his credit, glowered at Bredt with an expression of unbelievable ferocity. Ludwig and Weiss had their backs to Steiger, but he could sense the bitterness and anger in their slumped crumpled figures, and knew that any one of these men might throw his life and his crew away in a single useless gesture on the very next cruise, if only to prove himself better than Captain Bredt.

Steiger touched his scar gently. 'The duty of the U-boat Service is to destroy enemy shipping. As I see it we have already achieved more than any other form of offensive weapon in history. We know it, and the enemy knows it. The campaign of the Afrika Korps in North Africa failed, *not* because of the overwhelming successes of the Allied armies, but because of the dedicated and ruthless attacks by British submarines on our supply lines between Italy and Libya. In the same way, at the beginning of the war, Britain could not hold out in Norway because her big war vessels and supply ships were rendered impotent by our U-boats.' He lifted his eyes and stared slowly at Bredt. 'Even the convoys to North Russia are held in check by us. With more U-boats in Norway and a more concerted action against the long convoy routes to Murmansk we would soon have fewer of our soldiers killed by Yankee shells and bullets on the Eastern Front!'

Bredt stood up as if to hold on to his audience's attention, but already the others had turned and were watching Steiger's impassive face as he elaborated each point. They were well-known facts, but in Steiger's words each commander could visualise with sudden clarity his own part in the vast picture of war, and felt stronger because of this knowledge.

'I realise the importance of all this!' Bredt glared petulantly at Steiger's shadowed figure. 'It is all well known at Headquarters, too. It is possible for *me*, however, to see the more dangerous stresses and strains of our service which more loyal commanders are inclined to miss.' He plucked at his lapel. 'The Grand Admiral has told me that I am to be appointed as Deputy Head of Defence for this sector in addition to my flotilla duties, so you can see that I am much concerned by all these events!'

Steiger sighed. The Base had been operational for less than two months, yet already the pattern was clear. Bredt's personal advancement was blinding him to the real task in hand. Headquarters had offered him the post of Deputy Head of Defence like a carrot. It was meaningless, just an added spur of one man. As there was no Head of Defence for each sector, there could be no Deputy Head. It was a term, an expression of faith, a promise. The Grand Admiral had probably been advised to invent these meaningless appointments to give impetus to his local Group Commanders, but, as Steiger well knew, where it might prevent an efficient officer from becoming slipshod and adamant it would have an opposite effect on an officer like Bredt. He would risk everything and everybody to prove his own worth, to secure for himself the treasured title.

He had already shown himself unwilling to discuss problems. He seemed to think that if a problem was ignored it would cease to exist. While the U-boats of his Group had been at sea, Bredt had already built up his staff, duplicated paperwork to such a degree that the actual business of fighting the Battle of the Atlantic had become almost incidental.

Bredt continued: 'I have read your reports. By and large you have all refrained from making full use of your Snorchels, and thereby you have rendered yourselves more liable to detection by surface radar. . . .'

Lehmann stood up, his tired face completely white. 'If we use these damned breathing tubes our submerged speed is reduced to six knots, sir. More than that and the whole thing is liable to snap off! At best it fills the hull with gas, and if the tube dips into a deep wave you are liable to asphyxiate the whole engine-room staff!'

Bredt lifted his fist above his head and banged it down with such force that a ruler flew past the elderly Staff Officer's skull.

'Silence! I will not hear such defeatist talk!' His voice rose to a scream, and beads of sweat glistened on his flushed face. 'I do not want excuses, Lehmann! I want action! The Third Reich will not tolerate weakness or disobedience!'

Bredt looked suddenly at Steiger. 'And what about that man you lost overboard?'

Steiger regarded him coldly. 'I had to leave him. I could not sacrifice the safety of the boat for one man.'

Bredt smiled and nodded several times. 'I must read your report again, I may have missed something!'

Steiger heard the gasp of surprise which went up from the others, but controlled his rising anger with every power in his body. 'If, sir, you are suggesting that I might have acted otherwise, then I think this is a case for further investigation.'

Bredt glared at him, his pale eyes suspicious and angry. 'In what way?'

'I shall see Admiral Dönitz myself and demand a full enquiry!'

It was the oldest trick in the world, and Steiger felt no sense of victory as he watched the anger change to dismay and fear. He had found Bredt's weak spot and had used it to keep the respect and efficiency of the other commanders. He knew well enough that he had also made a bad enemy.

Bredt sat down and waved his hand nervously. 'Dismiss, all of you! I have a great deal to do.' He glanced quickly at Steiger. 'I think we can forget our little misunderstanding, eh? Nothing must interfere with our duty!'

Steiger picked up his salt-stained cap and nodded briefly. 'Nothing will ever do that, Captain!' His cold grey eyes flickered momentarily towards the officer's empty sleeve. 'Where duty is concerned I never allow my judgement to be clouded by sentiment.'

Long after they had all left the big office Bredt still stood by his desk, his body shaking as if from a fever. Then he picked up one of his telephones and waited impatiently for the operator to answer.

'Get me the Garrison Commander!' He stared unwinkingly at his reflection in the map case until Major Reimann's harsh voice rasped in his ear, and then said smoothly: 'The submarine crews will be ashore for local leave for the next few days, Major. I do not want your patrols to give them any preference over other serving men.' He waited for the words to sink in, and could imagine the surprise and pleasure on the soldier's piggy face. 'Any breach of discipline or any disorder in the town is not to be tolerated!' He put down the telephone, a small smile of triumph on his smooth features.

. . . . .

Rudolf Steiger paused halfway up the hill which sheltered the northernmost side of St. Pierre and forced himself to breathe slowly and carefully. It was a longer climb than he had imagined, but already he was feeling better because of the sharp air, the scent of wet grass and the weathered trees which contrasted so sharply with the grey sky.

Alex Lehmann grunted with exertion and halted beside him. His thin body was jerking at each painful gasp, and he peered at Steiger with disbelief.

'You certainly believe in punishment, Rudi! A walk with you is like a forced march!'

Steiger smiled and looked back at the town's dull rooftops. 'I just wanted to get a good look at the place. It is always well to know what one is defending.'

Far below the two commanders, beyond the town's limits and the sharp lines of the harbour breakwaters, the vast expanse of the Bay of Biscay stretched into the distance until its shimmering pattern of minute whitecaps was merged and lost in the misty horizon. A small patrol boat, its dull grey sides shining as it rolled sickeningly across the open water, moved with painful slowness towards the harbour entrance. It had once been the yacht belonging to a French millionaire, and even the grey paint could not hide its trim lines and frail beauty.

Lehmann watched the boat with indifference. 'When in God's name will it all end, Rudi?'

Steiger shrugged. 'Next year, tomorrow, it is not our concern.'

Lehmann laughed. It was a short bitter sound. 'In some ways I envy you. You are always so sure, so controlled. You never get sidetracked or discouraged by events!'

'The war as a whole is too big to visualize with accuracy.'

'Now you sound like Bredt!' Lehmann took off his white cap and pushed his sweat-dampened hair from his forehead. 'How that man sickens me! I wish to God *you* were in full command here instead of that dummy!'

Steiger eyed him thoughtfully. 'I am not, however, so you must not speak so haphazardly. Even if I were you would probably say the same of me. Command of anything always invites envy and contempt, *you* should know that!'

'There you go, you see? Everything cut and dried! I only hope that you still think the same when we are beaten!'

Steiger swung on his heel, his boots squeaking in the wet grass. 'Don't you ever say that again! You are my friend, but I expect you to remember your other responsibilities, too! We will never be beaten unless it is because of our own weakness and stupidity!'

Lehmann shrugged. 'Have it your own way, Rudi. Anyway, the Allies will not invade here. They are more likely to cut through Holland and Belgium.' He waved his arm. 'From what I have seen of these defences it is just as well!'

Steiger began to walk slowly up the remainder of the hill. He was disturbed by Lehmann's careless candour. Any man who never considered the possibility of defeat was a dangerous fool, but Lehmann actually sounded as if he fully expected, even welcomed, it. Evenly he asked, 'Do you hear from your wife?'

Lehmann nodded. 'She is coming here very soon. It will be the first time I have seen her for nearly two years.' He laughed. 'I am married in name only, really!'

Steiger stopped with such suddenness that the other man cannoned into him. 'Coming *here*? That is not possible!'

Lehmann thrust his hands into his pockets and eyed his companion with sudden stubbornness. 'How typical of you that is!

Of course it is possible! My brother is a Staff Captain in Paris with Army Transport. He arranged it weeks ago. Everything is possible if you have the right connection!' He stared at Steiger's questioning face and hurried on: 'You reacted just as I might have expected. You should have Bredt's command because you are dedicated *and* better for the job! You have a finer background than any of us, you could have done anything! Instead you have forced yourself into one groove and deluded yourself that you are just like the rest of us. You command a U-boat, you direct the Group, but you should have a say in far greater affairs!'

'Stop it! This is what I want, what I am best fitted for!'

Lehmann waved him down. 'You are a very good commander, but others could do the work as well. But less loyal and intelligent officers are thankful and content to let you believe your views. Brave and trusted men die every day, every hour, while pompous fools in high authority play games with living flesh and blood! We serve with blood and iron, Rudi, but soon only the blood will remain!' He glared with sudden hatred at the grey Atlantic. 'I love Germany as well as most, and better than many. But I want to stop this stupid waste of life, this complete destruction! I want to live and build again, not just sacrifice my life with the helplessness of a bullock in a slaughterhouse!'

'How can you talk of compromise? Either you win or lose. That is all there is!' Steiger found that he was shouting, his voice harsh and angry.

Lehmann spoke more calmly now, as if he was committed to a collision course. 'Germany is in the jaws of giant pincers. We are falling back on the Eastern Front. Italy and North Africa have gone, and the army is strung out across Europe so finely that when the Tommies and their friends burst across the Channel what can our men do? They will fall back and regroup, while all the time the damned Russians push into Germany from the east. We could still fight with honour if we joined with the Tommies and combined our strength against Ivan!'

'You're mad! If anyone else had said these things I would have killed him with these two hands! You're talking treason!'

Lehmann spread his hands. 'The British are much like us, you know that as well as I. If we carry out our present intention we will all exhaust ourselves. There must be good in both sides. The right men in each country would soon grasp the sane opportunity to save that good. Everyone is waiting for a gesture, and it *must* come from us. We have struck fear into everyone we have beaten, they prowl like jackals in the darkness, waiting for us to fall. We are strong now. We must bargain now. When we are weak we shall soon know the meaning of defeat! But unlike our enemies, *we* will have brought it on ourselves!'

Steiger controlled his features with a final effort. 'You are wrong. But whatever your private beliefs may be, you have your duty to the Reich and to the navy. Your oath excludes everything else. If the British were our allies I would fight for them with all my power. But they are our enemies, and they always will be. There is no way out!'

'How easy that sounds, Rudi,' Lehmann answered quietly 'You have only yourself. You have no family, no loyalties but your own code. You turn your back on weakness and ignore prejudice altogether when it clashes with your own ideals. You were born for all this, whereas I was a grocer's son, grateful for the chance to better myself when the new Germany was created. What will *you* do after the war, if you are still alive? I can see by your face that you have never considered the question! Well, *I* have, and I want the chance to live again. I lost my parents last year in the great fire raid on Hamburg, and my young brother died in Libya, I have a wife who is a stranger to me, and another brother who sits like us waiting for the inevitable!' He paused for breath and stared sadly at Steiger's set face. 'I said earlier that I envied you. I don't any more. I *pity* you. When you realize the real truth you will discover that your loneliness does not make you immune from the suffering of others. I hope I am not there when you find out!'

He turned on his heel and strode blindly down the hill. For several minutes Steiger watched the blue-clad figure grow smaller and smaller, his face still pale with anger, and shocked surprise.

He was angry because he had been unable to find the words to silence Lehmann's outburst. He was shocked, too, because although he had always been alone, he had until this day never considered the possibility of loneliness. The realisation moved in on him like a first heart attack, unfamiliar and alarming, and for once he could find no comfort or explanation.

▪ ▪ ▪ ▪ ▪

Heinz Dietrich settled himself deeper in the rear seat of the commandeered Citroën and idly watched the trees speeding past the closed window. A young naval driver swung the wheel with casual ease and sent the big car swinging off the main road towards St. Pierre and the Base.

Dietrich had spent most of the day in St. Nazaire on a mission for Captain Bredt, a duty he had welcomed if only to escape a while from his companions. He wondered what Luth and the others were doing as the evening shadows touched the tall trees with purple and a chill breeze stirred the bare branches with sudden movement. Reche was probably drunk in his room behind the Base Headquarters, and Luth was more than likely prowling around the docked U-boat. Luth had been more shocked than the rest of them by the loss of the man Steiger had left to drown, because the man had been one of his engineers. He had said nothing either against or in justification of the Captain's action, but had withdrawn into himself in a world of silence.

Lieutenant Hessler had wanted Dietrich to go ashore with him. He had explained that he had heard of a new and as yet unofficial brothel which had opened on the far side of the town, where the French girls were something to see, and their enjoyment must be sampled before everybody else got to hear of it. Dietrich had shied away from the suggestion, although he could not understand why. He knew he was attractive to women, but he had never been able to make contact with them. As the car roared down the cobbled road he wondered if his decision was the right one. Perhaps even a brothel was the best way to start. With his nerves screwed up in a tight knot, and the nagging worry of his brother's death never far from his thoughts, it might be one way of forgetting, if only for a short while.

He had hardly seen anything of Steiger since they had docked, but had caught a glimpse of him on one occasion striding alone along the waterfront, his boots almost touching the surf. It would just be a matter of time before he, too, discovered about his brother's death and then things would start to get even worse.

He toyed with the idea of stopping at the big café when they reached the town, but the thought of all the hostile French faces made him change his mind immediately.

Everything was unreal, there was nothing to hold on to any more. In St. Nazaire the place had been alive with rumours of an Allied invasion fleet building up in the English ports, of mass bombing at home and of mounting losses in Russia. It was all so distant, so difficult to comprehend, as if they were cut off from and forgotten by the real Germany.

They swung around a sharp bend and Dietrich saw his driver stiffen as he caught sight of a small struggling group of figures at the roadside. Dietrich recognised the steel helmets and breastplates of a military police patrol. Three men and an N.C.O. There was also an old grey-haired Frenchman on his knees in the middle of the group, and a young woman.

Dietrich waited until the car stopped alongside the swaying group and then leapt out. He did not know what was happening or what he was going to do, but all of his pent-up fears and anxiety seemed to propel him into the roadway like a spring.

The soldiers fell silent, and the N.C.O., who had been tugging at the girl's arm, let go and saluted, his angry face flushed and guilty.

'What is happening here?' Dietrich's voice sharpened as he saw the tears of anger and defiance in the girl's eyes. She was pale and very attractive, and even as the N.C.O. began to explain she pulled the old man to his feet and glared across at Dietrich, her mouth quivering.

'We were carrying out a road check, Lieutenant, and this old fool refused to show us what he had in his bag——'

'He's a *liar*!' The girl's voice was trembling with suppressed anger, but the clarity of her German made an even greater impact on those around her. 'They stopped us because they had nothing else to do! Then they saw this!' She thrust out her leg, and Dietrich noticed for the first time that she was crippled and had the leg encased in irons. 'They made jokes about it! The filthy beasts did not seem to think that ignorant French people would understand German. My father protested and they knocked him down!' In spite of her defiance two tears ran down her cheeks as she said more quietly: 'But I do not expect you to believe me. You are a German officer!'

The N.C.O.'s anxious expression changed to brutal confidence. 'Did you hear that, Lieutenant? *Insolent* swine!'

'Silence! Get about your business! Try to act like soldiers and not animals!'

The N.C.O. went scarlet. 'I shall report this to Major Riemann! I have my orders, Lieutenant!'

Dietrich felt an unreasoning anger sweeping through him like fire. The girl's pitiful defiance, coupled with the obvious brutality of the military police, had their effect. Police such as these had shot German soldiers in Russia, had probably been responsible for the death of his own brother.

'And *I* will report you, you insolent pig! They need men at the front now, I will make that suggestion to my own Headquarters!'

The N.C.O. saluted and gestured quickly to his men. All the bluster seemed to have gone from him in a second, and without another word the four soldiers marched hastily towards the town.

Dietrich picked up the old man's bag and handed it to him. Being careful to avoid the girl's astonished stare he said: 'I apologise for all this unpleasantness. I hope you understand that such things can happen in any country!'

'Thank you, *m'sieu.*' The man nodded gravely, his faded eyes moving quickly across Dietrich's uniform and his Iron Cross. 'It was fortunate you came along.'

'Perhaps I could see you to the safety of your house?' Dietrich stole a quick glance at the girl. She had violet-coloured eyes and her skin was pale against her auburn hair.

To her father she said: 'That will not be necessary. Tell the Lieutenant we are grateful but are quite capable of looking after ourselves!'

The old man smiled for the first time. 'I am Louis Marquet and this is my daughter, Odile. I am a clockmaker in St. Pierre. We can manage all right now, Lieutenant.' He saw the uncertainty and disappointment on the young officer's face and added, 'But we will be pleased to see you at any time you care to call.' He nodded again and moved off up the road.

The girl looked for a few seconds longer at Dietrich's face and then followed her father.

Dietrich stood by the idling car and watched her slim body until she turned the corner in the road. The painful limp seemed to bring a pain to his heart, and he wanted to go after her, if only to endure her scorn and contempt.

With a sigh he climbed into the car and stared at the driver's set shoulders. 'Drive on! There is no need to report this incident!'

The driver grinned inwardly but kept a straight face. 'Of course not, Lieutenant!'

6 : A Disgrace to his Uniform

The long harbour shed, open to the weather on three sides, rang to harsh commands as the seven submarine crews marched into their allotted ranks and positions, boots stamping and scraping while the men picked up their dressing and formed a hollow square on the damp concrete base of the shed.

The U-boat commanders and their officers formed a separate group behind a parked torpedo trolley and watched in silence as their respective crews steadied into firm ranks and settled into rigid stillness.

Outside the shed the March wind blustered across the small harbour and ruffled the sheltered water into a series of tiny breakers. The February weather had departed, the ice-cold replaced by short savage gales and damp mists, and even now, as the men of Group Meteor waited for their Commander, the gulls circled far overhead, tiny specks against the high colourless sky, a sure sign of another shrieking wind from the grey Atlantic. Two small minesweepers sheltered within the stone walls, their rust-streaked sides contrasting with the sleek newly painted hulls of the U-boats which lay nearby.

Rudolf Steiger entered the shed from the far end, his tall figure momentarily outlined against the glittering horizon, his white cap contrasting vividly with the sombre blue ranks which sprang to attention at his entrance, and with the grey stonework beyond.

He climbed stiffly on to the trolley and waited impassively until each crew had been reported present and correct by its coxswain. He half listened to the flat familiar statements, the sharp bark of commands, his eyes expressionless, his face set in a stern mask.

How different the seamen looked after a few weeks in harbour! The colour had returned to their strained faces, and the unfamiliar uniforms and jaunty blue caps gave the ceremony the appearance of a peacetime inspection. In a few more hours all this would be changed, he thought. These men would be dressed in the stained leather jackets, sealed up once more in their steel shells, helpless animals at the mercy of every whim of war.

A tense silence fell over the shed so that the distant harbour noises intruded with sudden clarity. The shrill scream of gulls, the clank of a winch and the hissing sigh of breakers against the jetties.

Rudolf Steiger glanced briefly towards the twin hills which guarded the harbour. How familiar they had become with their wind-swept trees and the tall ungainly flak-towers! Even the town had taken on a fresh personality. Blank French faces had become real people, indifferent-looking restaurants and cafés had become small havens for the land-starved seamen who nightly tramped the narrow streets with hopeful expectancy.

Steiger lifted his head and tried to dismiss the outside world from his mind.

'Comrades!' His voice echoed sharply beneath the high roof. 'We have all enjoyed a well-earned rest, but the time has come once more to play our part in the struggle at sea!' Just a few words, yet already he could sense the uneasiness which transmitted itself through the packed ranks like a chill wind. 'When you are dismissed you will go straight to your boats and prepare for sea. We will sail with the evening tide, and by dawn we will be well clear of the coast.' He ran his eyes quickly along the uptilted faces and wondered what his officers were thinking behind his back. The past weeks had been one long battle to try to draw the six other commanders and their men into one solid group. The actual commanders were the ones to watch, their efficiency and bravery was no longer enough. Their absolute loyalty and belief in *him* and his plans counted for much more now. Captain Bredt had used Steiger as an effective buffer between himself and the rest of the Group and had infected everyone with his fluctuating moods. One day he was abusive and insulting to every idea put to him, so that officers no longer consulted him about anything: the next morning he would be suave yet evasive, as if the whole action of the Group was almost unimportant.

Yet the operation ahead of Group Meteor was terrifying in its size and importance and needed every last ounce of planning.

German Intelligence agents working in Eire had reported a steady build-up of Allied shipping in and around the Bristol Channel. But this was no ordinary enemy movement, nor were they the usual type of ships. After months of investigation and careful observation the agents had stated that the Allies were about to carry out a full-scale invasion exercise in safe waters. Troopships, tank-landing craft, refuelling tankers, in fact every craft required for an all-out assault on German territory was to be put through its paces.

Another U-boat Group had already sailed from Norway and was making its way around the north of Scotland, slowly working itself towards the forbidden and heavily protected area of manœuvres off the Irish coast. The St. Pierre Group would attack from the south after passing through the vast minefield which guarded the approaches to the Bristol Channel and Irish Sea, and would strike deep into the packed mass of shipping beyond. Only two groups of U-boats were to be used. More than that might spark off the enemy's suspicion and counter-attack before they were even halfway to their targets. Every U-boat had been overhauled and fitted with a full load of the very latest acoustic torpedoes. It was a daring plan, and if successful it might well make the Allies postpone any idea of an attempted invasion for months to come. Every month was vital to Germany. In the summer the German armies in Russia would be able to hold the crumbling front once again and then launch the great counter-offensive. There would be no faltering, no mistake. Once more to the gates of Moscow, but this time the German soldiers would swamp the Russians with their new weapons and regained confidence.

Steiger remembered the faces of the other commanders as he had outlined their part in the new operation. So much depended on how each one of them would translate the complex order of battle into simple terms for his own crew once the Group sailed from St. Pierre. The seven U-boats would sail west and then north to get into position without exciting the attention of enemy patrols and aircraft. This would mean cruising at slow speed, submerged the whole time and using the hated Snorchels, and Steiger had seen the resentment in the other officers' eyes as he had explained this point. The Group would return in May at the latest, when good leave could be granted to the crews so that they might even return to Germany to see their families. It was a small temptation when separated from reality by the threat of the impending operation, but properly handled it might be enough to settle the men's nerves.

Steiger looked across the white-capped harbour, his grey eyes distant. 'In safer times we used only to think of our own ship, but now we must think of ourselves as a group, part of the whole which is Germany! I know that some of you are still very new to this service, but in a way you are more fortunate than the rest of us. You are able to face the future without sentiment or comparison. Your minds will be clear and fresh for the tasks which lie ahead! When we return, the boys among you will be men, and the men will be heroes!'

He cursed himself for his flat empty words. 'The High Command have seen what you can do. You are no longer a collection of individuals, you are one forged weapon, you are Group Meteor!' His eyes moved slowly across their wind-reddened faces. 'Let no man forget his allegiance, let no man bring discredit on our name!'

He stepped back so that the silence felt brittle like ice around him.

I am quite alone now, he thought. Even Lehmann avoids me now. They watch me warily and without envy, each man wondering when I will drag him down. With sudden anger he shut them from his thoughts. Let them be rebellious in their minds, but let no one doubt my authority!

He was startled as a tall grey-headed coxswain stepped from Alex Lehmann's crew, his cap folded in a huge fist. 'Three cheers for Commander Steiger! He will tweak the Tommies' tails for them!'

A great roar of cheering rolled across the shed, unsteady at first, then gathering momentum like a tidal wave, so that it engulfed the tall solitary figure on the torpedo trolley in a torrent of noise. The blue ranks faltered then broke as the man scampered across the gap, their caps waving, their faces wild with excitement and desperate eagerness.

It was almost as if they needed Steiger's reassurance in the way that a child needs its father. The unspoken fear was momentarily lost, the old dread was replaced by pride.

Steiger turned on his heel and looked down at his officers. He could tell that their minds were working like his own. They knew well enough that words were not sufficient, but in spite of this knowledge they stared at him as if seeing him for the first time.

He pushed through the cheering seamen, his shoulders numb to the eager hands, his eyes blind to the fervent, thrusting faces. Alex Lehmann saw his stricken face as he passed, and wondered if, after all, Steiger was like the rest of them.

Lieutenant Dietrich watched Steiger with something like awe, his throat tight with emotion. Of course the Captain was right, Germany was greater than small differences, more powerful than individual treachery. It was as if Steiger had suddenly opened his eyes for him so that he could view his brother's death calmly and without bitterness. Even here, in St. Pierre, things were changing. There was the French girl, for instance, and once the Group had carried out its mission there would be long leave for everyone. Leave which might yet have real promise for him. He pushed after Steiger's tall figure, his youthful face suddenly hopeful.

. . . . .

The blue mass of seamen surged from the harbour shed and swirled along the top of the main jetty wall towards the waiting submarines. Already the Base staff had piled the crews' small bags of personal belongings at the head of each narrow gangway, and the Base Gunnery Officer was making his last check of every vessel's long deck gun. There was a sense of grim expectancy in the keen air, and as the long column of seamen moved towards the final stone jetty the pace slowed and the men broke away into individual small groups, as if unwilling to accept the finality of their position.

Max König leaned against a worn stone bollard and stared down at *U-991*. His companions crowded around him in restless silence and watched as the last of the maintenance men sauntered up the steep gangway from the submarine's smooth whaleback.

Krieger, the man who had lost his nerve during the depth-charge attack, swallowed hard and wiped his lips with the back of his hand. 'D'you think this will be worse?' He flinched as the others emerged from their own thoughts and stared at him. 'I—I mean from what Steiger just said I got the idea that something special was planned . . .'

His voice trailed away miserably as Horst Jung grunted shortly, '*Captain* Steiger to you!'

Braun, the debonair hydrophone operator, once a waiter in Leipzig, looked at his well-kept hands and said calmly: 'Yes, it'll be the big thing this time. The last effort was just to get us all in trim!' He grinned unfeelingly at Krieger's taut face. 'So let's not have another show of nerves, eh?'

Horst Jung removed the small blackened pipe from his mouth and rubbed the warm bowl against his nose. Beneath the gentle pressure the boneless nose moved sideways across his face as if it were detached. Thousands of fierce punches in a hundred fights had left it a mere imitation of its original shape. 'The Captain'll see us all right, comrades, I've watched his career right through the service, and I well remember reading about his father, too. Yes, if anyone stands a chance to survive I reckon *we* do!'

Moses Rickover grinned cheerfully and puffed out his pink cheeks. 'That's it, Father, you tell them all about it!'

Jung settled himself comfortably against the stone wall and jammed the pipe back in his mouth. His eyes twinkled through the creased flesh. 'Young rabbit!'

Max König half listened to the bantering conversations about him as the crew crowded together on the wind-swept wall. The warm pressure of their bodies, the uneasy companionship of their complete dependence on each other, made him think of Steiger's set face when he had spoken to them. Was it possible to see the real man? Or were his words just the usual meaningless gabble to which every serviceman had apparently become immune? Yet the sudden cheering and the wave of excitement must mean something, he thought.

He heard the two seamen behind him talking about their recent exploits in one of the town's new brothels. Through their coarse, casual descriptions he could see some of the frightened French girls he himself had watched as they waited in the narrow doorways for the seamen to arrive. Usually thin and starved-looking, and always very young, they seemed to represent the misery and filth of war which had become international.

Everything we touch we dirty and defile! He tried to find comfort in his own recollections of the past weeks. He had tried to get away from the others as much as he could without rousing resentment or suspicion, and had taken long walks across the hills and through the woodland beyond the town. Mile after mile, until his boots were heavy with mud and his body wet with sweat, his feet automatically taking him clear of the isolated houses and farms, his mind painfully exploring the past and trying to find a memory without despair. It was as if he had *really* died in the air-raid, that he was indeed merely using Max König's body without owning it. Over and over again he had told himself, I am nothing, and nobody. I no longer exist, nor do I have any future!

Petty Officer Schmidt, a thin-lipped individual who maintained a permanent attitude of angry resentment, pushed roughly through the seamen. 'Right, you lazy bastards! Get aboard now and shift into your seagoing gear!' He glared down at Krieger. 'You can forget your snivelling escape ashore, this time we've work to do!'

Muller, the expressionless ex-coffin-maker, glanced quickly at the others. 'What news is there, Petty Officer? Something big?' He was trying to draw Schmidt's fire from Krieger, but to no avail.

'Ach, you gutless amateurs make me puke!' Schmidt swayed back on his heels. 'To think that the Fatherland must depend on the likes of you!'

Krieger blinked his eyes furiously. 'It was just one instant, I——'

'Silence!' Schmidt roared directly into the man's face. 'One more word and I'll have you on extra watchkeeping!'

König heard himself say: 'He's all right now! We were all pretty frightened during that attack.'

Schmidt swung round, his sallow face flushed. 'You speak when you're spoken to, Seaman High-and-Mighty König! I've met your kind before, born trouble-makers! Well, just you watch it in future, because I'll have my eye on you!' He gestured violently towards the pile of kit-bags. 'Now get that gear aboard! I'll teach you to act like a lot of farm labourers!' He clattered noisily down the gangway, his neck red above his tight collar.

König sighed and allowed his taut muscles to unwind slightly.

Jung raised his ragged eyebrows and shook his head. He seemed to be reasoning with himself. Eventually he commented, 'Still, he *is* a good seaman, Max!'

König shrugged wearily. 'Why is it that we breed that type in Germany? It seems that they are specially reared to become N.C.O.s. So damned ignorant that they can only do one job well and can find nothing good to say about anyone who knows anything else!' He picked up his bag. 'When he kept riding Krieger I *had* to do something. I can't stand seeing people humiliated. It is the worst cruelty!'

He said it with such sudden vehemence that Jung glanced up at him with quick interest. 'Petty Officer Schmidt was correct about one thing, Max. You are an odd bird, right enough. I think you are different from the rest of us.'

Moses Rickover leaned across them from the edge of the wall. 'Here, you two old men, let me give you both a hand.' Then he was gone, laughing and skipping down the steep gangway like a schoolboy on his way home for the holidays.

'God, what it is to be as carefree as that.' König stared after him.

Jung snorted. '*Old* men indeed! Just wait till he's got a bit of service in, then we'll see who's old!'

A figure joined the edge of the group, and König automatically tensed. It was Michener, the ex-policeman, his sour face still bloated from the previous night's trip ashore. He waited until most of the men had made their way down the gangway and then said importantly: 'I had to go over to the Headquarters building for the First Lieutenant. I think Lieutenant Dietrich rather looks to me. It's not every man who's had a bit of government service and knows the meaning of discipline!' Nobody answered, but Michener turned to König, his eyes eager. 'By the way, I just met an old friend of yours.'

König remained bent over his bag, his fingers hooked round the lanyard like claws. So it had happened, and Michener *would* be the one to break the first defence. In a flat voice he asked, 'Oh, who was that?' He waited, his heart pumping painfully against his ribs. Perhaps Michener was Gestapo? Maybe he had already discovered his secret and was merely playing his savage game in the way that only the Gestapo knew.

'A fellow called Fromm. He brought despatches down from Lorient, and I happened to show him the crew list which I was getting signed for Lieutenant Dietrich. This chap pointed to your name and asked if you were new, and when I told him you were the one who was rescued from that fire he became very interested indeed. He knew you before that, apparently, at the Intake Barracks, and heard all about your escape during the air-raid.' Michener paused for breath. 'He's pretty keen to see you again.'

König raised his eyes slowly in the way he had learned so well in the concentration camp, but Michener's face told him nothing. It, too, was blank but watchful. Perhaps Michener did not suspect anything. He was a naturally curious and interfering man, and maybe his additional knowledge about the fire and air-raid was just part of his hoarded information.

'Fromm, you say?' König kept his voice non-committal. If Michener was an agent it was not unlikely that he had invented even the man's name. 'I'm not sure if I remember him. A lot of my early service is a bit hazy. I completely lost my memory for a while.'

Jung rubbed his thick hands. 'Well, why not slip over to the H.Q. Block, Max? Dietrich is the Duty Officer aboard, he wouldn't mind. It would only take a couple of minutes.' He grinned, pleased with his idea. 'It might bring back a lot of happy memories for you!'

König shook his head. 'No, I'll see him when I'm up in Lorient. I'm not that interested.'

Michener picked up his bag, his face hidden. 'You'll see him when we dock again, König. Fromm is transferred to the Base as from today!'

König made himself walk with careful slowness as he moved down the gangway, but his brain was working in a whirl of desperate confusion. There had always been a chance of discovery, but as the months had passed he had hoped that his new identity would save him. Now a ghost from the real world had arrived, and the smell of death seemed to follow him down the slope to the gently rolling U-boat. Involuntarily he glanced back at the shore and felt the sweat cold on his forehead.

One thing is certain, he thought. They'll never get me back in that camp alive. The first chance, *any* chance, and I must get away.

Behind him he heard Jung say companionably: 'It's nice to find an old comrade. It helps to make life bearable.'

. . . . .

Rudolf Steiger paused in the centre of his small room and took another look around. It had probably been used by the hotel manager as an office in more peaceful times and was spartan in its simplicity. A desk, a narrow metal bed, two chairs and a long wall cupboard completed the furniture, and as the building itself backed on to the side of one of the twin hills there was little light from the one barred window to relieve the appearance of cell-like sparseness.

He looked absently at the long leather bag which lay packed and ready on the bed. His own life and possibly those of his men lay inside it. Diary, logbooks, action-charts, all checked and up-to-date. A few minor personal items. Very few. It was as if his whole life was neatly packed in the bag. In the room there was no photograph, nothing to give a clue to his identity for anyone who might take over the room should he not return. In the cupboard were his new shore-going uniforms, too stiff and unworn to help any newcomer to assess his predecessor. Nothing. He shuddered and glanced involuntarily at his face in the stained mirror. Commander Rudolf Steiger, Captain of *U-991*. Nothing else mattered. He reached for his long leather bridge coat and stopped as a hand rapped urgently at the door.

A messenger stood rigidly in the opening, his fingers straight down the seams of his trousers, his eyes aimed at a point over Steiger's right shoulder.

'Captain Bredt's compliments, sir, and would you go at once to the car transport park.'

One of Steiger's few weaknesses was that he liked time to prepare himself before each voyage. Like a matador outside the bull-ring, or a hunter setting out on safari. He liked to be alone for the few hours before sailing, to brood over each possibility, to readjust his plans like the complex pieces of a jigsaw puzzle. He frowned. There was still a lot to think about, yet Bredt wanted him for something or other which might have nothing to do with the operation at all. He sighed and reached for his cap.

'What is happening? Do you know?'

The messenger relaxed slightly and shifted his eyes to Steiger's face. 'Well, sir, I did hear that one of the U-boat's men has been found.'

'Found?' His brain clicked into place. One of *U-891*'s men had vanished two days ago, and Lieutenant-Commander Willi Ludwig, the boat's captain, had gloomily suggested desertion. It was a real possibility, but apparently he had at last been found. Poetic justice to be caught too soon to escape from sailing.

'Yes, sir. He's dead!' The man swallowed as Steiger's face darkened.

'Here, take this bag to my First Lieutenant and tell him to carry on until I return!' He jammed the leather bag into the man's fist and strode angrily down the corridor.

Three minutes later he was speeding along the straight cobbled road, his eyes bleak as he peered ahead of the camouflaged bonnet, but his mind toying with the vague information which Bredt had to offer.

'It appears that this seaman hanged himself, Steiger. Got too much for him, I suppose. The weekly service bus from Lorient discovered the body, or rather I should say some French forestry workers flagged down the bus and told the driver, who quite rightly telephoned the Base.'

Bredt lapsed into silence and Steiger watched the tall trees skimming past on either side of the car. Bredt gave the impression that it was all too irritating for words, and so it was. And yet if it was so trivial, why had he insisted on driving straight off to the scene of the wretched seaman's death? He glanced sideways at Bredt and wondered. Outwardly he appeared as bland and self-possessed as usual, yet Steiger had come to know only too well that Bredt could not be judged by a quick appraisal.

They rounded a shallow bend, and Steiger saw the long grey diesel bus parked beneath a tree, its driver chatting with some helmeted soldiers. Several service passengers peered impatiently from the steamy windows, and more soldiers and an army staff car were bunched further along the road. Steiger grimaced as he saw the portly, self-important figure of Major Reimann striding towards the naval car.

He saluted Bredt correctly, but his small eyes flickered quickly towards Steiger. Steiger plucked slowly at a button on his coat, his inner sense warning him that things were not quite so straightforward as Bredt imagined or pretended they were.

'He's through here.' Reimann gestured with his leather-covered stick and plunged immediately off the road, his polished boots grinding through the wet bushes and tangled weeds.

Some more soldiers stood apprehensively around the still form which lay a beneath a tall tree. The naval uniform was sodden from the previous night's rain, and the thin fair hair was plastered pathetically across the hideously distorted face with its bulging eyes and protruding tongue. A thin rope was still wound round the seaman's neck, and a corresponding piece fluttered from an overhanging branch to show where the soldiers had cut him down.

Bredt glared down at the blackened face with obvious distaste. 'Took what he thought was the easy way out, eh? Well, I shall have to replace him with one of the Base men, I suppose! The damned fool!'

Reimann shuffled his feet and looked from one officer to the other. 'Fellow's a disgrace to the service! A thing like this brings shame on his uniform.'

Steiger was on his knees beside the body, his eyes narrowed as he peered closely at the stretched rope.

'This man was *murdered*!' His words made the soldiers glance at each other with sudden alarm. 'He was a professional seaman, yet look at the way this noose was tied! No seaman would do that, for suicide or any other reason!' He ran his hands quickly through the dead man's pockets, conscious of the stiff, sodden limbs beneath his probing fingers, and aware too of Bredt's silence. He looked up. 'Empty! Robbed and murdered!' His eyes hardened so that in the dull light they shone like grey stones. 'A poor seaman caught alone and helpless, hung up and left to die like a dog, and you dare to call it suicide!' He could see from their stricken expressions that both Bredt and the Major knew this already.

Reimann gestured urgently and the soldiers shambled awkwardly out of earshot. 'I can assure you that we have made the fullest enquiries——' he began, but Bredt interrupted, his pale eyes flashing with sudden impatience.

'It is more convenient this way, Steiger. We can investigate the matter quietly when the Group has sailed. We will stand a better chance of catching the culprit.'

Steiger stood up and stared fixedly at his superior. 'Yet if I had agreed with your verdict you would have let this man be buried a coward! He was probably killed by some local men, and this is just a beginning unless you act now!'

Reimann waved his stick helplessly. 'You don't understand! If we make a big issue of this we will have the S.S. and the Gestapo down here in force!'

Steiger looked at him with contempt. 'And of course we don't want that, do we? They might discover that your control of this area is about nil! That your garrison are so well pleased with their assignment that they have forgotten their duty, have forgotten even that they are German soldiers!'

Bredt stepped forward, his face twitching. 'Control yourself, Steiger! This isn't organised sabotage! Probably some local thugs getting their own back! What do you want me to do? Arrest half the town as hostages? Shoot the Mayor and his family on suspicion?'

Steiger remained unmoved. 'If necessary, yes! Ever since the U-boats came to St. Pierre I have seen this danger getting more definite. It was only a matter of time before some token resistance was made. I expected it even if Major Reimann did not. As it happens, I do not think that a man, alone and frightened, murdered on a rope's end and left hanging on a French tree, *is* trivial. If we do not act now we will get more, *much* more!'

'I will be ready!' Reimann looked to Bredt for support.

'Of course we will be ready,' added Bredt smoothly. 'I will conduct the enquiry myself.'

'I am sure that the local people of importance will be as shocked as we are,' Reimann was recovering his self-control, 'and will do all they can to help.'

Steiger bent down and removed the U-boat clasp from the corpse's jacket. For a moment he looked at it and then slipped it into his pocket. 'I will give this to his commanding officer to be sent home with his effects. At least his family need not know how little we care for our *fighting* men!' Without another glance he thrust his way through the bushes and on to the road.

Upon his appearance the group around the bus came to life, and he said to the driver, 'Are you going to the Base at St. Pierre now?'

'Yes, sir. Can I give you a lift?' The man was not curious as to why an officer with three stripes on his sleeve should want to take his bus instead of the sleek staff car, any more than he cared about the corpse beyond the bushes. The irritating waiting was over, and that was all that mattered.

Steiger climbed on to the step as the big diesel coughed into life. As he felt the bus shudder into motion he saw Bredt and Reimann still watching him from beyond the bushes.

How alike they are, he thought with sudden fury. Reimann is bad enough, with his petty-minded stupdity, but Bredt is so desperately worried about his chances of promotion and all that goes with it that he is prepared to turn his back on real danger.

Steiger gripped at the safety rail as the bus lurched back on to the cobbled road. Well, let them be careful. One more chance like this and I'll go to Admiral Dönitz is necessary!

He swung round startled as a female voice said quietly: 'Would you care to sit here, Commander? I do not think there is any more room.'

Steiger's bitter thoughts still held his mind in a tangled web, and for several seconds he could only stare at the girl who sat watching him with grave interest. He glanced quickly at the other passengers, clerks, officers returning from leave, couriers and the like, and then lowered himself into the vacant seat beside her. He was immediately conscious of her closeness, the elusive perfume which seemed to lull the anger which had driven him on to the bus, and most of all the open way she was watching him. She was very dark, and her jet-black hair was piled on top of her head like a glistening crown. The raincoat she was wearing over her dress was crumpled, and her short boots were stained and spattered with mud.

'I must apologise for my appearance. I have been travelling for three days.' She gestured towards the wooded countryside. 'The French are so casual, so indifferent about their transport. I was grateful that I could get a German bus for the last piece of my journey!'

She glanced sideways as a horsedrawn farm cart trundled past, and Steiger turned his head to get a good look at her.

About twenty-five, wedding ring, and had casually accepted him as an equal. She had small, well-shaped ears, and the neck which disappeared into the shapeless raincoat was smooth and strong.

Turning suddenly she stared at him, her brown eyes very wide. 'How stupid of me!' Her face seemed to shine with her amusement, but Steiger thought he could detect something else. Nervousness? Embarrassment?

'I have just realised who you are! Rudolf Steiger! I have seen your photograph often enough in the newspapers, and, of course, Alex, my husband, has often written of you!'

A knife seemed to twist in his inside. 'Alex Lehmann?' In spite of his caution his voice sounded unsteady.

'That's right. I am joining him today. He has arranged some accommodation for me, although I have no idea what it will be like.' She laughed again. 'But anything will be better than sitting at home in Kiel!'

'Perhaps.' He controlled his voice with an effort. In just a few hours the Group would be sailing, and so far nothing had gone as he had planned. The dead sailor, his foreboding of danger, and now this. He tried to sneer at the uneasiness he felt at the girl's presence, but the feeling only helped him to remember Lehmann's serious face when they had quarrelled on the hillside above the harbour. With a girl like this, Lehmann could afford to be sorry for his superior officer!

'It's funny really,' her voice broke in on his thoughts. 'I shall only be here for a short while, and already I'm dreading leaving! I hardly know the man I call my husband, we were parted within weeks of being married, and yet I am expected to make some sort of new life in a few days, here in France!'

Involuntarily she laid one hand on his sleeve, and he stared at it without moving. In a strange tone he said, 'I am sure Commander Lehmann will do his best to make you comfortable.' Immediately he cursed himself. Lehmann might not be back from the next cruise in time to see her before she returned to Germany. He might not return at all.

The bus rolled slowly on to the town's open square and shuddered to a halt. Two sailors whom Steiger recognised as orderlies from the Base staff saluted respectfully and began to gather up the girl's luggage, while the rest of the bus's passengers climbed down and hurried towards the warmth and security of their respective quarters.

Steiger bit his lip. So it was all arranged, just as Lehmann had said. It was another world outside his own, and even though Lehmann faced the same dangers as himself, he was able to exclude even those perils from his own secret life, could cherish hope and benefit from such dreams as this girl could bring him.

A few heavy drops of rain slashed the side of the bus, and the girl turned up the collar of her coat.

'How I am looking forward to a hot bath, that is if the French can arrange such a thing here.'

All at once Steiger had a wild vision of her strong young body relaxed and rich in the steamy privacy of her bathroom, with the black hair no longer obedient and trapped, but hanging down across her smooth limbs.

Already she was moving away from him, and he remembered with sudden despair that Lehmann's boat was scheduled as the last to sail. It would be easy for the commanding officer to slip ashore for a few moments. No doubt that, too, was arranged. He briefly considered altering the sailing plan, but found no comfort in the idea. Instead he saluted stiffly and stared down at her upturned face.

'I hope you find everything as you wish it. Perhaps we shall meet again?'

She smiled and stepped clear as the bus moved away once more. 'Perhaps we shall.' But already she seemed to have forgotten him. 'It has been a pleasure, Commander.'

The rain began to fall, and the few onlookers melted into the walls of the nearby buildings. Steiger watched her cross the square as if half expecting her to turn and make some last remark. But she did not.

An army ambulance rattled on to the square, and Steiger recognised the driver as one of the men he had seen earlier on the road. The dead sailor was being brought in. There was still a lot to do. He glanced wearily at his watch and grimaced. It had been only an hour since he had left his room at the H.Q. building. Only an hour, yet nothing seemed the same any more.

7: Skating on Thin Ice

Lieutenant Heinz Dietrich leaned his elbows on the chart-table and braced his legs behind him to steady himself against the U-boat's sickening rolls, and tried to concentrate on the grubby chart spread before him. The pivoted electric lamp above his head cast a warm yellow glare over the vibrating table and gave the small illusion of warmth and privacy, so that Dietrich had to shake his head repeatedly to drive away the drowsiness which threatened to drag his mind from his calculations and at the same time allow him to be hurled from his feet by any unexpected lurch.

He stared fixedly at the criss-crossed bearings, the complex mass of tiny figures and soundings and, above all, their own feeble course shown by a pencilled line which wandered in what appeared to be an aimless and haphazard journey from the French coast to their present position, which as far as anyone could judge was about one hundred miles south of the Fastnet Rock. To the north lay the bulk of Ireland, and to the east the pronged coastline of England.

For two weeks the U-boat had manœuvred towards this position, an eight-hundred-mile voyage which should have taken them five days even under the necessity of using the hated Snorchel and thereby avoiding surfacing, but which in fact had dragged on and on until the dazed and weary watchkeepers had lost all count of time and distance. Only by looking at the chart, the positive proof of their journey, could Dietrich obtain a clear picture of what was happening. Even now the diesels were roaring and shaking in their efforts to hold the boat steady enough to remain at periscope depth while they sucked down great gulps of sea air through the raised Snorchel. Overhead a great gale raged with a fierceness which had dogged them for all but the first two days of the voyage, and which had made every watch a nightmare. For a few hours each day the Captain had dived the boat to a comfortable depth to allow his men time to feed, to snatch a few moments to change their dwindling stock of clean clothing, and to fall into an exhausted sleep. The rest of the time he drove the boat along just below the surface, saving the batteries, listening and waiting for the next contradictory signal from far-off Headquarters.

Every so often a mountainous wave would catch the porpoising hull unawares, and for a few moments the Snorchel would be submerged. Instantly the precious air was sucked into the hungry diesels, and men would roll about in agony, their hands clapped to their ears or their throats as the hull space turned into a deadly vacuum. Then the electric motors would be thrown frantically into life, and the diesels killed, while the Officer of the Watch fought to control the boat and bring her back to the correct depth, only to have the whole thing repeated perhaps minutes later.

And so it went on, until each officer could only think of the moment he would be relieved and be able to find a few hours' security in his bunk. Tempers frayed, and if a man was late on watch, even a few seconds, he was met with a face of real hatred. The weeks in harbour were already hard to remember, the brief escape from the Atlantic merely an elusive dream.

Dietrich swallowed hard, the sour acid taste of diesel fumes thick against the roof of his mouth. How long could this gale last? he wondered. Perhaps the operation might be cancelled and they could return to Base to await a better opportunity. Headquarters had already ordered countless changes of course for Group Meteor, so scattered and dazed by the weather the seven submarines had crawled painfully back and forth along the sides of a vast two-hundred-mile rectangle, charging their batteries, keeping clear of the known convoy routes, and just waiting. The Captain apparently thought that the British had delayed their manœuvres because of the gale, and Headquarters were waiting for fresh information from their agents. And what of Group Bruno? How were they faring? Dietrich wondered. They should have rounded the south-east corner of Ireland by now, and should have got themselves into a sheltered position inside the St. George's Channel itself. Group Meteor would have to make maximum speed to get into the attack area if and when the trap was sprung, and to do that they would have to pass right through one of the largest minefields yet laid by the British.

He shuddered and licked his dry lips. The gale could not have helped there either. Many of the mines would have dragged, and loose cables would be waiting to entangle a U-boat's propellers or foul any projecting piece of equipment.

He listened to Lieutenant Hessler cursing the helmsman as the deck canted sideways into a surging undercurrent, and wondered if he, too, was thinking of the future with dread. If the attack had been carried out as planned it would have been bad enough, but at least they had been rested and alert. But this waiting and soul-destroying misery had undone all that, they were living on their nerves once more.

Dietrich leaned his face in his hands and closed his eyes. Very slowly and carefully he began to build up a picture of the French girl in his mind, feature by feature, until he held her image in his brain like a tiny portrait. Her name was Odile Marquet, and he had visited her father's small shop two days after the incident on the road. He had ignored the amusement on the man's face when he had explained that his daughter was not at home. Dietrich had had the impression that the girl was within feet of him at that moment, listening through the woollen curtain at the back of the shop. He had made a little casual conversation, while the grey-headed clockmaker had nodded gravely or answered with polite interest. Every so often their conversation, such as it was, had fallen away, to be instantly replaced by the ticking of countless clocks and watches which were ranged like onlookers on every shelf.

Dietrich had made another visit, and had been invited to share wine with the girl's father. This time he had been luckier. She had sat alongside her father, her violet eyes averted from Dietrich's strained and eager face, her white skin making her look fragile and remote.

When Dietrich had taken his leave Louis Marquet had touched his arm and said softly: 'She is bitter because she cannot help me with my work. I wish she could get some little job, it would make her feel better, you understand?'

It was quite by chance that Dietrich had heard about Captain Bredt's scheme for employing some French clerical staff at the Base. They were necessary apparently because of the growing number of local people employed at the Base, and Dietrich took the information to the little clockmaker's shop with fresh hope in his heart. He waited two more days, and then when he had visited the small dock office within the harbour compound he had come face to face with her, and she had actually smiled at him.

Simply she had said: 'It was good of you, Lieutenant. I am sorry if I have treated you badly.' She had shrugged her slim shoulders, the movement stabbing at Dietrich's very insides. 'I hope you will understand. It is the war. Nothing is right any more.'

The office had been full of French clerks and a German overseer, but Dietrich had gently taken her hand and squeezed it. She had not drawn away, but had stared at him with shocked surprise.

Looking back now, while the U-boat staggered and groaned into each surging trough, it seemed uncanny how they had come to their arrangement with hardly a word being said. Dietrich knew well enough what the townspeople might say of a girl who befriended a German officer. Their words would be born of envy rather than loyalty to a cause, but they would be dangerous all the same. Dietrich's brother officers might also have something to say about the matter. A French countess was one thing, or even a girl in a brothel, but to take seriously someone like Odile Marquet, a cripple at that, was more than would be tolerated.

So without planning or fuss they met each other in a small café beyond the town on the lonely road to the north coast. It would be more difficult when the evenings became brighter, but in the days before the Group had sailed, Dietrich had known real happiness. Walking back towards the town, more often than not through the rain, her arm through his, with hardly a word between them. He walked slowly, his heart softened by the metallic click of her leg iron, his heart pounding with each successive pressure of her body against his.

An arm jolted him from his dreams, and Hessler snarled: 'For Christ's sake where is that bastard Reche? He's adrift from his watch again!'

Dietrich rubbed his eyes and groaned. 'Is it morning already?'

Hessler rasped his hand across his chin. 'Who can tell any more?'

. . . . .

Max König lay in his narrow pipe-cot, his nose only inches from the curved deckhead. Below him, crammed around the slung table, other members of his mess were listlessly playing a game of Skat, the frayed cards skidding on the scrubbed surface as the hull lurched and wallowed with irregular persistence.

König lifted himself stiffly on to one elbow and looked down at them. Most of them showed signs of physical rather than mental strain, and Muller, the coffin-maker, was well tinged with green as he fought his own battle with his stomach. Jung sat solidly at the head of the table, his powerful body rocking in an easy boneless motion, his face screwed in tight concentration so that his eyes had all but disappeared. For once he was without his cap, and his grizzled grey hair sprouted from his square head like a well-worn brush.

Braun, the hydrophone operator, winced as the water rumbled like thunder and the wire stays of the table hummed with sudden life. 'What a storm! All the same, I wish we were right up on the surface. At least we'd get a bit of air!'

Jung coughed, a deep painful sound, and shrugged indifferently. 'Always the same at this time of year. After March you can expect a bit better.'

Schultz, the ex-photographer from Dresden, picked gloomily at his stubbled chin and regarded the glittering metal compartment with loathing. 'Submarines! What a stinking life!'

Muller swallowed hard and clutched his stomach as a big roll heaved him hard against the edge of the table. 'At least the Tommies have learnt to respect us!'

Jung stared at him with surprise and then laughed, the laugh changing immediately to another cough in the foul air. 'What the hell are you yapping about? You talk like a damned recruiting poster!'

'Well, you know as well as I do that our successes have crippled them. How much longer can they hold out?'

Jung threw down his frayed cards. 'The sailor's dream! He's always hoping that something outside his own efforts will happen to shorten the war!'

Braun smiled his gentle, superior smile. 'Well, you tell us, Father. What does win a war?'

Jung picked up his cards and stared at the table. 'Endurance mostly,' he announced slowly. 'War is ninety per cent misery and ten per cent uncertainty. If you can stick that lot then you can hold on to the end.'

Muller scoffed. 'Everyone knows the British are softer than we are! They've not the stomach for fighting!'

Jung sighed and peered round at him, his small eyes glinting in the yellow glare. 'I can see you've been hibernating up to now! At the beginning of this lot I was serving in the heavy cruiser *Admiral Hipper* when she was rammed by the British destroyer *Glowworm*.' His creased face took on a faraway look. 'All alone she was, a little obsolete destroyer, against our ship, all ten thousand tons of her, *and* our escorts! She was on fire, blown to hell, yet she tried to *ram* us!' He grinned with sudden glee. 'She damned well did, too!'

Braun interrupted with impatience: 'Come on with those

cards, then! I say to hell with valour and self-sacrifice! It's all very well if you happen to be an officer, but for us it only means hard work and more belly-wrenching danger!'

The others laughed, and Muller lurched to his feet. He snatched one of the buckets from its rack and staggered into the central passageway, his face quite green and shining with sweat. They heard him retching and spluttering as he disappeared, and Jung nodded with mock gravity. 'It's as I said, comrades. Endurance is all you need!'

The bulkhead microphone crackled into life, and a voice filled the small compartment. 'This is the Captain speaking!'

. . . . .

Twenty feet forward of the gunners' mess the wardroom was still thick with the smell of stew and coffee, and as the deck tilted from side to side the uncollected dishes clattered against the wooden coamings, so that Luth, the Engineer, had to stop in his efforts to write a letter while he waited for Stohr, the messman, to clear away the debris of their meal.

Hessler wiped a piece of stale bread around his plate and belched contentedly. He cocked his head in the direction of Reche's bunk and winked at Luth. The Navigator's muffled snores were intermingled with groans and small squeaks, and Hessler said, 'Nightmare again!'

'I'm not surprised.' Luth locked his hands behind his narrow head and stared at Reche's blanketed figure. 'He's an angry man. Always getting worked up about something. It doesn't pay in this service!'

'Ach, what does?' Hessler rubbed his chin with distaste. 'I hate being unshaven. I can stand anything else, but a regular officer should always be clean-shaven and smart!' A slow grin spread across his heavy face as he realized the ridiculous content of his remark. 'God, I wish we could get to grips with something! In the old days you were on your own, not dragging about the damned ocean waiting for some poxy admiral to decide what to do!'

'Tch, tch!' Luth wagged his head. 'Now who's spreading dissension in the ranks?'

'Oh hell! *You* know what I mean! All this waiting and no doing. It makes it harder all round.' He grinned reminiscently. 'You should have come ashore with me when I asked you!'

'To that damned brothel? Not likely, I value *my* health!'

Hessler shook his head impatiently, the grin still on his face. 'You've got it all wrong, Franz. We've conquered all these people, don't you see that? It's been damned hard going, and now it's our turn!' He leaned over the table. 'Three little chickens I had, all in one night!' He roared with laughter as he relived each conquest, and Reche's snores stopped instantly at the sound. 'One of them was only fifteen, and she told me her father had sent her out to work for him!' He pulled at his massive eyebrows. 'At least, I *think* that's what she said. Damned Frogs, you can never be sure what they're gabbling about!'

Luth sighed. It was not difficult to imagine Hessler at work with his women. He could break any girl in half with those hands, he thought. 'Well, you just watch you don't catch something from them!'

Hessler pushed at the bell-button. 'Where's that bastard Stohr? No, my old bilge-rat, I told the woman in charge of the house that if anything like *that* happened I would make one more visit!' He gestured with a thick thumb towards the pistol rack. 'She knew what I meant, all right!'

Luth smiled in spite of his troubled thoughts. 'You're a mean-minded bastard!'

Hessler shrugged. 'Life's like skating on thin ice. Either the ice holds or it doesn't. It's no good worrying about it!'

The microphone squeaked, and then they heard Steiger begin to speak.

Reche's sleep-crumpled face appeared over the edge of his bunk. 'What's that? What's happening?'

Hessler lifted his hand. 'Shut up, man!' Then with a hard smile he added, 'I think I can feel a slight crack in the ice!'

. . . . .

Dietrich signalled with his thumb for the periscope to be raised, and settled himself more comfortably on the metal stool. The great lens broke cleanly through the side of a deep trough and then cut into the next fast-moving bank of black water. He sat higher on the stool and waited for the periscope to rise further above the angry crests, and then swung the long tube in a slow circle. It was just as he had imagined it would be. It was nearly dark, and there was only a hint of greyness to show where sea and sky met beyond the tumbling white-toothed waves, whose power seemed magnified by their silence. An empty sea, and another uncomfortable night ahead. And yet . . .

He crouched more steadily over the lens, concentrating fully on the angle of the crumbling wave-tops. The wind had definitely changed direction, had gone round more to the south. That explained the fact that the helmsman during this watch had found his task easier. Dietrich's heart jumped at the prospect of action. There was no doubt about it, he thought, the wind was falling away, the troughs in the black glassy waves were more rounded, less undisciplined.

'Down periscope!'

He walked to the compass and was staring at it as Steiger stepped across the high coaming of the watertight door and strode quickly to the chart-table. He laid his notebook on the stained chart and glanced again at a sheaf of signals, as if he could not trust his first scrutiny.

Without taking his eyes from the papers he gestured to Dietrich. 'I've just decoded the last signal, Heinz.' Steiger's voice was harsh, and Dietrich glanced at him with mounting uneasiness.

'Trouble, sir?'

Steiger snatched up a pair of dividers and a pencil and worked his way methodically across the chart. He sighed and dropped the dividers. 'Our estimated position,' he tapped a small cross, 'still well south of the Fastnet.'

Dietrich shifted impatiently. Of course that was the position. As it had been on and off for days. They had taken an eight-hundred-mile detour after leaving St. Pierre for a route half that distance. Then they had been forced to ride out the gale, back and forth, until no watchkeeping officer could be sure any more of any fixed position. Not once had they surfaced, not once had they seen a star to make a rough fix, nor had they any real idea of the wind's savage force matched against the strong currents.

Steiger added slowly: 'The British apparently intend to commence manœuvres at eight tomorrow morning. Group Bruno will attack half an hour after that!' He glanced at the black-faced watch on his strong wrist. 'In less than fourteen hours, to be more precise!'

Dietrich stared at the chart with disbelief and then at Steiger's cold grey eyes. 'But we're two hundred miles from the attack area, sir!' His voice rose in time with his mounting realisation. 'We can't get there in time! Those stupid swine at Headquarters have betrayed us!'

Steiger opened his mouth as if to rebuke him, and then stooped over the table once more, his pencil moving like a dagger across the furrowed surface. Half to himself he said, 'If Bruno attempts this thing without us they're finished!' He glanced briefly at his First Lieutenant, a small bitter smile on his lips. 'And if they do attack without us the British will be ready when *we* arrive!'

Dietrich staggered against the table, his blue eyes wide with helpless despair. 'We could signal Bruno, sir! Tell them to wait!' He paused, his hopes already shattered by Steiger's expression.

'No, Heinz. It will take our Group about thirty-three hours to get there. The manœuvres might have reached a different area by then. It would need about fifteen knots even to hope for a combined attack!' His eyes flickered with sudden excitement. 'But we might still make it on time!'

'How, sir?' Dietrich's face looked deathly white, and beside the Captain's tall figure he looked almost frail.

'Surfaced! Full speed, say fifteen knots to allow for the slower boats in the Group, we could be there, off the Welsh coast,' he tapped the Pembrokeshire headland with his pencil, 'just in time!'

Dietrich summoned up his reeling thoughts and grasped Steiger's arm. 'Please, sir. You know we can't do that! Have you forgotten the minefields? We must signal Bruno and cancel the attack!'

'Headquarters have demanded a radio silence from now on. There will be no more instructions from that quarter, unless something quite unforeseen occurs.' He looked down at Dietrich, but his eyes were distant and unseeing. 'No, Heinz, it is too late for withdrawal. It is passed to us to complete their plans, no matter how much those plans may have gone awry! The air force will make a combined attack on Plymouth after dawn, so there will be no air attack from the R.A.F., they will be too busy elsewhere!'

Dietrich withdrew his hand, shocked by Steiger's level tone. 'It's murder!' He kept his voice low, which seemed to emphasise the emotion that moved through him. 'One way or another, you'll kill us all!'

Steiger half smiled and then straightened his back. Once more his tired face was masked and impassive. Over his shoulder he barked, 'Pass the word to the radio room for the Chief Operator!' He took one more glance at the chart. 'Right or wrong, Lieutenant, I'll not let Bruno die without a fighting chance!'

He wrote rapidly on his order pad while Dietrich took three

strides to the helmsman and back, his face torn with uncontrolled fears.

In a strange voice Steiger said sharply: 'We will bring her about on to this course,' Dietrich's eyes followed the pencil as if mesmerised, 'as soon as we have contacted the rest of the Group on short wave. Surface in half an hour, and increase to maximum revolutions for fifteen knots.' Each unemotional order was like a hammer on Dietrich's aching mind. 'I want all guns closed up, and the Radar Search Receiver kept fully alert in case we run across an enemy radar picket.' He plucked at a loose button on his jacket, his face suddenly thoughtful. 'We should pass into the minefield just before dawn.' He watched the Chief Radio Telegraphist hurrying through the control room. 'Tell this man my orders. Contract the Group immediately, and call me five minutes before we surface!'

He turned away from Dietrich, his mind already filled with the next phase of his scheme. He picked up the hand microphone and pressed the button with his thumb. For a few seconds he stared down the length of his command, his vision channelled through overhanging boughs of brass and steel, of iron and waiting men.

'This is the Captain speaking!' He heard his voice re-echoed beyond his vision. 'Tomorrow morning we will attack the enemy where he least expects it!' He paused and stared stonily at the microphone in his hand as a burst of cheering floated through the swaying hull. He tried to dismiss Dietrich's words from his mind and continued evenly, 'We will surface in half an hour, let every man be ready and alert!' He paused, suddenly conscious of his hands. They were shaking. Very slightly. With one savage movement he thrust them into his pockets and allowed the microphone to fall on its lead.

As he strode to his cabin he heard a petty officer shout harshly: 'Bridge lookouts stand by! You don't know what you'll see the moment you surface!' Steiger bit his lip. The truest words you ever spoke, he said to himself.

▪ ▪ ▪ ▪ ▪

Steiger wiped the lenses of his powerful Zeiss glasses with a piece of tissue and took another look long at the dark waters ahead of the U-boat's wedge-shaped bows. The high bow wave, sharp and white, streamed back on either side of the invisible casing as the narrow hull thrust forward in response to the whining diesels. Overhead there were several long breaks in the clouds through which a few pale stars had helped with the navigation yet which appeared distant and hostile to the men on watch.

Steiger shrugged his shoulders more tightly inside his layers of clothing and marvelled at the sudden change of weather. The wind had dropped completely, and the black restless water was unbroken in a deep oily swell, marred only by the white arrow-shaped trail of the vessel's wake. The air was colder, but flat and moist, so that the shuddering conning tower ran with rivulets of water which mingled with the icy spray thrown from the bows. In the lenses of his glasses he could see the beginnings of a mist as his vision shortened and lengthened in a series of distorted pictures, so that the U-boat seemed to be cutting her way into a layer of steam.

The bridge lookouts crowded along the sides of the conning-tower, glasses sweeping through their arcs, feet straddled, faces pale against the sea beyond. Above their heads another seaman clung to the swaying periscope standards, his additional look-out made more perilous by the quick, savage lurches as the hull blundered over the uneven water.

Dietrich lifted his head from the voice-pipe and said quickly: 'Four o'clock, Captain. Lieutenant Reche is just bringing her round to oh-eight-five.'

Steiger nodded and lowered his glasses beneath the shelter of the bridge screen. 'Very well. Over nine hours' good steaming, and we're keeping to time.' He glanced at the pale stars. Soon be dawn, yet the night sky was as black as before.

Dietrich added quietly, 'We are approaching the south-west corner of the minefield.'

Steiger glanced briefly at Dietrich's outline and said: 'Yes. Should pass the first section in half an hour.' He shut out the immediate picture of his last command being blasted from beneath his feet, the screams and cries from the voice-pipe, and the towering column of water as the mine exploded from the empty sea. It was strange that he could keep so calm, yet at the same time so keyed up that every nerve felt like wire. In a flat voice he said: 'These minefields are highly overrated. If we cut across the corner of the field we should be as safe as if we were submerged.' At least it will be quicker, he thought. None of the agonising suspense of creeping along near the bottom at a dead slow speed and waiting for the sound of a rusted mine cable scraping down the length of the hull. This way was swift, and clean. The minefield covered a large area of the approaches to the Bristol Channel, and it was likely that the deadly seed were spread thinly over the ground. He bit his lip with sudden doubt. Perhaps I am endangering the boat merely to justify my own ends? Maybe I could not face a submerged approach? I survived one mine because I was on the bridge, as I am now!

He swung his glasses over the starboard side of the bridge. Some seventy miles away lay the long peninsula of the British mainland, Devon and Cornwall with their wave-washed rocks and high cliffs, while over the port rail, ninety miles to the north, the Welsh coast moved out to greet them like the other arm of a great trap. They were well inside the Bristol Channel now, it would soon be time for another alteration of course. He wondered how the rest of the Group were keeping their positions behind him, and if Lehmann was thinking the same as himself. It would fall to him to take command of the Group if anything went wrong.

'High-speed engines to starboard!' a lookout shouted hoarsely, and for a moment they all froze in one solid group, their ears straining above the hiss of spray and breaking water. The noise grew fainter even as they listened. A vicious, high-pitched buzz which ebbed across the hidden sea like a trapped hornet.

Steiger waited until the sound had been swallowed finally in the darkness. 'Motor torpedo boat,' he announced evenly. 'Probably a patrol making up-channel to base.' He felt the men around him relax slightly, and added quietly to Dietrich, 'Lucky fellows will be ashore and in bed by dawn!'

Another muffled figure struggled through the open hatch, and Torpedoman Stohr's voice announced, 'Fresh coffee, Captain!'

Steiger cradled the hot enamel mug in his gloved hands and held it close to his chin. He knew that the lookouts would be envying him every mouthful, but whereas they were relieved every two hours, he had been on the bridge since they had surfaced, ten hours earlier.

Dietrich shifted his position and peered down at the forecasing where the deck-gunners crouched miserably around their long-muzzled weapon. 'Mist's thickening, sir. It's definitely holding closer to the surface now!' Bitterly he added, 'It would be just our luck to get blown up in the minefield only to find that the Tommies had cancelled their manœuvres!'

'If we are blown up, Lieutenant, I suggest we will have nothing to worry about in that direction!'

Dietrich lapsed into silence, and Steiger returned to his thoughts. In his mind's eye he could picture the minefield as it was marked on the chart in the control room. Diamond-shaped and impressive in size, it was more as a deterrent to any foolhardy U-boat commander who might consider making his way right up the Bristol Channel for the rich pickings of Cardiff than for protecting the underbelly of the Welsh coast. By disregarding his orders from Headquarters and maintaining a fast speed on the surface, Steiger had been able to skirt the worst corner of the minefield and was now crossing from the south-west tip of the diamond to a northern point which would bring the Group right up to their originally estimated area.

The silence in the boat was electrifying in its tension, and when the watch changed, for once no one spoke, and the relieved lookouts seemed unwilling to leave the false safety of the upper deck. An hour dragged past, then two, and the strange unmoving mist thickened and hovered above the heaving water.

Dietrich had gone below, and Lieutenant Reche stood silently beside the periscope standards, his head jutting forward as if listening to some new sound. Steiger could almost smell the man's fear, and wondered how Reche had managed to hold out for so long.

Several times a lookout reported a sign of the dawn, but each time the man realised too late that it was merely a thickening patch of mist. As the U-boat's stem cut through the water the white mist vapour seemed to catch on the high stem-head and tear away like a canopy of silk to float high above the conning-tower. Again a man began to make a report, and Reche swung round, his voice loud in the still air: 'Silence, you stupid swine! If you can't see properly then for Christ's sake shut your mouth!'

The man mumbled miserably, 'Sorry, Lieutenant, I thought I was doing right.'

Steiger said sharply, 'Report *everything*!' More quietly he added, 'If you make them feel ridiculous, Lieutenant, they will be afraid to say anything, even if they see a torpedo coming at them!'

Reche sniffed loudly and withdrew into his shell of brooding silence.

Steiger rubbed his eyes. They felt raw and heavy. It *was* getting lighter. Already he could faintly make out the shape of Petty Officer Hartz's solid figure as he stood swaying behind the deck gun, and even the jumping wire was now visible as far as the bows.

He was about to remark on it and so draw Reche out of his misery, when the mist eddied and shivered down the full length of the hull. Simultaneously, there was a dull red flash from astern and a great roar blasted sullenly across the water. It was a loud, abbreviated explosion, so familiar in many of Steiger's dreams that the sweat flooded down his spine like droplets of ice.

Petty Officer Hartz was leaning over the guardrail, peering through the mist. 'Mine, Captain! Dead astern!'

Reche seemed to come to life. He leapt to the voice-pipe and screamed: 'Stop engines! Hard a-port!'

Steiger pushed him aside and tersely cut short the startled voice from the control room. 'Disregard that order! Maintain course and speed!' He swung round towards the rear of the bridge, his face set in a grim mask. 'There were seven submarines, Reche. On this course it was quite likely that one of us would hit a mine. We must have just missed it ourselves! There is no point in turning back now!'

Reche's face seemed to float before him like a carnival mask. 'You can't leave them to die! We must go back!'

'Don't be a fool, man!' Steiger spoke quietly, but his voice was like a lash. 'What do you think you'd find? Fifteen knots collision with a mine, and there's *nothing* left!' He gestured with his hand. 'Deck-party dead instantly. The rest straight to the bottom!'

Reche clamped his plump body and hugged himself, moaning softly like a child. 'Oh God! Oh God! We'll be next! I know it!'

Steiger seized his coat. 'One more word of that and I'll put you under arrest! Now get a grip on yourself and stand your watch!'

Reche tore himself free and walked to the front of the bridge. He peered through his glasses, and Steiger wondered briefly if he was actually seeing anything or whether his eyes were tightly closed.

The shock wave of the explosion would have been felt throughout the boat, in every other submarine in the flotilla. Every man would be wondering who had died, and who would be next.

Well, let them wonder, he thought savagely. It will give them all a chance to blame me! A sudden thought crossed his mind like a chill wind. Suppose it was Lehmann's boat? He dismissed the idea. The explosion was too close. Probably Otto Kunhardt in *U-765*. His mind persisted. Suppose it *was* Lehmann? Steiger saw again the girl's amused brown eyes and wide generous mouth. She would be waiting for Lehmann. Steiger withdrew his hand from his glove and laid it on his forehead. In spite of the cold moist air his skin felt hot and feverish. All at once the doubts came crowding in on him. He had made the final calculations for the attack, but who was to say he was right? They should soon be clear of the minefield, but could anyone be sure?

The voice-pipe squeaked and Reche answered dully: 'Control room reports we are clear of mined area, Captain. Turning on to new course now!'

Steiger nodded. He did not trust himself to speak just yet. He felt the pressure of steel against his arm as the boat heeled slightly and the wake curved away towards the starboard quarter. They were committed. The minefield was astern. Between them and the enemy coast lay the target.

As if in answer to his thoughts, the control room reported, 'Radar Search Receiver reports strong signal at oh-two-five!'

Steiger nodded again. 'Clear the bridge! Diving Stations!'

The game had begun.

8: The Attack

'Steady at fourteen metres!'

'Very well. Up periscope!' Steiger flexed his fingers around the training handles and waited for the lens to break surface. Around him the dimly lighted control room seemed unnaturally humid, although he had just seen the ice-cold condensation streaming down the curved sides. The low-pitched whine of the slow-moving electric motors sounded as if it was the only thing that lived in the enemy channel.

The grey light stabbed weakly at his eyes, and he held his breath as he swung the periscope around in a quick circle before bringing it back to the forward position. The water was pewter-coloured and almost flat. There was a slight undulating swell as if the sea was breathing, and above all else hung the wet, unmoving fog. It was almost frightening the way it hovered barely feet above the sea and left a wafer of misty vision for the slow-moving periscope. If there was any wind at all it must be in the south-west, Steiger thought bleakly. Driving the frail mist off the Atlantic and into the semi-landlocked waters of the Bristol Channel, where it drew together to mock their pathetic efforts and leave them groping like blind men on an unfamiliar road.

'Starboard ten. Steer oh-one-five!' He heard the helmsman's flat voice repeat his order and the scrape of Reche's oilskin coat as he leaned over the chart to time the U-boat's twisting journey towards the hidden Welsh coastline.

Steiger could feel his hands clammy against the periscope handles, and pressed his forehead hard against the rubber pad to muster his thoughts. Who could have expected this fog? It was just one more twist of fate turning against him. It could even be a warning. He twisted his buttocks on the stool with sudden frustration. 'Time check?' His voice seemed extra loud, and he could sense the others watching him and trying to gauge their fate from his reactions.

'Oh-eight-two-five, Captain!' The rating's voice trembled.

Five minutes to zero. Group Bruno must be in their position to attack, *if* the British ships were still there. The other U-boats had had plenty of time to find their selected areas, and even now must be stalking through the fog, as blind as he was. The sweat prickled around his eyes and trickled down his cheeks. He tried to see the whole plan as a clear-cut operation, but his mind revolted against it. All he could see was a line of U-boats strung along the Welsh coast, their crews nervous and strained after a long cruise from Norway and north about Scotland and the final days and hours of waiting. Group Bruno, commanded by another man like himself; experienced, desperate, yet stretched to the limit of human endurance. Behind them would be the hostile shoreline, and between them and safety would lie an armada of ships, any one of which might be a potential killer. And what of us? A minefield astern, the invisible enemy somewhere ahead.

'Zero, Captain!'

'Check your plot, Reche!' Steiger swung the periscope a few more degrees.

'I have, sir.' Reche's voice sounded shaky but sullen.

'Well, do so again—and, Lieutenant Dietrich!'

'Captain?'

'Go over the attack chart with him! I want the clearest possible check on our position!' Position? He peered ahead at the swirling vapour and gritted his teeth. They might be anywhere. It was too dangerous to use an echo-sounder to test the depth of the channel. There might be some wily destroyer riding nearby without engines, just waiting for some additional sound, some new hint of danger, to hurl itself into action. Blind or not, a destroyer's asdics would soon make up for a fog-hampered radar set, especially in these restricted waters.

He waited a few more seconds. 'Dead slow!'

The motors died to a tiny purr. 'Dead slow both, Captain. Course oh-one-five.'

I will have to surface now, action or not. I must try to rally our Group. God knows how the rest are managing. A thought moved through his racing brain. 'Hessler! Pass the word for one of the gunners to fetch an emergency flare!'

Hessler's guttural voice answered, 'At once, sir!'

Steiger drew a breath. Thank God for Hessler. No panic, no questioning in his answer. He would never be bright enough to hold a command, but his kind were worth their weight in admirals.

An ordinary flare would be useless, but the big emergency ones were just the thing. All the U-boats would be surfacing now, provided they obeyed their instructions, and just one great flash, thrice magnified by the fog like a great frosted lens, would be enough to rally them to their positions. Then the attack could begin. If there was anything out there in the fog, they would soon be on top of it. Intelligence reports had spoken of big transports, tankers and heaven knows what.

'Propeller noises ahead, Captain!' Braun tensed on his stool and moved his controls with delicate fingers. 'Powerful propeller noises, could be heavy vessel!' He tensed and adjusted the hydrophone headset over his ears. 'Distorted, Captain. Several vessels. From dead ahead to green four-five.'

Dietrich said sharply: 'Give me actual bearings! We must start plotting!'

Steiger felt the trembling in his hands again, and slammed the periscope handles into their grooves. 'Down periscope! Stand by to surface!' He glanced quickly at Luth and saw that he and his men were already checking the U-boat's trim in readiness for surfacing.

'Lieutenant Hessler, bring all tubes to the ready. You may

have to control the fire from down here when I am on the bridge. I am not certain of visibility yet.'

'Gun crews, sir?' Hessler was already cranking the handle of his telephone.

'No. If we have to dive there'll be little enough time for the bridge-party to jump clear!' He touched the officer's sleeve. 'But you can close up the Vierling and machine-guns on the bridge. They will have to be enough!'

'Very well.' Hessler glanced at his watch and then shuddered as a great explosion rumbled through the water and sighed against the U-boat's hull. The sullen detonation did not stop, but like thunder ebbed and grumbled until the hull was rocking like a toy boat. Some of the men in the forward part of the boat began to cheer but were cut short by their petty officers. *They* were too experienced to imagine that the great volume of noise was caused by German torpedoes.

Steiger strode to the ladder and began to climb. Over his shoulder he barked: 'Surface! Emergency speed!'

The motors whined into life, and the deck tilted towards the waiting day. Steiger grappled with the locking wheel, his mind tearing through his frantic preparations. They had to surface and open up the radio contacts again. God damn the regulations! This was no ordinary operation, and he *had* to know what was going on.

The lookouts and machine-gunners bunched behind him, and as the buzzer sounded in the tower he flung his shoulder against the hatch. Heedless of the water cascading over his body he fought his way on to the bridge. The escaping water surged around his seaboots and gurgled through the vents in the side of the conning-tower. The fog swirled over the glistening hull, sometimes grey, then pure white, like a cloudbank.

Even as he watched the nearest bank of grey fog closed in towards the sharp bows and changed colour yet again, but not to white. It seemed to flicker with a million fires, as if it was a curtain on to hell itself.

■ ■ ■ ■ ■

Max König listened to the far-off rumbling of the explosions and glanced quickly at his companions. He crouched with the other gunners in the magazine compartment just forward of the control room, and like them he had become almost dazed by the sour, unmoving air and the dull ache of waiting. Nothing seemed to be happening, yet nobody had found the time to explain the reasons for their slow progress or even if they were near their destination. König had been on deck with the gun up to the moment of diving, and even the soaking mist and raw cold had been better than this. Someone had said that there was thick fog above and the enemy was nowhere in sight. Somebody else said that even the Captain did not know what was happening, but König found the latter rather hard to believe. Steiger did not look like the sort of man who left things to luck or chance. And yet who was to know? It was as if they represented the whole of Germany, struggling forward to disaster yet still clinging to the old comforting assurances of supremacy and power. He shook his head and listened to the dying echoes of the explosions. Some of the men forward had cheered, but now there was silence. They hunched together for comfort, but each man avoided the eyes of the man nearest to him.

A seaman yelled from the control room: 'Here, one of you gunners! Captain wants an emergency flare from the locker!' He glared at the unmoving group. 'Well, come on, then. He's not going to wait for you bastards!'

A metallic voice intoned, 'Stand by to surface!'

Petty Officer Hartz struggled to his feet and pointed at König. '*You* go!'

König nodded vaguely, only half aware of what the other seaman had said, and followed him through the crowded control room. Already the deck was canting, and he could see the legs of the bridge-party vanishing up the polished ladder. Long gleaming belts of machine-gun ammunition hung alongside the ladder like evil snakes, and König could hear the gunners cursing to themselves as they cradled their weapons beneath strips of oilskin to protect them from the inrush of water when the hatch was opened.

'Here we are!' König's companion, a tall professional seaman called Bettelheim, caught at his arm and pulled him into a small brightly lit alcove abaft the control room. It was stacked with metal boxes brightly coloured and labelled according to their contents. Flares, signal rockets, small-arms ammunition, all were jammed tightly into metal slings which held them firmly in position.

König glanced down the rest of the narrow passageway towards the sealed engine and motor compartments. There was so much to see and know in a U-boat, yet he had hardly mastered the layout of his own small corner.

With nervous irritation Bettelheim snapped: 'It'll be in one of those cases! For Christ's sake jump to it!'

König undid the clamps of the nearest box and slid it to the deck. As he did so he noticed an additional canister which was sandwiched awkwardly below the next layer of flares. It looked out of place and untidy.

Bettelheim levered the box open and took out a long fat flare. 'Take it to the bridge!' His pale eyes followed König's glance and he frowned. 'What in hell's name is that?' He handed the flare to König and pulled at the cylinder with his fingers. It was about a foot long, crudely painted and without any marking. Bettelheim grinned savagely. 'Damned cooks again! Storing their spare food down here, I shouldn't wonder!'

There was a hollow thud as the conning-tower hatch opened, and König heard the scamper of feet on the ladder, followed by the harsh bark of quick commands. He tucked the flare under his arm and stepped over the coaming. His action saved him, for as Bettelheim tugged the cylinder from the rack there was a violent crack and the whole passageway was instantly filled with smoke. Even as König stared with horrified eyes the smoke changed to flames, and Bettelheim reeled back into the passageway, his hands scything the air, his face burned away to a frothing scarlet mask. He screamed and screamed again, his clawlike hands plucking at his smouldering body, while with each second that passed the space around him erupted into separate vicious little fires.

König could feel the agony of fear once more as he watched the tongues of flame licking against the nearest ammunition cases and setting alight the paintwork overhead. Tearing his eyes from the twisting figure, he snatched the communications telephone, and when a voice crackled in his ear he shouted, 'Fire in the aft magazine!'

He dropped the handset and stumbled towards the blackened figure which had suddenly fallen still on the blistered gratings. His eyes stung and poured with water as he groped for an extinguisher, and his boots skidded on all that was left of Seaman Bettelheim. Just before he fainted and the emergency fire-party burst in with their chemical extinguishers his reeling brain tried to connect this new disaster with the small cylinder which Bettelheim had torn loose. Even in his inexperienced eyes it had seemed all wrong, and Bettelheim had known immediately that it was out of place in the magazine.

A petty officer was pulling him clear of the flames and noise, and he heard the man's urgent voice next to his ear. 'What was it?'

Without pausing to think he said faintly, 'It was a bomb!'

. . . . .

Steiger coughed as the fog swirled in over the rim of the bridge, and half lifted the glasses to his eyes. It was useless. He could not even see the bows now. He opened the voice-pipe and shut his mind to the orderly confusion behind him. The torpedo sight was being mounted and telephones plugged into position. The machine-guns jutted from the still-streaming plating, and Steiger found a second to remember that they had surfaced in less than half a minute.

'Captain here! Tell the radio room to check all signals, then contact the Group!'

He watched narrowly as the fogbank slid sideways and allowed the U-boat to move into a strange dark patch of open water. Around it the vapour loomed like a cliff, and was lit every so often by dull orange flashes. There was noise, too, explosions long and short, which seemed to come from every direction at once.

He coughed again, the fog seemed to be thickening from astern. He frowned with tight irritation; that was impossible, they were making over six knots through the water.

An incredulous voice yelled, 'Smoke, sir!'

He stared at the thick column of black smoke which funnelled through the oval hatch to merge with the fog overhead.

The voice-pipe rattled, 'Fire in the after magazine, sir!' Even Hessler's voice sounded unnerved.

The bridge-party moved disjointedly round their tiny steel island, and for a few moments all discipline was gone.

Steiger sniffed the air like an injured lion, sensing the fear and rising panic as clearly as the smell of burning paint and scorched flesh.

'Keep silence there!' He deliberately turned his back on the hatch and roared, 'There'll be a break in the fog soon, so stand to!'

He tried to concentrate on the darker patches of water which marked their path through the fog-belt, tried to shut out the feeling of despair which clogged his mind like blood. It would not be long now. When the flames bit into the panniers of ammunition or ignited the rockets, the explosion would break the hull in two . . . if they were lucky. If not the fire would sweep through the boat from end to end until every man was fried in his own steel coffin.

The fog lifted slightly, like the hem of a giant curtain, and Steiger's desperate eyes stared at the long hard edge of grey metal which blocked the U-boat's course in each direction. The lower edge of the fog hovered just high enough to show him the double lines of sealed scuttles and the underbellies of the slung box-like launches which ran the full length of the vessel's boat-deck. It was a big ship, and if it was carrying invasion launches it was probably crammed with men, too.

He swallowed hard and peered through the lens of the attack-sight. Much too near, and the range closing. If he fired his torpedoes now the blast would engulf his own boat just as surely as the fire below. He coughed again and shouted into a telephone: 'Stand by one to four! Fire when ready!' Down below, Hessler's torpedo-party would be plotting the information fed down to them by the attack-sight, if they were not already suffocated by smoke. He leaned across the speaking tube. 'Stop both! Emergency full speed astern!'

He waited, gritting his teeth as the frothing propellers bit into the oily water and started to pull the hull astern. Slowly at first, and then he saw the other ship begin to fade into the fog. He pressed his eyes to the sight, the cross-wire firmly planted across the foremost invasion launch, above which he estimated was the vessel's bridge. He could feel the desperation like vomit in his throat as the enemy's outline began to disappear. In a croaking voice he called: 'Stop both! Slow ahead both!' Damn it, he had nearly lost sight of the ship!

Up the telephone wire he heard Hessler say flatly: 'Fire one! Fire two! Fire three! Fire four!' Each time the hull shuddered slightly, and Steiger could imagine the sleek torpedoes as they streaked towards the now hidden ship.

There was a great rumble from the port beam which momentarily broke his concentration. Depth-charges being dropped, and very close, too. A U-boat had been unable or unwilling to surface. It would soon pay the price.

'Starboard fifteen!' He peered through the fog and smoke. 'Steer oh-four-five!'

Dietrich emerged coughing and retching through the hatch.

Steiger glanced at him with a flash of sudden anger. 'What are you doing here?'

'Radio reports, sir!' Dietrich stared at him without recognition. 'Group Bruno, sir!'

Steiger looked past him at the rolling fog, his mind mentally ticking off the long seconds of the torpedoes' journey. Must have missed her! Aloud he rasped, 'Make your report from the control room!'

Stiffly Dietrich replied, 'I thought it best to confine the information to as few as possible!'

He paused, and Steiger glared at him with amazement. 'Well? What's happening?'

'Bruno is destroyed, Captain!'

Their eyes met and locked together. 'Destroyed? *All* of it?'

Almost calmly Dietrich said: 'There was still one left, but I think he has gone now. Surrendered or smashed!' He lifted his chin. 'Either way, we're on our own!'

A great breath of hot gas fanned across the bridge as an even brighter explosion blasted the fog into grey tatters around them. Then another, and then a third. They had scored three hits!

Steiger passed his hand across his wet face and peered down at the hatch. The smoke had been cut to a mere trickle, and he heard Dietrich say in that same empty voice: 'Sabotage, sir! There's a dead man down there!'

Steiger bowed his head and stared at the shining deck below him. This was a never-ending nightmare.

Another roar echoed through the fog, and Steiger pushed past Dietrich to peer over the port side of the bridge. 'Another hit!' The fourth torpedo must have found its own target somewhere else in the mad battleground where neither friend nor foe could even see each other. 'These acoustic torpedoes are really good!' Steiger grabbed the telephone. 'Have you reloaded yet?'

Dietrich swallowed hard. 'We must be cutting right into the enemy's shipping here, sir. We'll get run down if we stay surfaced!

'If we dive we're done for.' Steiger gave a forced smile. 'There's not much depth hereabouts, and the enemy is as blind as we are!'

Dietrich sucked in his breath and pointed fixedly to starboard. 'My God, look!'

For one moment Steiger thought they had run across a moored beacon of some kind, but as the realisation dawned on him he knew he was staring at the upended hull of a U-boat. The stern section pointed upright from the oily water, a black, slime-encrusted spire, like a memorial in some terrible and forgotten cemetery. The fog swirled about the stilled propellers and the one bright piece of metal where the rudders had been sheared off by the force of an underwater explosion. It hung quite motionless, suspended by trapped air or some fluke of pressure, and as it passed abeam and slowly faded into the fog, Steiger tried not to think of the men who might still be trapped within.

'Not one of our Group,' he said slowly. 'The hull had not had a refit for some time. Bruno probably.'

A lookout shouted sharply: 'Something there, Captain! Fine on the starboard bow!'

Steiger tensed and crouched over the sight. Dietrich seemed unable to move and still stared astern.

There was a darker patch in the fogbank, but hard to define, like smoke, or a shadow thrown by a water-spout.

In a flat voice he said: 'Stand by five to eight! Target bearing oh-five-oh!' He could hear the click of buttons below him in the control room, and cradled the handset carefully on the edge of his collar. Over his shoulder he said: 'Get below, Heinz! There'll be plenty to do in an instant!'

'What about that bomb?'

Steiger lifted his head momentarily and stared at Dietrich's drawn face. With deliberate cruelty he said: 'You were supposed to check the boat *before* we sailed, right? What do you want me to do now?' Dietrich still stared at him. 'Well? For God's sake get below and look after the men!'

A seaman on the starboard machine-gun yelled with sudden fear, 'A ship!'

Steiger swung back to his sight, but for the moment it was not needed. Like two impersonal eyes the twin anchors of a slow-moving transport loomed out of the fog high above the U-boat's bows, the rust-streaked stem cutting towards the half-submerged hull with the irresistible menace of a giant axe.

Dietrich felt his taut body relax, as if the very muscles were already broken. He could hear the seamen on the bridge around him cursing and whimpering with fear as the great silent ship towered over them. He could see the thin tracery of the high guardrails, and thought he could just see the massive grey bridge beyond. The men up there would only feel a slight shudder as their ten thousand tons of steel carved down on the trapped submarine which cruised so calmly to meet them.

All at once Dietrich's nerve snapped, and the rising fear swept over him in an uncontrollable flood. He could hear himself shouting unintelligibly, and then tasted blood in his mouth as a gloved fist smashed him down on to the rough deck-plates.

Steiger drew back his fist and shouted down the voice-pipe, 'Port five!' He watched the narrow bows swing so very slightly. 'Midships! Starboard ten!' The sweat was blinding him as he watched the two stems drawn towards each other as if by magnets. God, she was swinging too much! 'Port ten! Midships!' She was right overhead now, and the machine-gunners cowered back behind their thin plating as if to hide their faces from the great ship. The stern moved past, ten feet from the conning-tower. There was a savage lurch as the massive plates brushed indifferently against the U-boat's saddle tank. Thud! Another great lurch, and Steiger looked up to see the keels of slung life-boats passing right overhead. She had missed.

He heard Dietrich scrambling to his feet, but concentrated his whole mind on the endless length of the enemy transport. One more accidental nudge, one more panic, and they were done for with the same certainty as if they had been rammed.

The U-boat rocked violently as the ship's curved stern swung past, the huge propellers throwing up a slow-moving froth which seemed to be the only thing which lived against the grey backdrop. Steiger wiped the moisture from his brows and stared up at the vessel's name. *Wexford Queen*—Liverpool. Automatically he said, 'Hard a-starboard!' and as the slow-cruising hull shivered beneath him he added, 'Stand by five to eight!' The control room acknowledged his orders, and he found time to wonder at the prompt retort.

If it had been terrifying on the bridge, how much worse must it have been in the enclosed blind world below? The urgent helm orders, the shaking grind of steel, could drive some men mad in less time than it took to fire a torpedo. Steiger watched the long whaleback swinging towards the disappearing shadow of the transport. He tried to think, to concentrate. We must be right amongst the main concentration of ships, as Dietrich said. Except that he thought it was too dangerous, whereas I know it is the safest place, provided you can avoid being rammed.

'Midships!' Still swinging too much, and even with acoustic torpedoes it would not do to extend the bearing unnecessarily. 'Meet her! Steer one-seven-five!'

He settled down at the sight, his eyes watching the rounded shadow of the transport's stern. He frowned, the bearing had changed again. Either the ship's master had lost his way or he had decided to return to his base.

He shut his mind to the loss of Group Bruno, and refused to allow his bruised senses to contemplate the efficiency of the weapons and men which had dealt them the mortal blow. But for the fog *we* would have been here earlier, we might have broken the enemy's grip. He grimaced as if in pain. If only . . . perhaps . . . He was getting like the rest. 'Stand by!'

The cross-wires were pointing at an empty space, a swirling cliff which belonged in another world.

'Fire five! Fire six! Fire seven! Fire eight!' He tried to retain the complicated picture of their frantic manœuvring, but instead he could only see the upended hulk of the dead submarine. What was happening? What was going wrong with them all? Lehmann had been trying to explain, to find excuses for their sickness, their wounded pride. Even Dietrich seemed to have reached some indefinable point where fear of death was more terrible than fear of failure.

Another great salvo of detonations rocked the hull even as it twisted away from the last firing position. The fogbank was lit up with mingled scarlet and gold like the back of some rich tapestry, whilst above the roar of the exploding torpedoes Steiger could hear the rending of metal, the crash of machinery falling through bulkheads as the invisible ship rolled in her death agony.

Behind him his men stood at their posts, grey-faced and cowed, their eyes flickering with the flames of their prey. As the *Wexford Queen* plunged towards the bottom they heard the savage inrush of water and the bellow of scalding steam. Then beyond their tiny enclosed arena they heard, too, the disjointed sounds of battle and even the rattle of small-arms as the hunters and defenders stalked each other in a forest of fog and smoke.

Dietrich was standing close at his side, his pale blue eyes staring listlessly towards the bows, the blood from his lip more black than red in the unearthly light.

Steiger glanced at him coldly. 'You can go below. I will see you later on. I want a full report into that explosion, and many other things, too!'

Dietrich opened his mouth to reply, but in silence turned away and lowered himself through the hatch.

A freak gust of wind eddied into the rear of the long fogbank, as if eager to see the slaughter below. A pale watery sunlight glimmered momentarily on the pewter water, and the mist near the surface floated and writhed like steam, so that the icy air seemed all the more hard to bear.

A lookout shouted: 'Heads in the water, Captain! Survivors!'

It appeared as if the little clusters of men were floating in the mist rather than the water as they moved towards the U-boat's sleek bows. A machine-gunner muttered hoarsely: 'Christ! They're *our* men, look at those lifejackets!'

The survivors' thin cheers changed to screams and curses as the sharp stem parted them and carved them aside like so much flotsam. Frantic hands, gaping mouths, a terrible ballet which brought animal-like cries from the horrified bridge-party.

But Steiger was looking beyond the survivors in the water, his glasses cutting out the pitiful men he was leaving to die. The mist was parting in the shape of a giant triangle. In the cleared centre of the space, rocking gently on the darker patch of water like a graceful jungle beast pausing for breath, lay the destroyer. Her knife-like bows were slewing towards the U-boat, and even as Steiger jumped for the voice-pipe he heard the faint metallic jangle of engine-room telegraphs from far across the open space, followed by the answering surge of her forty thousand horse-power.

It was fascinating to watch, almost too terrible to understand, but Steiger's voice was expressionless. 'Hard a-port! Full astern port engine!' He glanced with something like surprise at the few remaining heads in the water as the throbbing hull scythed over them. He retched as he caught sight of the familiar uniforms and heard the choking cries in his own language.

There was a harsh stammer of automatic fire, and bright red tracers leapt from the destroyer's low deck to sweep overhead just clear of the periscope standards. The tracer looked so lazy and ineffectual as it lifted in a slow arc and then plunged down towards the heeling submarine. Then the British gunners found the range, and a long burst of twenty-millimetre cannon shells raked the forecasing as far aft as the conning-tower itself. The air was filled with the sharp crackle of exploding shells, the maniac scream of ricochets and the clang of metal as fragments whirred over the heads of the crouching men on the bridge.

Steiger watched with narrowed eyes as the destroyer backed one of her engines and seemed to spin round on her tail. Both hunter and hunted were turning in circles, the U-boat inside that of the destroyer. Because of the greater space needed for the British ship to turn and manœuvre, her captain was unable to make much use of his thirty-six knots against the U-boat's sixteen. But Steiger knew well enough from past experience that, like himself, the other commander would not be content to wait until his adversary made the first move.

'Midships!' He allowed some of the thrust to fall off the U-boat's turn so that the range between the two careering vessels fell away, and he could clearly see the white faces along the top of the destroyer's bridge screen and the long muzzles of her main armament as they were depressed to follow the low-lying grey hull which tore through the water like a trapped shark.

Steiger swung round with sudden fury. 'Open fire! Sweep her bridge!' And when the gunners still hesitated he jumped amongst them and punched the nearest man savagely in the shoulder so that he fell gasping across his gun. Steiger ran back to the voice-pipe, breathing fast as the Spandaus opened up, followed almost at once by the deadly rattle of the four-barrelled Vierling. The tracers leapt across the churned water, knitting momentarily with the searching fingers of the enemy fire before finding and holding the graceful shape of the spray-drenched destroyer.

Steiger could feel the ice-cold breeze fanning his cheek, and watched the mist swirling across the bridge. If it clears now, he thought with sudden despair, we are finished. There will be other warships nearby and then we will have to dive. Rammed or depth-charged, the choice left little room for hope. He watched with instant caution as the dazzle-painted sides of the destroyer glinted in the weak sunlight. She was turning again. He felt his mouth go dry and he cursed himself for allowing his mind to stray even for a second. The other captain must have put his charging engines astern, because the length of his ship had shortened and the high tapered bows were inched round just another fraction.

Bullets flayed across the bridge plating like a steel whip, and two of the gunners reeled back from their weapons, their twisting bodies already shapeless and splashed with scarlet.

'You there!' Steiger gestured at a lookout who crouched with his face pressed against the wet steel. 'Take over!' The man stared at him and then back at the rim of the bridge over which he could just see the tiny, stick-like masthead of the destroyer. Steiger fumbled for his Lüger, and the man whimpered as he dragged himself upright and groped for the silent gun.

Steiger's brain was working with a desperate precision, so that the very effort of thinking seemed to leave him breathless. The breeze *was* freshening, he had to act *now*. He watched the mad dance with unblinking eyes, and felt the deck canting as his engineers fought to give him greater speed, and still more speed. When they had completed another semicircle the wind would be astern, they would have to turn then. The U-boat was slightly ahead of the destroyer, which seemed to lie on the starboard quarter for most of the time. The British captain was dropping slightly astern and trying to open the circle so that he could bring his big guns to bear. Once that happened, he could pound the U-boat to scrap and then close in to ram. Steiger watched fascinated as the two vessels careered through the thinning curtains of fog.

If I turn suddenly to starboard he will not be expecting that. His mouth felt as dry as dust as he contemplated the move he knew he was going to take. The British captain would not expect such a manœuvre because the U-boat would have to turn towards him and would momentarily lie broadside across his bows. One mis-judgement, and two thousand tons of charging steel would thunder into the wallowing U-boat and slice it in two. At best Steiger could hope to pass down the destroyer's side and plunge into the fogbank once more. The other ship was going with such speed that it would be some time before the chase was renewed. By that time he might have thought of something else.

Another man fell from the guns, this time from the Vierling. A cannon shell had all but decapitated him, yet the body still threshed and pirouetted around the gun platform, its blood spurting over the grey plates and across the horrified faces of the other gunners.

Steiger spoke harshly into the voice-pipe, his ears deaf to the rattling crescendo of noise about him. 'Lieutenant Dietrich! Listen carefully to me!' He forced himself to wait a few seconds, seeing in his mind's eye the youthful, white-faced officer at the other end of the pipe, his chin still bloody from the blow his captain had given him. 'In a few seconds I will go hard a-starboard. When I pass that order I want the starboard engine put full astern and the port one to be kept full ahead. With the wheel hard over she should come about very well!' He waited, hearing Dietrich's voice as he repeated his instructions to Luth and the helmsman. 'Tell Luth to pump from forward!' If the bows were raised a bit more she should pivot more easily. 'And, Dietrich!' He waited and imagined he could hear the First Lieutenant's fast breathing, until with sudden shock he realised it was his own. 'You must be very quick!'

Dietrich's voice sounded small and faraway. 'Very good, Captain!'

There was a dull bang, and almost at once a shell screamed overhead, to explode in a tall water-spout barely a cable's length ahead. The British captain was starting to use his heavy fo'c'sle guns.

Right, it was now or never. From the corner of his eye he saw the fat careering shape of a bulky transport ship as it charged through the mist. In actual fact it was probably almost stationary and waiting its chance to slip back to its base.

Now! He could hardly find the saliva in his throat to croak, 'Hard a-starboard!' Immediately he could feel the changing thrust of the rudder, whilst below his straddled boots he could sense the terrible metallic clatter as the starboard engine was forced from full ahead to full astern. It was a dangerous and sometimes disastrous act, but in this case there was nothing left to try. Already the U-boat was swinging wildly across the frothing water, her course curved by a wake in the shape of a gigantic S.

He gripped the rim of the bridge harder with his fists, willing her to turn, his eyes fixed desperately on the destroyer. Its shape shortened, and then was bows on. Her captain was fighting to turn, too, and even now was heading straight for the tilting conning-tower.

The scar on his forehead felt white-hot, and he had to squint to see through the sweat which ran from under his cap. Still the U-boat swung round, while the towering stem of the enemy drove nearer and nearer. He could see the proud White Ensign streaming from her gaff, the levelled glasses on her upper bridge and the silent, impotent guns. The angle was changing, becoming more acute, forty-five degrees, twenty, both vessels were almost bow to bow, with the destroyer barely half a cable clear.

'Stop starboard! Full ahead starboard!' It was time to break out of the turn. 'Wheel amidships!' Luth's engineers would be watching their dials and gauges with horror, or perhaps they were beyond that now. Every rule was being broken, every safety barrier was down.

At thirty-six knots the destroyer surged past, the great bow wave breaking over the submarine as if it were a submerged rock.

Steiger saw the small knot of seamen running across the ship's quarter-deck and gestured frantically to the only gun which would bear. 'Quick! Get those men!' They were running for the depth-charges. If they could roll one off before the U-boat could get clear, the surface explosion alone would capsize her like a dead whale.

Again the Spandau stammered its vicious message across the minute gap. The hail of bullets cut through the running men like a scythe, so that they fell or scattered before they could release even one charge.

Steiger stood back and stared up at the destroyer's tall bridge and belching funnel. Bullets sang and whimpered from every direction, and he realised with sudden surprise that all the U-boat's guns were silent and sent no reply to the destroyer as it charged past and into the mist. He looked down at the crumpled shapes of his men, at the staring eyes, distorted faces and shattered limbs. He alone was alive on the scarred bridge, but even as he peered with shocked amazement into each dead face, one last burst of fire reached out from the mist-shrouded destroyer and found the unprotected rear of the U-boat's bridge.

It was like a great numbing hammer, which smashed into his shoulder and hurled him against the compass repeater, but before he touched the deck gratings he could feel the torture and agony of the wound drawing the strength and will from his body with claws of fire.

There was a mist across his eyes, but he tried with sudden desperation to pull himself towards the voice-pipe. The destroyer would already be turning. The U-boat was steering blindly into nowhere, her bridge filled with useless dead and a helpless captain. He thought of Dietrich's frightened face, and bit his lip to hold back a scream of anguish. Dietrich would not come. He rolled brokenly on to his side and felt the blood hot across his chest. They won't come, he thought weakly. They are all waiting for *me*! With a groan he stared at the riveted steel by his face and allowed the darkness to close over him.

9 : No Heroics

When *U-991* made her frantic turn at full speed to cross the destroyer's bows the control room deck canted over to such an angle that Dietrich had to fling his arm around the periscope to stop himself from being hurled from his feet. He blinked his eyes quickly to clear away the tears brought by the smarting fumes which still hovered around the burned paintwork and eddied through the passageway from the after magazine, where the seamen with the fire extinguishers lay in a helpless tangle, caught unaware by the sudden alteration of course.

The Coxswain spoke from between clenched teeth. 'Wheel hard a-starboard! Starboard engine full astern!'

Dietrich winced and glanced quickly at Luth's tense face as the engine screamed in protest. The hull was lying even further on its side, so that the men who still retained their feet appeared to be standing at an angle of forty-five degrees.

The tough plating of the outer hull shuddered as a stream of cannon shells tore across the smooth saddle tank, and Dietrich could feel his heart jumping in time with each vicious onslaught. The helmsman was answering Steiger up the main voice-pipe, but so great was the clamour of steel against steel, coupled with the thunder of water over the upper deck, that Dietrich could only guess at what was happening.

The growing roar of the destroyer's engines eventually blotted out all else, so that men who were not actually employed in handling the boat sat or lay like stricken corpses, their eyes and faces dulled and grey with shock.

Louder and louder, until every rivet seemed to be shaking loose. Dietrich found that he was biting into his gloved hand with such force his fingers were numb with pain. Soon now. A salvo of depth-charges or a well-placed shell would see the end of this terror and agony. He stared with sudden panic at the curving sides of the hull, and imagined that he could see the jagged stem of the enemy warship already biting deep into the U-boat's vitals, and the immediate inrush of frothing water.

The hull rocked violently from side to side, and Hessler said with disbelief: 'She's past! Missed us, by Christ!'

Luth licked his dry lips and spoke quickly into his handset.

He looked across at Dietrich. 'Both engines running well! May God reward the men who built this boat!'

Another flurry of gunfire pattered across the upper deck, muffled and impersonal like heavy rain on the roof of a car.

Dietrich tried with one last effort to control his shaking limbs and fight the nausea which swept from his stomach and clawed at the back of his throat.

The warship would soon be round and attacking once more. There was no time to be lost. He felt his eyes smarting again, but this time with frustration and naked fear. Up on the bridge Steiger held their lives in his hands, while they clung to each other like weak blind animals in a trap.

The helmsman said in a sharp, urgent voice, 'No further orders from the bridge, Lieutenant!'

Dietrich closed his eyes and pressed his head against the housed periscope. Damn him! He's probably already watching another target, and planning to attack. He will go on until he has killed us all!

As if to echo his fears, the Torpedo Petty Officer reported, 'All tubes reloaded, sir!'

Dietrich stared round the small world of the control room as if he expected to see contempt and disgust levelled in his direction. Hessler was expressionless, hunched over his fire controls, his earphones dangling from his thick fingers. Reche half lay across the chart-table, his bulging eyes fixed on some meaningless point as if he had already given up the struggle. Only Luth watched him, his dark eyes unwinking but pleading, trying to pass some urgent message to the desperate, bewildered figure of his friend.

Dietrich wrenched himself from his stricken pose and ran to the voice-pipe. 'Bridge?' His voice sounded strange and cracked. 'Bridge?' But there was no reply.

Braun looked up from his hydrophone receiver. 'More propeller noises, sir! Bearing oh-nine-oh! Several ships, moving very fast!'

The sweat ran down Dietrich's face as he stared fixedly at the bell-mouth of the voice-pipe. More destroyers! We must dive, try to get away *now*! Half of his aching mind still toyed with the shocked surprise he had felt when he had looked at his brother officers. He had expected advice, even an open challenge to his authority. They must have known about his collapse, his complete breakdown, yet they remained silent. Reche was terrified, but Hessler and Luth seemed unwilling to help him with his burden. His mind shied away from what he knew must be the truth. They were as afraid as he, and were looking to him to save them.

He shook his head like a dazed animal and ran towards the conning-tower. Over his shoulder he yelled, 'All spare gunners to the bridge!' He ignored the swaying ladder, the spindrift which spat over the rim of the hatch, and forced his unwilling legs to carry him up to that small oval of grey sky.

As his eyes rose over the rim of the hatch his nerve almost collapsed. His face was almost level with a staring, mutilated corpse, whose blood mingled with the spray which pattered noisily on the bullet-scarred steel and across the untidy pile of bodies beyond.

Even as he groped his way to Steiger's side he heard the banshee wail of a destroyer's siren, and he peered quickly over the stern rail towards the fogbank, expecting to see the white froth of a racing bow wave. There was nothing, and he stared down at Steiger's face and the blood which had soaked its way over the edge of his scarf. He was still breathing, but very unevenly.

With sudden desperation Dietrich tore off his gloves and opened the front of Steiger's coat. One bullet, he thought at length, and from behind. It must have passed right through Steiger's left shoulder, because there were two jagged holes in the leather coat, and the front of his clothes was soaked in blood.

He twisted round to see the seamen crowding through the hatch, their faces sick with horror at the bloody carnage which crammed the small space.

'Pass the word for the first-aid party! Quickly then!' He caught sight of Petty Officer Hartz's stolid face. 'Tell the control room I want Lieutenant Hessler up here, and at once!'

Steiger stirred, and then opened his eyes. Their greyness matched the sky and the sea, but the fire had gone out of them.

'Lie still, Captain! We will have you below as soon as possible!'

Steiger wriggled his shoulders and immediately sobbed aloud with pain. 'How long have I been like this? Have you altered course yet?'

Dietrich marvelled at the inner forces which were keeping Steiger alive. 'I will attend to all that, Captain. You are unfit for duty.'

Steiger stared at him with surprise. He could see Dietrich's set, serious face as if through a mist, but there was no mistaking the determination in his voice. He lay back and stared up at the grey sky. He felt numbed and weakened by pain, it throbbed and tore at his body until he was almost unable to think of the one important thing. The safety of the boat. The nearness of danger. He struggled again, but the tide of anguish almost smashed him back into unconsciousness.

'Dive the boat, Dietrich!' His voice was merely a hoarse croak. 'You've no time for anything else! Leave me here and *dive*!'

Dietrich stood up as the first-aid party clattered on to the bridge, the red crosses on their bags blending with the red-spattered steel around them. 'See to the Captain at once!' Dietrich strode to the voice-pipe. 'Slow ahead!' He ignored Steiger's moan of protest. There was no point in wasting fuel in careering blindly through hostile waters. 'Tell the Navigator I want our present position.'

He felt the wild desire to laugh at the clipped coolness of his own voice. Inside his outer skin his whole body felt twisted into knots of fear and stark terror. Yet Steiger's helplessness seemed to have given him an unnatural power, so that he moved from one decision to the next without pause or hesitation, like a man steps from sanity to the brink of madness.

'You wanted me?' Hessler spoke in a hushed voice, his deep-set eyes fixed on the empty sea beyond the bridge.

'Yes. Take over First Lieutenant's duties. The Captain is too badly wounded to keep command.'

Steiger's eyes flickered as Dietrich spoke. 'Dive the boat, damn your eyes!'

Dietrich regarded him without flinching. 'When I am ready, Captain! *I* am in command for the moment!'

Hessler swallowed hard and shook his head as if in a daze. 'Reche thinks we should get away while there's time.' He faltered. 'Of course, I'll do whatever *you* say, but I must say I agree with him!'

'Ready to move the Captain now, Lieutenant!' The seaman stared at Dietrich with concern. 'A bad wound, but if we can get him to hospital he will live!'

Dietrich gestured. 'Take him below. Be careful on the ladder, and call for all the help you need.'

He turned to watch the limp bloody bundles of the slaughtered gunners as they were rolled over the rail and into the frothing wake. He thought of his dead brother and his last moments on earth before the firing squad. This should have been *my* big moment. To prove them all wrong. To make one great gesture which would silence all the Bredts and Steigers of this world, just as *I* silenced Captain Maaze!

For one moment I almost ordered a fresh attack, just as Steiger was about to do, I was carried forward by the knowledge that the others were lost without him, just as I gained strength from his weakness.

The man in the first-aid party had changed all that. For a moment longer Dietrich played with the idea of pressing home the attack, but the thought of Steiger dying ignorant of his actions made his new strength fade like the blood on the casing washed clean away by the swirling water.

'Tell Reche to lay a new course to carry us clear of the minefield, and alter course at once. For the moment steer due west, and sound off Diving Stations!'

Hessler shrugged, as if he no longer understood anything. 'It's been hell, eh?' He clapped Dietrich lightly on the shoulders. 'But you'll see us clear!'

Dietrich strode to the front of the bridge and peered fixedly through his glasses. His hands were steady, and he could draw breath without tasting vomit. He rubbed the scar on his lip and frowned, wondering if Steiger had really known what he had done when he had struck him.

The voice-pipe said, 'Diving Stations, Lieutenant!'

'Very well, take her down to twenty metres!' He turned almost casually to the look-outs. 'Clear the bridge!'

It was like being drugged, he thought, or being under some outside influence. He must not think about it. All he knew was that if he broke again it would be final.

. . . . .

'Lieutenant Dietrich? Signal, sir!'

Dietrich lifted his head dazedly from his crossed forearms and rubbed his eyes. For a moment he stared uncomprehendingly at the messenger and then at the signal pad in his oil-stained hands. With a great effort he stood up and pushed himself away from the wardroom table and glanced at the bulkhead clock. He had fallen asleep barely half an hour previously, after nearly a day and a half of continuous concentration and strain. Beyond the door he could hear the even rumble of the diesel engines, and remembered that the U-boat was wallowing slowly along at six knots, her Snorchel raised to draw down the precious air from the night sky above. The batteries were weak from the constant pressure of manœuvring at full speed, diving, hiding and keeping them all alive. He took the pad and stared at it with dulled eyes.

The messenger said carefully: 'Lieutenant Hessler decoded it as instructed, sir. He said you would want to be told immediately.'

'Thank you. Carry on.' Dietrich re-read the signal from far-off Headquarters. He felt suddenly giddy, and allowed himself to sink back upon the bench seat.

They were not to be allowed to return. Group Meteor would re-form under Commander Lehmann and proceed to a fresh point some four hundred miles to the west of Ireland and render assistance to another wolf-pack which was shadowing a convoy bound for Britain.

U-765 would return unescorted to St. Pierre, having sustained severe damage to her hull and engines. Commander Steiger was to be transferred to her forthwith, and for the second time Dietrich would hold a temporary command.

Dietrich laid the pad carefully on the littered table and ran his fingers through his long fair hair. With the Battle of the Atlantic rising every month to a new pitch, it was often said in the U-boat Service that you were lucky to survive three patrols. The usual greeting to an old friend was, 'Still alive?' The farewell was, 'See you on the casualty list!'

And now they were off again. Not back to St. Pierre, but on and deeper into the Atlantic. A bitter laugh escaped his lips as he thought of the tersely worded signal. Group Meteor. Now there are only six of us, and one of those is returning to Base for repairs. Kunhardt, *U-765*'s captain, seemed to bear a charmed life. Everyone had thought that as the next astern he had been the one to blow up in the minefield. But it had been Helmut Busch in *U-983*. He had lost his position in the fog and had taken the death blow meant for someone else.

Stifling a yawn, Dietrich staggered to his feet and walked to the control room. Hessler greeted him with a weary nod, and then returned to the periscope.

Dietrich wrote briskly on his pad and handed it into the radio room. 'Send this signal to Senior Officer, Group Meteor.' The signal would pave the way for a quick rendezvous on some invisible spot where Steiger could be passed across to the damaged boat and sent home.

The periscope hissed down into its well, and Hessler moved

across to the chart-table. He wrote briefly in the dog-eared book, and then crossed to Dietrich's side. 'What does it all mean, Heinz?' He peered into Dietrich's pale face as if he expected to recognise some hidden meaning to the new orders.

Dietrich shrugged. 'The fight goes on.' He thought back to the previous thirty-six hours he had spent in control of the hunted U-boat. For one whole day they had been depth-charged by what seemed like a complete flotilla of destroyers. He had stayed on his feet, living and fighting back in an unreal world where orders and actions became almost automatic. To save air, only the men actually needed to control the boat stayed at their posts. The rest lay listening and sweating in their bunks, while the probing asdic tapped its metallic message along the outside of the hull, and the depth-charges thundered in every direction at once.

Once they had dived so far and so fast that the hull had ground along the shingle at the very bottom of the channel. Some men screamed, and others gabbled prayers like insane monks. But they had survived. Twisting and turning, dead slow or at full speed, at periscope depth or running deep, the furtive submarine had found its way around the edge of the minefield and into the open sea beyond.

Hessler smiled grimly. 'Feel the boat? Steady as a rock! It's like a millpond up top. Good visibility, and even the stars are bright. It's always the same, eh? When you need it, you get fog or gale. When you don't, *this* happens!'

Dietrich bent over the chart. 'It will make it easier for the Captain.'

Hessler glanced forward towards Steiger's cabin. 'I wonder how he feels about leaving? Too drugged to care, I expect.'

Dietrich smiled for the first time. 'He does not know yet!' The disbelief and surprise in Hessler's eyes brought a tremor of anger racing through him. '*I* have to make the decisions now. That is all there is to it!'

He strode back to the wardroom, and Hessler returned to the periscope. He was puzzled by the change in Dietrich, and more than a little uneasy. The First Lieutenant seemed to be moving and acting like a man in a trance, or one who knows himself to be invulnerable. Hessler thought back to the last depth-charging attack and licked his lips. Even with Steiger wounded it was somehow comforting to know he was here, in his cabin. Without him, and in the Atlantic, who could say what might happen?

He saw a hydroplane operator's head nodding and swore

loudly. 'Wake up, you dog's bastard! You'll get a good *long* sleep soon enough!'

. . . . .

Rudolf Steiger opened his eyes and tried to turn his head to see his cabin clock, but apart from the yellow light from the curtained door, the small airless cabin was in darkness. The effort of movement brought more pain through the haze of coma and faintness, and he could feel the hard pressure of the bandages across his chest and shoulder like tourniquets. He had lost all sense of time, and even by straining his ears he was unable to fit his mind into the boat's routine, to feel a part of the living, throbbing hull around him.

At the beginning of the last depth-charge attack, when the forced inactivity, the searing pain of his wound, had all but driven him into a state of frenzy, the sick-berth attendant had given him more morphia at Dietrich's instructions and, still fighting, he had fallen into another world of black weightlessness.

The curtain swayed aside, and he realised that Dietrich was standing beside his bunk and looking down at him. He, too, was unreal, like everything else. He had appeared without sight or sound, and Steiger could not be sure that it was not just another phase of a drugged dream.

'I am transferring you to *U-765*, Captain.' Dietrich's voice seemed to come down a long metallic tunnel, so that each word had an edge to it. 'Headquarters have ordered that we carry on under Commander Lehmann.'

Steiger's head fell back on the pillow, and he ran his tongue across his parched lips. Feet thudded overhead, and he could hear the muffled sluice of water within feet of his bunk. He had not even felt the boat rise to the surface.

The impact of Dietrich's words slowly penetrated his dulled mind, and a wave of unreasoning urgency flooded through his body. He tried to roll on to his side, but again Dietrich had moved without his seeing, and held him firmly against the blood-stained bunk.

'Easy, Captain!'

'I must stay aboard!' The words were jerked from his aching throat. 'I *must*!'

'*U-765* is abeam now, Captain. A dinghy will be here soon to ferry you across.' Dietrich's voice sounded tired. 'We have to obey orders.'

Dietrich watched his empty words play havoc with Steiger's desperate features. He wondered what was keeping him from collapse. What was making him fight against the inevitable? He heard Steiger ask in a strained voice, 'What of the Group, Heinz?'

Dietrich shrugged. 'Busch is dead. His boat hit the mine. Kunhardt has had a battering, so he is returning to Base with you. There are just the five of us left now.' A shudder ran through his body, and with a shock he realised that Steiger was staring at him, his grey eyes momentarily clear and bright.

'Be careful, Heinz. Don't take any risks.' Steiger studied Dietrich's pale face. 'No heroics.'

Dietrich turned his face away. 'You don't think I can hold down the job.' His voice was broken with bitterness.

Steiger freed his hand from his blanket and grasped the other man's wrist. 'No heroics, Heinz!' His voice was loud, but already the brightness was fading from his eyes. 'You did well back there. You could have left me to die on the bridge. There were already nine dead men up there. One more would have made little difference. You could have dived. Many would have done so.'

Dietrich tried to pull free from the steel grip. 'I have already lost one captain, sir!'

Steiger's white face twisted into a strange smile. 'Maazel? So he still bothers you?'

Dietrich felt trapped. 'No, Captain.'

'He would have probably died anyway. Perhaps it was better he went before he killed the whole crew!'

Dietrich stared down at the unwinking eyes and felt completely unnerved. Steiger knew everything. He must have known from the beginning.

Steiger's head lolled. 'It's war, Heinz. It's too big for mere men. We make mistakes, and others suffer. We look to each other for help and comfort, but alone each one of us is done for.' In a flat, resigned voice he added: 'Look after them for me, Heinz. They are still new to this work. You must not spare yourself. They are worth fighting for.' He tried to raise his head, but the final effort was too much. As his eyes closed he said: 'No heroics. Lehmann is a good officer, but . . .' The silence closed in on them like a curtain.

Kopp, the Coxswain, peered into the unlit cabin. 'Dinghy's ready, Lieutenant.'

Dietrich stood up and brushed his hand across his eyes, fighting back the fatigue once more. 'That man, the one who gave the bomb alarm. Send him across with the Captain. He is the only one who saw the thing. They might want to question him at Base.'

Figures crowded into the cabin, and hushed orders were passed as the men lifted their Captain through the doorway. Even drugged and helpless, to his men he still represented unquestionable power and strength.

A seaman almost brushed Dietrich aside to guide the stretcher party along the passageway, but he could find no resentment. He had wanted to shout at Steiger, to tell him that he *had* nearly left him to die, that no man was indispensable, but the impulse had died in his mind. Steiger had become a legend, and until that was disproved he was beyond the reach of mere words.

. . . .

Dietrich stood heavily on the crowded bridge, his glasses levelled on the thin black shape of the other U-boat. It merged with the darkness, and only showed itself when the cat's-paws rippled unconcernedly along its low-lying hull. Steiger and the seaman, König, had gone across, together with his own hastily scribbled report. A shaded lamp glimmered briefly across the uneasy water, and he heard the distant thud of a hatch being clipped home as the other boat's dinghy was stowed and secured. Two hulls in a hostile sea, afraid to part, yet conscious of their calling. Dietrich remembered Steiger's words, '. . . alone, each one of us is done for . . .' In his mind's eye he compared the beaten, pain-racked man who now lay in the other U-boat with the captain who had pressed home the attack on the enemy transports. He shied away from the realisation that few others would have done what Steiger had done. 'No heroics,' he had said. Dietrich shook his head. Steiger had been right there. It was sheer, cold-blooded bravery. A fanatical urge to fight and win.

A bell jangled below his feet, and a seaman reported, 'Secured for diving, Lieutenant!'

Dietrich nodded, and tried to see the other U-boat, but it had already vanished.

'Very well. Tell the control room to stand by!'

Petty Officer Hartz climbed awkwardly over the low rail from the Vierling platform and thrust his tools into his jacket. 'Guns are all in working order, sir,' he said gruffly. 'I've just had a last look before we dive.'

Dietrich looked quickly at Hartz's shadowed face. Calm, unmoved by the fast and terrifying pattern of events, he was as reassuring as he was competent.

'Funny thing about that man König. He didn't want to leave the boat any more than the Captain!'

'Oh? Perhaps he imagined we could not manage without him?'

Hartz shrugged indifferently. 'No, it was not that. He didn't seem to want to face an enquiry.' He laughed. 'He may be a new man, sir, but he's got a real sailor's attitude to authority!'

An uneasy thought moved slowly through Dietrich's mind. Why would a man not want to return to the safety of the Base? A prickle of resentment and bitterness made him turn away from Hartz's stolid shape. Did this man König have something to hide? He remembered Steiger's face when he had returned from seeing the hanged seaman. He had said it was only the beginning. The beginning of what? A feeling of ice moved down his spine. He thought of the Frenchmen in the town, the averted eyes and nauseating servility. Was that after all a mere guise for something else? In sudden desperation he tried to hold on to a picture of Odile Marquet. How would she react if she saw him in the hands of those faceless enemies? A more terrible thought followed just as quickly. *She* was as much an enemy as he. She had betrayed her country by befriending a German!

Hartz added thoughtfully: 'Yes, he's a queer one well enough. Well educated, too.'

Dietrich swung round, his eyes blazing. 'What the hell are you talking about? Get below and replan your gun crews!'

Hartz clicked the heels of his boots and trundled comfortably to the edge of the hatch. You could never fathom the workings of an officer's mind, and it was better to leave well alone.

His feet groped for the ladder rungs. All the same, he thought, it was a pity that petty officers were not allowed the luxury of temperament.

. . . . .

Rudolf Steiger eased his shoulders against the small mountain of piled pillows and kapok lifejackets which kept him wedged in the unfamiliar bunk. The drawn curtains at his side shone with the wardroom lights beyond, and he could hear the gentle snores of another officer above him. He could taste the harshness of schnapps on his tongue, which only added to his feeling of not belonging. He rarely touched alcohol at sea, and the drink, plus the warm comfort of fresh dressings and bandages, seemed to hold him suspended in the secret isolation of his new home.

He eased back a corner of the curtain and watched the hunched figure by the table. Lieutenant-Commander Otto Kunhardt, the boat's captain, was asleep in his chair, an open tin of stew grasped in his oil-stained hands. The boat was smaller than *U-991*, so that the captain was deprived of a cabin for himself. Even off watch he must stand the constant scrutiny and examination of his officers. Steiger thought momentarily of the captain he had once served under in the early days of the war. He had been a mere lieutenant, but he had ruled the tiny wardroom with a rod of iron. Steiger had hated him, but had learned later that the man was afraid of companionship, and frightened of showing favour even to the three officers with whom he shared his bread. Outwardly a tyrant, that miserable man must have dreaded every meal, every moment of silent relaxation.

Steiger watched the tin of stew fall from Kunhardt's hands and roll on to the salt-stained carpet at his feet. The people in Germany who waited for miracles, and applauded the actions and deeds of the U-boats, would never see the real picture, he thought. How could they compare the proud, arrogant figures of their newspapers with men like Kunhardt? Like himself? The smart uniforms, the handshakes after the presentation of Iron Crosses, the rambling stories of their exploits, and all the other fantastic ideas which maintained the morale of people desperate for safety.

Kunhardt groaned in his sleep and allowed his head to fall back, his gaunt, wolf-like features shining in the light like a death-mask. His hair was long and unkempt, his chin thick with dirty stubble, and his normally bright and fanatical eyes were hidden in dark hollows. Everything about him was stained and soiled with his trade, so that to Steiger he seemed to personify the very meaning of a U-boat commander.

The wardroom, too, was dirty and littered with discarded clothing, pistol holsters, chart folios, half-eaten food and pans of machine-gun ammunition. A picture of Adolf Hitler stared severely from one bulkhead, a small patch of colour against the greyness of war.

Steiger let the curtain fall and allowed his mind to wander drowsily to the future. Tomorrow they should reach port, even allowing for the uneven beat of the U-boat's one serviceable engine. And then he would have to face the torment of hospital, cut off from the last link with his own command. He had a vague feeling that Captain Bredt would be pleased to see him incapacitated, but he dismissed the thought as worthless. Bredt knew that his own position and advancement depended on the successes of his Group; for that reason, if for no other, he might now listen to sense. The wound began to throb again, and he closed his eyes.

Boots moved stealthily in the wardroom, and a shadow rose beside the curtain. He heard the protesting grunts from the sleeping officer as the newcomer shook him awake.

The voice whispered: 'Wake up, Hans! On watch in five minutes!' An answering groan and the sounds of boots being reluctantly dragged on. 'Never mind,' whispered the first voice. 'We'll get leave after this. You might be able to see your wife, eh?'

A short pause and the other voice said calmly: 'I'm afraid not. She got tired of waiting, you see. An S.S. officer, I believe.' A long sigh. 'Hope he keeps the bitch happy!'

There was a thud, and two shadows swayed alongside the drawn curtain. 'Look at the Captain, eh?' The newly awakened voice sounded baffled, his wife momentarily forgotten. 'How can he sleep, do you think?'

The other officer yawned. 'He's like the one in there!' Steiger stiffened as the two shadows turned towards his bunk. 'Cold as a damned shark! His sort are too inhuman to have personal feelings!'

They moved away, and Steiger heard the newly awakened one say with sudden vehemence, 'Roll on, death, and let's have a damned good rest!'

Minutes later he heard the hiss of air as the periscope slithered towards the surface. He wondered if the unknown officer was thinking of his unfaithful wife or, like Dietrich, was pondering on the invisible barrier between him and the men who controlled and drove him to and beyond the limits of endurance.

10: Then There Were Five

The arrival of another spring meant all things to all men. Along the thousands of miles of battered defence lines the German armies on the Eastern Front peered across the melting snow and waist-deep slush towards the Russian positions, where the growing might of the enemy drew its strength together and prepared for another great offensive. As the pale sunlight touched the shell-blistered tree stumps and raised steam from the waterlogged craters, the soldiers of Germany pulled in their belts, tended their worn and much-used weapons and waited. Thousands and thousands of their comrades marked every mile of their retreat and clogged each corner of their stubborn resistance. Divisions shrunk to battalions, then to companies, and the men who had started the campaign as callow privates now held the responsibility of command, and stared through their field-glasses across the rusted wire towards the empty land which they had once helped to conquer. Death was too commonplace for comment, survival as remote as home leave. A few still waited for the secret weapon, so long boasted of by the High Command, while others brooded over the vastness of the battleground which had made them all so puny and futile.

In Occupied France the feeling was different. Green came to the tall trees once more, and instead of black puddles along the cobbled roads, fine dust rose with the passing of every vehicle. Camouflaged tanks rumbled across fields, and sweating infantry practised every conceivable manœuvre under the eyes of their instructors and tormentors.

In the country districts Frenchmen who had not been recruited for forced labour or moved to the bigger cities to clear away the mounting bomb damage worked in their fields, their starved bodies grateful for the frail warmth and the smells of new life around them. Occasionally they would pause at their ploughs or lean on their hoes and stare upwards towards the high pale sky, where the slow-moving vapour trails of invisible bombers crossed towards Germany, to the homes of their hated masters. It was so remote, so casual, that the occupation seemed all the more unbearable. Everyone had become so used to the clatter of jack-boots, the tide of field-grey uniforms, that a Frenchman hardly raised his eyes when a German passed. It seemed the war, the real war, had passed them by, and had left them only with the shame and humiliation of defeat, which they wanted to forget.

Some Frenchmen thought differently, however. They carried on the fight, stabbed at the monster which held down their country, and with gathering momentum stirred the enemy into a tide of reprisals. A train would be sabotaged, a despatch-rider plucked from his motor-cycle by a single strand of barbed wire stretched across the road at throat level, and occasionally a home-made bomb would find its way beneath a parked lorry or munition dump.

Like swift tentacles from the main body, the powers of destruction moved in to stem these attacks by all and every means. The Gestapo and the S.S., aided by a formidable force of French informers and police, probed every incident, interrogated, tortured and executed suspects, and even killed hastily gathered hostages who were quite often ignorant of their alleged crimes. Innocent but for being French.

As the flowers blossomed along the hedgerows, so also did the new spirit of resistance. The few brave Frenchmen who defied the enemy were no longer regarded as terrorists and gangsters by their countrymen, but as patriots. Their ranks swelled, their organisation improved. Men joined the Resistance for different reasons. Some, like the first members, fought for pride and freedom, against the day when the Allies would launch their own counter-offensive and batter their way through Hitler's West Wall and on to Germany. Others did it to work off old scores, and killed for profit. Old enemies were labelled 'collaborators' and executed without question, goods were stolen, but never used beyond the hands of the thief.

On the other side other Frenchmen helped the Occupation Forces with equal dedication. Some because they were so involved with the Germans that they could not face an Allied victory with its inevitable reprisals, and others because they had found power for the first time.

Over and above all this the ordinary German forces lived a strange kind of existence, divided between defending the west door of their new kingdom and protecting their own way of life.

In St. Pierre the unreality of war was more evident than before. The tiny, remote corner of the Bay of Biscay echoed with activity, yet lay encircled by a town which hardly seemed to have changed in a century.

Two pairs of submarines were moored alongside a jetty, and

two more hulls were just visible inside the deep concrete bunkers. Group Meteor had carried out one more short patrol after the big attack in the Bristol Channel, and no one in any of the six boats could believe that they had not lost another of their number.

The Atlantic, too, looked different. Instead of the bitter harshness of winter, the deep blue-grey swells looked lazy, with the undulating power of a living desert. There was a lull in the endless battle at sea while both sides considered their next moves. But it was just a lull and not a stalemate. New measures would be used, and new weapons introduced to counter them, but every day the unseen war went on, and every hour at sea lessened a man's chances of survival.

When Commander Rudolf Steiger had been brought back wounded to St. Pierre he had been sent almost at once to the main hospital in Lorient. There had been several enquiries into the alleged sabotage of his boat, but Captain Bredt had decided to take no further action. The only witness, a seaman named Max König, seemed unsure of what he saw, and Bredt took the view that the damage might have been caused by a faulty signal rocket. After all, he repeatedly told himself, König was either too new to the service or too stupid to recognise a bomb if he saw one. Nevertheless, he commended the strangely silent seaman and sent him on leave, and then told Major Reimann to again check his security measures.

For Captain Bredt life in the town had become more than merely pleasant. He had found that his new position of authority seemed to give him extraordinary privileges, which, if he had retained his other arm and thereby stayed an ordinary naval officer, would have been not only denied him but also quite unknown. He had a very good house adjoining the Headquarters building, and six French servants. Through Major Reimann he had met the Mayor, who also owned the town's main factory, which made machinery for the German Army, and through the Mayor he had obtained a French mistress, whose ability and sexual delights still left him a trifle dazed.

He sent endless reports to the High Command, and complained to the Admiral if Group Meteor was excluded from any possible operation.

The men of the Group and the Base staff saw little of this side to their senior officer. Bredt ran the Base as much to peacetime routine as he dared, and he had even bullied his Staff Operations Officer into getting a band formed from the Headquarters personnel. On Sundays, and other special occasions, the band would march up and down the harbour approach or into the town itself, while the garrison troops and the townsfolk stared with a mixture of amusement and contempt.

In fact, with Rudolf Steiger safely away on enforced sick leave to recover from his wound, and a visit from the Admiral just successfully completed, Bredt could sit behind his wide desk with a feeling of justified satisfaction. He had never thought it possible that he would be able to cut himself from his former pathetic self, the role of the ex-submarine commander, the crippled hero, and become a real and vital person again. This was his true place in life. He was a planner, a wielder of weapons, rather than a mere unit in the great German Navy.

These were his feelings as he sat behind his desk in the third week of May, that is, until the telephone began to ring, and again everything changed.

* * * * *

The heavy commandeered saloon car rattled noisily over the cobbled square and swung right towards the harbour. The shaded headlights cut momentarily across wandering soldiers and their French girl friends and along the overhanging shapes of the old houses, and Steiger felt the depression grow stronger, mingled with the feeling of caution he had experienced since he had left the train and been met by a car from the Base. After being discharged from hospital he had spent three weeks' leave in Germany on the outskirts of Kiel, and whatever he might have been expecting to find in his homeland after being away so long, the shock of seeing the acres of bombed buildings, shattered streets and haunted people had left him dazed and uncertain. Old acquaintances seemed to have vanished, and the few faces he knew were too busy and worried to find time to share his company. In the hotels the young naval officers danced and sang to the tune of the enemy bombers, and there was an air of insane gaiety which made the return to St. Pierre and the waiting Atlantic seem welcome and reassuring. Each day he had read every newspaper he could get his hands on, and tried to find out what was happening in the wide theatre of war. There again it was not possible to gain comfort or understanding, as every item of news seemed to be constructed entirely for the civilian population. The news from the East was vague but optimistic, and in Italy, where the Allies advanced slowly into what Winston Churchill called the soft under-belly of the Axis, it was said that the Army was falling back according to plan. Only in the West did everything seem to be disciplined and well ordered. Across the English Channel the enemy could wait in vain for a chance to invade, for with the new system of coastal defences, shore batteries and fighter cover, the Allies would think twice before making such a gigantic sacrifice.

A sudden thought crossed his mind, and he leaned forward to tap the driver on the shoulder. 'Does Commander Lehmann still have a house in the town?'

The man nodded. 'Yes, sir. We are almost there now.'

Steiger sat back, his mind suddenly made up. 'You can drop me there, and take my case on to my quarters.'

The car swerved into a narrow, tree-lined lane where the houses were few and far between. A military police scout-car was parked in a lay-by, its wireless aerial swaying in the slight breeze, its helmeted occupants smoking and watching the last people along the road before curfew.

Steiger thought back to his weeks in hospital. At first it had passed quite well. Hazy days of anaesthetic and pain, of glaring lights and white uniforms. Then the waiting, the endless inspections of his wound, probing fingers, and empty comments which told him nothing. There had been photographers from the Propaganda Department, and two visits from an admiral, as well as a brief report about the Bristol Channel attack which was read to him by a secretary from Lorient Naval Headquarters. Various people came to shake his hand, and a top Nazi official asked him to stay at his house when he was discharged. None of these people meant anything to Steiger. He lay awake at nights fretting and wondering what was happening in St. Pierre, and cursing every delay which was keeping him helpless and useless.

Dietrich had visited him once and told him about the boat and about the last cruise into the Atlantic. But he seemed distant and evasive, and the Group's lack of losses was heavily countered in Steiger's mind by their apparent lack of successes against the enemy.

Steiger had forced himself to wait, driven himself to endure the slow business of recovery, so that upon his return to duty no one could mislead him or turn him from what he knew must be done.

Somewhere in the back of his mind he knew that Lehmann had failed him, and when they had argued that day on the hillside above the harbour he had been trying to tell him something more.

Well, it was better to get it over with now, once and for all. From what he had heard, it was plain to Steiger that apart from Otto Kunhardt's boat, his own was the only one to score any real successes against the enemy ships in that fogbound channel, and while Group Bruno had been slaughtered Lehmann had held back, and by so doing had prevented the rest of Group Meteor from pressing home the attack.

The car stopped, and the driver pointed to a small shuttered house which stood between two tall elms. 'There it is, sir.'

The gravel crunched beneath Steiger's boots, and he felt the cool salt air against his cheek. The car ground away into the gloom, and Steiger turned to face the house.

I will see him now, he thought finally. He was once a good friend, and could be again. But if he can no longer find the will to lead or the strength to fight, he must be replaced, and at once.

He pulled the ring beside the door and heard the ancient bell jangling deep inside the house.

After some moments the door opened to the extent of a safety chain, and a voice asked, 'Who is it?'

'Commander Rudolf Steiger.' He waited with a mixture of impatience and uncertainty as the servant closed the door and began to remove the chain. He thought he heard several voices and the sound of a door being slammed.

Eventually he was shown into a small, well-furnished room, which was lit by two ornate table-lamps and warmed by a cheerful log fire. Two army officers stood facing him as he entered, and another paused in the process of pouring himself a drink at a side table. Steiger's eyes moved past the three soldiers, none of whom he had seen before, and settled on the face he had so often remembered during his weeks in hospital.

'This is very unexpected, Commander!' She looked up at his stern face, her lips parted and glistening in the lamplight. She was exactly as she had appeared in his thoughts, but in her close reality the smoothness of her skin and the perfection of her beauty only helped to unsettle him further. She guided him to a chair, her back momentarily turned to him, and gestured to the three soldiers, who were already tightening their belts and groping for their caps. 'Friends of Alex,' she explained evenly, 'but I have just told them he is not back from Paris yet!'

The officers nodded to Steiger and clicked their heels respectfully, but only after they had filed from the room did Steiger realise that none of them had said a single word. He forced himself to sit calmly and consider what it all meant. Lehmann was on leave and had evidently gone to Paris, but why alone? He stiffened as he heard the girl's voice calling after the visitors, and was surprised to hear a car engine splutter into life behind the building.

She re-entered the room, her hands moving deftly to remove the empty glasses and pat into shape the cushions which were still warm from the silent guests.

Stooping over the fire she raked briskly at the glowing logs. Steiger felt his mouth grow dry as he watched the muscles at the back of her legs and the fullness of her breasts revealed by her red corduroy dress as it was pulled tight across her body.

She turned suddenly, her brown eyes steady and alert. 'I thought you would not be back for several days.' She sat easily on the edge of the chair opposite him, her hands smoothing unnecessarily at the hem of her dress. 'Are you quite recovered?'

'Well enough, thank you.'

'I came to Lorient to see you, you know.' She laughed quickly at the perplexed expression on his face. 'But they would not let me in. You were having a bad time of it!' Her eyes softened. 'I heard something of what you did. It must have been terrible.'

Steiger took the drink she offered him and drank it down quickly without noticing what it was. She had come to see him. She had remembered him, and cared enough to call. Hardly daring to hear her answer, he asked casually, 'Couldn't Alex have gone to the hospital instead?'

'I did not tell him I was going.' She dropped her eyes, and Steiger could feel the tension in the air as she added, 'After all, he hardly ever tells *me* anything these days!' There was bitterness, defiance too, and Steiger was immediately on his guard.

'Those three soldiers,' he paused, noting the sudden stiffening of her slim shoulders, 'friends of yours?'

'No. They came to see Alex.'

'Why is he in Paris?' He could feel the pain of his heart thumping against his ribs, and hated himself for following one question with another. He felt as if he was destroying something wonderful with each word, although he did not know what it was, and yet he was unable to stop himself.

'He went to see his brother.'

Steiger nodded, his mind racing as he recalled Lehmann telling him about his brother who was on the Army Staff.

'Without you?' He tried to make his tone gentle, but the suddenness of his question startled him beyond caution, and brought the girl to her feet.

'Well, why don't you ask outright, Commander?' Her eyes flashed with anger, and he could sense that she was only just holding herself under control. 'Has he got another woman? Or is he just changed so much that he is sick of the sight of me?'

She waved her hand around the small room which seemed to have fallen silent, as if listening. 'I tried to make this into a home. The first we have had since we married, but he does not care!' She took two steps towards him, her body shaking with emotion. 'He is not the same man! The one I married is only a photograph in a frame. Do you understand, Commander? I do not know *this* man!'

Steiger rose to his feet. 'I am sorry. I did not mean to probe. The war has changed so many things. Perhaps given time we might——'

She took another step, and stared directly into his face, studying his features as if for the first time. He could smell the exciting warmth of her body, the scent of her piled black hair, and could almost feel the extent of her desperate passion and anger.

'What have you done with Alex?'

The question hit him like a blow. 'What have *I* done?'

'How much do you think they can stand? Is it necessary to drive them all so much that even their wives don't recognise them?' Her body shook with a paroxysm of sobs, but her eyes remained bright and unblinking.

'*Look* at yourself, Commander! Take a mirror and have a good look! You have become so immersed in this bloody business of war that you have killed something in yourself!'

She stood swaying in the flickering light from the log fire, her hands held out to him as if in supplication. 'Please! Can't you even tell me it's going to end? Must we be expected to go on day after day, waiting and planning for something which seems to grow more remote with every hour?'

She turned away, the fire suddenly gone out of her, so that Steiger wanted to take her, to crush the protests, and if necessary to force his love upon her. The love of which he had been so jealous, yet which had been denied to her, as to himself.

'I think I will leave now.' His voice sounded strange and unknown. 'I think I can understand your feelings.'

She spoke across her shoulder, her voice low and broken. 'How could you understand? For you the fight is everything. If every living creature has to be destroyed to prove you wrong then you will say, "So be it!" '

She rested her hand momentarily on the silver-framed portrait of her husband. 'I believe Alex is trying to find another way. I don't know. There does not seem to be any more room for me in his way of life than there is in yours.'

'If there is anything I can do . . .' Steiger faltered, hating the stupid emptiness of his words. 'I would like to be of some help, of some use.'

She turned round, her face quiet again with surprise. After a moment she said softly: 'Perhaps I was wrong about you. Maybe you do care about people, after all!'

Steiger's face creased into an uncertain smile. 'I think I care *too* much.'

In silence she followed him down the passage to the front door, where he picked up his white cap. At the back of the house he could hear the French servant crooning an unintelligible song, and all at once he wanted to hold on to this moment.

She switched off the light and opened the door. Outside the trees looked black and hostile against the stars, and he felt a wave of disillusionment sweeping in with the night breeze. After he had gone she would probably laugh at his clumsiness and stiff stupidity. She was right, he did not belong anywhere but with his machines of war.

In a small voice she said: 'I was going to go back to Germany, but I feel I must stay now. I can't explain why. It's just a feeling.'

He groped for the edge of the door, and his hand brushed across her breast. Instantly he felt the tension run through her like a shock wave, so that her sharp intake of breath matched his own.

Very slowly she said, 'I think it would be better if we did not meet again.'

Without answering he turned on his heel and walked out on to the road. When he turned at the end of the lane and looked back the house had merged with the shadows, but her presence seemed to follow him and mock him at every step, and as he breasted the rise above the harbour the kiss of the sea-wind was like a cleansing breath, and the murmuring water seemed more like an ally than an enemy.

. . . . .

Heinz Dietrich opened his eyes and lay quite still for several long seconds. At first he did not know what had awakened him or even where he was, and then he heard the vague distant throbbing of an aircraft engine and briefly imagined it flying inland to the military airfield. Then as his recollections came crowding in on his newly alerted mind he held his breath and very carefully raised himself on one elbow.

The unfamiliar room was quiet and still, but the faint tinge of dawn light which filtered through the uncurtained window showed him the girl's dark hair on the pillow and the pale angle of her bare arm against his own. He listened to her gentle breathing and felt the tender longing rising within him like pain. They had both known that tomorrow was the last day, yet neither mentioned nor thought of it. Now, as the light strengthened and the creeper tapped against the window glass in the early breeze, he seemed unable to grasp its inevitability and its meaning.

The girl stirred and rolled on to her back. Dietrich could tell that she, too, was awake and watching him. Very carefully he lifted her chin in his hand and bent across her, his mouth tasting the salt of her tears and the sudden desperation of her need for him.

The last cruise had been almost too much for him. Something more than just fear had driven him ashore on his return. More than a loathing for the stink of the U-boat and the smell of death. He had been in a kind of daze as he had gone through the motions of making his report and seeing the crew away on leave. Even his visit to Steiger in hospital had seemed unreal, as if he were a spectator watching himself and listening to his own stilted words.

With methodical and deliberate calm he had spoken to the retired French coastguard who owned this isolated and semi-derelict cottage, and had made his arrangements. Then, and only then, did he go and see the girl, Odile Marquet. He had expected her to tear herself away from him, to show him anger or pity, but as he had talked he had seen her expression change from grave concern to one of understanding.

He lowered his head on to her smooth shoulder and ran his hand gently over her breasts and down across the curve of her stomach. Beneath the pressure of his hand he felt her body come alive once more, so that she twisted against him, the gripping heat of her thighs binding him to her with renewed fierceness until the mounting force of their love blotted out all else and left them momentarily safe and at peace.

She lay inertly in the crook of his arm, her breath still fast and hot against his chest, her mouth speaking soundless words into his very body.

'It is nearly light.' The words were wrung from him. 'We will have to go soon.'

She did not answer, but gripped his arm with such fierceness that he could feel the nails biting into his skin.

In a firm voice he said: 'This is only the beginning, Odile. Surely *we* are important? We matter as much as ideals and stupid beliefs?'

He stared desperately at the ceiling and noticed that he could now see the cracks which ran across it. He felt her hand on his mouth, and knew that she understood what he was trying to say, as she always did. Even when they had taken their secret walks together they had hardly spoken, yet when Dietrich was alone he could look back and seemingly remember an endless conversation, a complete matching of thoughts and dreams.

She freed herself from his hand and sat up on the rough blankets, her limbs white against the old furniture. For a long while she stared at the uniform which lay unheeded across a chair, and at the glint of metal where her leg-iron waited patiently for her to return to its own everyday world. She shivered as his hand moved blindly around her body and said almost to herself: 'Our two disguises are there, Heinz. Before, I hated them both, but I know now that without them this could not have happened, and we would have been like all the others!'

Somewhere in the far distance a dog barked with sudden surprise, and throughout the outside world men stirred and tested the new day.

In the cottage outlined against the dawn-silvered sea the French girl sat with her lover's head pillowed on her knees and felt the new strength which his need had given her. No one would understand, but that no longer mattered.

. . . . .

Rudolf Steiger forced himself to walk calmly to the group of officers and seamen who had gathered on the concrete platform at the side of one of the U-boat pens. He could see Captain Bredt's fair head bobbing amongst the excited figures, and the fact that he had forgotten to put on his cap made Steiger realise this was no ordinary crisis.

Steiger had been finishing a late breakfast when a nervous messman had come running with a message that Bredt wanted him urgently. That in itself had been curious, for Bredt had left no messages to welcome him back to the Base, and refrained from putting in an appearance in the mess, presumably so that Steiger should understand his position even more clearly. The converted hotel dining-room had been strangely deserted, most of the U-boat officers being still on leave, and the excited entrance of the messman had broken into Steiger's brooding thoughts like a minor explosion.

The crowd parted, and Steiger saw the Base Medical Officer bending over the spread-eagled corpse of a seaman. From the look of his ammunition pouches and discarded rifle, Steiger guessed he was either a sentry or a patrolman.

Bredt swung round, his face flushed and angry. 'Ah, there you are! Do you see this? As if there isn't enough to worry about!'

Steiger looked past him at the doctor. 'Well? How did it happen?'

'Stabbed from behind. He never knew what killed him!'

A petty officer stepped forward, his voice anxious. 'I was just inspecting the sentries, sir, and I found him here, just like this.' He glanced furtively at Bredt. 'I had been round the whole ring of patrols only half an hour earlier and he was all right then!'

'Excuses! That's all I ever get!' Bredt glared fiercely at the N.C.O. 'There's more in this than——' He broke off as Steiger stepped over the dead man, his grey eyes peering down the concrete ramp to the floor of the nearest pen.

'What of the next sentry, the one on the other side?' Steiger's mind had taken in the fact that the sentry's rifle was untouched. Whoever had risked his life to break into the Base had been after something more. With vivid clarity he remembered Dietrich's frightened face and the black smoke pouring through the open hatch of the surfaced submarine. Sabotage. The very feel of the word made him sick with anger.

'The other man is all right, sir.' The petty officer tore his eyes from Bredt's face and watched the tall commander with pathetic eagerness.

Bredt pushed after Steiger. 'Well, what do you think?'

'I think that somebody deliberately forced his way into this pen.' He stared at the newly painted stern of the docked submarine, the very one in which he had returned to St. Pierre. 'Whoever it was must have known the times and duties of these sentries, and the times of the petty officer's inspections.'

'I still don't see . . .' Bredt's voice was petulant, but Steiger was already moving down the ramp.

Over his shoulder Steiger shouted, 'The sentries change in half an hour, don't they?'

'Well, yes.' Bredt was completely lost, his face a picture of confusion.

'Get every man down here at once! There must be another bomb!' Steiger halted and stared back at Bredt with sudden fury. 'Do you understand *now*? For God's sake sound the alarm!'

The seamen stood in a ragged semicircle around the dead sentry, staring at their officers, only half aware of what was happening, but fully conscious of Steiger's anger.

Bredt suddenly noticed that the men had started to run, and felt the frustrated anger of one who has been cheated. In a firmer voice he barked: 'There's no need to lose control of yourself, Commander! I can see no justification for your——'

He stopped, his mouth still hanging open, as a muffled explosion lifted the sand and dust from the concrete slipway below. It was more of a sigh than a bang, and some of the running men who had almost reached the gaping entrance to the pen slithered to a halt, their faces blank and uncomprehending. The U-boat seemed to shiver, then with sad dignity began to topple sideways on its chocks. With gathering momentum it swayed against the rough concrete walls of the pen, the toughened hull screaming and buckling as the full force of its twelve hundred tons sidled clumsily across the buckled and blasted supports of the slipway. Then there was silence, and the little groups stood staring with awe at the tall column of dust and smoke which billowed slowly upwards over the shoulder of the green hill.

With his fists clenchd Steiger walked across and looked coldly into Bredt's stricken face. 'Are you satisfied now, Captain? Perhaps you realise what you have done, now that it is too late!' He could see Bredt's pale eyes blinking as each word struck his face like a lash. 'After this you might begin to understand that there is more to fighting a war than playing with little paper flags and coloured pins!'

Bredt's face reddened. 'How dare you! What gives you the right to speak to your superior officer like this!'

'*There* is your answer!' Steiger pointed at the crippled U-boat.

Steiger quickened his pace and climbed the steep path towards the Headquarters building. It would take weeks, perhaps months, to repair the damaged submarine, and the pen itself would be denied to all the rest of the hard-pressed Group Meteor. It was like a mad nursery rhyme, and the words kept repeating themselves in his brain in an irrepressible chorus: 'And then there were five! And then there were five!'

Well, this time Bredt's stupidity had gone too far. Even in large naval bases, peopled by hordes of foreign labourers, sabotage was almost unknown, yet here, in this backwater of the West Wall, it had already struck twice in two months, not counting the murder of a seaman whose death Bredt had chosen to ignore completely.

Steiger had always despised the adulation and praise showered on his exploits by the press and propaganda services, and had known it was because his seeming indestructibility had made him into a prop for their devices. He had never traded on his fame, but instead had endeavoured to remain isolated and unmoved with his puritanical dedication and faith in his own efforts for victory.

But for once he would make an exception, even if it meant going to the Grand Admiral as he had often threatened.

He was jerked from his grim thoughts by the swift approach of a shining black Mercedes which had just swept through the gate in the wire fence to the Headquarters compound.

Steiger's eyes narrowed as he saw the slim young officer in an impeccably cut uniform of olive-green alight from the back seat, and noted the Death's Head cap badge and insignia of the S.S.

The officer finished giving quiet instructions to his driver and then turned to face Steiger's scrutiny. He was about twenty-five, with such boyish good looks as to be almost effeminate. Above his round, open face he wore his cap at a casually rakish angle, and from beneath the polished peak his shadowed eyes were regarding Steiger with amused interest.

Incongruously he was carrying a large cat-basket, and this he changed from one hand to the other so that he could salute. This, too, he did with a casual informality, his lips parting to reveal a white smile of small delicate teeth.

'A very rough journey, Commander.' He glanced briefly towards the harbour. 'I am Major Claus Fischer. I understand that you are having a little trouble here?' He laughed gently, and for some reason Steiger was chilled by the sound.

The S.S. officer tested the weight of the basket in his grip. 'Poor Gottfried is probably sick from the journey. Like most cats he dislikes travelling. I had better go straight to my quarters.'

Steiger found his voice. 'You are expected?'

'I fancy not. But no doubt the excellent Captain Bredt will be pleased to afford me some comfort?' He smiled again as if at some inner secret. 'In fact, I am *sure* he will!'

Steiger watched him enter the building, then looked with sudden apprehension at his hands. They were shaking badly, and despite the pale sunlight across his back he could feel a bitter unnatural cold biting into his body.

11 : Sabotage

The flurry of a sudden rain-squall against the tall windows was the only sound in Captain Bredt's office. Max König was conscious of his own forced breathing and the air of hostility which had greeted his entrance, and which had remained hanging in the room like a threat.

He kept his arms at his sides and slowly dug the finger and thumb of his right hand into the fleshy part of his leg, so that the numbing pain acted like a brake on his racing thoughts and enabled him to stare at the charts on the opposite wall without faltering, and thereby avoid the casual scrutiny of the S.S. officer who sat near Captain Bredt's elbow.

Bredt said impatiently, 'With regard to your previous statement about the explosion aboard *U-991*.' He paused and glanced at his staff officers, who were careful to avoid his pale eyes. 'I have investigated the matter very carefully, but apparently another report is now called for.' He halted, and shifted his gaze to the slim figure at his side. 'Perhaps Major Fischer would like to ask you what you saw?'

Fischer crossed his legs and cocked his head on one side. For several seconds he stared at his brightly polished boots and then lifted his gaze to the tall seaman who stood unmoving in the centre of the carpet.

'Well now, König. You have just returned from a well-earned leave, eh?'

König kept his eyes on the charts and tried not to think of the last time he had been faced by an officer of the dreaded S.S.

'Yes, sir.'

Fischer leaned back in his chair and pressed his neat finger-tips together. 'To Cuxhaven, I believe?' His voice was very level, even friendly, but König's mind seemed to scream a warning.

'Yes, sir. I stayed at a small hotel there.'

'But your home is in Bielefeld, is it not?' Fischer's eyes were fixed on him with bright intentness. 'Well, isn't it?'

'Yes, sir.' His throat felt like dust, and he could feel the nausea of fear rising in him even as he struggled to control his voice. 'I did not want to go home. I wanted a change.'

Major Fischer nodded and showed his small teeth in a con-spiratorial smile. 'Ach, quite so! After the hazards of the Atlan-tic you no doubt looked for more pleasant company, eh?' He smiled across at Bredt's grim face. 'What it is to be without the weight of command!'

König swallowed hard. Fischer must have checked the leave passes of every man in the Group as a matter of course. Or did he know something already? Perhaps he was just playing the same hideous game for which his sort had become so well famed, and in a minute he would unmask the man who stood before him, the seaman who was someone else.

'Now this *bomb*, König. You saw it? And you said it was like a large cylinder or tin?' He nodded encouragingly to König. 'Did it strike you as being dangerous?'

'No, sir. I was not expecting anything like that.'

Bredt interrupted. 'He's new to the service! He would not have understood anything unusual!'

Fischer smiled lazily. '*You* have been in the service a great deal longer, Captain, yet you could not even bring yourself to recognise this as an emergency!'

König was jerked from his agony of suspense by Fischer's casual insult and by the intake of breath of every officer in the room.

'How *dare* you!' Bredt half rose, his face mottled with rage. 'I have never been so insulted in my life!'

Fischer shrugged indifferently. 'Then you are lucky, Captain!

But I have not come here merely for the good of my health. The success and survival of the German Reich depends on constant vigilance and security. You control a small part of the country's defence, and my department can, if necessary, control *you*!' Fischer was no longer smiling, and his hands rested warily on his knees as if he was going to spring directly at the one-armed officer who still stood foolishly behind his desk. 'So be good enough not to interrupt. This seaman has said what he saw, and his First Lieutenant was intelligent enough to grasp the urgency of the situation and salvaged what was left of the so-called bomb. That is all we have, but it will be enough.'

König realised for the first time that Lieutenant Dietrich was also in the room, his pale face and blond hair making him look like a child beside the elderly staff officers. The sight of Dietrich seemed to steady him, although he did not know why.

Fischer tapped his boot gently on the floor until Bredt had slumped back into his chair, then he continued evenly as if nothing had happened, 'I will now draw your attention to these items.' He flicked open a paper carton on the desk, and the heads craned to stare at the few blackened articles displayed.

Fischer lifted up a length of fire-stained metal. 'Now, König, do you recognise this?'

'Yes, sir.' It was all suddenly so clear in his mind that he momentarily forgot his own personal danger. He saw again the cylinder in its neat hideout, and the writhing, screaming shape of the man who had tried to move it. 'It was holding the cylinder in place.'

Fischer looked sharply at Dietrich. 'When would you normally use rockets from that rack?'

'When we return to harbour, sir,' Dietrich's face looked sunken with weariness, 'and as recognition signals with our aircraft.'

'I see. So at some time while your submarine was at sea a flare of some sort, or a rocket, *would* be used!'

Fischer sighed and put the metal strip back on the table. 'Very well, König. You can go. You have done well.'

Max König saluted and turned about, his eyes passing across the watching faces in a sort of dazed wonder. Fischer did not suspect him. Any flaws in his story had been forgotten, thanks to Bredt's timely interruption.

As the door closed behind him Fischer said thoughtfully: 'Of course, this recent sabotage is the same sort of thing. A local terrorist group, I imagine.' He was thinking aloud. 'My men have examined the perimeter fence, but there is no sign of a forced entrance. The last bomb was planted on a Sunday, and there were no workers in the harbour area but for a few mechanics, and I have personally interrogated those. There were, however, some unexplained marks below the slipway. I think the terrorists came from the water, across the harbour itself.' He watched the growing confusion on their faces and then turned to Dietrich. 'What do *you* think about that?"

Dietrich forced himself to sound non-committal. He felt calm and unmoved in spite of all the tension, and could feel no pity for Bredt and the others. He had heard many stories, seemingly exaggerated, about the methods of the S.S., but he could look squarely at this elegant young man without a tremor. 'It is quite possible, provided that these people are well organised.'

Fischer smiled at him. He and Dietrich were the same age, it was as if they had become allied by the other officers' unwillingness to face up to this new threat.

'That is so, Lieutenant. But the first bomb, *your* bomb, has afforded one small clue, and that was thanks to your prompt action!'

Dietrich saw Bredt's humiliated eyes glance at him with hatred. Fischer was thanking him for his brave deeds. It was lucky that Steiger was not here at the enquiry. He alone knew of his failure. Steiger had driven him below, had *forced* him to take the required action, had even beaten him like a dog, or a coward!

Dietrich glanced at the small wheel which Fischer twirled delicately in his fingers. 'Do you all see this? It is part of a clock mechanism. The bomb was also primed with a time fuse, just in case the other method did not work!' Fischer stared coldly at the wheel. 'The bomb was planted by a French worker in the harbour, probably while the stores were being loaded.' He did not look at Bredt as he added, 'Very careless supervision, I should say.' He carried on calmly: 'But the actual bomb was constructed by someone locally. Probably a clockmaker or the like. The bomb was crude, but effective. The mechanism is the only real lead so far.' He put the wheel carefully on the desk, his eyes hidden. 'My men will investigate this matter very fully. In the meantime I will ask you gentlemen to carry on with your duties in the normal way. I do not want these terrorists to be frightened off. This latest triumph will no doubt make them feel, as I do, that anyone stupid enough to allow sabotage *deserves* it!'

Dietrich stepped behind the other officers, hiding his stricken face, and groping blindly for one explanation, one reason to clear away the impact of Fischer's terrible revelation.

He thought of old Louis Marquet's shop and the ranks of ticking clocks. It had been Marquet who had approached him about helping Odile to find a job, and he had done just that, inside the harbour itself! He passed his hand dazedly across his chilled forehead. It was wrong, of course, it was sheer madness to think so stupidly. He thought of the lonely cottage, the girl's nearness, the ecstasy of their love, and hated himself for even a second's doubt. But suppose Fischer was right? Was it possible that Marquet was part of this ghastly business, and was even now congratulating himself on his success?

Right or false, Fischer's men would surely pay him a visit, would even question the girl. A shudder of sick anger ran through him. No. Odile belonged to him. He needed her, just as she did him. Whatever else happens *I* must deal with this myself!

Fischer's smooth voice bored into his brain like a drill. 'And when I find these carrion, gentlemen,' he paused to give his words effect, 'I will make them pray for death! But I will deny them that privilege for a long, long while!'

• • •

Rudolf Steiger stood beside the window of his small room and watched the freshening wind's advance up the steep slope of the hill, each gust making the tall grass bend and ripple like a green and yellow sea. He was glad that he could not see the Bay from his room, as it would only have added to his feeling of nagging uncertainty. Every day in harbour seemed infinitely long, and for once he found that he was unable to drive himself free from his brooding thoughts and his mounting frustration.

There was a tap at the door, and he turned to see Lehmann's tall figure framed in the opening, his thin face tired but watchful.

Steiger did not speak, so Lehmann said evenly: 'I have just returned from leave. I understand you want to see me?'

'You have been in Paris?' Steiger watched for some embarassment or defiance, but Lehmann merely nodded.

It was strange, almost unnerving, how each of them had changed towards the other. Steiger could look at his old friend with the detachment of any senior officer examining a subordinate, yet the familiarity of Lehmann's sensitive features added to the anger which was already moving his heart. He remembered Lehmann's wife, and her uncontrolled flood of words, her body made tantalising in the firelight.

'I suppose you have heard the news?' He forced himself to remain calm.

Lehmann glanced round the bare room before he replied. If he expected to see some sign, some link with its occupant, he was to be disappointed. 'Yes, I heard it. Sabotage is an ugly thing. I suppose we would have been the same under similar circumstances. It is not nice to have conquerors abroad in your own land.'

'I am sending Kunhardt and his crew back to Germany to commission one of the new electric boats. He will rejoin the Group when he has finished trials. It looks as if it will be some time before we can get the damaged hull moved from that pen. Whoever it was who planted that explosive did a good job.'

Lehmann tightened his lips at the sound of Steiger's bitter words, and groped for a cigarette. 'You take it all too personally, Rudi,' he said quietly. 'You have always been the same. You fight each battle as if you alone could decide the outcome.'

Steiger recovered quickly from the shock of hearing Lehmann use his first name once more. 'Well, what do you expect? It has been a long fight already. We are scraping the bottom of the barrel, yet instead of pulling together, some of our illustrious officers are whimpering like little boys, instead of behaving like Germans!' With sudden anger he added, 'They are all fine fellows when things are going well, but in defeat they sicken me!'

'If you are referring to me, Rudi, please say so!' Lehmann's face was impassive, but his eyes were bright and feverish. 'I disagree with your present ideas, as you know, but I am no coward.'

Steiger did not reply, but watched the grass rippling on the side of the hill.

'When I heard you had been wounded I was sorry, you know that?'

'Do I?' Steiger's voice was tired.

'You think that I deliberately held back the Group during the attack to spite you, is that what's inside you?' Lehmann's hand was shaking. 'Do you know me so little?'

'I don't think I know you at all. I don't even care what you think of me as a man, as I have said before! But *you* thought the attack was a waste of life, too great a risk! You damned fool, don't you see that we are halfway to being beaten when a commander succumbs to doubts?'

Lehmann flinched as if struck a blow. 'Is that all?'

'No, it's not *all*!' Lehmann's refusal to be drawn, his lingering familiarity, made Steiger forget his caution. 'What in hell's name are you up to? Why did you not take your wife to Paris with you?'

'So she told you about that?' Lehmann sounded weary. 'In my opinion, for what it's worth, this matter is none of your affair!'

'Well, it *is* my affair! I will not have any officer endangering himself and his crew because of his personal problems!' He swallowed hard. 'You must send her back to Germany!' He lifted his hand as Lehmann opened his mouth. 'And I don't give a damn how many brothers you have on the Army Staff to pull strings for you. I am giving you a direct order!'

'I was only going to say that I had already decided to send her back. I am afraid poor Trudi does not understand how things are here.'

Steiger faltered, momentarily caught off balance. So that was her name—Trudi. He held on to it a moment longer and then said flatly: 'You can go. I am expecting orders to sail tomorrow. Port leave will be granted to the ratings, and officers may go into the town if they so wish.'

'Thank you.'

Steiger made one final effort. 'Can't you tell me what is bothering you?'

Lehmann faltered in the doorway, his fingers playing with his cap. 'I love Germany. I will fight to the death for its freedom.' He lifted his eyes. 'But the old methods are finished, Rudi, and we are all being damned because of the actions of a few! With these leaders we can expect only a crushing defeat, from which Germany may never recover. We could still find a compromise. It might still not be too late for that.'

Steiger turned his back and stared at the hillside until he heard the door close. What did a man do when he was faced by this sort of problem? he wondered. In his puritan service upbringing there had never been any room, any necessity, for this sort of relationship with his comrades, junior or senior. Duty was duty, and orders were carried out without question. Steiger was an intelligent man, a shrewd observer, and he knew well enough that any system based on absolute obedience brought mistakes and waste. But there was no other positive way in peace or war for running a disciplined force, and therefore no allowance had been made for men who refused to become brutalised or broken by battle, who still saw themselves as individuals instead of parts of a master machine.

All at once he was sick of the room's watchful silence and the hovering memory of Lehmann's words. He had to get out, anywhere, before the final release from the land left him no time for misgivings and doubts.

As he strode through the gates of the perimeter fence, and stiffly returned the sentries' salutes, he knew that he would walk past the house where he had met Trudi Lehmann. He had expected Lehmann to argue with him, to refuse to send his wife away, but instead he had unwittingly turned his knife in Steiger's heart. The gesture had become a certainty, and the thought of her leaving made him feel a sudden sense of urgency.

· · · · ·

Heinz Dietrich pushed through the queue of French workmen who were filing wearily out of the gates and entered the small harbour office, his eyes moving quickly around the shelves of musty records and accounts books, and felt suddenly unsure of himself. The fat German clerk dropped his gaudy magazine and hurried to the counter.

'Can I help you, Lieutenant?'

'The French girl, Marquet,' he faltered as he saw the man's small eyes flicker with interest, 'has she gone home already?'

'She did not come at all today, Lieutenant.' He spread his hands in mock despair. 'There is no gratitude in these people! You found her a nice job here, yet she disdains to come when she is wanted!' He gave a sly wink. 'But no doubt the Lieutenant knows more of her than I!'

Dietrich said sharply, 'Perhaps she is ill?'

'No, she is not. I sent a man to her home, but she has gone.'

'Gone?' Dietrich's voice was harsh with a mixture of disbelief and alarm. 'Where?'

The man shrugged, enjoying the young officer's uncertainty. 'Who knows?'

'I see.' Dietrich strode from the office, blind to all but the urgency of getting into the town and finding out for himself.

His boots rang sharply on the cobbled road in time to his racing thoughts. The little fool! By running away she would immediately draw Fischer's attention, and then it would be too late!

The shadows were already lengthening across St. Pierre when he found himself breathless and apprehensive at the end of the road he had come to know so well. The shop stood on its own in a small plot of garden, and as he looked for the familiar landmarks, Dietrich felt his breath caught in his throat. With horrified eyes he stared at the silent black Mercedes which was parked opposite the shop and at the two S.S. troopers who stood beside the open shop door. He wanted to run to her, if necessary throw himself between her and Major Fischer, but his feet refused to move. It seemed as if he had been standing in that one spot for limitless time, with the blood roaring in his head like surf, his eyes fixed on the shop's misty outline until the sockets felt raw. Then with something like a sob he turned and blundered back along the darkening street, until sheer exhaustion pulled him to a gasping halt. Then he leaned against a wall and was sick, his retching mingling with the sobs which tore at his body. As he wiped his trembling mouth with the back of his hand he stared down the silent street and seemed to see her face, sad and accusing, in each empty window.

Then very slowly he began to walk towards the harbour.

. . . . .

Max König paused outside the café and listened to the sounds of laughter and music from within. It was dark in the street, and he could only just discern the café's painted sign, a grotesque rocking-horse, as it swung in the freshening breeze from the harbour.

He could not recall how long he had been walking, but his limbs were heavy, and he knew that if he stopped now he would not be able to move for some time. As if reading his thoughts, his fingers moved around the money in his jacket pocket, and with sudden determination he pushed open the swing door and groped his way round the blackout curtain.

As usual the place was packed with sailors plus a sparse sprinkling of army field-grey. In spite of the crush, the blue tobacco smoke and the bellowing voices raised above the martial strains from an old accordionist, he saw instantly the familiar face of Jung, the boxer, and some of the others from his own crew pressed round a tiny circular table, the surface of which was crammed with glasses, spilt beer and an assortment of wine bottles.

Jung was watching him even before he had started to push his way through the packed bodies and flushed faces, his expression watchful and concerned in spite of the red drinker's flush across his battered features.

'Well, hello there, Max!' Horst Jung's voice was unnaturally loud and hoarse. 'We thought you had become entangled with some of the local bitches!'

König sank into a drink-spattered chair and accepted the brimming glass which Moses Rickover thrust at him. It was strange how safe he felt with these men, how much a part of their uncomplicated world.

Braun, the hydrophone operator, peered across at him, his eyes glazed and half closed. 'How did you fare with the S.S.?' He shook with silent laughter. 'Still alive apparently!'

Schultz, the ex-photographer, grimaced and belched loudly. 'I wish I was in that lot. The S.S. *really* know how to live! Good food, plenty of everything! I bet they'll be sorry when the war ends!'

Muller, the coffin-maker, sniffed. 'Especially if we lose! The Tommies will string them up like onions!'

'*And* us, remember, children!' Jung wagged a finger across the haze. 'All U-boat men are criminals! They know no mercy and give no quarter!'

Muller groaned. 'You've been listening to the British radio! Don't let that Major Fischer find out!'

Jung regarded him bleakly. 'His sort don't need any proof of anything any more. Just put them against a wall and pull a trigger! Bang! Bang! That's all *they* know!'

Rickover lifted a long wine bottle to his lips, and the others stopped talking to watch his adam's apple jerking in time to his swallows. The boy eventually lowered the bottle and sat gasping for breath. 'Nothing to it!' He peered uncertainly at König. 'These old men only *think* they know how to drink!'

In spite of his thoughts König laughed and lifted his own glass. It would be so easy to give up the constant vigilance, to get drunk, to forget, if only for a short while. The noise of the room closed over his head as he thought of Major Fischer's casual questions. Well, he had not lied to Fischer. He had been to Cuxhaven, and had spent his leave in an hotel. For over a week he had bided his time and tried to build up his courage. As Fischer had remarked, the real Max König's home was in

Bielefeld, but the other forgotten man had once lived on the outskirts of Cuxhaven. Eventually, in spite of the inner cries of protest and reason, he had taken a bus ride to that other place, where he had once lived and laughed with a girl called Gisela.

There were plenty of sailors in the streets, and with his coat collar raised about his ears he had walked slowly through the evening shadows, his boots grinding on the dust from one of the town's many air-raids, his heart pounding as he waited for a shout of recognition or a hand on his shoulder.

It was madness, of course. He had risked so much to get away from these dangers, had sworn to himself that he would never return, but as he walked with painful slowness past the old house he could feel the tears stinging his eyes and a lump choking at his throat.

It was just the same. A little faded and neglected perhaps, but the same birch tree nodded beside his old room, and the double gates across the gravel drive still awaited repair.

Back and forth he walked, up and down the street, his body merging with the restless, aimless throng of men released temporarily from their duties who, unlike himself, were far from their homes and their roots.

Then, as the last daylight died, he saw a light appear in one of the tall windows. For about twenty seconds, before the blackout shutter was dropped into place, he saw his mother as she peered unseeingly into the dusty street. In those twenty seconds his last reserve almost snapped. It would have been so easy to run up the drive, to hold her in his arms, to tell her that he was alive. Then the shutter blotted out the frail little woman, and in a kind of madness he wondered if he had actually imagined what he had seen.

He had gone back to his shabby hotel, and had laid wide-eyed on the bed, a bottle of schnapps unopened by his side. Over and over in his aching mind he pretended that he had actually gone into the house, as if to torture himself still further.

His father would have come in from his library, his glasses on his forehead, and said: 'What's all the noise about, Mother? Who have you got in here?' And then they would all have stood in a tight group, arms together, not speaking. After that he could have borne anything.

Only when the dawn light glimmered around the curtains of his room, and a farewell siren in the far distance followed enemy bombers out to sea, did he turn his mind to reality, and then he was glad he had purchased the bottle of schnapps.

Half dazed he heard Muller say: 'I'll bet the Frogs will be sorry if we lose the war and have to go! They're probably making a fortune out of us!'

Braun grinned stupidly and spoke with the careful determination of the very drunk. 'I know that my little French girl will be sorry!' He belched, and his face was instantly covered with a sheen of sweat. Doggedly he continued, 'She says that the Frogs'll cut the throats of all their women who've gone with us!' His head fell back as he gulped at the air.

Jung grinned unfeelingly. 'Careful, or you'll spill a drop!'

Rickover frowned at the bottle as if unsure of his capacity. 'Why do people keep saying "if" we are defeated this or that will happen?' He glanced at König's thoughtful face. 'We *will* win, eh?'

Jung leaned between them. 'Our sort never win! And don't you forget it!'

Rickover shrugged. 'You're all crazy! I've never heard such a lot of old women!'

König reached out and touched the boy's sleeve. 'Good. Keep your faith, Moses. It'll be a help later on.'

Rickover grinned and lifted his bottle, but Jung's eyes were questioning as he faced König through the boy's crooked arm. 'What is the end, Max?'

König gazed across the smoke-filled room, his eyes distant. 'When all this hypocrisy and self-righteous murder is not enough for their appetites. When the cracks start to show and the beasts start to look at each other!' With sudden wretchedness he added, 'I hope I can stay alive if only to see that!'

Braun pitched forward into the glasses and lay still, while sailors at the next table began to fight with each other.

Jung brightened up at once. He jammed his cap in his belt and stood swaying amongst the broken glass. 'Come on, lads! This'll get the wind out of your guts!' So saying he reached out for the nearest stranger and punched him clean across the table.

Long afterwards, as the dazed little group staggered back towards the harbour, König thought about Jung's action and was strangely moved. The old boxer knew no other way to show he understood, and had helped his friend in the one method left open to him. In the yelling, stampeding brawl which had followed, he and König had stood side by side, everything else forgotten but the mad, primitive eagerness of the fight. Some of the pent-up despair had been battered from König's body, so that he had been unwilling to stop, even when the military police had broken down the door, only to be swept aside by the cheering horde of escaping sailors. A few of the less fortunate had been caught, but their own party was bodily intact. Rick-over's slim body was light across König's broad shoulders, while Jung and Muller carried the unconscious Braun.

As they swayed along the dark streets, Jung's instinctive sense of danger made him say, 'Look out, it's a damned officer!'

Guiltily they stood in the open street as the lieutenant hurried past. Only then did they recognise him as their First Lieutenant, Heinz Dietrich.

Muller groaned and released Braun's feet, so that they fell heavily on the cobbles. 'Didn't even see us! Probably drunk, the lucky bastard!'

Jung glanced at König. 'Whatever it was that drove him like that it certainly wasn't drink!'

König remembered Dietrich's drawn face at the enquiry, and found time to wonder. Perhaps his words were already true, and the cracks were beginning to show in the German structure?

Jung grunted and heaved the inert figure off the ground. 'Back to work, children! The first man to spew as we pass the guards will feel my boot!'

* * * * *

The door of the Operations Room banged open and an eddy of damp air seemed to force itself into each shadowy figure slumped around the main map-table. It was still not light, but the yellow lamps above the table were bright enough to illuminate the sharp, wolf-like features of Lieutenant-Commander Otto Kunhardt, who bared his teeth in a wide grin as he strode to the table as if he was about to devour the first meal of the day.

The three other submarine captains and their first lieutenants stared at him with a mixture of surprise and disbelief. Fritz Wellemeyer, the massive Berliner who commanded *U-1001*, was the first to speak. 'What the hell are you doing here? I thought Steiger sent you and your crew back home to commission a new boat?'

Kunhardt appeared to be studying the chart with sudden intentness. 'I am taking command of *U-891*, Willi Ludwig has gone back with my old crew.'

Wellemeyer tugged at his ear with astonishment. 'What's this you're saying? You've been taken off that job?'

Kunhardt answered calmly: 'I was not taken off anything. I

volunteered to stay, and I think Ludwig could do with a rest!'

Alex Lehmann sat unmoving in a deep wicker chair, his face framed in the shining collar of his oilskin. 'You're a fool, Otto! Don't push your luck too far!'

Konrad Weiss, a prematurely bald young lieutenant who commanded the smallest boat in the Group, leaned his hands on the chart-table and sighed. 'I wish you'd asked *me*. I'd like the chance to get back home for a spell. Just think, good old barrack routine. Breakfast at a gentlemanly hour, stewards to butter your toast who don't stink of diesel fuel, and all day to sit in a classroom hearing about the new new boats from instructors who've probably never even been out in a sailing dinghy! That's a fine life!'

Wellemeyer banged his hands together and winked at his First Lieutenant. 'No sense of patriotism, eh?'

Lehmann glanced at Heinz Dietrich, who was staring emptily at an unopened notebook in his lap. 'What time will your captain be here?'

'Soon now.' Dietrich glanced up at the clock and then at the blacked-out windows. 'He wants a dawn briefing so that all captains will have time to discuss things before we sail.'

'No more muck-ups, eh?' Weiss grinned without humour. 'Christ, I hope we can get better organised this time!'

The door opened and Steiger walked amongst them. He was freshly shaved, and nodded briskly to each of them, but he gave the impression of having been awake the whole night. He stopped beside Kunhardt and stared down at the wide chart of the Atlantic. Quietly he said: 'I appreciate your gesture, Otto. You've turned down a good chance, you know.'

Kunhardt's hard features twisted into a faint smile. 'Ach, I am sick of courses and new ideas. My own methods are good enough for me, and they will see the war out quite satisfactorily! Anyway, who is going to carry our Group Commander back to Base if he gets wounded again, heh?'

There was a ripple of laughter, and Steiger felt suddenly drawn to these haggard, brittle men.

'Well, let us get down to it, gentlemen.' He spread his log-book across a corner of the chart and gestured to the wide area to the south-west of Ireland. 'We will take up patrol areas here, starting at the position five hundred miles west of Brest. Usual box-patrol, forty miles between each boat.' He handed out the typed instructions and watched their faces.

Outside the building the dawn stillness was shattered by the measured tramp of booted feet as the newly awakened crews marched down towards the harbour wall. This time each man would·be carrying an additional burden to his kitbag. A memory of home leave, the worry of an unfaithful wife perhaps, or the ever dangerous twist of fear. The fear which had already cost the Group some twelve deserters, who even now were probably being hunted or were awaiting this dawn and the firing squad.

Steiger said slowly: 'No captain must take on a group of targets unaided. Even if it means losing several ships, we must try for a concerted attack. There are fewer of us now. We must make every torpedo strike home!'

Otto Kunhardt drew a long black cheroot from his jacket and stuck it jauntily between his thin lips. 'Where's Captain Bredt, then?'

Weiss shrugged. 'In bed, I expect. I gather it is becoming more difficult for him to leave it these days. The company is so attractive!'

Steiger bit his lip. 'That will do. You know well enough that I cannot stand here and listen to you throwing insults at a senior officer!' He felt his face split into an uncontrollable grin. 'So I shall leave the room for a few moments!' He walked to the door. 'Come with me, Heinz, I want to discuss the security check of the hull!'

It was still cold and faintly misty on the paved terrace above the harbour, and Steiger felt the usual sensation of exhilaration, the unspoken challenge. But this time there was something more, but he was unable to recognise it. He had returned from his walk through the town neither tired enough to sleep nor settled sufficiently in his mind to feel that he had achieved his purpose.

He realised that Dietrich was standing at his side, his eyes apparently watching the faint tinge of grey across the horizon. He waited a few moments. 'What has happened, Heinz? Are you still brooding over the last cruise?'

Dietrich jumped as if startled by Steiger's friendly tone. 'It's nothing to do with that, sir. It's something else.'

His voice trailed away, and Steiger said slowly: 'You didn't go home to Germany for your leave? What did you do?'

He saw Dietrich's head drop, and heard his voice broken and small, like a child's. 'There's nothing anyone can do. You least of all!'

'Why do you say that?' Steiger ignored the bitterness in Dietrich's voice. 'You are my responsibility!'

With sudden defiance Dietrich burst out: 'She's a French

girl! I thought—I thought . . .' He seemed to be lost and floundering in the secret which had become too big for him alone. 'And now I've betrayed her, I was too damned gutless to go to her when she needed me!' He reached out and seized the parapet, his eyes blind to everything but the picture of her face. 'Cowardice runs in our family, you know. I fought it. With her I might have amounted to something——'

'What happened to this girl?' Steiger was torn between an unexpected concern and pity and the sudden feeling of urgency Dietrich's admission had revealed.

The Group was to sail in two hours. That had to be remembered above all else. The five U-boats were being sent to one of the worst areas of the Atlantic, the congested approaches to the English Channel, where enemy frigates hunted in killer-groups, and destroyers worked with aircraft in an unending battle to escort the rich convoys into harbour.

Dietrich's grief was like a slap in the face, as if to tell him that he was not the only one hampered by a woman's attraction, an affair with no future, a nagging idea which might kill them all if it caught him off guard in the face of danger.

He heard Dietrich say quietly: 'Her father might be one of the saboteurs. But she did not know, *she* couldn't have known!' His last words were shouted at the sky like a challenge.

The door opened and Wellemeyer stood hugely in the yellow glare. 'Captain Bredt's coming down to the briefing. He glanced curiously at Dietrich's face and Steiger's own uncertainty.

'Very well. I will come at once.' Steiger thrust his hands into his pockets, his fingers balled into two tight fists. He had to concentrate, to make himself ready to lead, and to serve those who trusted him. 'We'll talk of this later. But right now there is more at stake than our particular feelings!' He seized Dietrich's arm and propelled him roughly through the door, his voice harsh but compelling. 'And remember that a coward is not born, Heinz! Cowardice breeds from something unknown. At least we know *our* fate!'

Afterwards Steiger wondered what had made him betray himself to Dietrich. It was as if he had broken some unwritten rule. He told himself that there were no such things as premonitions, onlv fears.

12: Atlantic Harvest

Max König turned up the collar of his waterproof coat and peered at the clear sky. A few gulls still swooped and circled effortlessly above the U-boat's sharp white wake, and on the lip of the starboard horizon König could just discern a faint purple haze, the French coastline.

Moses Rickover spoke through the corner of his mouth without lowering the powerful Zeiss glasses from his eyes. 'Pointe de Penmarch. The last we'll see of land for a bit!' He shot a quick glance at the restless figure of the Officer of the Watch. 'Still, this is more like it. A spell of lookout in this weather will soon blow away that stinking wine!'

König nodded slowly. It was quite fantastic that it could be the same Atlantic as before. In the sharp sunlight the sea glittered in one vast sheet of opaque green, broken here and there by unexplained patches of dark blue, but devoid of even a gentle cat's-paw to betray the power of the depths below. Every inch of glittering water seemed to act as an individual mirror, so that the men who crowded the bridge repeatedly blinked their eyes and readjusted their glasses against the glare. The sun was weak, but after the weather they had previously endured and survived, it was more than enough to lift the spirits of the men on watch as they felt its gentle warmth against their salt-coated faces.

The Group had sailed from St. Pierre in the dim morning light; now, two and a half hours later, they were well clear of the coast, with the open sea lifting and falling beyond the bows.

Rickover nudged König from his thoughts. 'There! See her? That's the next boat in the line!'

König steadied his elbows on the rim of the bridge. As he did so he felt the uneven ridge of steel where the destroyer's gunfire had flayed across this very place and had killed the gunners and lookouts. He shuddered, and then held the glasses on the spray-distorted silhouette of a conning-tower. He could clearly make out the bright red hammer painted on the side of the grey steel, and knew it was Wellemeyer's boat. The Group was steering in the formation of a giant diamond, with the senior boat dead in the centre. The lookouts took turns in finding their four companions as they pushed their sharp stems through the unbroken water at a steady fifteen knots, and found comfort in their closeness.

Rickover whispered, 'First Lieutenant seems worried!'

König shot a quick glance at the officer. Dietrich *was* looking strange. He hardly seemed to lift his head above the rim of the bridge, and his glasses hung unheeded about his neck. He strode back and forth across the tiny gratings. Three paces across then three paces back, like a caged animal.

'Woman trouble I expect,' Rickover added after a moment's thought. 'The officers seem to get rather entangled in that respect!'

'Silence on the bridge!' Dietrich paused momentarily in his walk, his eyes sweeping across the hunched figures silhouetted against the green sea. The watch settled down into an attentive silence, and Dietrich resumed his pacing.

König was pleased at the sharpness in Dietrich's voice. He wanted to make the most of the sea's freshness and impersonal beauty. Rickover still stood pressed beside him, and that was enough. Words were not needed to show that there was friendship nearby. He watched the narrow spit of headland merging with the horizon haze, and wondered what and where the next challenge to his security would be. It was strange that he rarely thought of the sea's dangers in such a personal way. If death came to the U-boat it would be sudden and violent, but there would be no humiliation, no last desperate pretence.

A light glittered above the mist on the headland. Probably a far-off car windscreen, invisible, beyond the reach of even the most powerful lens, yet still strong enough to capture the sun's rays and throw them back across the endless movement of the Bay.

The light reminded him of that solitary lighted window in his mother's house, and the silent figure who had stared past him into the street.

He felt a strange tremor run through him, so that he was afraid to draw his breath. Around him he could feel the companionable cluster of familiar figures, and through the open hatch he recognised the throat-catching aroma of bacon and coffee. Nobody else behaved as if anything abnormal was happening, and the other submarine cruised steadily abeam, its high stem throwing back an unbroken curtain of spray. Yet the tiny flashing light had been joined by two more, and already they were somehow below the blur of the headland, yet above the water itself.

König swallowed hard and then heard himself shout: 'Aircraft, sir! Bearing green nine-oh!' In spite of his experiences and the sufferings which had hardened him against most things, he realised for the first time that he had become more than just another person, he had become part of this boat. And as such he was still afraid of showing himself an amateur, just like any other new recruit standing lookout for the first time.

Lieutenant Dietrich was already at his side, and together they watched the three aircraft streaking across the water, their wings wafer-thin and lost against the shimmering background.

The gunners were swinging their steel-blue muzzles towards the intruders, and a warning Very light burst above Wellemeyer's U-boat as his lookouts found and reported what König had already seen.

Rickover said breathlessly, 'Probably ours!'

But there was no answering signal from the aircraft, which suddenly veered away towards the rear of the Group's wide diamond, their narrow shapes changing course with such speed and precision that they momentarily appeared as three silver crosses flung from the sea itself.

König waited for the order to dive, but heard Dietrich say into the voice-pipe: 'Captain on the bridge! Enemy aircraft circling the Group! Believed Mitchell bombers!'

König then remembered what Horst Jung had told him. If several U-boats were caught on the surface together, it was usually considered better to remain so. Together their combined fire-power was said to be more than a match for any medium or heavy aircraft.

There was a scrape of feet on the conning-tower ladder, and König felt the Captain brush past him and on to the forepart of the bridge. Steiger was hatless, and his short black hair made a marked contrast with the cruel white scar on his forehead. He glanced at Dietrich and then lifted his glasses to search for the aircraft.

Everyone was quite silent, so that the playful hiss of the parting bow wave and the confident rumble of the diesels intruded into the sun-warmed steel platform, giving an air of unpreparedness and indifference to the menace symbolised by the flashing shapes astern.

Steiger grunted. 'You're right, they are Mitchells. They are turning to get the sun behind them.' In a louder tone he said: 'Now watch them closely, you gunners, and remember what you've been taught! Don't waste shots, and try to keep a steady fire if they dive on us!' To Dietrich he added: 'Damned poor lookouts! How in hell's name did they get so close without being seen?'

Dietrich eyed him defensively. 'I don't know, sir.'

'Well, it's not your fault, Heinz. Fritz Wellemeyer's boat was nearer. They must be asleep over there!' He thought for a few moments, his eyes narrowed to slits against the playful glare. 'Open up R/T communication with the Group. No firing until they close to attack.'

He waited until Dietrich had pushed past him to the voice-pipe, and found time to notice that the lieutenant's face was completely without expression or emotion. He forgot Dietrich's troubles as a man called, 'Here they come!'

The three aircraft dived in a straight shallow dive, until they were skimming above the water as if on a tight-wire. When they were barely a mile astern of the last U-boat in the Group the rear pair of bombers separated and fanned towards the two outriders, Wellemeyer's boat and Otto Kunhardt's, which was at present hidden in a faint patch of surface haze.

Steiger watched the brief glint of silver as the first bombs detached themselves from their nests and plummeted downwards. He frowned at these tactics, knowing from experience that the bombs had little chance of reaching their slender targets. He lifted his glasses and watched as the bombers swung clear of the speeding U-boats and began to circle astern once more.

Petty Officer Hartz, who had come on deck to personally supervise the Vierling crew, called, 'What do you make of it, sir?'

'A waiting game, Hartz. They will either call up reinforcements or they are hoping that we will dive. The last boat to go under stands a good chance of getting bombed!'

Hartz dabbed his streaming eyes with his glove. 'Cunning bastards!'

Another ten minutes dragged by, with the three aircraft circling astern. The Group retained its course and speed, and the blur of headland fell behind the horizon, leaving them nakedly exposed on an empty, glittering sea.

It all looked so playful that Steiger felt a prickle of impatient anger rising within him. If they dived they would have to run deep. With five hundred miles yet to steam before they even reached the allotted patrol area, it could only mean waste of time and fuel. Yet if they stayed surfaced they would certainly be open to fresh attack. In the Atlantic their own Focke Wulfs played the same game with the enemy. For days they would circle a convoy, sending out homing signals to call up every U-boat within miles, while all the time the convoy twisted and turned, and made every effort to shake off their hatred followers. It was all a question of time and speed, of endurance and experience.

Lieutenant Hessler had arrived on the bridge and stood silently behind his captain. After a while he said, 'They are keeping well back out of range!'

Steiger nodded, his mind busy elsewhere. 'Make a signal to Headquarters,' he said at length. 'Request air cover immediately!' A few fighters from Lorient would soon send these insolent intruders running for home.

'Aircraft diving, sir!'

So they would make another attempt. 'Open fire when your guns bear!' To Hartz he added. 'Even if they stay out of range it will stop them from thinking we're asleep!'

The bombers tried another kind of attack. Two of them climbed like silver tridents towards the clear sky, while the other plunged straight for the U-boat which lay furthest astern. With a belch of black smoke the Vierling began to spit tracers towards the sun, and from either beam, as if rising from the sea itself, other tracers lifted lazily from their consorts and fanned across the path through which the bombers would pass. The low-level attacker had begun to weave a zig-zag course, its flashing propellers almost skimming the flat water, each second bringing it roaring towards the low black speck of the small conning-tower.

Steiger nodded. 'A clever move that! They are trying to divide our fire while they go for Weiss's boat together!' His voice was quite calm, almost matter-of-fact, but he was inwardly seething with apprehension as he watched the tracers groping vainly for a target. He wondered how the U-boat's young captain would stand up to this sort of attack. If his nerve failed and he tried to dive, he was a dead man along with his crew. If he held on his course he must be ready for instant action.

'Bombs falling, Captain!'

Steiger had been watching the low-level attacker with such fierce concentration that he was almost surprised to see the first stick of bombs fall from the sky.

Tall slender water-spouts rose on either side of the conning-tower, but after what seemed like minutes they saw the stick-like outline of the U-boat emerge apparently unscathed.

'Here comes number three!' Young Rickover was pointing excitedly.

The bomber which skimmed so wildly across the top of the water had turned with surprising suddenness and was now tearing towards their own boat.

The bridge vanished in a pall of smoke as every gun began to hammer and crack at the thin, twisting target. With an ear-splitting roar the twin-engined bomber lifted from its collision course and screamed over the periscope standards. Two small bombs seemed to bounce across the green water before they exploded with sharp suddenness on the port side of the hull. The air rang with splinters and whining bullets as the bomber's own gunners sprayed the boat's whaleback as a parting gesture.

But Steiger was watching the small orange flashes which rippled momentarily along the bomber's underbelly. Somebody had scored a hit, although with every boat firing as fast as its gunners could aim and reload, it was impossible to tell who had done the impossible. The bomber climbed swiftly towards the sun, but seemed to falter as a long trail of black smoke began to pour from its fuselage. The guns paused in their song, and Steiger could hear cheers from one of the other U-boats. The bomber was losing height, and even as they all watched, two parachutes appeared as if by magic against the pale sky. But no one else had time to jump clear before the aircraft dived, hit the water and then lifted in a final ricochet before disappearing in a welter of spray and smoke.

Steiger said calmly: 'Make a signal to Headquarters. We do not require air-cover after all.' He watched as the two other bombers dwindled into the distance. 'Then report survivors down in this area. A flying-boat can pick them up. They will spend the rest of their war without flying!'

He heard some of the seamen laugh and saw them grinning at him. It was amazing how easy it was to put new heart into them once they had been given evidence of their own strength.

Dietrich reported in a strained voice, 'No casualties or damage in Group, Captain.'

'Good! Now perhaps we can get on our way in peace!' He glanced at Dietrich's face and said quietly: 'I spoke to Major Fischer before we sailed, Heinz. His men have interrogated several suspects, including a clockmaker called Marquet.' He watched Dietrich's eyes widen with something like terror. 'But there was no girl arrested. He was quite definite about that!'

Dietrich rubbed his eyes with the back of his hand, and then stared blankly across the empty water towards the faint cloud of smoke and the tiny yellow specks of the airmen's lifejackets. 'No girl at all?' His voice was a mere whisper.

'No girl.' Steiger watched him closely. 'And even the others are only suspects. They will not be punished if they are innocent.' His voice hardened. 'But if they had anything to do with that sabotage I personally will demand their execution! There is far more at stake now than your personal pride!'

Max König, who was bending to pick up a glove, stiffened as he listened to the officers' tense and urgent voices. He glanced quickly at Dietrich's stricken features and remembered him as he had looked in that other place, in that street when he had stumbled blindly towards the harbour as if running away from something too terrible to face.

König turned guiltily away as Dietrich stared past him with unseeing eyes and said in a low voice, 'If anything happens to that girl I shall kill myself!'

Steiger stiffened. 'If anything happens to this boat because of your negligence I shall kill you first!' He said it without anger or contempt, but his grey eyes were fixed on Dietrich's face and left no doubt as to the sincerity of his threat.

All that day the five submarines drove steadily westward, and the sea remained empty and without menace.

Watchkeepers joked and laughed, and from the forward messdecks came the cheerful sound of a mouth-organ.

Steiger alone mistrusted the enemy's silence, and he spent most of his time on the open bridge, his face turned towards the western horizon as if to find a clear, safe way for his command and the men he was beginning to recognise as individuals.

He repeatedly tried to stamp out these ideas and to retain his old detached hold over the men he had once regarded as a mere weapon in his hands. Dietrich's grief and fear of fear made him realise only too well what would happen if he once released his hold over them. Yet as the time dragged by, and each turn of the propellers drove them all nearer another challenge, he found he could no longer depend on his self-discipline, his past faith in himself.

The sun dipped towards the still calm sea, and he found that he had become unsure, and the realisation of his bared weakness made him sweat with sudden panic. Others before him had gone through this. Some through carelessness or strain, and others because they had simply driven themselves too long and too hard.

The hunter's moment of weakness, when his back is suddenly laid open to the weapons of an adversary. It was all the same thing. The first night stars shone palely above the crisp bow wave, but for once Steiger could find no comfort or reserve of understanding.

. . . . .

'All torpedoes running, sir!'

The hydrophone operator's voice intruded briefly on Steiger's thoughts as he peered through the sun-dappled lens and held his forehead firmly against the rubber pad on the periscope.

The first kill of the cruise, and everything was dropping into place. The flat green sea with its leisurely swell and small glittering wavelets seemed to swim towards his eyes as he watched the distant alien shape of the big ship. Yet around his cramped body he could feel the penetrating chill of the control room and the watchful tenseness of his men. The electric motors purred in such a fine key that Steiger could almost imagine the U-boat congratulating itself on another successful chase which was soon to be completed.

For three days they had followed the damaged tanker, and now the waiting and the manœuvring was almost done. Steiger had ordered the remainder of the Group to stay in their patrol areas, lest a sudden gathering of U-boats excited the attention of more enemy escorts. He swung the periscope slowly to watch the tiny silver shape which seemed to hover on the horizon itself. For three days he had managed to dodge the faithful Sunderland flying-boats which had flown one at a time from their English base to keep watch over the labouring tanker.

He watched the ship with something like sadness, a feeling he often experienced on these occasions. It was a small intimate picture he held in his sights, a peaceful sea, a big listing ship with its attendant tug, a sense of timelessness and tranquillity.

Even now the four torpedoes would be reaching their maximum speed and streaking through the quiet water to shatter the small illusion.

The Sunderland was beginning to turn once more, the sun gleaming momentarily across the tilted wings. It too looked peaceful, distance hiding the searching airmen and the racks of depth-charges which waited for men such as Steiger.

He was about to order the lowering of the periscope when the first torpedo struck home. He watched the bright orange glow which was followed immediately by a towering column of water and its attendant pall of smoke and flames.

Seconds later the drum-roll of an explosion thundered against the U-boat's hull so that the periscope quivered in his hands.

'Down periscope! Ninety metres!'

A muscle jumped in his cheek as other explosions followed the first. Already the U-boat was diving deep, but in his mind's eye he could clearly see the dreadful sequence of events he was leaving behind. The tanker rent and blasted, the peaceful afternoon changing to an inferno of hell.

Steiger had seen tankers burn before in the Atlantic. One he had watched from the surface in the middle of a warm summer's night. He had seen the blast of the first torpedo open the bowels of the heavily laden ship so that the blazing oil fanned across the sea itself in a field of bright fire. Men had been swimming nearby, dark anonymous heads and thrashing arms, who made for the only solid thing they could see illuminated in the savage glare. Steiger had ordered his deck party to stand by on the forecasing to pull the wretched survivors aboard, but even as he watched he had realised that the blazing oil was gaining on the sodden swimmers, and that one by one they were being overtaken and burned alive.

With the mounting heat scorching the paint on the front of the conning-tower he had steered his boat just a little bit nearer. It had suddenly become terribly important that someone should survive, that he should beat the oncoming fire.

They had at last pulled one man aboard, his body soaked with oil fuel, his eyes white and staring in his blackened face.

With the engines thrashing, the U-boat went astern from the holocaust, while the men on deck shaded their faces from the heat and peered across at the tanker's tilting shape as it lifted its stern towards the sky. Even the plates of her hull glowed red, and she shimmered in her own steam like a terrible phantom ship.

Some of Steiger's men had gone forward to catch hold of the one survivor, who still stood staring at the end of his own ship. But as they advanced along the narrow casing he turned towards them, his eyes gleaming in the dying fires. He had screamed one word, as if the sound had been wrenched from the dead throat of every other man in the tanker's crew.

Then he had evaded the outstretched hands and had leapt over the side, his small figure immediately lost in the black waters.

Steiger had remained staring at the empty casing, his ears still ringing with the man's last cry. '*Murderer!*'

It came back to him now as further explosions, muffled and indistinct, sighed against the hull.

He did not need to hear Braun's report as he readjusted his earphones, 'Ship breaking up, Captain!' to know that this latest prize was already on its way to the bottom.

He shook himself and tried to wipe the picture from his mind. 'Well done, lads! That's one load of fuel the Tommies won't get!' He heard the word passed down the hull, and listened to their cheering.

Luth said quietly, 'Steady on ninety metres, Captain.'

The Coxswain reported, 'Course oh-four-five, Captain.'

Steiger walked slowly to the chart-table and stared down at the faded pencilled lines. 'Bring her round to her original course, Reche. We will rejoin Group Meteor's area as soon as possible.'

He glanced up to see that Lieutenant Reche was watching him with something like fascinated horror. Of course, *he* would understand. He was an ex-merchant seaman, he knew that a ship was more than just a target or a pile of scrap metal. Only the amateurs and the desperate were without feeling of any kind. Far, far away they heard the dying thunder of exploding depth-charges as the Sunderland groped vainly for the attacker.

Another hundred miles and the tanker would have reached port. That was a long way, but probably little after the thousands of miles they had already come. With home so near and safety so assured, it was little wonder that a man's mind might wander. The pilot of that last flying-boat may have been thinking of a job almost completed, and a girl who might be waiting in Plymouth. A lookout might not have been watching as the deadly salvo had been fired.

All small distractions after days of strain and vigilance. But small or not, they allowed the unseen enemy his one chance. And that was enough.

. . . . .

Group Meteor had only another twenty-four hours to go before a fresh alarm was raised. A signal from Headquarters, followed almost immediately by a short-wave transmission from a scouting Focke Wulf, brought the five U-boats to an instant state of readiness.

Steiger tightened the scarf about his neck as he mulled over the brief fragments of information. A small convoy with six escorts was approaching their area, having just successfully fought off another U-boat attack in mid-Atlantic.

Six escorts. If the facts were right it meant that there was almost one warship per merchantman. He wrote his plan of campaign on a pad and pushed it across the chart-table to Dietrich.

'Pass this at once to the Group. We will close the convoy just about dawn.' He watched his words pass across Dietrich's pale face. Nothing. If I had said that Winston Churchill was personally in command of the convoy it would have made no difference. Aloud he said sharply: 'Lower the Snorchel, Chief! Have your engine-room staff informed of all that is required!' He saw Luth nod, and he added to the control room at large: 'A good fast target. But I don't want to get sunk by one of our own zealous commanders!' There was a faint spread of laughter and he relaxed slightly.

He glanced at the clock. Four hours to go. He found that he was wishing the time was now. Or never.

'See that a good meal is served at once!' A petty officer hurried away to pass his order to the galley. The men were always better with full bellies.

Lieutenant Hessler was at his side. 'Surface attack, Captain?'

Steiger bit back his annoyance. It was an oversight, but he should have remembered. It was his own fault. 'Tell the First Lieutenant to add it to my Group signal, Hessler.'

Damn this waiting! Steiger's fingers groped for the button of his bridge coat and began to tug in short, angry movements.

A surface attack at dawn. A straightforward table-top exercise with small metal counters and gay flags. Except that here the counters were real. He stood heavily against the chart-table, his fingers jerking at the button, his face set in a grim frown, so that the passing seamen avoided his eye, thinking that their captain was merely displeased.

Without studying the chart further Steiger knew how it would appear. The silver line of the dawn, with the unknown convoy coming straight out of the darkness. Five conning-towers with the rising sunlight behind them. It was dangerous, but the report said that the enemy ships were fast. There was no time for complicated manœuvring at periscope depth. There was no time for anything.

Dietrich appeared at his elbow. 'Reply from Captain Wellemeyer, sir. He asks permission to skirt the convoy and attack submerged.' He waited as Steiger took in the import of Wellemeyer's message.

The big Berliner was experienced and clever. He knew the dangers, and was tactfully reminding Steiger of what might lie ahead.

'Reply in the negative!' Steiger's anger felt sour in his throat.

'Nothing else?' Dietrich's eyes were fixed on his face.

Steiger swung on him. 'What do you suggest? Would you like to tell everybody to forget the whole thing? Perhaps you imagine the war would end and the Allies would come and shake our hands, eh?' He was still glaring after Dietrich had gone to the radio room.

Damn them all! All watching and waiting! Well, let them, he thought savagely.

He peered down at the chart and thought briefly of the old-time jousts with mounted knights in armour. A line of ships was steering straight for the Channel Approaches, and a line of U-boats was waiting to match their strength. In a few hours the world would know who had been right and who had made a victory. And a few hours after that the world would have forgotten the whole incident.

He stared incredulously at Seaman Stohr's red face. 'Well?'

'I've laid your breakfast in your cabin, Captain. There's a fresh tin of gherkins for you, too.'

Steiger shook his head. Even Stohr had his worries, so there was no point in keeping him in suspense, even if the thought of tinned gherkins made his stomach turn over.

'Thank you, Stohr. That was very considerate.'

Petty Officer Hartz stepped aside as his captain passed down the centre passageway. To one of his gunners he said proudly: 'Take a lesson from your captain! See him, did you? Cool as ice, and not a care in the whole damned world!'

. . . .

Rudolf Steiger climbed quickly through the hatch as the water surged and gurgled from the bridge, and the U-boat bared itself once more to the dark sky. He shivered in spite of his thick coat, and fumbled with his night glasses as the lookouts and gunners scrambled up behind him.

'Keep silent there!' His voice was low but harsh enough to accentuate the silent hostility of the dawn, and he looked for the first time at the open sea beyond the slowly moving bows.

Hardly a ripple, with the black, glassy water cruising towards the low-trimmed hull in an endless procession of silent dunes. God, it was cold. He swung his glasses slowly across the curtain of sky and sea, and heard the soft chink of metal as the gunners unlimbered their weapons behind him. Lowering his head he peered at the luminous dial of his watch, and wondered if the other boats were yet in position.

Another glance through the glasses. Empty, yet full of movement. Any minute now, and somewhere out there a British radar operator would peer at his screen and rub his sleep-starved eyes with alarm. Sooner or later the five pin-points symbolising the conning-towers of the Group would begin to show themselves, and then what? He readjusted the unfamiliar blue cap on his head and tried to think through the mind of the Convoy Commander. He had discarded his white cap on surfacing. Even a small thing like that might betray their whereabouts when action was joined.

He rested his hand on the attack-sight, feeling the damp cold and the rasp of salt.

The British Senior Officer would order an alteration of course for the merchant ships and detach half or more of his escorts to attack the submarines. He might also signal for additional support, but that was unlikely. Too far out for heavy air cover, and no other convoys in the vicinity. Yes, it was very unlikely. The detached escorts would charge at the U-boats, possibly under the impression that they had surprised a German wolf-pack surfaced to recharge batteries. Then they would expect the startled Germans to dive, to begin the usual desperate game of hide and seek. Depth-charges versus U-boat cunning.

A metallic voice whispered from one of the telephones which had just been plugged into the bridge's nerve system, 'All tubes at the ready!'

Five submarines, twenty-six torpedoes in the first salvoes. No escort commander would expect a concerted attack on his own ships. The merchantmen were the real prizes, but they would have to wait.

Another disembodied voice: 'Strong radar echoes, Captain! Confused but steady!'

He heard Hessler passing instructions to his men, and wondered what the seamen behind him were thinking. He thought, too, of the new homing torpedoes which now waited behind the opened bow doors, and tried not to contemplate the possibility of faults or failures.

'Stop engines!'

The electric motors were so quiet that he could only tell by the boat's sluggish motion that his order had been obeyed. The enemy radar would be surprised at this. Unmoving targets. He could almost imagine the suspicion and the tense expectancy on every bridge. Petty Officer Hartz stood quietly at his side. He could not see him, but he could hear the man's heavy breathing.

'Soon now, Hartz.'

'Too damned dark to see anything, sir!'

Steiger was glad the man could not see the anxiety on his face. The cloud had thickened before the dawn. There was no light. This fact might be a help, it might be an enemy. It was too early to decide.

The lookout who swayed precariously on the periscope standards stiffened and leaned forward like a figure-head. 'Listen!' His voice was a loud whisper, so that every man froze. 'Something moving ahead, sir!'

Steiger closed his eyes and strained every fibre in his body. There it was, far off but steady, like unfettered water pouring over a sluice. He could well imagine the destroyers or whatever they were tearing through the black oily sea, with every man staring straight ahead into the darkness.

'Right, Hartz. You know what you have to do!' He counted seconds as the man hurried over the side of the conning-tower and landed with a thud on the forecasing. The enemy would be expecting the Germans to dive or to run away. Surprise was always the greatest weapon, and to catch basking U-boats stopped and surfaced was every destroyer captain's dream. He found that his legs were shaking uncontrollably, and he knew that he alone must act, if only to drive away the growing seed of doubt.

'Fire!' he shouted down at the invisible deck gun, and waited for the agonising seconds to drop away.

He heard the snap of steel, and Hartz's brusque, 'Shoot!'

The gun roared back on its mounting, yet the flashless powder of the charge hardly showed beyond the muzzle. The sharp explosion made Steiger's head reel, but he still remained staring dead ahead. One, two, three, he counted.

Harshly he snapped, 'Close your eyes!' Then as the star-shell burst above the oily water he ducked his head beneath the bridge screen. Within seconds the other surfaced U-boats fired their star-shells, and between the low clouds and the unbroken sea the night changed to arctic brightness.

Some of the star-shells went wide, so that the falling flares seemed lost in the vastness of the night, but others threw their eerie glow full across the four creaming bow waves, the starkness of their power illuminating every mast and every gun as the blinded ships dashed into their silvery arena.

Steiger tried to concentrate on Hessler's thick voice and the swinging arm of the attack-sight. He ignored the sudden bark of gunfire and the scream of a shell ripping overhead. The British gunners were momentarily blinded. In a few more seconds they would have fired their own star-shells to fall over and beyond the surfaced U-boats. Steiger had seen it all before. He had played a very dangerous game, and he could feel the sweat pricking at the wound in his shoulder.

'Fire one! Fire two!'

The orders were rapped out until the six tubes were empty. The torpedoes, released from their parent ship, gathered way and fanned out across the glittering water. The enemy escorts, three destroyers and a frigate, were already re-forming and wheeling into line ahead like the armoured knights of Steiger's imagination.

But the British had recovered from their surprise, and gunfire rippled and spat from each heeling deck, and shells screamed overhead with the sound of tearing silk. Two tall columns of water erupted alongside the conning-tower, and Steiger tasted the raw salt tinged with cordite. He heard Hartz's rapid orders, followed by the insistent roar from the deck gun. This time it was armour-piercing shell. There was little chance of a hit, but any additional confusion and noise would help.

The first destroyer quivered and slewed round as two torpedoes exploded deep below her keel. She staggered, all fierce dignity gone, and seemed to crumple with the force of the twin detonations. Even as Steiger watched her through his glasses he saw her funnel dip towards him, and found that he was looking straight into the tilting bridge, where seconds before her officers had been planning his own destruction. He could see their tiny oilskinned figures slipping and sliding like beetles down the tilting deck as the destroyer lost way and began to heel on to her side. The frigate, slower and separated from her fast consorts, received three torpedoes at three-second intervals. She did not heel over or lift her bows to the clouds. She simply erupted in one jagged sheet of flame, which painted the low clouds with reddening gold as far as the horizon.

'Full ahead both! Hard a-starboard!' Steiger rapped out his

orders as the second destroyer swung in a tight turn. Maybe she was about to ram him, or perhaps her commander was trying to avoid the next salvo of torpedoes. With her guns firing she received her death blow full in the fo'c'sle, so that the bows dropped clean away like the front of a bombed building. Briefly illuminated in the dying flares, Steiger saw the criss-cross of her bared bulkheads, with one solitary figure clinging like a fly to the severed deckhead.

The sea boiled and bucked with sudden fury, as if shocked into action by the savagery of the battle. But in fact, the erupting water was caused by the first destroyer's depth-charges exploding as the stricken ship plunged towards the bottom. Steiger gritted his teeth and felt the hull shiver beneath his feet from the force of the explosions. He shut out the picture of the few survivors caught in that terrible vice of destruction, their bodies hurled skywards, gutted like so many dead fish, and thought instead of what would have happened to those charges had he waited too long. A great hush seemed to fall over the water as the last flare hissed dying into the uneasy swell. Steiger realised with sudden shock that the fourth ship had gone without his seeing her. A whole ship, a builder's pride, a home for her crew, men like Dietrich and Petty Officer Hartz. He shook his head, dazed by the enormity and suddenness of their destruction.

'Dawn coming up, sir!' a seaman called out, his voice cracked with either shock or relief.

Steiger rubbed his eyes. 'Midships!' He peered at the luminous compass-repeater. 'Steer oh-nine-five!' Dazed, he crossed to the rating with the handset. 'Tell the First Lieutenant to contact the Group. We will re-form and carry on with the attack!'

Hessler reported, 'All tubes reloaded, Captain.'

Steiger drummed his fingers on the spray-dappled steel. Four ships sunk within minutes. If the enemy expected one thing, you must hand him another! They might still catch a straggler or two, but in any case they had struck a good blow for Germany.

'Signal from Headquarters, Captain!'

Steiger stared at the rating who had materialised out of the gloom. He realised that the grey light from the horizon was at last thrusting its way through the low, full-bellied clouds, and showed the vague outlines of his boat, the men on her bridge and the empty sea beyond. To himself he asked: Why am I so surprised and shocked? Did I not expect to see another dawn?

He realised that the seaman was still standing mutely with the pad in his hand.

'Well, has Lieutenant Dietrich had it decoded?' Damn Headquarters and their aimless battery of signals!

'No, sir. It's a Restricted Signal.' He was watching Steiger's wild face with something like awe. 'For you, sir!'

Steiger's teeth gleamed momentarily in his haggard face. 'I'll see to it later! There's work to do, or hadn't you noticed?'

The man gulped and hurried below.

'First Lieutenant reports signal from *U-1001*, Captain!' A messenger's face glowed in a sudden ray of watered sunlight, and Steiger could see the deep lines of tension around his pinched face. 'He is attacking one merchant ship at extreme range!'

Steiger nodded, and strode to the side of the bridge. Fritz Wellemeyer was the extreme limit of the patrol area. If he was having difficulty in securing contact with the rest of the scattered convoy, there was little point in continuing the chase.

'Make a signal to the Group, excluding Wellemeyer. Disengage. Resume previous patrol.' He hesitated, remembering the horror of their sudden slaughter. 'And say, "Well done!"'

He turned away as Reche, the Navigator, clattered on to the bridge for his new orders. It was always 'Well done'. Empty, meaningless words.

He narrowed his eyes to watch the sun probing through the cloud-bank above the horizon. Time to hide. To dive and reassess the night's work, to wait and prepare.

His fingers touched the crumpled signal in his pocket, and he thought of Captain Bredt and all those like him who waited by their maps and their statistics. 'Well done!' It was like a mockery, an insult to brave men who died without knowing why.

'Orders, Captain?' Reche's face looked a pasty yellow in the sunlight.

Steiger tore his mind free from his confused thoughts and opened his logbook.

13: So This is the Enemy

Torpedoman Stohr, the wardroom messman, placed a fresh pot of coffee on the table and slowly gathered up the pile of greasy plates.

Lieutenant Hessler leaned back on the leather cushion and gave a long-drawn sigh of contentment. 'Well done, Stohr! One of the best meals I've had for some time!' He waited until the rating had left the wardroom and then grinned at the other officers. 'A good meal before an action, and another immediately after, that's the right way to fight a war!'

Lieutenant Reche lifted his cup to his nose and savoured the coffee's strong aroma. Like the others he looked dazed, and seemed unable to accept the peaceful routine which had replaced those short terrible moments on the surface.

U-991, like her four consorts, had turned her back on the bright sky of day and was cruising slowly and comfortably at a depth of ninety metres. Occasionally a figure would pad purposefully past the wardroom entrance, but otherwise the boat seemed silent and relaxed. Most of the men would be asleep in their bunks, or like their officers, dozing over a last cup of coffee before sleep finally relaxed their taut bodies and gave peace to their minds.

Hessler shook his head in silent admiration and then said: 'The Captain is a real genius! The way he scuppered those destroyers! I still can't believe we are alive to remember our victory!'

Lieutenant Luth toyed with a slide-rule and watched the surface of his coffee shimmering to the electric motors' silent vibrations. 'No wonder the Tommies hate the name of Steiger. They have probably put a price on his head! I never thought I should see the day when submarines and escorts fought each other like that. I suppose that with convoys getting harder and harder to attack, we shall get a lot more of that sort of thing?'

Hessler shook his head, the excitement still bubbling in his voice. 'No, Franz. Before long we shall be sinking both supply ships *and* escorts! Even the Yanks will be unable to keep up with the rebuilding and launching of replacements!' He closed one beefy hand in a tight squeeze. 'When that stranglehold closes, that will be the end. No more fighting.' He gave a great sigh. 'All we will have to do is pick up the pieces, and show these idiots who is the real master!'

Luth smiled. 'It really is amazing what a little bit of success can do for our morale! On the last cruise we were nearly ready to cut our throats! Now everything is bright and sunny again!'

The Torpedo Officer drained his coffee noisily. 'Just think, Franz. We might even get sent to the Pacific when we've settled the Tommies and Ivan. If we worked with the Japs against the American Navy, imagine the time we could have!' He rolled his eyes. 'Little brown girls to wait on you hand and foot!'

'You'd like that!' Reche's red-rimmed eyes watched him with sudden bitterness. 'Don't you ever stop to *think*? One victory, and you seem to think *you*'ll still be alive to see it.'

Hessler's grin faded. 'Because that is how I keep going,' he said calmly. 'If I lived on my nerves like *some* people I'd have given up four years ago when I heard the first bang!'

Luth shifted in his seat. 'Live for the day. What else is there?'

All three looked up as Dietrich entered the wardroom and without speaking poured himself a cup of black coffee.

Luth asked quietly: 'Hello, Heinz. Is the boat steering itself?'

Dietrich glanced up momentarily and then concentrated on the enamel coffee-pot. 'The Coxswain is in control for the moment.' Then as the others still stared at him he added: 'The Captain wants all officers in here. Now.'

They all looked at each other, and Hessler said at length: 'What can be happening? Another attack, do you suppose?'

'Hell's teeth!' Luth leaned back and closed his eyes. 'Just when I was thinking of the Pacific and old Karl surrounded with dancing-girls!'

Dietrich remained standing, his pale eyes slitted against the steam from his cup. He ignored the lively banter between Luth and Hessler, although in some way he knew that they were doing it for his benefit. It must be another attack. That Restricted Signal to the Captain was probably the answer. He felt the anger being fanned into flame as he imagined all the countless staff officers and planners who might even now be directing the submarine to some new menace. He ran his eyes around the small wardroom. Like everyone in it, it was soiled, stained and worn out with use. There was neither warmth nor personality. It was merely a part of the main weapon, a tiny cog in the great machine. All over the Atlantic other men would be sitting or sleeping in their little steel boxes, and waiting. There was always something to wait for.

Stohr poked his head around the curtain and whispered confidentially, 'The Captain's just coming, sir.'

When Steiger entered he found them all on their feet facing him. Once again their faces had changed, and he could see the anticipation, mixed with anxiety, which confronted him in a hostile barrier. He placed his cap on the table, and found himself envying them their little haven of comradeship. It was strange how one damp, riveted portion of the hull could become so detached from the rest.

'Please sit down, gentlemen.'

It was strange, too, to see them all together like this. Usually they were either split into watches, asleep, or keyed-up to the agony of the chase and the kill. Now they sat, stiff and unsure of themselves, although *he* was the interloper.

How should he translate that bald Restricted Signal from Headquarters? How could he begin? Every U-boat commander at present at sea would have received that short coded message, or would do so the next time he was within radio contact. Each captain would be faced with the same task.

He cleared his throat, and realised with a start that the four pairs of eyes had dropped to his right hand, which had unconsciously begun to pluck at a button on his coat.

'Firstly, let me say again how satisfied I was this morning with your handling of the attack. It will shake the confidence of all escort ships in future if they know what might be expected.' He hesitated and then came to a decision. 'The signal I received from Headquarters affects you all, as it does every German wherever he may be. At first light this morning the Allies landed in France. Three main landings have been forced, and by now I expect the enemy have made some gains.' He watched his words sink in. 'This war has gone on for so long that the prospect of a full-scale invasion across the English Channel has become rather remote and even unlikely. Yet it was inevitable. War has never been won by stalemate, whatever the so-called historians would have us believe. We must accept what is happening, and face up to all its new problems. In a moment or two I shall inform the crew, but before I do, I want to impress upon all of you the importance of your own bearing and manner. An invasion has commenced. Successful or not, it will be contained, and Greater Germany will be able to withstand it. But in any case, our task remains the same. Every man, every enemy bullet, must be carried by sea, and we are the means to stop them! Any questions?'

Surprisingly, it was Hessler who spoke first. His square face was puzzled, with the expression of a man betrayed. 'How did they manage to get ashore, Captain? I mean, what of all the defences we have been hearing about?'

Steiger smiled. 'Defence in depth, Hessler. The old days of barricades are gone for ever!'

Reche was rubbing his chin, his protruding eyes fixed on some invisible chart. 'Northern France. Normandy, most likely, just as I always thought it would be!' He banged his hands flat on the table and bent his head in a convulsion of despair. 'They'll drive a wedge between us and Germany! We'll be cut off!'

Luth interrupted quietly, 'There's a lot of France to cover yet, my friend!'

But Reche said with a groan: 'Have you never seen an ice-berg when a crack starts from its top? It goes right through, and the two halves fall apart!'

Dietrich's voice intruded on Steiger's thoughts. 'Will we return to Base now?'

He shook his head. 'We will carry on with the patrol as before.'

Dietrich nodded. 'I see. Then there is a possibility that St. Pierre will be attacked while we are at sea?'

Steiger shrugged. 'There has always been that possibility. Air attacks throughout France will be stepped up. Sabotage and murder may become commonplace once the civilian population think we are relaxing our grip.' He eyed each officer in turn. 'So you can see how important it is to carry on whatever the setback may be. Our comrades in Russia have been fighting a bitter and merciless war for many months. They would laugh this French campaign to scorn. We must see that we are equal to their past efforts.' He picked up his cap, suddenly wanting to escape from their uncertainty. 'As you well know, the U-boat arm is the cream of the service. If ever our country needed us it is now!' He stepped into the passageway and strode towards the control room.

He had told them. Now he must prepare his signal for the Group, and rally them. Fighting a war in the Atlantic had always isolated them from their homeland. In the past, wherever and whenever their feet had touched European soil they had retained a contact. But now, as Reche had observed, they might be cut off. Supplies would be difficult, but at all costs Germany had to retain her Atlantic coast bases. If U-boats were forced back to German or Norwegian bases it would add thousands of hazardous miles to their passage routes, and cut their patrol time accordingly. He gritted his teeth. This was ridiculous thinking. The invasion would be smashed, just as in the coming summer the Russians would be finally thrown back. There was no other way.

In some ways this new threat might improve the situation in France, he thought. Captain Bredt and the others would be drawn together for their own security if for no better reason. He stopped in his tracks, so that Dietrich who was following almost collided with him. What of Trudi Lehmann? Would she still be at the Base, or had she already returned to Germany? He remembered the methodical sabotage and the hanged sailor with sudden anxiety. France would no longer be an apathetic and down-trodden country now that the Occupation Forces were on the defensive. It would be like a disturbed ant-heap, a killing-ground.

He felt Dietrich put the microphone in his hand. 'Loudspeaker system switched on, Captain!' Dietrich's face was empty, giving nothing away.

Steiger swallowed, his mouth suddenly dry. What in God's name is happening to me? Why should this news affect me so much? As I told them in the wardroom, the invasion was inevitable. He glanced quickly over the bowed heads of the men on watch. But so is death inevitable, and none of us can take *that* for granted either!

He pressed the button. 'This is the Captain speaking!'

* * * * *

Rudolf Steiger's voice penetrated every inch of the slowly moving hull, and until he had finished speaking hardly a man moved. In the gunners' small mess the men sat or lay like waxwork figures, each wrapped in his own interpretation of his captain's words.

'. . . and until that time no man among us must do less than his duty!'

Steiger's last words still hung in the damp air even after the routine voice of a petty officer snapped, 'Duty part of the Watch muster in the control room!'

The loudspeaker above Max König's head buzzed and went dead.

'Well, that's that!' Schultz, the ex-photographer, lay back on his narrow pipe-cot and glared angrily at the deckhead. 'Let's have a crack at the bastards!'

Muller, the coffin-maker, guffawed hollowly. 'Hark at our hero! He can't get enough damned fighting!'

Max König got slowly to his feet and walked across to Horst Jung's bunk. He could hardly contain the excitement which Steiger's announcement had given him. At last the dreadful period of nerve-racking limbo was over. One way or the other the pendulum had started to swing. He had to pinch himself to understand the full impact of Steiger's words. Allied troops on soil which had come to be accepted as Germany's by right of arms, by the power of fear and brute force. The Allies must have made quite sure of their preparations before attempting such an attack. They must be more than confident, they must be certain of victory. Perhaps it would be over sooner than he dared hope. It would seem strange, the streets full of alien uniforms, more regulations, fresh masters to serve. But this would be nothing to him, and those like him. Whatever the hardships, he would be able to survive, to breathe freely again. To the conquerors he might appear as just another bewildered ex-serviceman, an enemy from the past. But he would know that he was different from the rest, and that would be enough. He forcibly checked his excited thoughts. This was ridiculous, it was far too early to drop one's guard.

He leaned on Jung's bunk and looked down at the man's battered features. They were covered with a thick fuzz of grey, almost white stubble, which gave him the appearance of shabby old age. He was staring bleakly at the pipes which ran above his bunk, his face momentarily unguarded and bewildered.

König's elation stilled as he saw the change in the man. He had forgotten about people like Jung and Rickover and the rest of his comrades who had shared danger with him. While he had been thinking of his freedom, they had been staring at the door to a strange and frightening captivity.

'Well, Horst? What did you make of that?' He watched Jung's eyes re-focus, and saw the man's mouth turn down at the corners.

'The Captain did well to warn us. Times are going to be a bit hard, I reckon.' Jung grimaced and rubbed his hands down his thighs. He forced a grin, his uneven teeth making a cheerful crescent in his untidy face. 'Damned rheumatism again!'

König said cautiously: 'You should apply for a transfer, Horst. You've been in U-boats too long perhaps.'

'Ach, lot of nonsense! I'm as fit as I ever was!' He suddenly closed his eyes and said with unexpected fervour, 'God, what would happen if we lost, after all we've been through?'

König tore his eyes away. He felt like a traitor, a hypocrite. 'There is another life outside the navy, you know.'

Jung shrugged wearily. 'For the likes of you maybe. You've got education, a trade.' He shrugged again. 'I've got . . .' His voice trailed away into nothing.

König stared desperately at the dripping bulkhead. God, they're *all* like poor Horst! Living a giant delusion. They've believed in it firstly because they had no choice, and now because there is no alternative. Even the Captain must soon realise what is happening. And when he does, what then? Will he and his kind still struggle on into oblivion, or will they face their real responsibilities? He thought of Steiger's slow, measured voice, and wondered. Tradition and training had made the Captain what he was, just as he himself had been moulded by fate and personal disaster. With roles exchanged could they have been any different?

Jung was saying: 'I've a sister living in Emden. I was going to her when my time had expired. She has a small shop, you see, and now that her husband's been killed off she'll need someone to run it for her.' He gave a bitter laugh. 'We've never got on together, in fact I sometimes think she hates me. But, still, there it is!'

König said gently, 'That's not much of a future, is it?'

'When you've had an upbringing like mine, Max, it's all you can reasonably expect. Just a place to lay your head, and a few marks at the end of the day for a smoke and a glass. You hate this life. But later on, like me, you'll look back and remember all this differently.'

Jung sighed. 'Now leave me be, Max. I'm going to have half an hour's sleep before I go on watch.'

But later as König sat thoughtfully at the table, he could still see the overhead light shining in the boxer's eyes.

. . . . .

The flaming red stallion with sightless white eyes rose again and again on its hind legs, flailing the air with a mounting frenzy before crashing the hoofs down in a burst of exploding lights. Each time the hoofs seemed to be getting nearer and nearer to the body of Trudi Lehmann, which lay transfixed like a marble statue beneath the towering, crazed beast.

The figures faded into oblivion as a telephone buzzed above Steiger's bunk and jerked him awake from his nightmare. He sat dazed and uncomprehending for several seconds, the handset in his fist, his eyes blinking in the gloom of his cabin.

'Yes? Captain here!' He had to swallow hard to clear the croak from his voice.

'Officer of the Watch reports object in the water ahead, sir!' The communication rating's voice was clipped and without expression.

'Very well. I'll come at once.' He swung his long legs over the rim of his bunk, his mind still hazy as if reluctant to release the brief picture from his dream.

A quick glance at the clock. An hour to sunset. Only two hours since his head had touched his pillow. All day he had been planning and making arrangements. Signals to the Group, and answers from his four captains to study and digest. The Allied invasion was still not a day old, yet already it seemed as if he had thought of little else.

His feet took him rapidly to the control room. Another quick glance to tell his reawakening mind what was happening around him. Periscope depth. Dietrich standing beside the greased tube, his eyes on the clock. He felt some of the tension unwind within him. The Watch was still behaving in a routine manner. There was no immediate emergency apparently.

'Well? What's happening?' He kept his voice gruff and non-committal, and saw the shoulders of the hydroplane operators stiffen as they became aware of his presence.

'Object dead ahead, Captain.' Dietrich glanced at him warily. 'I think it is a rubber dinghy.'

'When did you last take a look?' Steiger knew the danger of unnecessary periscope work.

'Fifty seconds.' Seitrich was watching the clock again as if gauging his very life by minutes.

'Up periscope!' Steiger bent over the eyepiece and waited for the lens to break surface.

The sea looked just as before. Long unbroken rollers of pale green, but with shallow troughs already darkening in the fading light. A quick look around and overhead. Nothing.

He steadied the lenses on the small lifeless object which bobbed sluggishly over each successive roller, its bright orange sides making a violent contrast with the dark-edged water around it. He watched it for several seconds. Three heads were just visible above the curved edge of the dinghy. Probably dead. The Atlantic was littered with forgotten lifeboats and their skeleton crews, airmen in dinghies and lifejackets, and all the other flotsam of war.

'Down periscope! Stand by to surface!' He listened to the scream of the klaxon. 'Close up the forecasing-party, and get ready to haul that relic alongside!'

Men were scampering to their stations, and Steiger leaned his back against the periscope. 'Not one of ours. Most likely British.'

Reche had appeared blinking from the wardroom to hear the last part. 'Is it worth the risk, Captain? Leave the swine where they are!'

Steiger ignored him. 'Surface!' Already his feet were moving across the control room and up the long vibrating ladder. Lookouts and members of the deck party were crowding after him, their faces averted to avoid the inrush of spray as the hatch was opened.

The wet, cold slap of salt air against his face caught Steiger by surprise, and he cursed himself for his feeling of mental and physical exhaustion. Perhaps tonight there would be quiet and more time to rest. But not now.

'There it is, Captain! Dead on the starboard bow!' The man realised the double meaning to his words and grinned uncomfortably.

Steiger lifted his glasses and spoke from the side of his mouth. 'Stop both!' The dying thrust of the motors carried the U-boat's still streaming hull straight for the dinghy, and Steiger saw the seamen already preparing to throw their grapnels as the two contrasting craft moved to meet each other. Two strangers meeting in an empty sea. No-man's-land.

He steadied his glasses. Three figures sitting around the circular dinghy, their feet entwined over the crumpled body of a fourth. He watched their heads nodding and swaying in time with the playful rollers, and experienced the familiar chill across his neck. They seemed wrong and out of place here. Young, immature faces ashen from exposure and made pathetic by the ridiculous moustaches favoured by the Royal Air Force.

A grapnel dropped amongst the airmen's legs, and a heaving line tautened to bring the sagging dinghy squeaking alongside the starboard saddle tank.

A lookout murmured, 'Poor bastards!'

But a petty officer grated: 'Pay attention to your duties, you dolt! Just remember that they must be members of an anti-U-boat patrol plane! They would have laughed to see *you* go up in smoke!'

Petty Officer Hartz's red face moved along the forecasing and peered up at the swaying conning-tower. 'One of them's still alive, Captain!' He seemed for once uneasy. 'What shall I do with him?'

The caution, the apprehension and fear in Hartz's tone, made Steiger's throat contract with bitter anger. Hartz, a bluff, competent regular sailor, who must have seen every sort of hazard and danger at sea, was afraid of his captain's reply. It was as if he expected Steiger to scream 'Shoot him!' or 'Throw him back in the sea!'

Harshly he said, 'Keep him there for the moment and pass the word for the canvas stretcher so that he can be lowered safely down the tower.'

'Aye, aye, sir!' Hartz's face split into a grin. 'At once, sir!'

Steiger jerked himself from his brooding thoughts. 'And send a man into the dinghy to check the others! They won't be carrying any secret information, but check all the same!' He saw the uneasy shuffling amongst the deck party and enjoyed a flash of cruel pleasure. They were nearly all recruits down there. It would do them good to get a closer look at the cause of their sentiment.

The U-boat fell heavily into each low trough so that the small dinghy rose and fell with short, impatient jerks on the end of the heaving line.

Hartz leaned his gloved hands on the guardrail. 'Right, two men over the side. Pass that officer up here first. But take it easily. He's all but done for!'

Max König saw Rickover skid down the curved tank and leap into the centre of the dinghy, and as the hull rolled once more followed him down. All at once the submarine seemed huge and far away, and König remembered that it was supposed to be a common feeling for U-boat men to experience once they were temporarily released from their steel shell.

Rickover sat awkwardly between two of the crumpled figures, his youthful face suddenly defenceless and frightened. The dinghy rose and fell, yawed and staggered, and to König it appeared as if the dead airmen had drawn Rickover into their macabre dance.

With sudden urgency he rasped, 'Give me a hand with this one, Moses!'

Rickover retched and groped across the corpse in the bottom of the dinghy. Its face was under water, but the dead eyes still glared with fixed hostility at the tall conning-tower which swayed overhead. The hunter hunted. The eagle torn from the sky. König's thoughts were vague and troubled as he struggled with the airman's limp frame. He was a young officer, with two stripes on his waterlogged tunic. Probably the captain of the aircraft. His hair was long and fair, like Lieutenant Dietrich's. König shuddered. It was like pulling your own kind from the water.

Rickover's face was beside him as the other men reached down and grabbed the airmen from them. 'It's all different,' he stammered. 'I never thought they'd look like this!'

König tried to give a smile of assurance. Rickover had spoken of the enemy. What had he expected to see? He had been nearly two years at sea, yet he was only eighteen now. Months of fear and bravado, or tension and brief exultation. But, like the others, he had never *seen* the enemy. The enemy was sound, and destruction. The enemy was the stalking aircraft, or a wisp of smoke on the horizon, but not flesh and frailty like themselves.

Rickover sat in silence as König searched quickly through the tunic pockets of the dead men. 'I've been in the service longer than you, Max, yet you are as cool as ice. I was nearly sick just then!'

König bit his lip. That was careless. Rickover might remember later about the recruit who casually ripped the tunics of gaping corpses and ignored the accusing, empty eyes. 'You forget, Moses, I am older than you!' He hoped his voice sounded right.

'Get a move on there!' Hartz looked deformed against the setting sun. 'And bring up their watches as well! They're too precious to waste!'

König shrugged. It was easy to him. The concentration camp had taught him one lesson often and well. Dead men were harmless. They meant nothing. They were nothing.

Then he and Rickover were scrambling aboard again, and with the others stood looking down at the aircraft's one survivor. He lay on an oilskin, his eyes open, his blue hands shaking like frightened animals across his chest.

König stooped beside him and passed a blanket over his body as the stretcher was passed from the bridge and on to the forecasing. He cradled the man's shoulders in his arm, and saw a fleeting recognition pass across the shocked, vacant eyes.

A seaman said: 'Should have left him with the others! Off a bastard bomber, I shouldn't wonder!'

Another said: 'Careful with that stretcher! He's gone through enough by the look of him!'

König thought, So young, so lost and broken without his comrades and his machine. Something made him turn his head and look up at the bridge. Against the purple sky he could see Steiger's hunched shoulders and head bent in concentration. He is watching every move, thought König. Perhaps the Captain had seen what he had seen, and recognised himself in the limp, broken warrior.

They carried the man along the swaying deck, their uniforms dark against the airman's pale blue, but their faces merged in common suffering.

A knife flashed briefly and the line was severed from the dinghy. A small patch of colour, it drifted alongside, and as the submarine gathered way bobbed astern and vanished.

Steiger watched the airman pass, and heard himself say, 'Put him in my cabin, and do what you can for him.'

Some of the men nodded, all at once grave and protective, and Steiger despised himself all the more. It was an act, a cruel parody. The airman would be dead before dawn. Somehow you could see a thing like that if you understood the signs. Perhaps it would have been kinder to leave him with his comrades on that last endless journey.

He yawned and stretched his arms wide. 'Tell the control room to start charging batteries when ready. We will remain surfaced for the present.' Then, as an afterthought, 'Send my food up here to the bridge.' He would sit on his steel stool and stay with the night. Others could watch and worry. He would sleep in the open and perhaps that weird dream would return.

• • • • •

Six days after Steiger's Restricted Signal from Headquarters, *U-991* turned warily on another long beat of her patrol. Overcast skies and sudden vicious gales of wind swept away the memory of sunshine and success, and the ominous brevity of further signals helped to add to the tension which dogged every man aboard.

Day after day the business of war continued, however. Otto

Kunhardt and Fritz Wellemeyer on the extreme wing of the patrol area had together cornered and attacked a complete section of a broken convoy. They had torpedoed three ships and badly damaged an escort before escaping on the surface under cover of darkness. Lieutenant Weiss in *U-895* had sunk a damaged straggler, and Lehmann had torpedoed a small tanker at extreme range. The nerve-wrenching suspense mounted as every torpedo left its tube, as each weather-beaten ship lifted its broken stern to the sky or rolled in its final convulsion. *U-991* was no exception. With all but two tubes empty and fuel tanks half consumed, she seemed to have reached the end of her endurance for this patrol.

Heinz Dietrich clambered up the shining ladder and on to the bridge. He touched Reche's shoulder and relieved him of his Watch without even listening to his mumbled report. What did it matter? It was always the same. A good lookout. Listening and watching until every nerve screamed out for rest. A few hours' exhausted sleep below, and then on watch again. God damn this waiting! Get rid of these torpedoes and return to St. Pierre.

Dietrich felt almost faint with the exhaustion of worry and anxiety. Steiger had assured him that Major Fischer had not arrested a girl. Not *then*, but whole weeks had passed, a way of life was changing in Europe again, and who could say for sure what was happening? Even if she had been spared, was it likely she would look at him again? With her father arrested she would see him as just another enemy.

'Light, sir! Fine on the port bow!' A man's voice close by his ear made him start with surprise.

He fumbled with his glasses and peered through the dark grey turmoil of heaving water and white-capped waves. The hard light of the dawn as yet only filtered through the low clouds and seemed to accentuate the immensity of their task, the completeness of their loneliness.

He caught his breath. There it was. A brief pinpoint of light, like a torch close to the water. For one instant Dietrich imagined that it was another airman flashing his final signal for assistance. But in spite of his inner torment he was too hardened by experience to trust his first impressions at a moment like this. The open sea jeered at a man's humble beliefs, made mock of training and tested instruments.

'Strike me blind, sir!' The petty officer had shinned up the gyrating periscope standards and was peering through his night glasses. 'It's a ship! Right down in the damned water like a waterlogged raft!'

Dietrich bit his lip. A wreck most likely, with a few miserable survivors still aboard.

The excited voice above him added, 'By God, she's a tanker!'

Dietrich jerked himself alive. 'Call the captain! Sound off Action Stations!' With only two torpedoes left it might be necessary to use the gun.

Steiger seemed to be at his side before he had time to peer ahead at the low-lying ship. But as the U-boat lifted over the lip of a curling wave crest he caught one brief glimpse of the long, wedge-shaped hull, mastless and listing, with a fire-blackened bridge stark against the tumbling water like a burned-out building.

Steiger was rubbing his eyes, his face sunken in the dawn's unearthly light. 'Five and six to the ready! Range one thousand metres!' To the wind-swept bridge he added, 'She must be well loaded or she'd have gone down by now!'

A lookout called: 'All her boats seem to have gone, sir. Perhaps those men aboard climbed back after they were torpedoed and——'

Steiger stiffened. '*What* men?' He glared at the seaman behind Dietrich. 'What the hell are you talking about?'

'There was some sort of flashing from her, Captain.' Dietrich stared at him with surprise. 'Perhaps it was a deadlight left unclipped and a cabin light flashed as the ship rolled?'

Steiger licked his lips. 'Hardly. There'll be no power aboard *that* ship!' With sudden force he added, 'I wish to God you'd tell me everything when I come on the bridge, Lieutenant!'

'There it is again, Captain!' The man's voice was hushed because of his captain's outburst. 'It *is* a signal!'

A metallic voice intoned from the control room, 'Five and six tubes ready, sir!'

A silence fell over the open bridge so that the sea and wind intruded right amongst the small spray-dashed group of men who stared with watering eyes at the uncertain stammering light.

The petty officer read the feeble message very slowly, his voice almost lost in the hiss of spray as the U-boat's high stem sliced into a long unbroken roller. The wave broke and tumbled along the shining saddle tanks, its impact shaking the foot of the conning-tower and swirling around the feet of the deck-gunners.

'S O S!' The man's voice faltered. 'S O S!' The light paused and then flickered once more. The petty officer's mouth moved stiffly in the cold wind as he slowly translated the message. At length he reported: 'There are five men aboard, sir! Four of them too badly injured to be moved. Whoever is using the lamp must have seen us before we saw them.' He paused, and Steiger lowered his glasses to look at him. 'The message ends by asking you to spare them, sir. They're helpless. They might die anyway.'

Dietrich stared from the petty officer and back to Steiger. 'Well, sir?'

Steiger staggered against the steel side of the bridge, caught unaware by a sudden lurch, and felt something like raw madness exploding in his brain. They are helpless. They might die anyway! He tried to shut his mind to the picture of the wretched and wounded men as they sat somewhere on that battered superstructure and watched the slow approach of their executioner.

The airman had been bad enough. He had lingered on for three days after the U-boat had pulled him from the sea. Three days in which Steiger had found himself unable to stay away from his cabin and its attendant smell of decay and death. In his few moments of sanity the young pilot had talked of his home in England, quite clearly and without emotion, so that Steiger had seen the green trees and quiet Surrey lanes. Then at other times, as if he realised his time was running out more quickly, he had started to question Steiger. It was uncanny, almost frightening, to hear a dying enemy speaking your name with ease and familiarity. 'Oh yes, Captain, we all know about *you*!' Two red spots of colour had formed on the airman's cheeks as he broke into a fit of coughing. 'You are famous, so I suppose I should feel honoured to be your prisoner!'

Dietrich's voice made him turn. 'Do we *fire*, sir?'

They were all watching him, and in his desperation he could imagine the men in the control room and throughout the boat sitting and listening for the order he must give.

Must? What good was the ship? Waterlogged, with much of the cargo ruined, it might even sink if this gale persisted.

But if the weather moderated the salvage tugs would find her, and within days the rich cargo would be pumped into bombers and tanks to send them on their way across the English Channel.

He stared quickly again at the tanker. It was clearer now, the scars of a previous encounter clearly displayed in the growing light.

God, somewhere out there they were waiting for him to answer! If his own decision was hard how much worse the waiting must be for them.

The white spray lifted and fell across the tanker's wallowing bulwark as if to chase away the brief hope he might have fostered for saving the five survivors by dinghy. There was no way. Either fire or turn aside. A moment of sanity, or was it weakness?

He remembered the airman who had died in his cabin with such a swift finality. Steiger had been drowsing in his chair when the man had struggled up on the bunk, his eyes huge in the shaded lamplight. 'You can't win! Don't you see that now? You've turned the whole bloody world against you!'

Steiger had called for the messman, but the airman had died with a twisted smile of relief on his bloodless lips.

You've turned the whole bloody world against you!

He bent over the attack sight, his heart painful as he watched the cross-wires fasten around their prey.

There was no other way after all.

'Fire five! Fire six!' *Forgive me!*

He made himself stand facing the gusher of fire and spray which blasted the tanker to fragments, and when the grey sea had eventually extinguished the blaze he said slowly: 'I suppose that you are wondering why I hesitated, Heinz? When so many men are dying every hour why should five more make any difference?' He had intended his voice to be harsh enough to dispel his own doubt, but his words merely sounded defensive and wretched.

Dietrich stared at him for several seconds before replying. 'Just *one* man can make all the difference, Captain.' He eyed Steiger challengingly. 'All the difference in the world!'

A shutter seemed to fall behind Steiger's cold eyes, and he appeared to pull himself together with one final effort.

'In war a wrong decision can often be better than no decision at all. Duty allows little room for inner grief!'

He stared hard at Dietrich, but the latter dropped his eyes as Steiger added: 'Resume patrol. Call me if you sight anything. *Anything!*'

Dietrich walked back to the side of the bridge and groped for his glasses.

Just for a few seconds he had seen below Steiger's guard. Once he might have felt pity, but when he thought of how much they all depended on this strange, remote man, his nev knowledge unnerved him.

14: Homecoming

Rudolf Steiger stood high up in the forefront of the bridge, his cap pulled down to shield his eyes from the warm afternoon sunlight, as *U-991* glided alongside the grey stonework of the harbour.

Heaving lines snaked ashore to the waiting dock party, and Steiger noticed how sunburned and smart these shore-based sailors looked compared with his own haggard and pale-faced men.

Hessler's harsh voice goaded the deck-parties into renewed effort until at last the rebellious mooring wires were reeved through the fairleads and hauled ashore to be secured to the massive stone bollards.

Steiger glanced briefly at the four other U-boats of Group Meteor. They had arrived earlier, and already looked lifeless and deserted. The bright red of their ensigns, each with the black cross and swastika, made colourful contrasts with the slime-streaked and rust-dappled hulls. Every one of the hundreds of miles they had patrolled had left some mark, some scar, so that they looked as unkempt as Steiger's crew, who stared so hungrily at the green shoreline and the whitewashed buildings around the town square beyond the harbour.

'Finished with main engines!' He heard his order repeated, the jangle of telegraphs, and then felt a great shudder as the submarine's hull fell silent and inert after what seemed like a year.

'All secure fore and aft, Captain!' Hessler's black-stubbled face was squinting up from the oil-smeared casing. He seemed to have shrunk since they had sailed from this place. But his manner was still the same.

'Very good. Inform the First Lieutenant, and then clear the boat. Fall the men in on the jetty and march them to the Base. I don't want a disorganised rabble this time!' He was surprised at the sharpness in his own voice. Amazed even that he was still able to concentrate on these small details. But small though they might be, they still had to be remembered.

He glanced up at the crisp ensign overhead, floating in the steady Atlantic breeze which probed above the harbour wall. Like the flag, for instance. To his men, who were too worn out to care, it might be just another piece of trimming. But Steiger knew well enough the impression it made to watching eyes ashore. A prick of pride, a touch of awe, even envy, which was the very stuff of discipline and endurance.

Dietrich appeared at his side. 'Ready to clear the boat, sir!' He looked even paler in the bright sunlight, his oil-smeared jacket and scuffed seaboots making him appear unreal against the smiling shoreline.

Steiger touched his chin and thought, I must look even worse. 'Right, Heinz, carry on.'

Steiger stepped off the grating and felt his legs quiver beneath him. It was as if he was suffering from delayed shock coupled with near exhaustion. He peered across at the Headquarters building, and then stiffened as he saw the smoke-blackened walls of some houses beyond. St. Pierre had not escaped an air-raid of sorts, it seemed. He tried to vanquish the quick feeling of bitter pleasure, but it returned as his men started to climb through the hatch and over the side of the scarred conning-tower.

Life had gone on just the same in St. Pierre, with the Base staff and civilians alike grumbling about their rations and their lot. While at sea these wretched, brain-weary scarecrows had endured every sort of strain and fear, and been stretched to the limit of human survival.

Each man glanced briefly at his captain, a grubby hand raised in a hasty salute as he stumbled towards the friendly, unmoving jetty.

Steiger watched each man, picking out names and personalities, remembering how each had acted and worked on a hundred different occasions. The deck-gunners, Muller, Schultz and the ex-policeman, Michener. Then the old seaman, Jung, his face screwed up in pain as he hoisted his leg over the coaming, accompanied by his friends König and the boy, Rickover. Braun, the prim-faced hydrophone operator, and Stohr, the messman, who looked after his officers with the bluff competence of a mechanic. Still they passed, seamen and engineers, torpedomen and gunners, until only the petty officers were left.

Kopp, the Coxswain, his face ferocious beneath a massive beard, reported, 'All ashore, Captain!'

Petty Officer Hartz was pushing his men into three disciplined ranks on the jetty, just like that first day Steiger had seen them so long ago.

The Base staff was watching the last of the crews to come home, their faces interested but without understanding, and probably thinking that the sooner they could get the submarines back into running condition and their crews on their way to sea again, the sooner they could settle down to the quiet life once more.

Lieutenant Hessler waited until the other officers had joined him on the bridge and then held out his hand. 'Thank you, Captain.' He seemed unable to find the right words. 'You got us back home. Thank you, sir!'

Luth wiped his hands on his filthy overalls, and then changed his mind about offering one to Steiger. 'I second that, Captain.' He forced a grin. 'It was quite a patrol!'

Reche said nothing, but kept his eyes fixed on the twin hills and the baked road which ran away into the distance.

Dietrich saluted, and after the briefest hesitation held out his own hand.

Steiger stared straight into the young officer's eyes, reading the emotions of shame, pride and anxiety all mixed up together. He did not wait for Dietrich to speak, but said quietly, 'I should thank you, gentlemen.' He looked at each man in turn, and knew that each one was holding back time for a few more seconds, reliving small stark episodes, and probing the memories like men will test the progress of old wounds.

The blazing ships and fire-blackened men. The airmen, and the one who had shared their lives for three days. The thunder of depth-charges and the nerve-wrenching detonations of torpedoes. The hiss of escaping steam and the scalding roar of exploding boilers. Each a separate, terrifying moment, but all linked together with their own endurance and suffering.

Steiger realised with sudden shock that he was still gripping Dietrich's hand, and grinned with discomfort, the unaccustomed movement of his face muscles jerking at his nerves like cramp.

Dietrich stood back, and all four officers saluted.

Steiger watched them walk along the jetty, and then lifted his hand to the men who still stood mutely in a long colourless rank.

Petty Officer Hartz bellowed an order, and the crew of *U-991* marched heavily between the watching groups of smartly dressed sailors from the Base.

Hartz turned as he marched, so that he could look along the whole of his hollow-eyed charges. 'Come on then, you idle bilge-rats! At the count of the three let me hear "We are marching against England!"' He glared redly down the column, his feet still in perfect step although he was marching backwards. 'Left! Right! One, two, three!'

Steiger heard the old familiar marching song ripple along the swaying ranks, weak and resentful at first, and then with sudden power as if each exhausted man had become determined to shout away the fears and turn his individual weariness into a kind of defiance.

Steiger's hands shook, and his mouth felt suddenly choked. He stared unblinkingly after the dusty little column until it was swallowed up amongst the Headquarters buildings, and the voices were merged with the cries of the gulls and the sigh of wavelets against the moored hull.

They would all be waiting for him. Bredt and the other commanders. Watching him, assessing his resistance. like engineers inspecting a well-tried bridge.

With swift determination he swung his legs over the hatch coaming and climbed down into the silent hull. He walked very slowly through the control room, his eyes still seeing the accustomed figures at the controls and watching the motionless dials, although he was alone. The periscopes lay shining in their beds, the chart-table was empty. As he passed the gunners' messdeck he saw the fading pictures of buxom film stars already peeling from the lockers, and a forgotten tobacco pouch lying in one of the empty cots. The wardroom with its scratched and stained furniture, the bunks where his officers slept or hid their private fears. The galley and the reek of stale cabbage. The radio room, for once silent and in darkness.

Then he groped his way into his cabin and opened his small locker. His fingers touched the cool glass, and he stood the bottle on his table. As he poured himself a large measure of brandy he paused to finger the table and marvelled at its stillness. No vibration. The very life had been drained out of the submarine.

He leaned back in his chair and listened. No, of course the

life was still there. The boat seemed to be silently watching him, yet without criticism or malice.

Steiger felt the spirit raw and burning in his throat, and closed his eyes. Overhead he could hear the shuffling footsteps of the Base staff crossing the forecasing, and knew that his peace would soon be shattered. Then he would have to force himself into motion once more. But just for this moment he would sit and listen. It seemed as if he and the boat had become one. And that each was grateful to the other.

He drank another full glass and then locked the bottle away. He stood up and peered at his gaunt reflection in the smeared glass. With sudden care he brushed back his hair and fitted the white cap carefully over his forehead to hide the jagged scar. Like an actor stepping from the wings he pushed the curtain aside and walked towards the foot of the conning-tower ladder, where a pool of sunlight awaited him like a spotlamp.

* * * * *

The evening was warm and oppressive with a hint of thunder in the air as Lieutenant Dietrich strode hurriedly across the town square and turned into the first familiar street. After a quick bath and shave he had made his excuses and left Luth and the others in their quarters, still dazed and unsteady from their weeks of sleepless patrol. Dietrich ignored their curious glances and was not even conscious of the feel of his shore-going uniform and clean shirt, two things which in the past had given him immense satisfaction upon returning to the safety of the land.

As he neared the small side street his feet slowed, and he had to forcibly steel himself against the mounting uncertainty within him. He turned the corner and stopped. All the way from the harbour he had been remembering the black Mercedes outside the shop, the lounging S.S. men and the unseen eyes behind the curtains of the silent houses. Now, the street was little different, but this time was completely empty. Not even a stray dog explored the deep shadows thrown by the setting sun, and the shop itself was exactly like the one in his memory.

He lifted his chin and advanced towards the flaking door with its old advertisements of forgotten Swiss watches. His heart jumped as the bell jangled, but he pushed his way into the dark interior and closed the door behind him. His feet stumbled against a jumble of broken glass and pieces of splintered woodwork, and as his eyes became accustomed to the gloom he could feel his brain flashing a warning. The outer shop was a shambles. Every shelf and partition had been torn down and systematically smashed, and in some places even the floor boards had been ripped completely out of place. It looked as if it had only recently happened, but Dietrich could tell from the thick layer of dust that the scene of destruction had been left untouched, probably from that very night when he had seen Major Fischer's car waiting outside.

He swallowed hard and groped instinctively for the shape of his Lüger. A prickle of alarm explored his scalp when he remembered that in his hurry he had left it in his room at the Base. There was something evil as well as pathetic about the broken shop, and at the same time Dietrich had the feeling that he was not alone. Glass crunched beneath his feet as he stepped carefully towards the curtained door at the rear of the shop.

Somewhere very close a man chuckled. The sound was so unexpected and horrible that Dietrich staggered against the wall, his eyes straining across the littered room where he had once sat and spoken with Odile and her father.

A shadow bobbed in the corner, and Dietrich heard a voice say, 'Is that Lieutenant Dietrich?' There was another unnerving chuckle. 'Ah good! Excellent! You are just in time for our evening meal!'

Dietrich moved another step, the sweat cold on his forehead. 'Monsieur Marquet?' It was the same voice, yet different. He faltered as his knee collided with a broken table. 'What is happening? Shall I put on the light?' He felt stupid and on the edge of panic.

Louis Marquet gave a little giggle. 'Only an oil lamp of sorts, Lieutenant. But light it if you wish.'

He began to hum a little tune as Dietrich groped his way towards the only shining object in the room. The match flared, and Dietrich fumbled with the lamp as he adjusted his mind to the picture of devastation the light revealed, and wondered what worse thing was to come. He turned, and had to grit his teeth to prevent a cry of horror.

Dietrich was young and already hardened to the ways of war, but the sight of the small hunched figure who sat grinning at him in the flickering lamplight was almost too much.

Marquet bobbed his head again. 'Very gratifying to have you here once more!' He half turned so that the light fell full on his scarred cheek and the glistening, empty eye-socket. His hands, too, were like things from a nightmare. Turned into claws, yet without purpose or uniformity. Broken, useless pieces of flesh and bone which made Dietrich choke and taste the vomit in his throat. Hands which had once been so delicate and firm. Hands of a craftsman.

In a strangled voice he asked, 'Who did this to you?' Already he knew, but he wanted Marquet to break, to scream abuse at him, to curse him along with every German who had ever allowed such things to happen.

Marquet merely shrugged. A small, playful gesture like a child's. 'They asked me questions. I could not answer them, so they broke up my shop.' He grinned across the littered room. 'Then they started on me!'

Dietrich forced himself to speak slowly. 'Where is Odile? Is she safe?' He waited, and watched the meaning of his words sinking into Marquet's maniac face.

'Gone.' He nodded emphatically. 'Gone. Gone!' His voice ended in a sharp scream, like that of a trapped animal, so that Dietrich fell back, sickened yet fascinated by the unwinking socket.

'*Please*, I must know! Is she safe?'

Marquet was mumbling to himself, his lips wet with bubbles of saliva. In a different tone he added more loudly: 'I cannot answer, Herr Major! I do not know what you are asking!' He gave a great shriek, so spine-chilling that Dietrich could feel his hands quivering. 'I do not *know*!' The dreadful claws lifted as if to cover his face. 'Please, Major, not *again*!' His broken body twisted wildly as he relived the nightmare of torture and horror. Then he slumped sideways in the chair, his grey hair spilling across the old sack about his shoulders. In a more normal voice he said: 'Odile betrayed me. *She* gave me to the Boche, just as she gave herself to you!'

Then he was on his feet, clawing and spitting, struggling to find Dietrich's throat, his eyes, to destroy him, and thereby end the terrible waiting.

A door crashed open, and two military policemen, their faces startled and alert, burst into the room. But Marquet was already spent. With a little grunt he slumped down amongst the shattered remnants of his life. Dietrich shook himself and suddenly wanted to get out of this room. Marquet had died still thinking his daughter had betrayed him to the enemy. He had waited all this time for Dietrich to come to him. His mind had been broken like his body, but for the one remaining spark of revenge and hatred.

One of the soldiers stooped over the body. 'The old bastard's dead!'

The other said, almost reprovingly: 'You should not walk about here alone, Lieutenant. It is not safe any more.'

Dietrich stared at him wildly, only half hearing what he had said. She had gone, but where? He saw the interest in the soldiers' eyes and said quickly, 'Nothing is safe any more.'

He walked back up the deserted street, and when he stopped to look back he could see that the two military policemen were still watching him.

. . . . .

The high sliding doors which normally separated the main lounge from the large dining space were pushed right back to the walls, and the whole area seemed to shimmer in a semi-tropical heat as the room's humid atmosphere thickened and became more intense behind the drawn blackout curtains. All signs that this was the Headquarters building of Group Meteor had practically vanished, and large bowls of fresh flowers, draped signal flags and coloured lights added to the gay holiday atmosphere. A small orchestra comprised of Base sailors supplied a steady accompaniment of Strauss waltzes, while the floor space was crammed with officers, naval and military, a few French dignitaries and numerous women.

Rudolf Steiger paused at the entrance hall and ran his eyes quickly over the noisy and seemingly carefree crowd. There was an unmoving group of senior officers in one corner, well served and protected by a small army of white-coated stewards, and from his position at the top of the marble stairs Steiger could see the continuous movement of officers who wished to be noticed by their superiors moving in and around the important-looking group like workers in an ant colony.

With his ample buttocks resting against a table crammed with gold-topped champagne bottles, Rear-Admiral Reinhart Opetz from the Headquarters Staff at Lorient was holding sway over his attentive listeners, while Steiger's four U-boat commanders stood in a small honoured crescent on his right hand. Steiger could see again the striking difference between their strained, gaunt faces and the well-nourished ones around them, and he knew with sudden loathing that he, too, would soon be amongst the noisy, sweating mass of brother officers. For this Social Evening was in honour of Group Meteor, and that meant in his own honour.

Two heavily painted French women paused at the top of the stairs and stared at him. There was a sort of animal lust about them in the brazen way they held his eyes with their own, and in Steiger's mind there was almost a desperation, too. They had started something which could not end well for them whatever happened. They would be fêted and used, and then discarded. Steiger smiled grimly to himself. Perhaps that is why they look at me? We have the same end in view! He tugged his jacket into place and stepped into the sea of noise and excitement.

A petty officer in white gloves stepped forward and touched his sleeve. 'Excuse me, sir!' He signalled to another of his assistants, who immediately banged on a small table and continued to do so until the great concourse of uniforms and gay dresses was in silence.

Steiger felt a twinge of alarm. It was going to be even worse than usual.

The petty officer stood stiffly at attention like an old-world footman. 'Captain Rudolf Steiger!' He even sounded like a footman.

Steiger walked stiffly down the stairs as an avenue opened for him between the smiling or sentimental faces. That fool of a petty officer, he thought. Calling me *Captain*! Although every commanding officer was always known as captain aboard his own ship, his true rank was the one used when being correctly addressed.

He reached the Rear-Admiral and felt his fingers sink into the man's plump, perspiring hand.

'Well done, Steiger! Well done, *Captain*!' He gave a conspira-atorial wink and grinned at the closely packed ring of watching faces. 'Your promotion was brought forward, Steiger. You have indeed earned it!'

Automatically Steiger glanced at Captain Bredt. I shall be equal to him in rank. Perhaps now we can work together! He looked round at the eager, smiling faces, most of whom were completely unknown to him. They were actually *pleased* he had been promoted! Outside in the dark harbour my five boats lie and wait. Whilst in here I am treated like a conquering king! He shrugged. The world must be going mad!

Rear-Admiral Opetz was saying: '. . . and your last patrol does more than justify the Grand Admiral's strategy! Your efforts have been an inspiration, a great encouragement to everybody throughout Germany!' He raised his voice, so that his stiff white collar bit into his thick neck and turned his cheeks to an even deeper purple. 'My friends! Captain Steiger is the ace of submarine commanders! With leaders such as he we have no need to fear for the Fatherland's future, which has never been more assured! Just this forenoon I heard of more successes by our army comrades against these insolent invaders in the north! In Normandy we are already smashing the spearheads of their forces, and next we will cut through and destroy the remnants!! It will be another Dunkirk for the enemy, but in such a magnitude of death and destruction that he will never recover!! Soon, and who knows *how* soon with men like this,' his eyes moistened as he laid a hand on Steiger's shoulder, 'our flag will fly over Buckingham Palace, and for all time, the world will be ours!'

Steiger's head rang to the mad cheering, the fierce hand-clapping and stamping which seemed to rock the very building. A glass was thrust into his hand, and all at once he was being patted, congratulated and numbed by the stifling force of their demonstration. He forced his way towards the other commanders, and shook each of them by the hand. Immediately a series of flash-bulbs exploded and he glanced up in time to see a small smile on Alex Lehmann's lips.

With sudden anger Steiger realised that Lehmann was thinking he was acting, making a false gesture for the purpose of propaganda and self-praise. He took Lehmann's hand and deliberately turned his back on the cameras. 'I am glad you are here, Alex.' Their eyes met, and then Steiger moved back into the press of figures around the Admiral.

'Congratulations, Captain!' The soft voice made him start with surprise. He turned and found that she was pressed almost against his arm by the people around them. For a few moments it was like being on a small island surrounded by a raging impersonal typhoon. Trudi Lehmann was wearing a plain dress of black silk, sleeveless, so that the bare smoothness of her suntanned arms was all the more startling. Her hair was just as he remembered it, glistening in a black coil above her small ears.

'Thank you.' He stared down at her and saw the concern in her dark eyes. 'I had no idea you would be here!' He bit his lip. The words sounded so stiff and clumsy. He was making himself just as idiotic as the last time.

'I saw your boat arrive today. I was up the hill.' She gestured with one shoulder, the casual movement making his mouth dry. 'I thought you would be too tired for all this!' She eyed him gravely. 'You look worn out, you know.'

He took a glass from a tray and handed it to her. 'Let me see *you* drink my health!'

The Admiral's voice intruded like a clap of thunder, and the island was swamped. 'Isn't she a lovely little thing, eh?' Steiger stiffened as the man's plump fingers caressed the rounded curve of her shoulder. 'Enough to quicken the heart of any man!' He squeezed a bit harder, and Steiger saw that the girl's body was completely unmoving, but tense like a spring. She lifted her eyes, but she was looking neither at the Admiral nor at her husband, who must have been somewhere behind Steiger. She was looking at *him*! There was a strange expression of pleading in her brown eyes, as if she was looking at him through a mask.

He could see the tiny beads of perspiration on her forehead, and the faintest movement of her perfect breasts. He heard himself say, 'I think I will ask her to dance with me!'

As if in response to his decision the distant orchestra struck up yet another waltz, and without waiting for further comment Steiger held out his hand to her. She moved to meet him, and he saw the Admiral drop his hand reluctantly from her shoulder. The crush thickened as more couples moved into the whirlpool of music and laughter, and Steiger gave up trying to concentrate on the waltz and held her body close against his own, conscious only of her presence, the perfume of her hair and the strange expression on her upturned face.

'You must be very proud?' She moved closer as a drunken lieutenant skidded on the polished floor.

Steiger grinned with unexpected embarrassment. 'It's absurd. The war goes on without this sort of thing.'

Her mouth lifted in an amused smile. 'The Admiral seems *very* pleased!'

Steiger looked at the pink imprint of the Admiral's fingers on her skin. 'Well, look at the opportunities it gives him!'

She twisted her head to look. 'I bruise very easily.'

Steiger stared fixedly over her head as he moved her carefully in the press of dancers. Just a casual remark, or was it? Everything she said seemed to have such hidden meaning, such concealed promise. He tried to clear his mind, to imagine life just as it would be once more when the music stopped and the flags and the flowers were taken down. The shock it gave him brought a real pain, a desperate longing which almost made him exclaim aloud.

You fool! She will laugh in your face if you ever even thought of touching her! But another inner voice insisted, You are touching her now!

Steiger tightened his grip, every nerve straining to detect the first sign of displeasure or resentment. She moved closer, so that her breast was pressed hard against his tunic. But she no longer looked up at him, and kept her face close to his shoulder.

Once as they gyrated near the edge of the floor Steiger looked for Lehmann, but he had vanished.

Through the mists of his dazed senses he heard her say softly: 'Do you remember when you called to see Alex? When I was so rude to you?'

He shook his head. 'It was my fault. You must have thought me a pompous idiot!'

She did not seem to have heard him. 'I am so glad I did not go back to Germany. I am forbidden to travel while there is this trouble in the north. I hope we might meet again soon?'

Another couple cannoned into them, and the young officer opened his mouth to say something, but shut it again as he saw Steiger's angry eyes on him.

The girl laughed, and Steiger looked at her questioningly. 'Everyone is so afraid of you! But you are really just like a little boy!' She frowned with sudden seriousness. 'But you really should not be here. I think it is dreadful to expect it after what you have been through!'

'Does it show so badly?'

'You must take care. You cannot be expected to do everything!'

He laughed. 'I am not alone out there, you know!'

She touched his chin with her hair. 'When I hear people like the Admiral spouting such utter rubbish I sometimes think you *are* alone!'

She looked up with characteristic suddenness and caught the startled expression on his face. She laughed and threw back her head, so that he could see the clean line of her throat. He could feel the hunger and desire welling inside him like a flood, so that coupled with his state of semi-exhaustion he felt like a man on the verge of intoxication.

The music stopped, and there was a noisy display of applause. As Steiger guided the girl back to the waiting line of shining faces he felt the sudden pressure of her fingers on his own.

There was little time left. The Admiral was just signalling for the stewards, and the tempo seemed to be quickening as if everyone felt a sudden need to show open defiance to the war which had been brought to their midst by Steiger and his officers.

'Can I see you tomorrow?' He saw her shoulders stiffen. 'Alone?'

He immediately regretted his words. He had committed himself and left no room for manœuvring. If she rejected him now there was no other chance.

She lifted her hand to return the Admiral's jovial salute. In a very quiet voice she said: 'I would like that. I will be alone.'

A great torrent seemed to be roaring through Steiger's ears, and with it came a new wave of strength to sweep away the despair of uncertainty and longing.

The surrounding smiles no longer seemed empty and trivial. He could even look at Bredt without anger, and face the future without bitterness.

* * * * *

The iron bedstead creaked as Steiger sat upright with startled suddenness and groped for the light switch. The knock was repeated at his door and he shook his head to clear his aching mind, and at the same time tried to remember how long he had been asleep. He peered at his watch. Two hours since he had left the noisy celebration. Two hours since his slow walk along the foreshore past the sleeping U-boats and the black muzzles of the shore batteries as they pointed blindly out to sea. He rubbed his eyes with sudden violence. 'Come in!'

He stared with surprise at Luth's thin figure framed against the harsh lights in the hallway. The Engineer was still wearing his best uniform, the front of which was spattered with droplets of champagne.

Steiger checked the anger which surged through his sleep-starved body, and looked instead at Luth's anxious expression, the nervous uncertainty in the man's sad eyes.

'Well, what is it?'

It was nearly dawn, and when Steiger had broken from his deep sleep he had momentarily imagined that he had heard the clamour of alarm bells, the clatter of running feet and the shouted orders from the control room.

Luth swallowed. 'I am sorry to call you, Captain.' He faltered and glanced quickly round the bare room. 'I had not gone to bed when this man came to me.'

Steiger became aware for the first time that another shadow hovered behind Luth. He swung his legs over the edge of the bed, but remained staring at the floor. It must be serious. Whatever it was, Luth seemed too overcome to tell him.

'What man?'

Luth gestured with his hand and a helmeted seaman muffled in a thick watchcoat shuffled into view. He clinked as he moved, and Steiger saw that he was hung about with gasmask, sidearms and bayonet. There was an unexplained snuffling sound, too, which only added to the unreality of the scene. Even as Steiger craned his head a big Alsatian dog peered round the edge of the door and glared suspiciously, the steel chain about his neck glinting in the electric light from the hallway.

There was something familiar about the seaman, and then Steiger saw that the man had only one arm. Like Bredt, a figure from some past encounter in a forgotten battle.

The seaman nodded his head uncertainly. 'You won't remember me, sir. Huntz is the name. I was a torpedoman in *U-75*.'

Steiger stood up. Of course he remembered now. So many months, years ago. The man had been strafed by a fighter plane off the Hook of Holland. Steiger had been on deck. Somehow he had stopped the loss of blood until they could get the man properly attended to.

He smiled slowly. 'Yes, I remember you.' There must be more than this. A lot more.

'I've never forgotten *you*, sir. You saved my life.' He looked to Luth's hollow face as if for support. 'Helped me, too, when it was over.' He took a deep breath. 'I've got a job here at St. Pierre, sir. A security guard on the perimeter fence.'

Steiger ran his fingers through his ruffled hair. Surely this man had not awakened him just to tell him this? He glanced at Luth. 'What has happened, Chief?'

The man interrupted. 'I was out on patrol tonight, sir, with old Prinz here. I had been up the hill listening to the music, and all the goings-on at your celebration, when I heard this car.' He licked his lips. 'It was well after curfew, and I guessed all the officers would be at the party anyway, so I ran down the hill to investigate. This car stopped at the cross-lanes and, and . . .' he dropped his eyes, 'they threw out this body!'

Steiger felt himself go suddenly cold. 'Body?'

'A girl it was, sir. All cut about. Terrible! She had a card pinned to her, sir. It was addressed to your Lieutenant Dietrich.'

Steiger walked to the window and pulled open the curtains. A blue-grey sky showed the hardening skyline above the nearest hill.

'Go on, Huntz.' His voice was expressionless. 'What did it say?'

'It said: "Nazi whore! Traitor!"' The seaman's voice was hushed, even shocked. 'She was just a slip of a girl, sir, crippled, too!'

'Have you told anyone about this?' Steiger glanced at Luth.

Luth shook his head, and suddenly looked very old. 'No, sir. This man said that he thought you should know first. He thought it was only right!'

Steiger felt a prick behind his eyes and turned towards his piled clothing. While he and the others had been losing their minds in that pointless celebration, Heinz Dietrich had been out looking for that girl. *Thank God this one disabled seaman had had the sense, the decency, even the courage, to find me first!* In the German Navy it was no small feat to rouse a full captain from his sleep.

'I'll come at once.' He reached for his coat and looked levelly at the other two men. 'I shall not report this. We will bury her now, up there on the hillside. You, Huntz, go and get some spades. Luth, you go and rouse Lieutenant Hessler.' He held their eyes with his own. 'I will take full responsibility. There is no cause to tell anyone else.' He reached out and touched the seaman's shoulder, so that the guard dog quivered threateningly. 'Thank you, Huntz. I will not forget this!'

Half an hour later he leaned against the cool bark of a bent tree and watched the first hint of sunlight across the brow of the hill. Luth was idly kicking stones across the damp grass, and Hessler crouched quietly smoking a cigarette. The seaman with his dog was outlined against the sky like a medieval warrior, his face shadowed by his helmet. Between them lay the patch of freshly dug earth, and two spades. A small broken body. But the savage wounds had given her a strange dignity, so that Steiger felt more than merely moved. He felt humble.

Hessler said quietly, 'Time to be getting down, sir?'

A bugle alerted the damp air with strident determination.

Luth kicked one more stone. 'Will you tell him, Captain?'

Steiger turned and lifted his arm to the watching seaman on the hill. 'I will tell him part of it.'

He followed the other two down the hillside, his boots squeaking in the grass. The sun was already warm across his cheek, but he realised that he was shaking all over, like a man with fever.

15: Change of Allegiance

Beyond the wide windows of Captain Bredt's office the endless expanse of the Bay of Biscay gleamed and shimmered invitingly in the bright sunshine. The heat, magnified by the large area of glass, seemed to hold the room in an air of dazed indifference, so that the officers who stood or sat around the big desk appeared listless, even bored.

Bredt had just entered the room, and as the officers settled back into attitudes of tired watchfulness he began to leaf through a pile of documents which were piled neatly on a clean blotter. His movements were quick and nervous, and Steiger, who remained in his favourite place by the windows, noticed that Bredt's pale eyes were unusually restless and that he was not in fact concentrating on the papers at all.

Steiger's mind was blurred and weary from the wretched burial-party that morning, yet in his dazed condition it seemed as if even that had been merely a part of the whole condition of homecoming. The noisy but false reception in his honour was still stale in his mouth, just as the traces remained evident about the building. Even here, in Bredt's efficient office, there was a forgotten champagne bottle on a window-ledge, and a glass, well smeared with lipstick, lay unnoticed on the rich carpet.

'Gentlemen, I am afraid that I have bad news for you.' Bredt looked up for the first time, his face puffy and flushed as if from drink. 'The Group will be required to sail within twenty-four hours!'

Steiger heard a mingled gasp from the assembled officers, and glanced quickly round the circle of faces. He had half expected something like this, although in his mind he had believed such a decision impossible. He waited, noting the disbelief and resentment on the faces of his four commanders and the anxiety shown by the Base staff officers. Major Reimann, the Garrison Commander, was also present, and his bloated red face was set in a fierce mask which only barely concealed the man's alarm.

Bredt continued harshly: 'It cannot be helped. Despatches have been received from the north. The Front has been broken in many places. Our army has fallen back to re-group, and there seems to be some confusion as to what the position really is!' He darted a vicious glance at Reimann as if he was in some way responsible. 'Every boat must be made ready for sea at once. Maximum fuel and stores must be taken aboard. There is some doubt as to when we may get fresh supplies.'

Steiger turned his back and watched the white lines of gulls paraded along the harbour wall. So the worst was happening after all. With the Allies gaining ground after the first assault, it was obvious that they would soon make use of every captured air base to harry supply columns and dominate the roads and railways. He closed his tired eyes to visualise better the dangerous geography of the new battleground. The enemy would try to cut all supply lines first, and then isolate the west coast of France. Every garrison and naval base would be slowly strangled into uselessness. For them defeat would be inevitable, surrender a matter of months, even weeks. He shook himself and tried to concentrate on Bredt's hand as it moved vaguely across the wall-chart.

'Every available U-boat in this area must be used at once to attack enemy shipping in the English Channel approaches. More landings will be tried, and every day will see fresh convoys crossing the Atlantic to supply them. They *must* be held up,' he dropped his eyes, 'regardless of our own losses!'

Steiger thought of Admiral Opetz and his bland optimism. Why do his sort think we have to sustain our strength with lies? Any man can face temporary disaster if he is prepared and trained for it!

The room was silent, and Steiger realised that Bredt was staring at him.

'Well, Captain? Have you anything to add?' Bredt's tone was uneven, as if he was out of breath.

'Nothing.' He saw the dismay in Lehmann's eyes, but continued calmly: 'One move leads to another. The invasion has happened. It is reality, but not the end of the world.' He walked to the chart. 'The Group will sail separately. Weiss and Wellemeyer tonight, Kunhardt and Lehmann at dawn. I will follow last. Sailing and operational procedure will be as laid down. I will see each commander beforehand and discuss final details.' His cold eyes excluded the others in the room and swept quickly across the four weary faces. 'Questions?'

Without looking he knew it would be Lehmann who would speak. He had seen the anger and open defiance on his face. He recognised the signs only too well. Steiger hardened his heart and waited.

'They're asking the impossible!' Lehmann was on his feet, his tall frame swaying as he gestured towards the chart. 'Supplies could be cut while we are at sea! We might return here to find nothing, and then we will be useless, and trapped!' Lehmann's voice grew louder as he faced Bredt. 'We are being betrayed! What is the use of throwing away lives *now*? We should get back to Germany before we are cut off!'

Instead of shouting him to silence Bredt dropped his eyes again. In a strange voice he said: 'U-boat Headquarters has already been moved. We will continue to operate from here until the end.' He tried to put new strength into his voice. 'Our Leader has ordered that there shall be no retreat, no weakening now that the battle has begun!'

Lehmann spread his hands. 'The battle has *begun*? In the name of God what do they think we have been doing in the Atlantic for five years?' His long face seemed to collapse. 'This country is being run by madmen!'

Bredt's face reddened. 'How dare you speak like that! I'll——'

But Steiger's voice interrupted him. 'Sit down, Lehmann! That is an order!' He turned to face the room at large. 'Now listen to me, all of you!' His voice was low, but so hard that every man stared at him as if fascinated.

'I shall not say this again. For one thing we will all be too busy, and another, I will have arrested, and if necessary executed, any man who dares to weaken our cause to suit his own ends!' His scar shone white below his dark hair. 'When our Leader lifted Germany from the dust and shame of world scorn, and gave us a purpose, a new hope, there were few of us who thought he could do it. Germany became great in spite of outside enemies and the traitors who tried to destroy us from within! In those days every German was a leader, and every day seemed like the dawn of some new victory!' His mouth hardened. 'Now that the tide is turning against us there are plenty who will weaken and be eager to forget their allegiance!

'You may think this is such a small part of the war here in St.

Pierre that I am over-dramatising the situation? If so I can assure you that you are mistaken. Even now the French Terrorists are more open in their movements, less unwilling to face combat. Given a chance the whole of Occupied France will become an ant-heap which will take badly needed men from the Front to control and garrison. Our Group Meteor has done well, but has never been more needed. Its efforts have never been so vital to the Fatherland!' He turned his back on them and stared across the glittering water.

'If Germany falls it will be our shame. There can be no second chance. This time the enemy means to destroy us, utterly and completely. They failed in my father's day, but this time they will not turn from anything but brute force and our combined determination!'

He realised that they were all staring at him, and he had to bite his lip to relieve the tension in his mind. Words, words, words. These men had to be held together whatever the cost. Perhaps in Supreme Headquarters they had some master-plan to overwhelm the Allied advances, or maybe the army would fall back to the Rhine in one unbroken wall of strength. Either way, the West Coast bases would probably collapse. It had to be faced. But every U-boat must fight from its base until it was no longer possible. It was useless to plan in terms of defeat. Each obstacle must be overcome as it arose. If you avoided a minefield and thereby lost a target you should not command a U-boat. Grand strategy ashore should also have its yardstick, even if the men who lived and died by its findings were never consulted. It was useless to become entangled in uncertainty and supposition. They had their weapons. They would use them.

Bredt was saying: 'The Base is well protected. Major Riemann's men are on constant patrols, and the batteries are manned day and night. No one will go outside the town area, and shore-parties must always be armed.' He lifted his eyes dramatically to the ceiling. 'Captain Steiger is right. We must only think of our duty! Our Leader is biding his time. He knows when and where to strike!'

He gathered up his papers and seemed uncertain what to do next.

Major Reimann spoke for the first time. 'Gentlemen, let me add my own assurance. My troops are ready and willing to face the enemy! They will not falter if their time comes!'

Steiger knew that every man in the room was seeing a picture in his mind of Reimann's elderly soldiers. Not least, Major

Reimann must have had them constantly in his thoughts. For once Steiger felt something like pity for the fat, stupid soldier. His little world had been so remote, so safe from war, that in his ignorance he must have imagined it would last for ever.

Steiger reached for his cap, his mind suddenly bitter. Nothing lasted that long. He thought of Dietrich's stricken face when he had told him of the French girl's death, of the naked horror and disbelief which had rendered him speechless and empty.

All small things, but in war they could become so vital, and in their own way could become the only reason for living, or dying.

With startling suddenness he remembered Trudi Lehmann, and knew that his words to his officers had been a sham to cover his own despair.

• • • • •

A warm wind fanned the harbour stonework as Steiger walked slowly back towards the town. Twice he stopped and looked seawards where the rim of the sun shone like a sliver of burnished gold above the dark horizon line and cast a warm path across the calm evening waters. But the two outward-bound submarines had already lost their outlines and merged with the sea.

His limbs felt like lead as he walked along the edge of the wall, his boots ringing loudly as if to spell out the air of desertion and quiet which hung over the small harbour. He passed the moored shapes of the next two boats to sail, their darkening decks alive with swarming figures as their crews prepared for yet another patrol. The air above them shimmered with diesel fumes and the vibrating murmur of generators and fans. Steiger had spoken to their commanders, and wondered as he passed if Lehmann was watching him from his bridge, hating him. Despising him.

He quickened his pace until he reached the solitary shape of his own command. Like the others she was already manned, and hummed with urgent activity. Even in the fading light he could see the outline of the angry mermaid on the narrow bridge and the long finger of the deck gun. The boats had only time for the briefest inspection, and they were still suffering from the strain and shock of that last venture into the Atlantic. In any new engagement or danger who knew what might happen? Their crews had become hardened to a point of frailty, as brittle as iron with an unseen flaw.

Dietrich would be down there in the hull, concentrating his outward attention on the mass of preparations before sailing, but his soul and mind lost in his inner torment. Luth and Hessler might still be watching him, remembering perhaps that moment of peace on the dawn hillside and the bare patch of raw earth.

They had all trusted their Captain Steiger. He alone would bear their resentment and bitterness for their sacrifice. For that is what it would be. Without rest, with hardly a break, they were being flung back into the battle. Yet they were required to be as alert as a crew which had come straight from a training squadron!

He cocked his head to listen to the murmur of distant gunfire. It ebbed and flowed across the shadowed hills like thunder, merging with the surf on the beach and the sigh of wind in the trees. It never stopped, it was like a tide. A tide of battle.

Steiger stared up at the pointed roofs of the town and tried to imagine the forces of destruction sweeping through the quiet streets. It seemed impossible. But it must have seemed that way to the people of Rotterdam and Warsaw and the countless other towns laid waste by an invader.

He walked through the perimeter wire and found himself counting the number of patrols which moved purposefully along the streets, their equipment jangling, their boots awakening the echoes. The town itself seemed dead, and even the fields appeared uncared for and forgotten. The people were hiding, or had gone altogether.

He stopped and looked at a tall mound of fresh earth at the side of the square. A notice board was erected at one corner with the long list of names for all to see. Sixty-five hostages executed by Major Fischer's firing squads. As punishment for the town's indiscipline. For the maintenance of law and order, For the honour of the Third Reich.

It had all happened while the Group had been at sea. Major Fischer had continued his search for the saboteurs, but had met only a wall of silence. His victims had been grateful for his final punishment. Each of them had been interrogated at his headquarters. Nobody had seen what had happened. Or had they merely closed their eyes?

Steiger tore his eyes from the silent cairn and walked slowly on. The innocent and the guilty. The strong and the weak. It made no difference to this war-crazed machine which no one could stop.

He wondered what Major Fischer and his S.S. men would do now. They had moved clear of the town and were searching outlying villages. More interrogations and more torture. Yet with unnerving regularity the sabotage went on. And with it Fischer's rage would fan like that of a mad dog's. It was said that he sat with his pet cat on his lap while his men tried to wring confessions from their helpless victims. Steiger thought of the man's eyes and believed the story.

He shook himself angrily. What is the use of recrimination? What can *we* do about it? It is part of a system which has grown up with violence and danger. We cannot ignore it, yet we can do nothing to prevent it. Yet by our helplessness we have shared the guilt.

He stopped outside the house, aware of the silence and the feeling of breathlessness which made him touch the cold wall as if for support.

It was only after he had rung the bell that he felt the return of uneasiness. She had not intended him to come. It would be the final weakening of his strength.

The door opened and he was inside the small dark hallway before he realised what was happening. She did not switch on any light until they were in that low beamed room he remembered so clearly. He half expected to find the three army officers waiting there, but the room was empty and very quiet. In spite of the warm summer night, a small fire rippled in the grate, the final touch required to roll back time to the night of his first visit.

She led him to a chair and walked quickly to a side table. She poured out two drinks, again without asking his choice, and he noticed the quick nervousness of her movements, the high colour in her cheeks. She placed the glass in his hand, and then unexpectedly knelt on the rug at his feet. Over the rim of his glass Steiger watched the movement of her throat and the moistness of her lips.

The windows rattled momentarily, and she twisted her head with alarm.

Steiger thought it might be because of their shared guilt, but she said suddenly, 'Guns or bombs?' She did not wait for an answer. 'It's been going on night after night! They say it's Lorient and St. Nazaire. There can't be much left of either!' She placed her glass on the carpet. In a low voice she said, 'I'm so sick with fear I don't know what to do!'

The realisation of her plight came to Steiger with the force of a bullet. If the fighting did reach this far south, what would happen to her? The anger he had been feeling for Lehmann fanned through him like a fire. The man who had ignored his wife and did not even care what happened to her now that she was in real danger. He cursed himself, too, for being so blind.

'It will be all right.' He tensed as she laid her hand on his knee. 'The war is still a long way off!'

She lifted her head, so that the thick black coil gleamed in the firelight. Her eyes were wide and desperate. 'Why won't anyone speak the truth any more? Every time I think of the stupidity of all this I am nearly driven into hysteria! I am married to a man I do not know, a man who walks alone like a ghost!' She raised her hand as Steiger opened his mouth to speak. 'I am not afraid to die, but I want something *more* to hold on to! I am a woman, I need love as much as I need to love someone!'

Her mouth quivered in a small uncertain smile. 'You seem shocked? That is the last thing I want. But you will be away at sea soon. Those left behind will be thrown to the wolves. That is how I see it!'

The silence moved closer into the room, then she said quietly: 'I think you understand me, Rudi. If we had more time I would not risk your despising me. But we have so little——'

He saw his hand on the nape of her neck and felt the smoothness of her skin beneath his palm. His fingers moved clumsily into her hair, and then all at once he was pulling it free, so that it cascaded over her shoulders in a black wave. Her eyes were closed, but her body seemed to writhe against his legs as he twisted her round and fumbled with the front of her dress. He let it fall to her waist, the realisation that beneath the dress she was naked making the blood roar in his brain like the distant gunfire.

In a choking voice she said: 'We have so little time. I could not wait!'

He twined his fingers into her hair so that she cried out with sudden pain and arched her body back across his knees. For a moment longer he tortured himself by filling his starved mind with the picture of her perfect body, and then allowed his other hand to move like something detached over her straining breasts, the motion making her shudder, and then suddenly fall quiet and still.

Almost savagely he picked her up and carried her up the stairs, the darkness making her body a white crucifix in his arms.

Later he lay staring at the curtained window and half listened to the whisper of gunfire. He was afraid to close his eyes in case he was to be mocked by yet another desperate dream.

He could feel her leg hot across his body and the heat of her breath against his shoulder. He ran his hand down her spine, so that she moaned and pressed closer to him.

By straining his eyes he tried to see her in the darkness. This woman is mine. He repeated the words over and over again, until with the fierceness of their passion sleep swept aside his defences and left him as helpless as the girl at his side.

. . . . .

Max König turned up the collar of his watchcoat and eased the rifle sling across his shoulder. The forecasing was slippery with dew, and the morning air was still sharp, without a hint of the warmth the sun would soon bring over the twin hills.

The moored hull moved uneasily on the rising tide and squeaked against the frayed rubber fenders. As the grey light filtered more strongly across the small harbour König enjoyed momentarily the sense of isolation and peace As deck-sentry of the Morning Watch he seemed to be the only living soul in St. Pierre. Even the gulls still nodded on the weed-encrusted buoys, like old men reluctant to face another day. All the other berths were empty, the second half of the Group having sailed before the first hint of light in the clear, colourless sky. The harbour was at peace, and for once the distant gunfire was temporarily stilled.

He tilted back his regulation helmet and rubbed the weariness from his eyes. He wondered just what was the truth of the enemy's position, and how soon St. Pierre would feel the power of running men and the vibration of racing armoured columns. I will probably be at sea when that time comes, he thought. How will the others accept the news, and how will they react?

A figure moved slowly along the top of the wall, and automatically König's fingers groped for the rifle sling. He relaxed as he saw that it was a shore-patrolman, a seaman like himself.

The man halted on the top of the stonework and grounded his rifle. He glanced along the jetty towards the shadowed Headquarters building and then cautiously lit a cigarette. He grinned companionably at König and then said: 'Off to sea again soon? Rather you than me!'

König smiled. 'It's a living, comrade!'

The other sentry yawned hugely. 'I hear that one of your seamen has gone sick. Some poor bastard is being sent from here to replace him!' He chuckled unfeelingly. 'Glad they didn't choose me!'

König shrugged. He had heard that a man had indeed been removed from *U-991* with appendicitis. There would be another new face for this patrol.

The man added: 'Nice fellow, by the name of Fromm. He tells me he's got an old friend on board already, someone he knew in the Intake Depot.' He squinted down at König's stricken face. 'His friend is called König. Do *you* know him?'

The harbour seemed to have faded into a red mist. König turned away from the other man and said hoarsely: 'Yes. I know him.'

'Well, it's nice to have a friend in a new ship.' The sentry stiffened and said irritably: 'Must get on. Duty Petty Officer will be after me otherwise.'

König watched him go, his mind swinging madly from one desperate plane to another. It had happened, just as he had always feared. Out of the blue, and at a time when safety might almost be within his grasp. He peered quickly at his watch. Half an hour before a bugle roused the Base and a train of events would be set in motion. He could see the perplexity in the man Fromm's face changing to disbelief and then suspicion. The alarm would be raised, and he would be immediately isolated in terror and panic.

An inner voice seemed to be screaming a warning to him, yet he remained stockstill and rigid, his eyes vacant as he faced his own destruction. There is *still* time! They will never take me again! Never!

All at once he had crossed the wooden brow, his boots crunching on the sanded stone. His mind worked frantically in time with his pounding feet. To the end of the jetty, then left behind the sheds. There was a sentry beyond the perimeter fence, but he would take little notice of an additional patrolman. In any case he would be watching for someone trying to break *into* the Base, not out of it. Where the hill faltered and crumbled into the sea there was a way round the end of the barbed wire. At low water there was another sentry with a dog on the beach, and at high tide the rusted wire dipped down below the surface. Right now, at this very moment in time, there was a way round.

He walked quickly into the shadow of the loading sheds and then broke into a run.

Behind him, *U-991* lay quietly alongside the jetty, the tips of her periscope standards already glinting in the first sunlight. No one kept watch on her upper deck. No one called the Officer of the Watch as a second U-boat cruised slowly and quietly round the end of the long breakwater.

. . . . .

Rudolf Steiger closed the door of his room behind him and walked slowly to the window. As he moved, his fingers reached out to touch the sparse but familiar objects, but his eyes stayed fixed on the fine yellow sunlight which glinted across the dew-soaked grass and threw strange shadows from the line of ragged trees.

Lying across his unused bed was his other uniform jacket, the extra stripe of gold lace bright above the three more tarnished ones. Absently he threw his coat down and slipped into the other one. The Base tailor must have seen the bareness of the room and wondered about its occupant.

Steiger sat down heavily on the bed and hugged his body as a convulsion of cold shudders ran through him.

He had dressed quietly beside the girl's bed, his body weak from the fierceness of their love. He knew she had been watching him in the grey dawn light, and when he had stooped over her he had tasted the salt on her cheeks. He could not remember speaking, nor could he recall the actual moment of leaving her. Outside the house he had faltered, his mind suddenly heavy and despairing.

Footsteps echoed along the corridor, and he tried to compose himself. Dietrich had probably sent a messenger from the boat to tell him it was time to sail.

Suddenly he could not face them. Neither the boat nor the Atlantic. He had seen the glittering sea, so deceptively kind in the dawn light, as he had walked through the town's deserted streets.

The door opened, and Steiger stared with surprise at the bearded lieutenant who stood framed in the ever-burning corridor lights. A sense of alarm crowded into his aching mind. This officer was Lehmann's First Lieutenant. Lehmann was at sea. Something must have gone wrong already.

The Lieutenant licked his lips. 'Would you accompany me to

the Operations Room, Captain? Commander Lehmann sends his respects, and asks that you come at once.'

His manner was strange, strained to the point of animal desperation. Steiger darted a quick glance at the clock. No bugle yet. Something was really wrong. Almost without thinking he reached for his locker.

In a flash a Lüger appeared in the Lieutenant's hand. A wild gleam shone in his deep-set eyes. 'You do not understand, sir. You are under arrest!'

Steiger stood up very slowly. One unexpected move and he knew the man would shoot. He was obviously frightened of Steiger. But he was more frightened of failing in his mission.

'You know what this means, Lieutenant?' Steiger kept his voice very level, although inwardly his thoughts surged back and forth in baffled turmoil. 'This is mutiny! Nothing good can or will come of such madness!'

The pistol-barrel shone brightly as the sunlight filtered through the window. 'Come, we are wasting time!' The man gestured urgently towards the corridor.

Steiger walked down the passage and into the fragile warmth of what appeared to be a perfect July morning. Everything seemed unfamiliar now, like items in a disordered dream. Armed seamen stood guard outside the buildings, and Steiger recognised them as members of Lehmann's crew. Perhaps Lehmann had gone berserk? Steiger had always maintained that the commanding officer of a submarine could easily hold sway over the minds of his men. For good or evil, it was easy for the one man who was able to control their very right to live.

The gunfire had started up again, the urgent whispering almost lost in the crisp brightness of birdsong and the sigh of the high water against the beach.

He turned his head to look along the harbour. Lehmann's boat lay at the far end near the harbour entrance, the ensign limp in the calm air. His own boat was empty of life, but for a small group on the open bridge. Suddenly Steiger's heart felt heavy and tired. Whatever this madness meant, his own men must be a part of it.

Steiger could hear the officer's heavy breathing behind him, and lifted his chin with sudden determination. Whatever lay ahead he must be ready. For a few hours he had turned away from watchfulness. In those precious moments his world had changed. And it was still changing.

* * * * *

Captain Bredt's office seemed to be exactly as it had been the previous day, and Steiger glanced quickly across the room as if to see if the empty champagne bottle was still in its place by the window. The fact that it was only helped to add to the unreality of the scene, and he looked at the small group of assembled officers to reassure himself that the other U-boat commanders had not in some way returned with Lehmann to complete the picture.

Bredt sat behind the desk, the top of his sleek head gleaming in the bright sunlight as he stared at his hand on the blotter. Lehmann was standing beside him, his eyes fixed on Steiger's face, whilst along one wall the Base officers and Major Reimann stood in a line of unmoving statuary.

Steiger waited until the door closed behind him. He could feel the sun hot across his face, and he sensed the frightened tension which hung in the air like the dust transfixed in the rays from the tall windows.

He stared coldly at Lehmann. 'Well? I suppose I am entitled to some sort of explanation?' He waited, aware that Lehmann was the most composed person present. 'You must realise that you have committed a serious crime by returning to Base without orders?'

Lehmann's thin face quivered in a tight smile. 'I am sorry about this, Rudi. But under the circumstances we are forced to act without delay.'

Steiger kept his face set. 'I would prefer you to address me by my rank, Commander!' From the corner of his eye he saw an army captain he had not previously noticed. He caught his breath as the magnitude of the nightmare suddenly came to him with startling clarity. It was one of the three officers he had seen at Lehmann's house. The conspiracy, whatever it entailed, was more serious than he had dared to imagine.

Lehmann's voice was heavy. 'I still say I am sorry about this. You are a brave man, and no one doubts it for an instant.'

'Then perhaps you could inform me why I am under arrest? At the same time you might tell me by what authority you have dared to act as you have?'

More seconds passed, and the figures around the room remained motionless.

Lehmann shrugged. 'We have assumed command here. For months we have been planning this, but the sudden decision to send the Group to sea rather hurried things. By this time tomorrow the whole of Germany will be under new leadership!'

Steiger turned slowly and walked to the window. He ignored the sharp movement of the officer with the pistol, and tried to concentrate his mind on what was happening. New leadership? What did it mean?

Lehmann continued evenly: 'I have tried to get you to understand, but you have never listened. Germany is being destroyed by a maniac. We are all being sacrificed at the whim of one man. By tomorrow the world will know he is dead!'

Steiger caught his breath. So that was it. Groups of officers might even now be seizing control of ships and garrisons in a mad bid of revolution.

'*You* are insane!' His voice was calm. 'I hope you have considered what will become of you now?'

'We have considered everything, Captain. You have said yourself that St. Pierre is important in spite of its size. I agree with you. From now on your example will spread throughout France and across Germany itself!' Lehmann's face was shining with sweat. 'With Hitler dead and his criminal accomplices under guard we can present a fixed front to the Allies! *We* will make the bargains, and discuss our own terms!'

Steiger gave a thin smile. 'I can imagine!'

Lehmann tightened his lips. 'Don't mock, Captain! What can be attained by throwing our men away as we are now?' He shook his head. 'We will come to an agreement with the Allies. Together we will make *one* front against Russia in the east, and together we will rid Germany and Europe of them once and for all! That will satisfy the British and their friends. It will also give us a free hand to cleanse our own country and live as we choose!'

'And you hope to do this on your own?' Steiger turned and stared at the other man with contempt.

But Lehmann met his stare, his eyes hot with anger. 'Oh no, Captain! Tomorrow we will all be obeying orders from the men who really count! There are many General Staff officers on our side, and right now they are putting our plan into operation!'

Steiger felt his hands trembling. 'How did you know I would not send you to sea before the others in the Group? If you had been in the Atlantic you might have found it difficult to betray your country!' His voice stung like a lash, and Bredt lowered his head even more.

Lehmann laughed quietly. 'Because I knew you were a man of honour, Captain! I knew that you could never make love to my wife knowing that her husband was at an unfair advantage!'

His words hung in the air like echoes. 'It is because I know you *so* well, Captain, that I was confident of success!'

Steiger felt the colour rising to his face. So it was all planned even so far ahead as that. He tried to see her face in his mind, but it was impossible to imagine her betrayal.

Lehmann shook his head. 'No, Captain, she did not know about this. I think she might have forgotten her first loyalty to her husband, had she known!'

Steiger found that he was suddenly quite calm. 'You mean *your* loyalty, surely?' He faced the room at large. 'Well, have *you* nothing to say? Do you realise that you are shaming Germany by your madness?'

Bredt raised his head, his eyes red-rimmed. 'I wanted no part of this!'

But he looked away as Lehmann said sharply, 'But you reconsidered very quickly, didn't you, when you realised that by tomorrow you might be out of a job?'

Steiger took a pace towards the desk. 'Remember this, Lehmann. The rest of the Group is at sea. Even now they may be contacting the enemy. They will be relying on our support, and it will be denied them! Kunhardt, Wellemeyer, Weiss and all their men may be killed because of your actions!'

A shaft of pain showed itself in Lehmann's eyes, and Steiger continued calmly: 'You acted against me because you could not rely on my support. You knew I was too loyal to my country for this sort of treachery! By God, Lehmann, you jeer at my sense of honour, but what of the man who risks his wife's very life and sanity? Who is prepared to sacrifice his comrades because he is too weak and too vile to act like an officer!' He turned his back. 'No, Lehmann, I am very glad you did not confide in me! I feel unclean just to be sharing this room with you!'

Lehmann's voice sounded tired. 'Take him to his quarters. He is not to be out of the guard's sight for an instant!' Then after a pause he added: 'I always said you were different from us. Your sort never change. You obey, you fight, without question. You have never learned to move with the times!'

Steiger felt the nausea rising inside him once more. He forced himself to face the watching officers, and ground his teeth together to hide the misery from their gaze. Of course, it must have been easy to convince Bredt. Reimann would obey whoever was in command of the Base, and the other officers were too frightened to resist either of them.

'Believe me, gentlemen, you will live to regret this day!' And to Lehmann he said quietly: 'If any harm comes to the men under my command because of your actions I swear that I will kill you!'

Lehmann eyed him coldly. 'And if I choose to have *you* shot, Captain?'

Steiger walked towards the door. 'I would rather shoot myself than live to see Germany in your hands!'

He hurried from the room, his eyes blind to his watchful guard, his head splitting to the realisation of his own helplessness. Lehmann's betrayal was nothing compared with his own. The men who were depending on him were without a voice. He had been trusted and at the most important moment had left his back unguarded.

. . . . .

Heinz Dietrich gave a sharp cry as a hand jerked urgently at his shoulder and pulled him from the depths of an uneven sleep. He set up blinking, his eyes wide and startled as he stared first at the wardroom clock and then at Luth's gaunt face beside the bunk.

'What is it?' Dietrich controlled himself with a major effort and pushed the hair back from his forehead. For a few seconds the shock of being suddenly awakened held him in the same old state of suspended anxiety, with every nerve tensed and waiting for disaster. His eyes dulled as the rawness of his recent experience crowded back into his brain, and he looked down at Luth with resigned weariness. 'Well? Is it time to get under way?' He realised for the first time that the generators were still and the normal signs and sounds of an awakening submarine were quite absent.

Luth held his finger to his lips. 'Quick, Heinz!' Something in his tone made Dietrich swing his legs down on to the deck. 'There's real trouble of some sort!' He watched anxiously as Dietrich threw on his jacket and trousers. 'You had better bring your pistol. I think it's a mutiny!'

Dietrich shook his head, his mind clearing reluctantly to face this new impossibility. But as he hurried from the wardroom he knew that something unusual was indeed happening. Small groups of newly awakened men stood awkwardly in the passageway, their eyes watching him as he passed with the grim-faced Engineer, and in the control room Lieutenant Hessler was standing at the foot of the conning-tower ladder, his rough features illuminated in a patch of sunlight.

Dietrich glared at Hessler's dazed expression. 'What in Christ's name is going on?'

But a new voice boomed from overhead, the words magnified by the metal sides of the conning-tower. 'This is an emergency, Lieutenant! No one is to leave the boat, and no attempt must be made to use the wireless!'

Dietrich squinted up towards the oval of sunlight. It was broken by the head and shoulders of an army lieutenant, of all people, and Dietrich could hear the scrape of feet as other figures moved on the U-boat's bridge.

'I am coming up!' Dietrich could feel the insane anger rising again. It was as if this was the one chance he had been looking for. An opportunity to let go of his inner torment, a final chance to stop himself from going mad.

The soldier shook his head. 'If you act foolishly you will die, and so will your men! Until I hear to the contrary from my superiors this boat is under arrest!'

Dietrich paused with his foot on the bottom rung. 'Do you know what you are doing? If you prevent our sailing you will jeopardise the whole Group!' He felt Hessler's quick breathing beside him. He added loudly. 'When Captain Steiger knows about this you will be sorry!'

'Steiger is under arrest!' The words stopped every movement in the control room, and Dietrich could not believe that he had heard correctly. The voice continued, 'Our forces are taking over control, and very soon will be in command of all the forces throughout the Reich!'

Hessler whispered: 'It can't be! It just can't be happening!'

'How dare you give orders to us? Dietrich's voice shook with sudden rage. 'We have been fighting for you! Who are you to command *anything*?'

'Control yourself, Lieutenant!' The head and shoulders moved clear of the hatch. 'You know what to do, and I would advise you to consider your men before you act foolishly. If you try to rush the bridge we will drop a few grenades down to cool your eagerness!'

Dietrich heard the soldier's voice fading as he barked a few orders to the men on deck, and then there was silence.

Hessler rubbed his eyes furiously. 'I still can't believe it!' He stared foolishly at Dietrich and Luth.

Dietrich threw back his head and laughed. His laughter

seemed to engulf the control room, and then the whole boat, as he stood clutching the ladder for support, his body bent in helpless convulsions.

Between sobs he shouted: 'This is priceless! The Fatherland fights for its life! But *we* have to fight ourselves as well!' His laughter stilled just as suddenly as it had started, and Luth saw Dietrich's expression change to one of cold anger and determination.

'The sentry must have seen this happening. He was probably a party to this crazy plot!' Dietrich held up his hand as Hessler made as if to speak. 'No matter! It's too late for recriminations now!' He glared up at the sunlit oval above his head. 'Dear God, let us get back to sea! I'm so sick of this damned place!' Then in a more normal tone he said sharply: 'Right, muster all the petty officers in the wardroom. Issue them with machine-pistols and grenades. I want our own men to go to their quarters.' He dropped his voice. 'There might be some hotheads aboard who would want to go along with this ridiculous revolution!'

Hessler strode away, his face tense. But he seemed relieved that he had been given an order. It was something to hold on to.

Luth said softly, 'Before I called you, Heinz, that damned soldier told us Commander Lehmann is behind this business.'

Dietrich's eyes narrowed. 'You mean he left his patrol? Returned here and left the others to fend for themselves?' He passed his hand across his pale face. 'At least *our* captain is not a party to it!'

Luth's shocked face cracked into a short smile. 'Did you imagine he would be?'

Dietrich stepped back from the ladder. Half to himself he said, 'There have been times when I could have killed Steiger, but I think you know that!'

'I also know that we'd all be dead but for him!' Luth watched the orderly bustle of armed men by the wardroom.

Dietrich gave a small bitter smile. 'Well, now is our chance to prove that we can also die *because* of him!'

16 : Patriotic Mutiny

Max König peered through the hedge and then stepped out on to the cobbled road. He had thrown away the helmet and was wearing his blue cap which he considered to be less conspicuous. The rifle was heavy on his shoulder, and he again thought of discarding it, too. But the touch of its smooth stock gave him a small comfort, so without further hesitation he strode up the deserted road, his face set in a determined mask.

They would have discovered his absence by now, and even if the submarine had already put to sea the shore-patrols would be out looking for him. He plucked thoughtfully at the rifle sling. They would not take him alive. That was certain.

He increased his stride, his eyes busy on the isolated houses which dotted one side of the road, his ears pricked to detect the whine of a car engine or the grate of marching feet.

He would have to get some civilian clothes and a small store of food. Then he could make his way north and either surrender to the advancing Allies or merely melt into the inevitable aftermath of confusion and disorganisation which must follow any conqueror.

His glance fell on the last house in the road. Beyond it lay the open road and at least one army check-point. He slowed down and examined the building with great care. Windows closed. No sign of life. Probably owned by a St. Pierre shopkeeper who had already made himself scarce.

With a pounding heart he pushed open the sagging gate and crunched up to the front door. He glanced up. No faces at the windows. No telephone wires. So his desertion would not have preceded him, no matter what else lay in store.

He circled the house and pushed gently at the back door. Surprisingly, it opened, and in three seconds he was standing in a low, cool kitchen listening to the sounds of his own laboured breathing. The house was quite silent. He laid the rifle on the scrubbed table and began to examine the cupboards. A few tins. They would do for a beginning.

There was a small click behind him, and he swung round to stare down the barrel of a glinting Lüger.

For a long moment neither of them moved. The tall, broad-shouldered seaman in crumpled watchcoat and stained boots.

The slender, black-haired girl whose hand seemed lost around the big pistol.

'What are you doing? Are you a mutineer, too?' She shifted her position, as if the weight of the gun was too much for her. But the muzzle did not waver. Only the quick movement of her breasts beneath her dress betrayed a dangerous nervousness.

König accepted the first surprise only to be staggered by the second. The girl was obviously German, and vaguely familiar. He drew in his stomach muscles. German or not, it made no difference. He had to overpower her, even kill her if necessary. He heard himself ask in an unfamiliar tone, 'Mutineer?' He decided to hang on to the precious seconds. 'I did not realise that the house was occupied!'

She moved slowly round the kitchen, so that the table was between them. 'Who is your captain?'

The question was so unexpected that König was again caught off guard. He moved his legs, and instantly saw the girl's finger begin to tighten on the trigger.

Quickly he answered, 'Captain Steiger!'

Her lips parted, and for an instant he thought she was going to break down. But instead her eyes flashed with sudden anger. 'You lie! You were sent here to arrest me! I'll kill you before I let you lay a finger on me!' Her voice seemed to awake the old house, and König could feel the desperate tension which the girl appeared to give off.

He sighed and dropped his hands to his sides. 'I *am* one of Captain Steiger's men.' He half smiled, aware that further pretence was pointless. There was always a chance that he might think of something else. 'But I should have added that I deserted from the boat this morning!'

She took a pace towards him, her eyes fixed on his face as if to find some other truth. 'This morning? Then you do not *know*?'

König saw the gun muzzle droop very slightly. 'Know what? I left just before reveille and cut inland across the little wood. You are the first person I have seen, apart from a patrol on the hillside!' Perhaps she was mad? Or maybe she was just killing time until someone arrived.

The girl's mouth seemed to crumple. 'A deserter! How lucky you are!'

'Lucky?' König moved his right foot very slowly. A quick lunge across the table and he might throw her off balance.

In a strange flat voice she said: 'There is a mutiny at the Base!

Some officers have taken over control and have arrested your captain and his crew!'

König tensed as a motor vehicle rattled past the house, and then tried to reassemble his thoughts. What in God's name was happening to him? A mutiny, some sort of madness by the sound of it, had followed in the wake of his escape. But why? And who was behind it?

Aloud he said quietly, 'Why should they do that?'

'There was a plot. Some officers have assassinated Adolf Hitler!'

She glanced desperately at the window, and in that instant König acted. He did not remember leaping across the table, but his groping fingers seized the pistol, and the weight of his body sent her backwards against the wall. Surprisingly, she did not struggle, and the pistol when he examined it still had the safety-catch on.

In a beaten voice she said: 'Take what you want from the house. I no longer care.' Then she lifted her face, and he saw that she had already forgotten the reversal of their positions. She was urgent, pleading and frightened all in one long glance.

'Please help me! There is no one else now!'

König stepped away from her, the perfume of her hair still on his face. He must get clothes and food *now*, and get away!

Far away the drone of aircraft mingled with the insistent mutter of gunfire. Like the drone of bees on a lazy afternoon, it seemed to rob him of the will to think and act. *Hitler was dead,* yet he still could not grasp the significance of the news.

'Are you in trouble, too?' He looked at her slowly, seeing the tiny flame of hope his words had produced.

Before he could smash the stupidity of his question she said: 'I must help Captain Steiger! He will think I knew of this plot! Even now he will be hating me for something I did not do!'

Suddenly her eyes filled with tears and her body began to shake. It was like a knife turning in König's heart as he remembered Gisela's face when the Gestapo had seized hold of her.

The free, clean sense of escape he had enjoyed on the deserted hillside and when he had run through the sun-shadowed wood seemed to vanish with the finality of a door's closing. He bit his lip with sudden anger and tried to resurrect the memory of his old way of life. He had sworn that he would never again risk his freedom for anything or anyone! And yet . . . He stared down at her so that she dropped her head away from his grim features.

In a choked voice she said: 'I will give you everything I have. I will help you to escape if you will do this for me!' Her hands were bunched into two small fists. 'I will give you my body if only you'll help me!'

König placed the pistol very carefully on the table within her reach. He took her by the arm and led her to the only chair in the room. Quietly he said, 'Even if I agree what can I do?' He tried to smile. 'A deserter cannot be expected to fight the whole German Navy!'

'They have taken him to his room at the Base under guard. That is all I know. But together we might be able to think of something.'

He stared at her with uneasiness. 'How did you know about all this, if you had no part in it?'

She shrugged. 'My husband is Commander Lehmann. He is the ringleader!'

He started to speak, if only to erase the shock her words had given him, but his voice was drowned by the sudden crackle of anti-aircraft fire. The house quivered as the guns spoke to the sky, and their numbers multiplied until every gun on the coast seemed to have joined in. Upstairs a window-pane tinkled on the floor, and König was aware, too, of the mounting roar of aero engines.

He ran to the door and shaded his eyes against the bright sunlight. Stupefied he watched the tiny silver specks which glinted against the pale blue backcloth. Rank upon rank, but high and indifferent, like comets en route for another universe. The puffs of exploding shells looked sparse and ineffectual, but König pulled the girl back into the kitchen as whining fragments of shrapnel bounced down from the roof.

He had developed a way of life for so long that this seemed all the more unreal now that it had arrived. The waiting was over. His own small spark of defiance and injustice was nothing when matched against the terrible majesty of those invincible bombers.

'Quick! Over the road and into that ditch!'

He snatched the Lüger from the table and seized the girl by the wrist. All at once it seemed terribly important that they should stay together. Unprotesting, she ran with him to the ditch, and together they crouched against the crumbling side of sun-warmed clay to listen to the chorus of engines and gunfire.

König glanced sideways at the girl's determined face, and tried to match her with Captain Steiger's aloof hardness. Whatever had happened at St. Pierre that morning the Captain was a lucky man to have someone like *her*!

Her eyes widened with alarm as he pulled her roughly against his body, but then tensed as she saw his expression. Like an unearthly wind through a forest, or the maniac howl of a typhoon, the first curtain of bombs began to fall.

König shielded her body from the ground, knowing that within seconds the undisturbed countryside would be writhing in agony. He rested his chin in her hair and counted.

As the land erupted around him he remembered thinking how strange it was that so near the end of its endurance St. Pierre's own moment had arrived.

* * * * *

Dietrich was still standing below the conning-tower when Hessler reported that the petty officers and other key personnel had been armed and were standing by. An air of nervous expectancy seemed to pervade the humid air of the control room, and Dietrich had to take a conscious grip of himself to keep the rising fury restrained and at the back of his mind.

He quickly ran over the hurriedly conceived scheme which had startled him with its simplicity. As he had stayed at the foot of the ladder, his hands like claws on the rungs to prevent them from shaking, he had noticed the telephone handset rigged beside the helmsman's seat. The Captain always used it when the boat was entering or leaving harbour, so that he could stand right up on the bridge screen, a handset in his fist, and still be able to speak directly to the helmsman below in the control room. It saved the precious seconds when delay caused by passing and repeating orders to the voice-pipe might make all the difference. A sudden eddy or unexpected current around the harbour entrance, even a sharp gust of wind, and a slow-moving submarine might easily swing on to the ragged stonework or collide with another craft.

Hessler was panting noisily, his eyes white in the shadowed control room. He was watching Dietrich uneasily, his thick-set body framed against the gleaming dials and brass wheels at his back.

Dietrich straightened himself. 'That handset,' he spoke very quietly, 'is it still connected?'

Hessler nodded, his face mystified.

'Good. In two minutes I am going to call the bridge and tell the fools up there to go and tighten the mooring wires or something.' He smiled briefly. 'Then while the bridge is unguarded I will go up and resume command!' His smile broadened to a humourless grin. 'Simple, eh?'

Hessler spoke in urgent disjointed whispers. 'Why should they go? Anyway, the moorings don't need to be tightened, *you* know that!'

Dietrich glanced upwards at the bright blue oval of sky. He had seen a brief movement a few seconds earlier. A patch of field-grey. 'They are soldiers up there. I am relying on their thinking that the telephone is connected to the shore and not to here! In something as mad as this mutiny no one will have had time to instruct a lot of stupid soldiers in the mysteries of a U-boat!' Hessler's jaw dropped as Dietrich continued calmly: 'I am also depending on the German's ability to obey orders. Provided you shout loudly enough, he will obey anyone!'

He picked up the handset, and stared at it. 'Now this is what we will do.' He gestured to Luth and Reche who was standing anxiously in the background. 'Lieutenant Hessler will take command of the boat. You, Franz, will stand by engines and controls as usual, except that you will be a little short-handed.'

The Engineer nodded, his expression still dazed.

'You, Reche, will come with me. I want a petty officer and ten men, armed with machine-pistols and spare magazines. I will take them ashore as a landing party, while you,' he stared at Hessler, 'will take the boat to sea. Get clear of the coast, in case some fool has taken over the batteries on the headland, and stay out there until I give either a visual signal or call you on R/T. Got it?' He ended sharply so that the other officers started.

Hessler said slowly, 'Suppose the men on the bridge don't fall for your idea?'

'Then I'll go up myself and finish them with a grenade!' He grinned suddenly, so that his face looked like that of a mischievous boy.

Hessler nodded. He knew now that Dietrich meant what he said. Even although a grenade would kill the thrower as well as the soldiers in such a confined space.

Dietrich cleared his throat, and took a machine-pistol from Petty Officer Hartz. 'Right, Hartz. Select your men. I suggest that you take the gunners to save time. When we get on deck, release the mooring wires, and shoot anyone who tries to stop you!'

Hartz hurried away, his face grim.

Reche spoke for the first time. 'I'm not going, d'you hear?' His voice was shaking with fear. 'You're only doing this because you hate me!' He turned to the others. 'Or is it because of that French tart? You think I'm stupid, but I'll show you!'

Dietrich eyed him without emotion. The stillness in his pale eyes made his face like a mask, and all the more frightening.

Reche added loudly: 'I'm not going ashore! If there's a mutiny we may be involved! The whole of Germany may be against us!'

'For God's sake keep your voice down!' Hessler spoke hoarsely, his eyes on the blue muzzle of Dietrich's machine-pistol.

Dietrich shrugged, and his voice was almost matter-of-fact. 'You will obey orders, Reche. We are going ashore to get the Captain. Our place is at sea with the Group, and higher politics and mutiny are not our affair!' He tightened his mouth as he saw Hartz and his men making their way through the control room. 'Hessler will take over the bridge as we leave and con the boat clear of the harbour. Man the bridge guns and rake the jetty if they try to stop you!' He held Hessler's eyes with his own. 'Lehmann's boat is somewhere up ahead, but I doubt if they will be expecting this!'

Luth said quietly, 'and if *they* try to stop us?'

'Kill them! Germany can well do without their kind!' A spasm of despair passed momentarily across his face. 'I know the crew are only obeying orders! I *know* that! Just as our men are waiting like dumb beasts to obey us. They will suffer, but there is no other way.' He smiled bitterly. 'Captain Steiger would have said the same.'

Hessler nodded several times, his features heavy with the meaning of Dietrich's words. 'He would indeed!'

Reche was almost whimpering. 'Not me! Please let me stay behind!'

Dietrich tested the weight of the handset and turned away from the white-faced lieutenant. Almost to himself he said, 'And to think that my brother died with men better than you!' He cranked the handle viciously and listened.

Overhead a voice asked dubiously: 'Who is that? Corporal Knopf here!'

Dietrich shouted, 'Officer of the Guard speaking!' He felt his limbs quivering with uncontrollable excitement as he heard the soldier's feet click together. The plan was working. Aloud he said: 'Get down off that conning-tower and run to the hut on the jetty! I will join you in a moment! I believe someone is hiding there!'

There was a long silence, broken only by the sudden shriek of a passing gull. Then the voice said miserably, 'My orders were to stay here, sir!'

Dietrich glanced quickly at the others. They were all watching him with dazed fascination. 'How dare you question my orders! Do as I say at once!' He took one more gamble. 'We will cover the U-boat from here!' He slammed down the handset and held his breath.

For a moment nothing happened, then they heard the soldier's boots scraping down the ladder to the deck. One man, then a second. The bridge was clear.

Without looking to see if his party were following, Dietrich clawed his way towards the hatch. He ignored the pain in his shins as he threw himself over the rim and stumbled to his feet, the long pistol already gripped in both hands. The others blundered up behind him: Reche, whose face looked like paste, Petty Officer Hartz, with his head drawn into his shoulders as if he expected to be greeted by a fusillade of shots, old Jung, Rickover, and all the rest of the deck-gunners, until the bridge was swamped with figures.

There was a shout from the jetty, and Dietrich flung himself over the ladder and down on to the casing without noticing how he did it. One of the soldiers, the corporal, was running towards him, waving his rifle, his helmet jerking on his head like a coal-scuttle. Dietrich did not wait to hear what he was saying. He could not stop himself. He fired one sweeping burst across the sunlit jetty, so that the bullets cut across the man's middle like stitching. The force of the burst flung the man down, the helmet rolling noisily across the stonework and into the sea. He was an old man, bald-headed and fat, and Dietrich noticed briefly a thick gold ring on the man's hand as it clawed at the gushing torrent of scarlet and then fell still on the jetty like a discarded glove. The second soldier took to his heels, and as Dietrich fired after him leapt over the side of the wall. The weight of his boots and equipment carried him down, and only bubbles showed where he had tried to avoid Dietrich's vengeance.

Dietrich realised that the U-boat was already coming to life behind him. The diesels coughed into life, and the severed mooring wires snaked dangerously across the blood-spattered jetty at his feet. Seamen scampered along the narrow casing, and with savage desperation heaved at the jetty, dragging the fenders along the saddle tanks as the boat began to sidle clear.

'Petty Officer Hartz, up the jetty at the double!' Dietrich blinked at the sky, aware for the first time of the growing rumble of aircraft. With added urgency he yelled at Hessler across the widening gap of threshing water: 'Air-raid! It is for the Base this time!'

He did not know if Hessler understood, and at that moment the anti-aircraft guns began to fire beyond the town. He watched the growing pock-marks of shell-bursts, the exhilaration fanning through him like champagne. No time to wait. Must get on.

He gestured with the pistol to Reche, who was staring after the U-boat. 'Come on, man! We must get off this jetty before somebody cuts us down!'

Together they ran after the seamen as the air filled with the roar of engines.

▪ ▪ ▪ ▪

Unopposed by fighters, the first wave of enemy bombers cruised sedately across the headland, their lordly course marked by clear-white vapour trails like ships' movements on a blue chart. They shone momentarily in the sunlight as if struck by some secret weapon, while the whole force turned slightly towards the south-east and at a given signal released their bombs.

The first salvo blanketed the town square, exploding on the hard-packed cobbles and scything outwards into the dejected-looking houses, so that the walls seemed to buckle even before the full force of the detonations reached them. The tall grey church, the most imposing building in the town, staggered before the onslaught and then flew apart before the terrible wind and burst into a sea of flames. One bomb plummeted deeply into the tree-shaded churchyard before exploding at the foot of the steeple, so that, too, swayed and then collapsed in a towering cloud of dust and smoke.

Two lorries raced through a narrow street, sirens screaming, soldiers clinging like beetles from every handhold, when the street itself leapt skywards and then sucked the buildings down into a crater to swallow both lorries and the screaming men who burned even as the earth closed over their heads.

But there was no time for fear or conjecture. Stick after stick of high explosives screamed down into the packed buildings, each salvo more devastating than the last, and each getting nearer and nearer to the harbour itself.

Rudolf Steiger coughed in the thick dustcloud which started to filter into his room with the first explosions. He beat again and again on the door, his ears straining for some sound of life beyond. It was as if he was the only person left alive, a creature imprisoned and tortured by the savage bombardment which blanketed the town.

When he had been locked in the room, and only after the guard had departed, did he feel the true shock and impact of his position. Crowding into his mind, the implications mocked him like phantoms, so that he reeled about the room, sometimes shouting aloud, sometimes too dazed even to know what was happening.

He tried to compose himself, to weigh up the strength of Lehmann's actions. But it was useless. Viewed from any angle they seemed only to accentuate the hopelessness of their position. Did Lehmann really believe that the war would stand still and wait for him? No matter how sure and how dedicated were his followers and fellow conspirators, they could never hope to stem the tide of war which even now seemed to be breathing a sort of vengeance on the town itself. As if to boost up his own morale, Steiger's guard had talked loudly of the vastness and the strength of their plan. Hitler had failed them, so he must die. One plan had misfired, so another had to be implemented. It was like a child talking, or the confident tones of a raving lunatic!

Steiger had tried to reason with the young officer, even though his very soul seemed to scream out that he should throw himself at him, make one last gesture in the face of so much crude stupidity.

No matter how long they had been planning this coup, it had taken merely minutes to put into practice. If only half what the officer had said was true, right now in Paris the Gestapo and police officials would be under guard along with less reliable officers, and the armed forces would be turning to face their new masters. Bewildered, resentful or indifferent, it did not matter. Germany would be in the hands of men who were prompted by emotion, even cowardice. They would never admit failure, and Germany would be smashed piecemeal, her soldiers and sailors dying because of the foolishness and stupidity of a mere handful of idealists like Lehmann.

Somehow Steiger managed to remember his father's grave face and his words he had so often repeated when he had tried to explain the folly of his own war. 'You cannot fight without honour, Rudolf! There is no cause so important as the integrity of the German fighting man, and there is no duty higher than that of a German officer!'

The Headquarters building rocked to its very foundations, and he had to fight for breath as the air was sucked from the room. Through the barred window he could see the smoke clouds rolling like fog along the hillside, so that the sunlight was quenched and the grass seemed grey and lifeless.

He banged again on the door until his knuckles were raw. He thought of the U-boat helpless and dead beside the jetty, a target for the next salvo, if not already a mass of twisted steel, a coffin, as Hessler had so often prophesied. And at sea the rest of the Group, the last loyal survivors, would be patiently waiting for him to lead them into battle. Even they might already be pinned down by a killer-group of frigates, or swimming for their lives in the Atlantic they had fought for so long.

Suddenly calm, he sat down on the edge of his bed, his hands entwined in his lap. Like drowning, there was perhaps no point in fighting when the end was inevitable. He tried to shut out the picture of the open sea, of order and discipline which prevailed even when all else failed. To die like an animal in a trap, even a trap made by his own kind, was still only death in another guise.

A great roar of falling masonry shook the walls and brought part of the ceiling crashing at his feet. It could not be long now.

He closed his eyes and tried not to see the picture of the girl's face. Perhaps she was already dead, or even now crying out her life beneath that small house while the world went mad around her. Lehmann had said she knew nothing of the mutiny. It was strange that such a man could deny himself the pleasure of torturing Steiger even further. Perhaps he had known it was useless to pretend that the girl he had neglected could have given herself to another man, or maybe deep down he was still the same man Steiger had once known and admired.

Steiger quickly hardened his heart against Lehmann. Anyone who could use his wife in such a way must be worthless and unreliable. If the plot worked, she would be shamed for ever. If it failed, she would be arrested by the Gestapo as an accomplice. It was strange how her position resembled that of the murdered French girl. An enemy of no one, a lover of only one, she had been the first to suffer.

He stared suddenly at the four gold stripes on his sleeves. Patterned with dust and falling plaster, they still symbolised something real. He had gained the same rank held by his father and many of his ancestors. Yet, unlike his father and so many of his family, he was not facing the worst moment of his life on his bridge or matching his brain against what he could see through a periscope lens. The thought seemed to steady him and burn through his veins like a forgotten fire.

The air was acrid now with burning woodwork and scorching paint, and the thud of bursting bombs was mixed with the hissing roar of fire. The sudden rattle of gunfire in the passageway made him jump to his feet, his stinging eyes fixed on the door. Perhaps the enemy had broken through Reimann's clumsy defences even while the defenders argued and changed sides. Even that would be better than dying in shame and humiliation. He stood very still as the door opened slowly, his gaze dropping to the muzzle of a machine-pistol which poked round the doorway like the head of some vicious reptile.

For a long moment he stared at Dietrich's smoke-blackened face, and then at the feet of the dead officer who lay sprawled in the passageway. Over Dietrich's shoulder he could see Hartz and the boxer Jung. They were all watching him again, gauging his reactions as before. He bit his lip hard, the emotion only just held in check by the pain, and then stepped into the smoke-filled corridor. For another moment he looked down at the dead lieutenant, whose staring eyes were still alive to surprise and bewilderment. Just one of the victims. Like a lone survivor from a stricken ship who too late sees his momentary escape fading in the loneliness of despair and final death.

He allowed Dietrich to lead him through the smoke, only half aware of the great cracks and fissures which criss-crossed the walls and the broken glass which appeared on every side. Shadowy figures loped to meet them, more familiar faces, yet all different. Out of their element they looked hunted and wild. Like released animals.

Dietrich dropped on to one knee and pulled Steiger down beside him as the air was again torn by the shriek of bombs. As they crouched and blinked away the spurting dust Dietrich related what had happened, and once more Steiger felt the unnerving pain of gratitude and disbelief. The submarine had escaped, and yet Dietrich had come back for him.

He found that the others were on their feet again, and with a great effort he broke into a run as Dietrich shouted: 'Round the other side, Hartz! Cover the main entrance!'

Steiger realised that they were standing in what was left of the Headquarters building, a sagging, blackened shell ripped open on the seaward side, and all but roofless. Medical orderlies were plunging through the smoke, their Red Cross armbands clean against the chaos and desolation, their faces squinting as they searched for survivors. An armed sentry was peering from behind a sandbagged barrier, and he saluted as Steiger and his party hurried by. Dietrich lowered his pistol a mere fraction and showed his teeth. 'The new order changeth, apparently!'

Steiger glanced at him with fresh surprise. Dietrich sounded as if he was cheerfully sorry that the sentry had not resisted. He would have killed him in one more second.

With that thought still in his mind, Steiger pushed open the door to the Operations Room and stared at the two storm lanterns which cast a feeble glow over the broken glass and plaster, which, mingled with the filth from fire extinguishers, had been ground into every inch of the room's thick carpet. The steel shutters had been drawn across the tall windows, and Steiger thought briefly of the cheerful sunlight which had been filtering through these windows such a short while earlier.

Bredt was still at his desk, and for a few more moments Steiger thought him to be dead or unconscious. A telephone was buzzing impatiently in its leather case, and a red light winked from another. The same staff officers were still there, too, and stood listlessly by the wall, their eyes on the tall figure in the doorway.

Steiger noticed, too, that there was a bright clean rectangle on the empty wall, where Bredt's precious chart had hung until a bomb blast had scattered it to the wind.

Of Lehmann there was no sign, but as Steiger strode into the room Bredt looked up, the lamplight glinting on his tear-stained face. In a strange voice he said: 'It was not my fault! I *had* to do what I was told!' He blinked and then rubbed his eyes with his hand. 'You do understand, don't you?' His tone was pleading, and he seemed unconscious of the men around him and the levelled pistols of Steiger's sailors. Bredt continued brokenly: 'I did what I thought was best. Now it is too late!'

Steiger controlled the rising anger with an effort. 'What has been happening?' And when Bredt stayed staring at him, he leaned across the desk and slapped him hard on the cheek. '*Answer* me, and stop thinking of yourself!'

Bredt fingered the red mark on his cheek with surprise. 'Lehmann assured me it was all going to be all right!' He sounded baffled and shocked. 'There have been signals.' He gestured towards the telephone which had suddenly stopped buzzing. 'I could not act because Lehmann said they were not ready.' He shook his head. 'Now it is too late!'

Steiger gripped the rim of the desk. '*What* signals?'

'Supreme Headquarters have ordered us to evacuate the Base. Boats at sea must make for German ports or scuttle themselves if they are out of fuel.' He stared round at his shattered room. 'People who are caught in the Base are to destroy all installations and make their way across France and try to join up with the main army!'

Steiger took a deep breath. 'So the Front has collapsed?'

Bredt did not seem to hear. 'Major Reimann is with his men on the main road. A report came in to say that parachutists have been dropped and have joined up with the French Terrorists.' With sudden vehemence he lifted his voice. 'Lehmann said it would be different! I did not pass on these signals because I *believed* him! Now the Terrorists have blown the main road bridge and mined the side roads! We are trapped here like pigs for the slaughter!'

Steiger tensed as another stick of bombs lifted the floor like the deck of a ship. The Base was cut off at last. It had already been forgotten by the High Command, who were no doubt busy enough with the main assault. In spite of the urgency he felt, he forced himself to ask, 'And what of the Great Plot?'

Bredt shrugged. A hopeless, broken gesture. 'Hitler lives. The plot failed!' He glared at the telephone through which the message must have been passed. 'Lehmann *lied*!'

Steiger spoke to the room, 'And where is *he*?'

An elderly commander spoke from a corner: 'Dead! He shot himself!'

Dietrich perched himself on the edge of the desk and wiped his eyes. 'God! Aren't these precious characters superb? Even now they speak with such reverence of their own destroyers!' He choked back a laugh which seemed about to break from his throat. 'Christ protect Germany from Germans!'

Steiger said sharply: 'I must find Major Reimann! We must reorganise here and try to contact the Group!'

Bredt said half to himself: 'Reimann will surrender in half an hour. If they will let him!'

Steiger felt suddenly sick and tired. 'Nobody surrenders!' He gestured to Dietrich. 'Come on, we will head inland to Reimann's command post! And you,' he glared at the silent officers, 'stay here until I return!'

Lehmann was dead. Everything was collapsing. 'Is Lehmann's boat still at the jetty?' It might still be possible to evacuate by sea.

Dietrich stretched himself. 'Done for! The first bombs on the harbour ripped the side out of it!'

So now there were only four boats left. And they were without a leader.

Harshly he said: 'Later there will be a lot to answer for! But now we have a great deal to do!'

Dietrich took a last look at the shattered room. 'By then it might be too late to matter!'

■ ■ ■ ■ ■

Leaving the outskirts of the town was like emerging from a fog, and as the file of blue-uniformed figures made its way slowly along the scarred road and into the protective woodland, Steiger found a moment to marvel at the suddenness of the destruction which the bombers had left behind. He signalled a halt and stood in silence as his men threw themselves thankfully on the sun-warmed grass. Overhead the trees spread a little shade, yet across the blue the remains of the vapour-trails still hung motionless and threatening.

Steiger felt the sweat running down his spine, and glanced down at his weary men. They had been too long in U-boats to be a match for this sort of thing. Even a single patrol rendered a man useless for a forced march over unfamiliar ground. Hollow-eyed and breathing heavily they sat or lay in the grass, seemingly indifferent to the occasional crackle of small-arms fire somewhere ahead, and totally oblivious to the rumble of distant gunfire which had now become constant and part of life.

The twin hills looked peaceful and inviting from this different angle, linked together by the silver horizon of the Atlantic, so that the shimmering water looked like that in a giant dam. Between the hills lay the smoking remains of the town, outlined against the sea, blackened and shattered and burning fiercely in several places at once.

Across the still air Steiger could hear the occasional scream of a siren and the clatter of falling stonework. Figures moved briefly against the terrible backdrop, small and pathetic, lost in the vastness of their tragedy. Craters pitted the fields, and dead cows lay with their legs in the air, stiff and obscene in the warm sunlight.

Steiger looked again at his men. Dietrich was leaning against a tree, tapping his boot with the barrel of his pistol. There was something unfamiliar and disturbing about him. He seemed impatient, even eager, for whatever lay ahead, as if he was controlled by some alien force.

Lieutenant Reche, his plump face blotchy and perspiring, sat crouched on his haunches, neither relaxed nor vigilant. He stared straight ahead, his mouth hanging open as he gulped at the air like a fish.

Petty Officer Hartz stood a little apart from the ten seamen, his set features giving nothing away as he slowly filled and lit a small blackened pipe.

Steiger thought briefly of the seaman who had deserted. But for him none of this might have happened. Even if Lehmann had returned as before, the alarm might have been raised, and Steiger doubted if the complacent Base officers would have been so eager to obey Lehmann had they time to consider the consequences. And it was all in the space of hours. Hitler was dead. Hitler was alive again. Twin rumours which had never even reached the bulk of the people who mattered. Steiger found that as before he was strangely unmoved by the possibility of the Leader's death. No one man was that important. Each one should play his part, give his contribution to the whole, and then move on. Like his own father, and his father before that. Steiger plucked at the button on his jacket. And now me.

Wearily he passed his hand across his stubbled chin. There was so much to think about. So much planning.

The harbour had seemingly vanished, so that the battered wreck of Lehmann's boat was mingled with the semi-submerged stones which had once been jetties. Cranes lay broken and useless by the isolated bunkers, and even one of the flak-towers had been lifted cleanly from its perch to lie with its gunners in deep water.

If Hessler tried to bring the U-boat back it would be very dangerous to approach in daylight. Surfaced and amongst the broken harbour works it would be a sitting target for any sudden air attack. He looked at his watch. There was still a lot to do before nightfall, and by then it could be too late, as Bredt had said.

Suppose Hessler did not choose to return? No one could blame him if he took the submarine into open waters. He remembered his feelings when Dietrich had burst open the door of his prison and felt ashamed. Hessler would return, with or without a signal. What he might find was another matter entirely.

He walked over to his two officers. It was ridiculous, of course. There was no reason at all why Major Reimann should obey his orders. He cursed inwardly as he thought of Fischer and his S.S. men. Even their additional support would have been welcome now. He pictured Major Fischer's smooth, elegant features and felt an unreasoning surge of anger. But for him and his sort things might have been different. If only . . . He shook himself and said sharply, 'We must get ready to move!' He watched the misery on Reche's face. 'I want to get Reimann to reopen the road. The Base personnel can still get through then.'

Dietrich yawned. 'It will be like joining the Army for them!'

'For all of us!' Steiger added, smiling tightly in spite of his tensions. He waved to Hartz, who immediately tapped out his pipe and moved over to the men.

One of the seamen, Muller, stood up and stared back at the town. 'I'll bet they'll be needing some coffins down there, eh? I should have stayed in my trade!'

Jung tottered to his feet and rubbed his thighs vigorously. 'It's the same in every war, comrade. Only the undertakers can win in the end!'

Joking and complaining they picked up their weapons and waited obediently to move off.

A spent bullet from somewhere distant whistled over their heads and cut down a handful of leaves.

Dietrich seemed to come alive again. 'Keep those men spread out! There'll be snipers most likely!'

Steiger realised, perhaps for the first time, what he was leading his men into. Perhaps he was wrong. What after all did it really matter if a few German troops did surrender, or some useless installations fell into enemy hands? He tightened his lips as he remembered the French girl's mutilated body. It was no longer quite as easy as that. He glanced sideways at Dietrich and wondered if he, too, was thinking the same thing.

17: Blood for Blood

They stood in what had once been the main bedroom of a tall villa above the harbour. Now, like the façade of a film set, it offered its empty windows to the glittering sea, while the rear of the building gaped hollow and shattered, with the bomb-scarred beams and rafters still smoking and charred in the sunlight. The old-fashioned and heavily patterned wallpaper hung in shreds, and the wide brass-railed bedstead which had once dominated the room hung at an angle over the narrow street below. It was hot in the room, a sun-trap below the roofless cage of broken beams which threw great bars of black shadow across the litter and debris which was left in the wake of the bombers.

König balanced himself precariously on the cracked window ledge and peered across the littered harbour. It seemed quite impossible to recognise anything which was familiar, except for the wrecked U-boat and the sea beyond. It had become a dead town already, a place which waited for another assault or some other disaster to complete the final destruction.

Behind him the girl leaned heavily against the wall, her eyes closed against the sunlight and from the exhaustion of their dash through the wrecked streets. The plain grey dress was ripped in several places, and one shoulder was completely bare and patterned with tiny droplets of blood. In one hand she still clutched a small bag, while the other lay across her breast as she tried to regain her breath.

After a while König said slowly: 'The boat has gone. The Captain must have made his own plans, after all.'

A fresh cloud of dust swirled in the street below as a lorry full of sailors rocked around a corner and then vanished towards the main road. 'The Base personnel seem to have gone, too.'

With something like despair König sat down on the ledge and looked at the girl. But for her he might have left the town far behind. After all his high intentions and blind sentiment the facts were worse than before. Even Captain Steiger had managed to get away. The small struggle for power had shifted once more, but to the enemy they would all seem the same. The complete ruthlessness of the air-raid still left him dazed. In spite of their certainty of victory in France, the Allies had blotted out this town with the ease of an elephant crushing a beetle. To destroy a small German base they had smashed a whole town and wiped out a way of life. Yet even now the French Resistance would be rallying to help the new invaders. Did they hate the Germans so much they could ignore their own personal losses so completely?

König said, 'I think we should go down and try to find someone who will take you on one of the lorries.' His words sounded empty and he knew that she recognised the defeat in his voice. No one would stop for either of them now. This was no orderly evacuation. It was panic at its worst.

She shook her head so that her hair shimmered in the sunlight, in spite of the dust which had settled on it. 'I am not running away any more.' She shrugged. 'I only wanted to tell him that I did not betray him. But, of course, in his eyes I must seem already false!'

'I think you are mistaken.' König grounded his rifle and rubbed his hands against the warm metal. The girl had turned her face away, and he could sense the sudden barrier her words had thrown between them. Suddenly it was all very clear to him. By knowing of her husband's part in the plot to overthrow Hitler she had become partly guilty herself. Yet in spite of this terrible knowledge she had nursed the belief that Rudolf Steiger at least would be saved. Out of the Atlantic, away from the war, he might after all be spared from destruction. König knew that she had wanted to share her thoughts with him, to gain comfort or be condemned. But even she must have realised that Steiger's pride and hard-bred devotion to duty were too strong for the ties of emotion. Even love.

König watched a single gull circling above the building. Steiger believed too much in his cause. He *had* to believe. But with or without Lehmann and his fellow conspirators Germany would be made to suffer and realise something more than just defeat. When that time came Steiger would need all the strength possessed by this strange, desperate girl. His own power would die with his convictions.

As if reading his thoughts, she said suddenly: 'I will be waiting. Somehow, I will be waiting!'

König opened his mouth to reply, but realised that she was speaking to herself. He shrugged and turned away. She was right in one sense. What was the point of running away? For years he had hated and feared men like Major Fischer, whose barbarity had torn Germany apart. Now, perhaps for the first time, he realised that other men, dedicated like Steiger, were as helpless and deluded as he had been.

From the corner of his eye he saw a movement amongst the ruins of a small shop. He thought it might be a wounded survivor or somebody searching for lost possessions, but as he watched he saw a group of men emerge on to the street and stand watchfully amongst the fallen bricks and broken glass, the sun shining brightly on their levelled weapons and gaily coloured armbands.

König's mouth went dry as a German soldier, hatless and tattered, ran round the corner of the street and then skidded to a halt in front of the waiting men.

Once more König reached across to the girl and held her against his body. He pressed his hands around her ears so that she should hear nothing of the hideous drama which had started with such unexpected savagery below.

With dulled fascination König watched from around the scarred wall, his mind once again adjusted to all the horror he had known before. The Frenchman in the armbands had seized the soldier, and the sunlight had shifted to their knives as they began to work on their prisoner's twisting body.

Soon it was done, and the men moved away down the road to leave the soldier glistening in the dust. In a short while there would be other killings, and more terrible tortures to free the spirit of revenge. The collaborators, the prostitutes and the last of the fleeing Germans, all would know that terror. König felt the girl tremble beneath his hands as if she was reading his mind. The men in the streets would become beasts. What would they do to a German woman before they let her die?

He glanced across at his rifle. As she had said, there was no point in running away.

. . . . .

The sun was high above the western sea so that inland beyond the town the hills and trees were masked by haze and smoke. On the humid air, sporadic and indistinct, echoed bursts of machine-gun fire and the occasional thud of a grenade, but down by the harbour the water hissed and lapped against the warm stone-work with playful indifference.

Steiger sat with his back against a fallen slab of masonry and stared up at the gaunt outline of the Headquarters building. Fire had gutted the main structure, and apart from a few rooms, the rest was hollow and empty. It was odd to think that beneath the shattered bricks, in the deep, strengthened cellars where the useless radio lay unwatched and broken, there were still several living beings, like characters in a world of madness.

Two or three staff officers, spent after a last orgy of drinking, lay staring at the walls, while a few French officials, including the Mayor, sat with their women and their late masters, still unable to grasp the finality of their position.

Petty Officer Hartz appeared round the edge of the rubble. Like everything and everybody he was coated in dust. 'Sentries posted, Captain. I have made the remainder of the men take some rest.'

Steiger nodded. 'Have they been fed?'

'There is not much left, sir. There's been a lot of looting.' He forced a grin. 'There seems to be plenty of drink available!'

Steiger closed his eyes. Hartz might be making a joke, or perhaps he was trying to voice the bitterness he must feel at the behaviour of some of the leaders he had obeyed and trusted for so long. 'Very well, Hartz. Go and get some rest yourself.' When he opened his eyes the man had gone.

He listened to the vibration of gunfire and tried not to think of Trudi Lehmann. Perhaps she was already speeding to safety on one of Major Reimann's lorries to find the main bulk of the retreating army. Safety? Who could tell even that any more?

Steiger had found Reimann in his concrete command post beyond the town's limits after a weary search amidst dis-organised troops and careering transport. The roads were lit-tered with shattered vehicles which had found some of the cunningly concealed mines left by the Terrorists, or had been caught in the inferno which had followed the bombing.

Reimann had been sitting on an upended ammunition crate consuming a tin of beans with a rusty spoon. Even now Steiger could not accept the change which had come to the fat soldier, and he could remember clearly the anger in the man's eyes when he had asked him what he was doing to clear the road and keep open an escape route.

His voice, too, was different. He was no longer the down-trodden, resentful soldier. 'I have prepared my men, Captain!' His thick voice had echoed round the small bunker. 'The soldiers you all chose to ridicule, remember? Now that's all different! My stupid, *cowardly* troops are preparing to fight their last battle for Germany!' For a moment his piggy eyes had clouded over. 'All except for twenty who got lost while those fools at the Base were playing at saving the Reich!' Without waiting for Steiger to ask he had added viciously: 'Twenty deluded soldiers! They were hanged in a neat line beside the road!'

Across Steiger's shoulder Dietrich had asked sharply, 'Terrorists?'

And then Reimann had laughed. Just as Dietrich had laughed in the Operations Room when Bredt had shown his despair and bitterness. 'No, my young friend! Major Fischer's S.S. men hanged them! While the German Army pulls back, and I am asked to hold this road until my last bullet is spent, Fischer's butchers were hanging my men! They even found time to paint little signs to hang around their necks!' He had scrambled unsteadily to his feet, and Steiger had caught the bitter tang of schnapps. '"German traitor!" Or sometimes the signs said: "I was a dupe of the enemy!"' The piggy eyes had glowed in the shaft of sunlight from a weapon-slit. '*There's* a real soldier's end for you!'

'And where is Major Fischer?' Steiger had felt the same sickened disgust he had experienced that night in the square beside Fischer's cairn of victims.

Reimann was reaching for his helmet. 'Dead, I trust! My sergeant neglected to inform him that the road he was taking was heavily mined.' He threw back his head and laughed again. 'He was running away, too! His magnificent work completed.'

He had stared for a long moment at Steiger's grave face. 'So here *we* are! You, the cream of the Navy, depending on me and my men, the dregs of a forgotten army!'

He had pushed past the two naval officers and blundered into the sunlight. Over his fat shoulder he had called: 'When we met you told me my coastal batteries were useless! You said that the enemy would come down this road! Well, you were almost right. Except that right now the bastards are all round us! Parachutists, Terrorists and any ill-advised swine who can pull a trigger! By God, if I am going to be killed I am going to give them a run for their money!'

Steiger had watched him go. A fat, shambling figure in helmet and stained uniform. A caricature of German arms, but a soldier.

He passed his hand across his eyes and listened to the sudden crackle of small-arms close at hand. Perhaps even now Reimann was coughing out his blood on that damned road. But at no time had he mentioned surrender.

. . . . .

Dietrich lay on his stomach, a long blade of grass between his teeth. Surprisingly, it tasted of salt and he knew that if he twisted his head he would see the empty waters of the Bay.

It was odd when you thought about it. With my back to the sea, he thought. Like heroes of Ancient Greece, except that they fought on their own ground. He watched some starlings circling angrily above a smouldering building. Disturbed and baffled. Well, they are not alone.

He tried to picture the cool efficiency of the U-boat's control room, but the vision eluded him. Here it was quite different. There was menace and latent danger, like the smouldering buildings, but nothing moved which he could recognise as openly hostile. If only something or somebody would move. He reached out to touch the machine-pistol, its smooth barrel warm as if from firing.

Petty Officer Hartz slithered down at his side and with him stared at the deserted town. Quietly he said, 'Lieutenant Reche is missing, sir.' No emotion, just this strange air of bewildered calm which they all seemed to have inherited.

He heard himself reply. 'Have you informed the Captain?'

'Yes, sir. He says for you to remain here and watch our front.'

Watch our front. Dietrich stirred restlessly, like a gun-dog. Already we are acting like land-creatures. Watch our front. Aloud he said, 'Where would he go?' He imagined Reche's untidy body crouching and doubling through the crumbling streets. Going where? North, or east? Behind lay the sea, but elsewhere who could be sure?

'He might be making for Army Headquarters, sir.' Hartz sounded almost disinterested.

He could not run fast enough to keep up, Dietrich thought savagely.

'How are the men?'

'Ach, they are all right, sir.'

'I suppose they are blaming me for bringing them ashore?' Dietrich turned to look at the older man.

'If you had not acted as you did,' the petty officer jerked his thumb towards the broken U-boat by the jetty, 'we would be like that!'

Dietrich shrugged. The U-boat had settled itself upright amongst the debris of the jetty, a broken memorial to Lehmann's dreams and ideals. 'I hate this place.' He spoke calmly, but his fingers were hooking into the sandy soil which felt so warm and friendly. 'I can't fight something which I can't see!'

Hartz rose on one knee and then fell flat as a bullet whined overhead and splattered against the brickwork. 'Christ!'

Dietrich lifted himself on his elbows. 'They're here!' He laughed shortly at the emptiness of his words. Who were here, and how many? An army perhaps, or maybe the combined wrath of France had decided to force them into the sea and purge their country of the enemy.

Poor Odile. He had not even been with her at the end. He thought of Steiger and the strange burial-party on the hillside. What had they been trying to save him from?

A sudden gust of small-arms fire raked the ruins nearby and brought a few shots in reply from the hidden seamen. 'Tell them to hold their fire!'

Damn them all, he thought. I wish to God I was down there in the cellar with those stupid bastards and their women! One last orgy, one final display of power!

A bullet hit the bank in front of his face, and he felt the grit patter against his forehead. Perhaps the men who murdered Odile were trying to get him, too. The thought inflamed him like a raw wound and he groped for the pistol.

All over France it must be like this, he pondered, as calm restored itself to his taut mind. There must always be the few who are on the very end of a retreat, just as the few are always on the prongs of an attack. The rare, lonely ones who never survived. How could they understand that they were expendable like the cartridge cases and the discarded weapons? Flesh and blood. Hopes and fears. Perhaps my brother was like that. Even Odile.

A seaman called hoarsely, 'I can see a group of them up that alley, sir!'

Dietrich blinked. Of course, that was Muller. He had picked

up a pair of field-glasses as a souvenir. They might be useful, after all.

'Right! You, Muller and Jung move off to the right and we'll head them off!' Enough of this waiting. He looked towards the sea. 'And *you* come with me!' The third man showed his white face. It was Moses Rickover.

The boy nodded violently, his head moving like a puppet's. 'Very good, sir!'

Dietrich crawled through the grass, his elbows grating on the small pieces of bomb-blasted rubble. Before each move he lifted his head to watch the shadowed street. They were probably looting while they waited for the cover of night.

Dietrich's heart began to thump again, and he quickened his pace. It was no longer ship against ship, or even German against Frenchman. It was man against man. Blood for blood.

He heard Rickover's fast breathing and bared his teeth like an animal.

. . . . .

Lieutenant Gunter Reche broke into a clumsy run as he cleared the harbour limits and turned into a narrow street where the buildings seemed to lean to meet each other against the sky. Already he was out of breath and his shirt was clinging with sweat. He knew that he had no time to rest or falter, he *had* to find an army outpost and get through to the last of the retreating forces. His eyes were blinded with perspiration and tears as he thought of Dietrich's insane cruelty. To bring him ashore against his will and then allow him to be left for slaughter! The Captain, too, with his sense of duty! Well, let them rot in this place! Stupid, arrogant fools!

He stared foolishly at two soldiers who sat by the roadside, their dead eyes already hidden by eager flies. We will all be like that! The panic gripped him once more and he forced himself into a run.

Further along the street a dead woman lay with a child in her arms, her body covered in brick dust, while at her side stood a vase of flowers quite untouched.

A figure stepped out into the sunlight, and Reche thought for a second that his heart had stopped beating. His dazed mind was swamped by several realisations at once. It was neither a German nor a Terrorist. As he stood gulping air and peering at the stranger he managed to take in the unfamiliar camouflaged smock and alien helmet, and then he realised that he was confronted by an enemy soldier. For a moment they stared unwinkingly at each other.

The soldier's expression of startled anxiety slowly changed, and a lazy grin spread across his unshaven face. He was tall, and the chinstrap of his paratrooper's helmet hung unfastened across his chest. Reche watched it fascinated as it swung in time to the man's breathing.

It was all finished. No more fear of death. There would be no humiliation in captivity, but just somewhere to hide, to sink into oblivion until the worst was over.

He lifted his hands and tried to smile, but the man took a pace back, his high-laced boots creaking in the dust. Then he lifted the small carbine from his side and levelled it at Reche's stomach. Too late Reche realised what was happening and let out one last desperate scream.

There was no pain, but he realised that he was lying on the warm cobbles, a great numbness squeezing his body until he could feel the veins swelling in his head and shutting out his vision.

He lifted his face and tried to see the soldier. It was all a mistake. Perhaps there was still time.

The effort of movement brought the pain and with it the unending scream which he could not control. Frantically he rolled on to his side, his fingers groping for the soldier's leg. His arm stiffened in mid-air, the fingers still pointing at the smoking carbine.

Trapped by the cobbles his blood formed a bright crucifix which shimmered in the sun, as if still alive.

The soldier relaxed again and stood for a moment looking at the corpse at his feet. Unbeknown to Reche, he had been afraid, too. Lost and searching for his comrades, he had met the running officer merely by chance.

A ray of light glistened on Reche's wristwatch, and the soldier reached out to remove it. His movement was automatic and without conscious thought.

Above him in the shattered villa König held his breath and squeezed the trigger of his rifle. The sound of that single shot once more awakened the dead town and made the startled birds circle angrily overhead. The blue smoke hung in the air, while below the soldier embraced Reche's body as if asking for forgiveness.

König turned wearily to watch the girl. She was looking beyond the two figures in the street.

'I know that man!' Her voice was a mere whisper.

König nodded dumbly. 'Yes. Some of the others must be here, too.' With sudden urgency he gripped her wrist and started towards the sagging stairway. 'Come on! We'll make a run for it!'

After all, it was better to be with your own kind at the end, That was where Reche had made his last mistake.

. . . . .

A single, long-drawn-out explosion engulfed St. Pierre and for a moment blotted out all other sounds. A few pieces of brickwork shook themselves free in the blast from the top of the Headquarters building and thudded on to the flagged terrace, whilst the solitary sentry who sheltered behind a cracked pillar stared uncomprehendingly at the stately column of brown smoke which rose straight up towards the clear sky.

Steiger paused in his dash across the terrace and stared at it. The arsenal. Somewhere on the far side of the town Reimann's remaining sappers had fired the fuses. A signal for destruction as well as their own defeat.

Blinking away the dust, Steiger groped his way down the steps and into part of the building's labyrinth of cellars. Without electric power the rough-cast stonework was lit by storm lanterns, and in addition, near the entrance a bright bonfire of confidential books and papers was pouring out such heat as to turn the normally cool place into a furnace.

Captain Bredt was crouching over the fire, raking the embers with a long steel rod, his face set in a concentrated frown.

Steiger watched him warily. 'You wanted me?'

Bredt jumped to his feet, his eyes glittering like a sparrow's. 'Yes. Yes, of course I wanted you!' He sounded petulant, and Steiger wondered what on earth the man could find to complain about with his whole world collapsing about his ears.

Bredt took another lunge at the fire and threw the rod aside. His cheeks were scarlet from the heat, and he seemed to be unable to control a twitch at the corner of his mouth.

'Yes, Captain. Now let me see.' Bredt frowned hard, so that his eyes disappeared beneath his brows. 'I want to be quite sure that everyone understands what is happening.'

In a tired voice Steiger said: 'The arsenal has been blown. They will be attacking us next.' He saw no understanding in

Bredt's eyes so he continued, 'My men are keeping a lookout for *U-991*, and as soon as she is sighted I will signal her inshore with the battery-operated projector.'

'*U-991*?' Bredt looked up sharply. 'What about the other boat?' He chuckled and rubbed the palm of his hand against his ribs in a quick circular movement. 'Aha, Captain, I see you had overlooked that one!' A look of cheerful cunning crossed his sweating face. 'Still, you cannot be expected to remember things like that. You see, Captain, *I* have been trained for such things. Method, planning and discipline!' He smiled condescendingly at Steiger's impassive face. 'Well, no one can say I have not done my best here! *And* it has been without much help, I can tell you!'

Steiger flinched as a withering burst of Spandau fire echoed down the steps. One of his men must have seen someone trying to get near to the defences.

Bredt did not appear to notice. 'I hope they appreciate in Berlin what I have been doing!' He patted Steiger's sleeve. 'Never mind. You can leave such matters to wiser heads. You play your part and I will be satisfied!'

Steiger took off his cap and ran his fingers through his hair. His whole being was screaming out for reprieve, and he wanted to give in, to let himself drop at Bredt's feet and just wait for the end. What was the point of anything any more? It had been bad enough with the uncertainty of a mutiny and being locked in a room while the bombers razed the town to the ground. What was the use of trying to explain to Bredt that the other U-boat was useless, when he must have seen it for himself?

Bredt was fumbling with his coat, his single hand moving like a crab across the bright buttons. '*I* will personally take command of *U-985*!' He grinned roguishly at Steiger's shadowed face. 'I may be an old hand, but I never forget my tricks, eh?' All at once he was serious again. 'As Senior Officer I will be the last to leave. I will take over Lehmann's boat and cover your withdrawal!'

Steiger turned away. Oh, God! The shock and suddenness of events has destroyed Bredt's mind. Steiger could hear him talking excitedly as he groped vaguely amongst the equipment which was scattered on the floor. I could put him under arrest and forcibly remove him when we leave. . . . *If* we leave.

Another series of explosions shook the walls, and Steiger felt the sickness of defeat crowding his brain like blood.

He moved clear as Bredt ran lightly up the steps.

Well, why shouldn't Bredt stay here if he wants to? It would be a merciful end for him. If he returned to Germany he would be crucified when his part in the mutiny became known. The High Command would never accept his explanations. He would be the only remaining scapegoat. Perhaps it was that terrible knowledge which had finally unhinged him.

For the first time Steiger looked at Bredt with something like compassion. All those plans for promotion, his stupidity in a role he would not admit was too big for him. Even his absurd personal standards had cost him dear. He was nothing. Not even a man.

Bredt disappeared up the steps, and could be heard shouting orders in a loud, strident voice.

He is calling for his men. Steiger shrugged and walked slowly after him. Apart from Dietrich and his Landing Party and a few wounded men from the Base, the place was deserted. Yet Bredt was quite convinced that he was at the peak of his power.

Petty Officer Hartz was staring after the one-armed officer. 'Shall I look after him, Captain?' He sounded shocked.

'Leave him. He is happy the way he is. God knows, there will be enough to do here in a moment!'

They both stiffened as a voice shouted, 'She's coming, sir!'

They looked up at the seaman, Michener the ex-policeman, who was gesticulating and pointing from the naked frame of a blasted window. Even from the terrace Steiger could see the tears on the man's face as he capered and shouted, his eyes fixed on the glittering sea.

Steiger felt sick and shaking. At the very last moment. Yet even this was earlier than Hessler should have dared. 'Man the projector, Hartz! Signal the boat into the bottom of the slipway. It's deep water there, and she stands a better chance of avoiding the wreckage!'

There was an unexplained lull in the rumble of explosions, and in that moment they both heard a single rifle shot. Like the crack of a whip. Without a sound Michener, the lookout, dropped from his precarious perch and plummeted down into the rubble. The last thing he saw in life was the pencil-shaped hull of the U-boat as it wended its way around the headland.

Steiger stared hard at the empty window where the smoke from the sniper's bullet still hung in the air, and shouted with sudden anguish, 'And signal Hessler to open fire on the town!'

Hartz swallowed as he watched his captain's features. 'Which part, sir?'

Steiger still stared at the empty window. '*All* of it, I don't care!'

He thought suddenly of Bredt's pathetic madness and Reimann's last-minute invincibility. Of all the men who were depending on him, and the girl who was denied to him. His voice seemed to still all other sounds as he shouted, 'God damn them!' But then as the smoke drifted clear of the building he saw what Michener had seen.

The U-boat was close inshore, and he could see the flash of her signal lamp as she answered Hartz's message. He saw the ant-like figures around the gun and the flash which preceded the scream of its shell overhead. The projectile exploded somewhere in the mountains of rubble, its destruction lost in a ready-made wilderness.

But Steiger waved his cap as if to encourage the tiny figures on the sleek casing of the submarine. 'Shoot, Hessler! Shoot!' His voice was swallowed in a fresh tide of gunfire, but he still continued to shout until he became exhausted.

They were not beaten. They could still hit back.

. . . . .

The tall façade made by the buildings on one side of the narrow street acted as a bulwark against the thunder and roar of fighting which covered the rest of the town.

The sudden rattle of machine-pistols had cut into that comparative calm like saws, and no man who had pulled so desperately on his trigger could now say how long that burst had lasted, or how long it had taken them to crawl into position.

Now the street was quiet again, but the haze of blue smoke hung thick and unmoving like a cloud above the disordered jumble of mutilated and distorted bodies.

Dietrich and his three men had surprised seven Frenchman with a completeness which still left them inert and gasping beside their smoking weapons. Even now Dietrich half expected one of the corpses to leap to its feet, to fight back. Nothing moved.

Without giving an order to his men he climbed down the slope of rubble from the front of a caved-in shop and walked through the harvest left by his guns. He peered into each face as he passed, his features a mask as he looked into each pair of horrified eyes and bared teeth.

He heard a sob behind him, and turned to see Rickover staring at a mere boy who had been almost cut in half by one savage burst. He lay with his mouth open to cry out, his fingers interlaced across the scarlet mess which even now forced itself through the front of his leather coat.

Perhaps Rickover thought he was looking at himself. Dietrich forgot him as a figure at his feet gasped and rolled on to his back. Even with death's mark already on his bloodless features, he was recognisable. Dietrich remembered him as a man he had seen calling on Marquet, the girl's father. The street and its hot stench of death faded, and he saw again the cool shaded interior of the shop with its rows of clocks. The vision was replaced by one of Louis Marquet gibbering in the wreckage of his life. Major Fischer's S.S. men had tortured him certainly. But who was it who had betrayed him, had killed his daughter, Odile?

He gestured to Rickover. 'Quick, hold him up! He's still alive!'

Misunderstanding Dietrich's intentions, the boy slipped his arm under the Frenchman's shoulders and tried to raise him. Instantly the man shrieked with pain, and Dietrich saw the widening patch of blood below his spine.

He knelt very close at the man's side. 'You know *me*, don't you?' Dietrich watched the dazed recognition move into the man's pain-filled eyes. 'You remember me, don't you?' He repeated the question more loudly, unaware of Rickover's stricken expression.

The man nodded weakly.

'Well, tell me why you killed her!' He gripped the man's jerkin in his fist. 'Tell me, damn you!'

A horrible grin showed itself on the white lips. 'I-fought-you-in-Spain.' Each word was dragged through the man's blood. 'Everywhere-I-have-fought-Fascist-swine!'

Dietrich stood up. 'Get away from him, Moses!'

Rickover saw the expression in Dietrich's eyes as he lifted his pistol. 'Please, sir! Perhaps he only thought of his own patriotism!'

Rickover saw the muzzle waver as Dietrich answered: 'Perhaps. But people like this will use anyone for their own ends, Moses! They don't believe in a cause or even a flag. They just believe in themselves!'

With a sob he shouted, 'Why did you have to kill *her*?' But as he lifted the gun to fire he saw that the man had cheated him. His teeth were bared, his eyes still filled with hatred as he lay amongst his followers.

Jung and Muller were watching from the side of the street, and Dietrich could only gesture with his hand. They followed him back down the street, their boots loud on the warm cobbles.

. . . . .

U-991 sidled between two fallen cranes and manœuvred slowly into the entrance of the big concrete bunker. Her gun was unmanned as she made the last dangerous approach because every inch of the way was marked with a deluge of bullets from ashore. Steel clanged against steel and then whined away in fierce ricochets as hidden marksmen made a final effort to prevent this pitiful evacuation.

Steiger watched the first heaving lines snake ashore, and then as the raked bow passed behind the protective wall of the slipway's edge he jumped down on to the forecasing and ran to meet Lieutenant Hessler. All the strain and suspense of conning the U-boat through the rock-strewn harbour, the fear of what he might find, seemed to fall away from the lieutenant's face like a curtain as he grasped Steiger's hand and stood staring at him, wordless and shaking with obvious emotion.

Steiger looked over Hessler's shoulder, beyond the staggering wounded men who were already being assisted towards the main hatch to the blue-eyed mermaid with her hatchet who still guarded the conning-tower. At the deck gun which shimmered with heat, and the bearded, familiar faces which peered at him as they scurried back and forth along the narrow deck. It was like a homecoming.

Trying to control his voice Hessler said: 'We will have to get clear soon, Captain. There are aircraft about. The whole coast is going up in smoke!' He followed Steiger's eyes towards the shattered town. 'But then you know all about that, sir!'

Steiger turned to watch two elderly Reserve officers of the Base staff being roughly assisted over the bows. Dazed with shock and drink, they hardly seemed to know where they were.

He turned on his heel and climbed the ladder to the bridge. The deck trembled impatiently below his feet, and he had to drag his eyes from watching the faces of the few survivors from the Base. A handful, but it was better than he had dared to hope.

He could feel the ache growing in his heart and he said

urgently, 'Ready to get under way?' The waiting was the hardest part. 'Get that hatch secured for sea!' For sea. Open, clean, impartial. He tried to lose his mind in preparations. It would be difficult to get clear. Stern first to the broken breakwater, then ahead on one engine to swing around the wrecked U-boat in the entrance.

It was no good, his mind rebelled against every detail, seemed clogged by the fierce sequence of events. How could he begin all over again, take up the threads of his life, when at this very moment he could see no future at all?

There was a clatter of feet on the bridge ladder, and Dietrich's grime-streaked face appeared above the worn plates. Steiger made another effort to control himself. He could feel his limbs shaking, as if he was naked in a strong wind, and he had difficulty in focusing his eyes on Dietrich's dazed but excited face.

'Is everyone aboard?' Steiger heard his own voice but hardly recognised it. His head felt as if it was splitting, and the staccato bursts of small-arms fire were almost unbearable.

Dietrich peered into his face. 'I found her!' He nodded violently. 'She was trying to get past those damned Terrorists, and I *found* her!'

Steiger dug his fingers into his palms to control the nerveless shaking and tried once more. 'Found who?'

Dietrich touched his arm and pointed down on to the forecasing, where some of the seamen were waiting by the main hatch.

She was standing quite still, her eyes fixed on the bridge, her hair unheeded across her face and whipping in the breeze.

From afar off he heard Dietrich's voice, 'Are you all right, Captain?' No longer excited, but anxious and concerned.

Steiger saw the girl touch her fingers to her lips, watched the fading sunlight playing on her bared shoulder, and tried to speak, to call her name. But he could no longer trust himself to do anything.

For another few seconds they held each other's eyes, then she allowed herself to be lowered to the unseen hands below. The hatch rasped into place, and the deck was empty. With a sudden movement Steiger leaned over the front of the bridge, his eyes wide and desperate. Perhaps he had joined Bredt in madness? There was no girl on the scarred deck. Nothing.

But Dietrich spoke very close to his side. 'She is safe. She has got where she wanted to be!' Then very carefully he added: 'Shall I take control, Captain? Until we are clear of the harbour?'

Steiger looked past him, his features haggard. 'No, Heinz. We will get under way at once. Ring on main engines!' Then as Dietrich turned as if to go below he said, 'But stay with me.' He half listened to the frothing rumble of the diesels and the splutter of exhaust gas against the jetty. 'You see, Heinz, I need *you* now!'

Dietrich spoke sharply into the handset, 'Slow astern both!' and watched as the last mooring line slipped through the fairleads. Beside him Steiger slumped against the screen, his eyes unseeing as the boat sidled clear. Dietrich shuddered as some of the aftermath of killing and filth moved through his thoughts. It had been a baptism, he thought. I at least have emerged whole, and a man.

He glanced quickly at Steiger. Whereas, *he* is afraid of his new-found happiness. He has lost it once. He cannot face the possibility of a second time, for he has never been taught to lose.

18: Vigilance is Not Enough

Trudi Lehmann lowered herself gingerly from the high bunk and reached out uncertainly as the deck gave a slight lurch beneath her feet. For a moment longer she stared at the small overcrowded wardroom, her nostrils rebelling against the foul air and the smell of oil and sweat.

All at once she shivered, made conscious of the rough seaman's jersey and serge trousers which she wore over her tattered dress, and was reminded with brutal suddenness of those last few hours in St. Pierre. She sat down at the small table, her head on one side as she listened to the unfamiliar murmur of the motors, the soft click of machinery and the occasional pad of feet in the passageway through which she had been guided like a helpless child. The clock above her must be wrong. It told her that she had been aboard the U-boat for fourteen hours, but surely that was not possible? She peered at the packed sleeping figures in the other bunks and tried to match them against the frightened desperate people she had seen being dragged aboard like herself.

She leaned her head in her hands, conscious of the grime on her fingers and the feel of dust in her hair. So it was over. Or perhaps it was only beginning.

She closed her eyes and saw with sudden clarity the semicircle of waiting figures around the bombed house, the glint of sunlight on their weapons, and above all, the naked barbarity in their faces as she had stepped from the shadows. The seaman who had watched over her, and had lost his own bid for freedom for her sake, lay helpless and unconscious in the building behind her. The stairway had collapsed and he had fallen even as he threw her to safety. Perhaps the noise had drawn the French Resistance men to the place, or maybe they were waiting there in any case. But it had suddenly become quite clear to her what she had to do. She had failed Rudolf Steiger, and now a helpless and injured sailor would be killed because of her selfishness and stupidity. She knew that if she walked out alone they would soon forget to look for another, and König might be spared the treatment they had meted out to that lonely soldier.

She clenched her fists as she relived that moment of silence in the desolate street. The brief, terrifying moment before Dietrich's hidden gunners had swept the road into a bloody carnage almost at her feet.

The rest was like a numbing dream. From noise and terror, the crash of gunfire and the last-minute dash for safety, to this other world of quiet orders and timeless efficiency.

She had seen Steiger only twice. Once on deck, and later a mere touch of hands, a look, a moment held in time before he had been called away to the world he shared with no one.

When she tried to think of her husband, nothing formed in her shocked mind. There was neither sorrow nor anger, and she could only see him as a stranger.

She swallowed hard, tasting the acrid tang of diesel, and wondered how König was feeling about his own return to this strange, impersonal life. She had never imagined that her husband and all the others she had met had endured conditions such as these. The boat seemed to be a power of its own, the men merely servants who moved quietly about its length as if afraid to arouse its wrath. The deck hardly moved, but there was the constant shiver and vibration of steel all about her to remind all within the hull that only it could protect them from the crushing force of the sea around and above them.

Someone groaned in a bunk, and she knew it would soon be time to face the others who had survived the end of St. Pierre. The handful of wretched Frenchmen and their wives, who because of their torn loyalties were more afraid of their own people than the common enemy. Two or three members of Captain Bredt's staff, and a larger number of wounded who had been packed away throughout the boat. Like stores and spare equipment, they had to be fitted in where there was a space.

If only there was some way to be with him alone. Just for a moment. If not like that other time, then just for a few seconds so that they could share even the strangeness of silence and peace.

Beyond the stained curtain she heard a man begin to cough, and then the rattle of dishes. Her stomach contracted and she thought she was going to be sick. Food and conversation she could not face. Like a frightened animal she climbed back into the bunk and pulled the blanket over her head.

All of a sudden she was terribly afraid, and the more so because she could find no reason.

. . . . .

Steiger finished writing in his logbook and rubbed his eyes. Apart from the yellow glow of his desk lamp, the cabin was in darkness. One of the elderly Base officers lay in the single bunk, his mouth a black hole as he snored away the hours and enjoyed the safety of sleep.

Steiger felt his eyes drawn again to the small pile of signals which Hessler had left for him. Try as he might he could not turn his mind from their contents, nor could he yet appreciate the full force of their cold inhumanity.

He would not rejoin Group Meteor, after all. *It had ceased to exist*. Again and again he tried to see more than just the bald operational statement in the signal, but the answers would not come. All three boats were finished. Weiss and Wellemeyer had been sunk attacking an unexpected convoy, and Otto Kunhardt and his crew had perished in an air-attack. In the twinkling of an eye. While Lehmann had tried to make a different Germany, and Bredt's small empire had crumbled amidst the bombing, these three commanders had been wiped from the slate. Preserved in the timeless silence of the Atlantic.

He touched the other signal with his fingers. He was ordered to return to Germany with all despatch. He was only to engage targets which were unavoidable, as he was required at Kiel at the earliest opportunity. There was a small and casual addition about the possibility of passengers which he might have on board, and that was all.

Steiger glanced at the compass repeater on the bulkhead. The luminous card showed that every turn of the U-boat's screws was taking her further and further to the south-west, *away* from Germany!

How could he be sure he was acting correctly? The signal was normal under the circumstances. Or was it? Suppose Major Fischer or one of his colleagues had got through to the High Command in Germany? After the attempt to assassinate the Leader there would be massive and terrible reprisals, so why should St. Pierre be spared? Any small piece of information, even a rumour, would be enough. And if it was known that *U-991* was carrying some of the very people who had been infected by the plot, the inevitability of what would follow was stark and sickening.

He thought of the injured seaman, König, who had seemingly deserted only to reappear with Trudi Lehmann. Both of them would be immediately suspect, as would the Base officers who had meekly stood by while Lehmann had assumed command.

The more he tortured his mind with the alternatives, the more he was sure he was acting rightly. With luck their fuel would be enough to carry them back to Kiel, even around Scotland and through the dreaded Denmark Strait before attempting the last dash across the North Sea. But before he turned to the north he would find a neutral ship and put the girl on board. The wounded men could be sent across, too. Some of them were in no state for a long and dangerous trip across the Arctic Circle. But he knew in his heart that the dazed and delirious wounded were only an excuse.

The curtain moved, and Hessler's face appeared in the doorway. 'Faint light on the horizon, Captain. Bearing one-nine-oh.'

The two men looked at each other. Steiger stood up and reached for his cap. Was it possible that only hours ago he was ducking amid the ruins of the old hotel with bullets ripping at the dust by his feet? He remembered, too, the last desperate dash for the harbour entrance, both engines going at full speed, the suction from the racing screws swirling the silt from the shallow bottom like liquid gold. But most of all he remembered Captain Bredt. A lonely, erect figure standing in the conning-tower of the wrecked U-boat, his only companion a dead sailor who hung over the bridge rail like a bored spectator.

Steiger had momentarily forgotten the hazards which loomed ahead of the quivering bows and the spatter of bullets alongside as he stared across at the unmoving hatless captain on the gutted bridge.

Already small figures were creeping along the breakwater, while others were leaping across the submerged stones towards the wreck.

For one moment Steiger had considered going alongside the hulk and removing Bredt by force. He was glad now that he had left him. In Germany Bredt might have been an ideal scapegoat for a situation he could never have foreseen. But in his madness Bredt had been allowed a last moment of glory. He had even tossed Steiger a casual wave as the two boats parted for the last time and the smoke from the dying town rolled over the harbour.

Steiger realised with a start that Hessler was waiting for an answer.

Sharply he said, 'A light, you say?'

'Yes, sir. But it's still a bit too soon for the dawn, and it's more steady than a signal flare.' He faltered as Steiger's face lightened.

'A neutral perhaps?'

Steiger saw Hessler nod thoughtfully. Of course, that would be it. There were many Spanish and Portuguese ships about this section of the Bay, and they invariably kept themselves clear of convoys which might be attacked and showed themselves bathed in arc lamps during the hours of darkness.

'Very well. Alter course to intercept. I will take a closer look.'

Hessler faltered as if to question Steiger's judgement. He knew well enough what was in the signals, and while he was sorry to hear of the destruction of Group Meteor, he was no longer surprised. He was far more sorry to think that Steiger might be risking his own life and reputation by disobeying orders. But he sighed and shambled back to the control room.

* * * * *

'This is the Captain speaking . . .'

Throughout the length of the submerged submarine men paused in their tasks to listen, heads raised, expressions momentarily exposed and unguarded as they waited and wondered.

The hull was swaying slightly in a lively cross-current as it moved sluggishly through the water at a bare six knots while the raised Snorchel sucked down precious air to the pounding diesels, and the newly awakened crew sat blearily contemplating their breakfast plates. The boat's atmosphere was thick with cooking fat but was nevertheless cold and damp, so that the crowded men sat hunched together for comfort, their faces still lined with sleep and weariness.

Unseen by all but the Officer of the Watch, who took quick and regular inspections through the periscope, the sky above the dark sea was already lightening, so that the stars seemed pale and indistinct. Small whitecaps moved independently to the freshening breeze, and already there was a hint of bitterness in the water as summer loosened her grip on the Atlantic for another year. There was no autumn in the world's most treacherous ocean. Just the hurried warmth and too-bright sunlight of a few months to break the savage weather and lull man's defences for a short while.

'. . . the mounting pressure throughout France has made our position there impossible. But we will carry on the fight as before from other bases, with new comrades . . .'

In the wardroom the girl lay staring at the deckhead, her eyes unblinking as she listened to his voice. He must be holding the microphone very close to his mouth, she thought. His voice was so clear that she could hear his controlled breathing and sense the emotion beyond the words. Around the table the other passengers sat stiffly and uncomprehending, their eyes avoiding their companions as they listened. Here a hand toyed with a cup or rearranged a fork on the stained table; there a man stared with downcast features at the vibrating coffee as if to see his own fate. The Germans looked dazed and resentful. The French seemed empty and lost, as if realising that they were excluded and belonged to no one.

She turned to watch the only ship's officer who was present. The Engineer, a narrow-faced man with sad, thoughtful eyes. He sat with the others, but was apart from them. She wondered what he was thinking as he listened to his captain.

She stiffened as Steiger continued quietly: '. . . we have sighted a Spanish ship, and as soon as we have made contact with her the wounded and certain other passengers will be transferred aboard. As captain I speak for all the men of this company when I say I will be sorry to see them go. . . .'

She twisted a corner of the blanket and bit it hard with her teeth as the tears scalded her eyes. He is speaking to *me*! He is trying to tell me . . .

A few feet away in the gunners' mess Horst Jung paused with a spoon raised in his fist. Wrapped helplessly like a baby in a blanket, a wounded seaman stared upwards at the spoon, his mouth open for the soup, his eyes shadowed in suffering.

In his own bunk König tried to turn his head, but the pain in his broken ribs made him fall back exhausted. No one had spoken to him since he had recovered consciousness. But he had expected that. He had betrayed their code and their trust. He had run away for his own purposes, and although they all wanted to do the same, they were bound by something too strong, a strange discipline which he did not understand.

The girl would be put aboard the Spanish ship. There she would be safe. He would be returned to Germany to face a fate more terrible than any of these silent seamen realised. Perhaps he could write a quick letter and smuggle it to the girl before she left the boat. His heart quickened at the idea. His mother would get it long after it was all over, but at least she would know he had tried to get near to her. To comfort her.

Nearby, Muller and Rickover watched Jung with the spoon and listened to the Captain's words. An unused plate and mug stood in the rack, and unbeknown to each other they were all thinking of Michener, who had died with the returning U-boat in his eyes.

'. . . in all wars there is treachery and confusion on every side. Historians may find men right and far-sighted whom we have condemned or destroyed. We cannot be held responsible. We must do our duty as we see it *now*. If we destroy it is because war is itself destruction. If we kill it is out of necessity and not out of conviction!'

In the control room Steiger's voice was closer and more

personal. Dietrich stood near the helmsman's seat, his eyes in shadow as he watched the ticking gyro repeater. There was hardly a movement in the control room, but for the occasional shift of a hydroplane wheel or the telltale flicker from one of the white-faced dials. Hessler stood beside the sheathed periscope, his eyes on the brass clock as he waited for his next look at the world above, his stocky body swaying to the deck's uneasy motion.

Petty Officer Hartz was just outside the oval door, his head cocked like an old dog's as he listened to Steiger. He was newly awakened like the others, yet already his uniform was pulled into place, his face stolid and competent as he heard his captain talking about men like himself.

Dietrich glanced at the chart-table and imagined that he could see Reche's body hunched over the chart, his lower lip protruding as he manipulated the ruler and dividers. He thought again of Reche as he had last seen him in an unnamed street, his bloody hand pointing towards the sea. Perhaps at the last moment he had wanted to return.

Something made Dietrich look again at Steiger as he said: 'Whatever may lie ahead, I will never forget your loyalty to me. Sometimes you will hate and despise the things you must do in the name of duty. But one day you will be proud to say, "*I* served with the Grey Wolves!" And when that day comes the whole world may understand as you will . . .' He handed the microphone blindly to a seaman and stared upwards at the grimy steel.

Muffled at first by the diesels, and then stronger even than the U-boat's own power, Steiger heard his men cheering.

Dietrich was watching him, his lips parted in a smile, but his eyes troubled. Steiger looked at the bowed heads of the watchkeepers and Hessler's face beside the shining periscope. Worn faces, forgotten faces. Like those in Group Meteor who lay in the Atlantic and waited for their last companion. Otto Kunhardt and Fritz Wellemeyer. Weiss and Busch. Karl Schubert, who had surrendered, and Alex Lehmann, who had died in spite of the Atlantic, if not because of it.

Now we are going back to Germany. To a homeland we may not recognise. He thought back over his words to his crew and tortured himself a moment longer. Do we really know what we are doing? The world will never understand. How can they if we doubt ourselves?

He forced himself to walk to the periscope. It would soon be time to act. To separate from the one person who understood, yet who would now be denied him for ever. Perhaps that would be better than this terrible limbo of uncertainty and want. Of a yearning which could never now be rewarded.

'Up periscope!' He reached out for the handles, his mind clogged with the emptiness of his words to his men.

I wanted to tell them. To explain. Because no one ever explained it to me, and I am paying for my ignorance with every minute I stay alive.

He blinked away the film which seemed to cover his eyes and peered through the misted lens.

There she was. Tall and unreal against the paling sky. The red and yellow flag painted on the hull, the bright arc lamps of neutrality in a world of darkness bent on destroying itself.

He stared wildly at the ship as he had so many before, the cross-wires across the bright flag, but for once harmless and without hostility. Soon it would be over, and the grey hull would turn away again while the little steamer carried its unexpected passengers to safety.

He pressed his forehead against the cool pad, feeling the pain in his scar, the sudden exhaustion which moved over his body.

'Down periscope! Stand by to surface!'

The orders were repeated throughout the hull, and with reborn obedience the men hurried to their stations.

. . . . .

Nervous and uncertain, the U-boat's passengers were once again shepherded into the centre passageway, a few of them glancing for the first time at the boat around them. The wounded, some on improvised stretchers, others propped between members of the crew, were ushered to the control room where they waited in silence as the seamen of the bridge-party gathered at the foot of the shining ladder.

Steiger walked amongst them, and then stopped as the girl moved to meet him.

'Steady at fourteen metres, Captain!'

'Ready to surface, sir!'

The voices and familiar noises crowded around them, but for a few more seconds they were alone together.

Dietrich said quietly, 'Shall I take over, Captain?'

Steiger heard himself reply: 'No, Heinz. I will be all right.'

The hiss of the periscope. One last look, and then there would be no more time.

Her lips moved. 'I shall be waiting.'

He nodded. Waiting? We are all waiting.

'Up periscope.' I must hold on. Dear God, she is standing so close I could reach out and hold her.

The small Spanish freighter was very near. As yet unaware of them. Hardly a ripple for a bow wave, she stood like part of the sea. An island.

He tried to concentrate on the misty picture, to hold back the wall of despair which seemed to be grinding him down.

'Down periscope!' He turned to hold her gaze. To give her some message.

Around him the waiting figures stared up at him, blank and without understanding.

He reached out and touched her arm. That was all. He moved to the ladder and waited.

'Surface!'

The air thundered into the tanks and the boat seemed torn with noise and sudden urgency.

Steiger climbed the tilting ladder and reached overhead for the locking wheel. Behind him the lookouts crowded the narrow shaft, and he could feel them reaching up to steady him as he opened the hatch.

The explosion when it came threw him back across the lip of the hatch even as he heaved himself on to the dripping bridge, and he fell gasping with pain as something clanged against the conning-tower and screamed away into the pale sky.

Still shocked, he dragged himself upright as another blast rocked the hull, and with disbelieving eyes stared at the billowing cloud of brown smoke which streamed abeam from the U-boat's bows.

Muffled and distorted voices crowded into his reeling brain. 'Fore-torpedo-compartment flooding! Hydroplane out of action!'

Men shouted as two tall columns of water rose alongside the shivering bridge, and through the flung spray Steiger saw his adversary for the first time.

He tried to bring the last of his strength to bear, to concentrate on what had to be done, but all the time his inner being seemed to be taunting him, jeering his one moment of unguarded weakness. He had seen it happen so often to others.

He had tried to warn them, prepare them but, always there came a time when vigilance was not enough.

Dietrich was beside him, his mouth working as he shouted above the din. 'What shall we do, sir?' More explosions.

Steiger tried again. We cannot dive. Hydroplane out of action. It was a miracle that the torpedoes in the forward compartment had not been ignited. Even now the deck felt heavy as Luth struggled to control the inrush of water through the gaping wound in the bows.

He felt himself slipping, the pain almost unendurable.

He saw Hartz and his gunners scrambling over the bridge, the gleam of a pistol, a mad scramble of scarred boots under the falling spray. Somewhere a man screamed in pain, and Steiger thought of the packed men below. In minutes, even seconds, they would all be paying for his frailty.

Steiger still could not believe it was actually happening to them. To *him*.

One moment the sea had been empty but for that solitary ship. Already the Spanish freighter had vanished in the smoke, perhaps a spectator, as he had so often been, at the death of a ship.

I must fight! Perhaps if the gun can be brought to bear, or even the stern tube fired, we can still survive! But his thoughts refused to steady or form into any plan which he could recognise.

Dietrich was bending at his side, his face white against the rust-pitted plates. Steiger did not remember falling, and stared up at the bright sky with surprise.

The explosions ceased and a great silence fell over the small oval world encompassed by the tall sides of the bridge. Steiger saw the desperate faces, the impotent periscope pointing at the sky, through which he should have seen the one flaw in the lens' picture. Perhaps he only saw what he wanted to see. Maybe this was how it was always intended.

Vaguely he heard the clang of the breech-block, and he again tried to struggle to his feet. With sudden anguish he called, 'Don't fire!' He saw the understanding flood across Dietrich's face and added: 'It would be pointless! There is more than a gesture needed now!'

The explosions started again, and Steiger winced as each shock wave passed through the wallowing hull. It was as if he was receiving the death-blow, too, yet was powerless to help.

Men were scampering through the hatch and hurling themselves over the side of the bridge, while beneath his body the engines' vibrations quivered, then ceased altogether.

Dietrich said: 'She's taking water fast, Captain! Shall I give the order to——'

With a soft cry Steiger pulled himself the last few feet to the front of the bridge. 'Damn you, *no*! I'll give the orders!'

Dietrich stepped back and saluted, his ears deaf to the whine of gunfire, his eyes smarting as he stared at the tall, pain-racked figure on the bridge, which even now leaned more heavily towards the sea where, facing her mortal enemy, the British destroyer shimmered beneath a haze of gunsmoke.

. . . . .

U-991 gave a violent lurch and settled more heavily on to her port side, whilst within the pressure hull the rumble of escaping compressed air was magnified to such a degree that it sounded as if the hull was being hammered across an anvil.

At the first detonation some of the main lighting failed, and with each successive explosion splintered glass from shattered lamps and instruments rained down on to the heads of scurrying figures as the damage-control parties stampeded from one source of danger to the next.

Max König strained himself into a sitting position, his eyes blinded with the sweat of pain as his broken ribs grated beneath the tight bandages. He was half deafened by the explosions, and could feel panic gripping his insides as the air around his bunk became choked with a fouler and more terrifying reek of gas. All the stories and horrors he had heard about a U-boat in its death-agony flooded through his mind as he struggled over the edge of the pipe-cot, and he stared with added disbelief at the deserted messdeck and the table which even as he watched tipped its contents on to the steel deck.

A flashlight cut across the flickering lamps and smoke-filled air, and he saw Lieutenant Luth and his Chief E.R.A., Richter, crouching in the open doorway. They glanced at him without recognition, their faces strained and filled with apprehension, then they were gone, and König heard the distant thud of hammers and the hiss of inrushing water.

It was useless to struggle. Those still below had enough to do without worrying about him. König lay on his side, his eyes misting with pain and despair. Yet the wounded seamen had gone, and he could no longer hear the terrified cries of the Frenchwomen in the wardroom. He had heard, too, the crash of boots overhead and the metallic grate of steel as the deck gun had been unlimbered and swung towards the enemy.

I should be up there with them. I belong with Jung and Rickover and Petty Officer Hartz. Anything is better than dying down here, gassed or crushed to death.

He thought of Steiger's face and tried to imagine the submarine's last moments. The Captain would fight. He would not care about the crazed women and helpless wounded. He would see his duty to himself first. The honour of dying in battle regardless of the cost.

He felt someone beside the bunk, and blinked at Jung's lined face which seemed to hang in the thick air like a grizzled fruit.

Jung said sharply: 'Come on, Max, my son! We are getting you up top, and quickly too!'

König let his body go limp as more hands pulled at his blanket and hauled him on to the tilting deck. Dazedly he stared at the legs and the impossible angle at which his friends were standing. The boat must be going down! Yet these men were risking their lives for him! Through the mists of pain and gratitude he saw Jung's teeth bared in curses and angry orders, Moses Rickover as white as death and shaking with fright, Muller whose pouchy face was sweating but grimly determined as he led the way to the control room.

A necklace of blue sparks, blinding bright like diamonds, danced madly across the switchboard and shattered yet another dial. The wheel jerked unattended and forgotten, the helmsman dead beside the Coxswain, killed when the gyro repeater had exploded in their faces.

König felt more hands guiding him to the foot of the ladder and he stared upwards at the oval patch of sky, still unable to understand what was happening.

Then the bridge, empty but for a dead seaman, the First Lieutenant, who was calling to the invisible men on the casing, and the Captain. Steiger was framed against the sky, his head tilted, his eyes fixed on the ensign which floated from the periscope standard.

A shell exploded alongside the hull and more splinters scythed screaming into the conning-tower. Steel against steel.

The men laid König on the rough plating, and he heard

Dietrich call, 'They will keep firing while the flag is flying, Captain!'

König listened with sudden understanding, his mind clear of pain. There was no panic in Dietrich's voice, nor was there any sense of reprimand. Someone had hoisted the flag. If it was to be a battle to the death, it was a final gesture. To remove it now would mean not defeat, but surrender!

König raised himself on his elbows to watch Steiger's face. He knew that he was seeing something far more terrible than the loss of just another ship, and if he lived, he knew that he would remember this moment for ever.

The U-boat lurched more steeply, and through the open hatch König could hear the splutter of fuses as the water greedily explored the broken hull.

Steiger spoke: 'Clear the boat, Lieutenant! Get those other men on deck!'

Then with slow deliberation Steiger groped his way to the flag halyards and fumbled with the spray-soaked cord, his eyes still lifted to the great scarlet ensign with its black cross and swastika.

König saw Dietrich move as if to help his Captain, and realised for the first time that Steiger was injured. He saw, too, the emotion and helplessness on Dietrich's pale features as he stood back and stopped himself from helping in the one action which Steiger would never share with anyone.

The halyard gave, and in one swoop the ensign cascaded into the bridge and covered the rusted plates like blood.

The firing stopped, and König knew it was finished. Across the water he could hear cheering. Far off and unreal, yet strangely sad.

He heard Hessler shouting: 'Over you go! Watch your life-jackets!' There were cries and shouts as the crew began to leave.

As König was lifted up into the sunlight he heard Dietrich say, 'Will you come, sir?'

And Steiger's answer: 'In a moment, Heinz. I must have time to think. . . .'

Then Dietrich said: 'You did rightly, Captain! There is no other way!'

Then Steiger walked to the front of the bridge, the flag under his arm, his hand pressed against his side. For another moment he watched the heads which were already bobbing alongside and the bright orange lifejackets. Then he saw her. She stood on the exposed saddle tank, her figure tiny between the two seamen who stood ready to swim with her to safety.

She struggled as she saw him, but the men held her tightly, their faces already watching the grey ship and the oared boats which danced across the white-capped water.

Steiger lifted his hand and walked stiffly back to the rear of the bridge. When he looked again the hull was clear.

Dietrich stood with him, a lifejacket in his hands. Steiger suddenly shrugged as if he had just come to a decision.

'Keep with the men, Lieutenant. They will be looking to you!'

Then he was alone on the bridge, but for the dead seaman who lay with pillowed arms as if asleep. It was over.

* * * * *

The destroyer yawed heavily in the rising swell, her decks dotted with watching men and the discarded shapes of empty shell cases. From her high bridge the Captain, a stocky, red-faced commander in a faded duffel coat, watched the final scene through his powerful glasses.

The last whaler was being pulled alongside crammed with German survivors and the mysterious civilians who had poured on to the U-boat's deck soon after the destroyer's first salvoes.

A young sub-lieutenant standing nearby said excitedly, 'By God, sir, what luck!'

The Captain smiled wryly. What *luck* indeed. The destroyer, stopped with engine trouble in the bleak and hostile Atlantic, had waited and watched the dawn with apprehension and fear. Across the lightening horizon had steamed the brightly lit Spaniard, so that the watching British seamen had swallowed their envy and stood to their guns once more and waited for the stranger to pass. The Spaniard was not part of their world, they must keep their thoughts for the dangers which the daylight would bring.

Then in the fresh sunlight they had seen the shadow beneath the surface, and the listening asdic men had heard the telltale echo which could only be a submarine.

Two things happened at once. The destroyer's engineer reported his engines ready for use once more, and against the dawn light the U-boat began to surface.

But for the Spanish ship which unwittingly had blotted out

the destroyer's shape for those few vital seconds, the roles of the two enemies might have been reversed.

The Captain sighed. 'I have been fighting them for five years, yet this is the first time I have laid eyes on them!'

He heard the gasps and cries of the rescued men and the rough encouragement from his own sailors. They look so like us, he thought. And yet . . .

'Permission to get under way, sir?'

The Captain nodded, caught off guard. Was it all over so soon? The boats were already hoisted in their davits, life rafts secured. He explored his mind, knowing that this moment would be important to him in later years.

There should be a feeling of exultation and pride. Yet as he watched the tall lonely figure in the white cap and sodden leather jacket who stood motionless by the guardrail he could only feel a sense of embarrassment.

In war it was better when the enemy remained faceless and without shape. Brought into close contact, stripped of danger and mystery, he could make the victor feel as if he had been deceived.

The telegraphs jangled, and a great wash surged beneath the destroyer's stern.

Rudolf Steiger tore his eyes momentarily from the sea and looked upwards at the tall bridge. For a few seconds the eyes of the two captains met. Across the dazed survivors and busy British sailors the one glance was enough. Both were captains, and each understood the other if for this moment alone.

When Steiger looked again towards the sea the U-boat's stern was high in the air, the propellers still, the scarred plates ugly with weed and slime.

Yet as it stood suspended in the sullen turbulence of air bubbles and thick-spreading oil, the dying submarine seemed to hold a kind of beauty.

He could hear the girl crying very quietly behind him, and knew that she alone would find a way for him in the future. But now he could share with no one.

Dietrich's voice sounded hoarse and far away as he said, 'She's going!'

And as the destroyer began to move through the great oil-stain the submarine quivered and then dived deep for the last time.

For a while longer the scarlet ensign floated on the seething water before it, too, was sucked down, and the Atlantic once more smoothed its surface and tidied another of man's follies.

Steiger turned his back and walked slowly towards a British officer who waited by the bridge ladder.

It was over.

Yet in spite of his grief he knew that life could begin again. Even for him.